AMERICAN
LOVE STORY

ADRIANA HERRERA

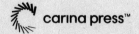

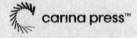

carina press™

ISBN-13: 978-1-335-21597-0

American Love Story

Copyright © 2019 by Adriana Herrera

Recycling programs for this product may not exist in your area.

For those who put their bodies in the struggle. For those who are brave enough to speak truth to power. For those who overcome. You have always mattered.

AMERICAN
LOVE STORY

"Power at its best is love implementing the demands of justice, and justice at its best is power correcting everything that stands against love."
—Martin Luther King Jr.

Chapter One

Easton

He made my heart stop.

Over a year had passed since I'd seen Patrice Denis for the first time, and still, he was the most beautiful man I'd ever seen. Too bad I was so inconsequential to him that he'd been in Ithaca for over a month and was yet to send me a text with as much as a "fuck you."

I stood there observing him from a distance, once again feeling spooked by what Patrice's presence did to me. He had his locs coiled on top of his head and was wearing glasses that I'd never seen before, distractedly talking to a man who seemed a lot more invested in the conversation than he was. As I watched the guy lean in close enough to brush against Patrice's shopping cart, I gripped the handle of mine so tight it squeaked. An unexpected flare of jealousy, coming out of nowhere, just from seeing someone in his space. I shook my head, amazed at the feeling. I'd spent my entire adulthood thinking I just was not the jealous type.

That was before Patrice Denis walked into my life.

I was still trying to decide whether I should just keep moving or go say hello when the man he'd been talking to walked away. Patrice looked after him, his face stony. The relief loosening my chest did not go unnoticed.

I headed toward him, knowing there was a good chance I'd get the same icy reception, but I wasn't strong enough to stay away. When my cart was only a few feet from him, he turned around and the smile he gave me was…everything. After a second, he must have realized he was beaming at me and schooled his expression.

But it was too late. I'd seen it.

He'd been happy to see me. I was *certain* of it, and it gave me the last push I needed to jump back in. I leaned on the handle of my shopping cart and smiled up at him while he held a shiny red apple in his hands.

"Professor."

He turned fully facing me and just having his body so close made a shiver run down my spine. He had on a Cornell sweatshirt with some cutoffs and leather flip-flops on his feet. I noticed he'd switched the stud in his nose for a small silver hoop. That big body as imposing and powerful as ever. An image of that carved chest looming over me flashed through my head and it was all I could do not to gasp.

I was staring. I knew that, but I couldn't help it. At least he seemed a bit flustered too; shaking his head as if trying to clear his thoughts before answering.

"Easton. Good to see you," he said with a sheepish look, such a contrast from the serious one from a few minutes earlier. "So is this place like a major hangout in town? It's eight on a Sunday and I've already ran into like three of Nesto's relatives and half of my department."

No mention of his ghosting me. Banter then, I could banter. "To be fair, his uncle and his sister do work here."

He conceded my point with another smile, but he didn't reply, and so I kept rambling.

"Philmans is pretty busy most days, and everyone shops here. It's actually pretty calm compared to how it is during the day on the weekend. That's why I come here at this time. Get my shopping done faster."

He nodded distractedly as he gave me an appreciative look, as if he was starting to remember how things had been between us. His eyes assessed me closely, his body leaning toward me. When his gaze finally locked with mine, they were full of heat and a hint of humor. Suddenly the man I'd been pining over for the last year was right in front of me. "Are you sure you're not just avoiding disgruntled customers?"

I scoffed at the jab, but there was no hiding the smile which seemed to be a side effect of being around Patrice. "For your information, Professor Denis, I happen to have one of the best conviction records in the state."

He raised an eyebrow about a hundredth of a centimeter, which I guess was his version of acknowledgment, then spoke in a more serious tone than I was hoping for. "I'm aware, counselor."

I nodded, feeling unsure of how heavy this conversation was about to get and desperate to come up with something to make it lighter.

I brought out my grievances instead.

"I was wondering if you'd made it up here," I offered, lifting a shoulder, the unsaid *since I never heard from you again after you fucked me on every flat surface in my apartment* hanging in the air. "Welcome to the Finger Lakes."

He bowed his head and started to look uncomfortable, but before I could interject, he opened his mouth.

"Sorry I didn't get in touch. Things have been a little crazy this year. The job market was hectic and unpredictable and I didn't decide on this position until late in the game." He sighed and fidgeted. Almost unsure, which seemed so out of place.

In the time I'd spent with him, Patrice seemed to be the walking embodiment of self-possessed, so seeing this new side of him was...endearing. "It's been an adjustment, to say the least."

I dipped my head in response, not sure how to proceed, the pull I felt toward him on the verge of undoing my ability to carry on polite conversation. All I could think was *I want to touch you so badly.*

I had no right to it though, on that at least I was very clear. Patrice's lack of interest had not been exactly subtle. Last summer we'd been incendiary, coming together over and over again. From the start, the attraction between us had been undeniable. We'd see each other by chance while he was in town helping his best friend with his food truck, and inevitably we'd end up back at my place tearing each other's clothes off. I'd felt a hunger for Patrice, that seemed insatiable and those few weeks, it seemed like it'd been the same for him. But in the year after, his silence had been almost complete.

Despite our connection, once Patrice was gone, *he was gone.*

I knew he'd been back over the winter to visit Nesto, but he never made any efforts to get in touch or let me know he was in town. So when I heard from a friend in common he'd taken a job at Cornell, I was elated, thinking we'd be able to reconnect. A part of me even foolishly thinking his decision to take a job here had something to do with me. I'd texted him to congratulate him, but he'd responded with a thank-you, and never contacted me again. It stung, but once I received the message he wasn't interested, I'd vowed to keep my distance.

Now that he was here in front of me, I realized staying away from Patrice Denis was going be much harder than I'd anticipated.

Patrice cleared his throat and I realized I'd been spacing out.

So smooth.

I looked up at him and managed to produce a smile as I tried to read his expression. "No worries. I know how it is. Never thought you'd end up here. It's a nice surprise." I dearly wished I could sound neutral when I was around Patrice, but "thirsty and parched" seemed to be my only settings when it came to him.

This time he averted his eyes before answering me. I wondered if he was a bit more affected by me than he let on. "Hard to say no to a job offer from an Ivy League school."

Okay, not exactly a romantic revelation. I barely contained a frustrated sigh before I nodded. "Sure. Congratulations on that. It's a big deal. How are you getting on? Did you find a place?"

He pursed his lips, decidedly unhappy at the mention of his living situation. "Yeah, but I won't move in there for another week or so. I'm staying with Nesto and Jude until then." His best friend, Nesto, was coupled off with Jude, the local hottie librarian, and living in pre-marital bliss.

"How is Nesto? I haven't been by the restaurant in a while," I said, barely repressing a groan. "I've been acting as interim DA since my boss had to take leave after having heart surgery. Not much time for longer lunches lately."

That was the understatement of the century, but I did not want to deviate the conversation and my mining Patrice for intel on his living situation to talk about my work stress. But to my surprise, Patrice raised an eyebrow.

"Congratulations to you. Is the plan for you to run?" Patrice sounded genuinely interested, so I considered what to say for a moment.

He wasn't the first person to ask me this of course, half of Ithaca was of a mind that I was a shoo-in for the position, but I was still not sure I wanted to take that step. I was good at my job, but I wasn't sure that I'd be good at the politics, and I didn't want my work tainted by bullshit.

"Honestly, I'm not sure. Cindy, my boss, is still considering coming back." I shrugged and looked up at him. He was only a couple of inches taller than me, but his massive frame made me feel almost dainty. "Politics is not my thing, but I can't say I won't throw my hat in the ring if there's a special election."

He nodded, considering my answer in that way he did. That was something that had captivated me about Patrice from the first—he took his time with things. He mulled them over, letting silence stretch out for minutes sometimes as he found the words he needed.

"You won't take your job lightly," he proclaimed, catching me by surprise. Then he grinned, and it was all I could do to not get closer. "And I can't say seeing posters of you all over town is going to be a hardship."

"Thanks for the vote of the confidence," I said sincerely. I had no idea if it was a joke or not, but I was very fucking close to shoving my cart to the side and making extremely salacious propositions. I wasn't in the mood to get shut down, so I went with something benign instead.

"Is your place in town?"

Also, I had no shame.

He gave me a funny look, but after a second he nodded. "Yeah. It's that old building behind the co-op, I rented the apartment on the top floor."

I kept my expression neutral but was surprised. That place catered more to students than faculty. He didn't look very excited about the apartment, and I didn't blame him.

"I signed the lease months ago, but they've been delaying the move-in date for weeks now." He scowled, obviously frustrated, an interesting departure for someone who always seemed unfazed by what was going on around him. When he spoke, it was clear he wasn't happy about the situation.

"They seem to have some issues with the building. I'm starting to think I may need to look for something else. But housing here is such a hassle. I'm not sure I'll be able to find something close to campus this late in the game. Classes already started."

I should have left it alone, but the temptation was too strong and before I knew it, I was blurting it out. "Landlords in Ithaca can be a pain in the ass. If you do want to look for other options let me know." This time I was the one clearing my throat and feeling awkward, but I pushed through. "My building has a couple of units open."

He perked up at that but almost immediately went back to his calm, cool and collected demeanor. I could tell he was interested though. He'd been to my place a

few times last summer and knew it was in a nice loca-
tion and that the apartments were pristine. Still, I braced
for him to turn me down.

In the interest of not coming off like a full-on creep,
I decided not to offer up the fact that I owned the building. I fidgeted with the kale I had in my cart as I figured
out how to proceed. It wasn't like "my money" was a
secret; Patrice and I had talked about my family's vineyard when we met, he'd seemed interested, but not exactly impressed by my status within the one percent. I
didn't want to give Patrice one more reason to run in
the opposite direction by reminding him about that, so
I kept my mouth shut while he considered my offer.

He thought about it for another minute and then nodded. "I might call you up to ask for the landlord's info.
If I can't move in this week, I'm going to start looking
for another place."

"Sounds good. Listen—"

I was about to take my shamelessness to the next
level and ask him out for a drink or something when I
saw him jump and then pull his phone out of his pocket.
He smiled when he looked at the screen, and spoke before I could.

"It's my mom. We're supposed to Skype tonight. I
should get going," he said, giving me another smile, but
this one was not at all inviting.

"It was good seeing you, Easton," he said, as he hurried away without giving me a chance to say goodbye.

I stood there wondering if I really could read people
as well as I thought. Because from the first moment with
Patrice, I thought we'd shared something big, something
worth exploring. I could lie to myself about how it had
been the same for him when he was a few hundred miles

away, but with him here maybe it was time for me to accept I was probably the only one who'd felt that way.

Patrice

"Well look who finally made it into town."

I heard Nesto call out as I walked into his restaurant. It was 8:00 a.m. on Monday, and he'd run out the house at 7:00 a.m. so he could be here to receive an order. He'd left Jude, his partner, and me home to take our time before we each headed to work. But he'd forgotten his iPad, which he apparently needed. So I stopped by on my way up to campus to drop it off.

"Did you drive in, P?" Nesto asked, looking a little too amused at my expense. I was not fond of driving and had only bought the black Audi SUV I now owned after much prodding from my friends.

"Yes," I said with a groan, making Nesto laugh with my very unenthusiastic answer.

"I assume you got my man to work in one piece." His humorous tone almost, but not quite, masked the fact that he actually wanted to know if I'd safely delivered his lover to work.

I'd lived most of my life in New York City and never had a need for a car. It was a big milestone to now be someone who needed to drive everywhere. Only my friend Camilo was sympathetic to my dilemma, but even he told me to face the fact I would need one if I was living in Ithaca. Juan Pablo and Nesto just told me to get over it.

My mom, on the other hand, had been very reluctant about the car purchase. She was usually all for the flex, but me driving a car upstate was not sitting well

with her. She kept saying it made her nervous. I tried
to temper her uneasiness by reminding her that I wasn't
going to be driving in the city, and would most likely
not get into a head-on collision with a yellow cab going
eighty on the wrong side of a one-way street. As one
would on any given day in Manhattan.

She acquiesced, begging me to be careful, but still
not fully at ease. I usually joked around with her whenever she got overprotective—I was her only child and
sometimes that meant she was a bit more in my business than necessary. But this time I didn't push because
I knew what she worried about was not me getting into
a fender bender. She worried about what the mother of
every black man who got behind the wheel of a car in
this country worried about.

Hell, I worried about it too, and it pissed me off, because I refused to live in fear. But I wasn't delusional
either, and still spent the night before I picked up my
car watching YouTube videos on what to do if you got
stopped by the police. I also made sure I kept my license
and registration on the visor above the driver seat where
it was fully visible and easy to get. I hated having to do
that, and how paranoid it made me feel, but I wasn't a
fool. I was pretty good at avoiding things I didn't want to
deal with, but some things you ignored at your own peril.

"Dude, you look mad emo right now." Nesto's re-
proachful tone finally pulled me out of my fretting.
"I've been standing here for five minutes waiting for
you to talk. The fuck, Patrice?"

I rubbed a hand over my face, a little embarrassed.
"Sorry. Just got distracted. Yeah, I gave Jude a ride, so
he needs one of us to drive him back home." At the mention of his partner, Nesto's face lit up as usual.

"Good, he's been on a carpool kick lately. He's been taking the bus, trying to be more mindful of the environment."

Jude had changed Nesto in so many ways. He and I had always been the intense ones in our foursome. Nesto, Camilo, Juanpa and me.

Like me, Nesto had never made time for romance or indulged in situations that could end up messy. He'd taken huge chances when he'd left the city to come here. Put it all on the line with his business *and* his heart, but it had paid off. Here he was living with a man he loved. His whole life on a different track.

I wanted to talk with Nesto about seeing Easton. I knew I needed some advice, but still couldn't make myself open my mouth. Why was it so hard for me to talk about this stuff? Nesto was like my brother, we'd seen each other through everything.

Why couldn't I open up to him about this?

Before I talked myself out of it, I did it. "I ran into Easton last night." As soon as I mentioned him, an image of how he'd looked filled my head. He'd just been in jeans, a sweater and sandals, but as always it all looked like it was tailor-made for his lean body. The only little bit of imperfection had been his adorably ruffled hair. His dark brown, almost black hair was usually perfectly styled, but last night it had been messy, which only made him that much more appealing to me. Those green eyes flashing with want and something else when he saw me. Surprise and apprehension. Like he'd expected me to be an ass to him.

I knew I'd run into him eventually. This was a small town and we knew a lot of the same people. And no matter how many times I told myself I was here because no one could say no to a tenure track position at an Ivy League school, I couldn't lie to myself. The fact that Easton lived here *had* been on my mind in a big way while I was deciding to take this job.

He was so fucking fine and seeing him last night had been sobering. Everything inside me seemed to realign when I was around him. Easton made me feel like I was the center of the universe, like I could be however I wanted and he'd be into it.

Being myself in front of people I didn't know was not easy for me. Even with my friends I was closed off and guarded at times. I was always on the lookout for what was going on, mindful of the space I was taking up. Aware of all the different ways people were looking at me. How I was coming off, and the assumptions people were making about me.

A black man had to always think about the space he was in.

Most of the time it seemed like people were looking right through me. Not Easton.

He looked at me like my friends and my mother looked at me. Like he could see *all* of me. The me on the outside and the me on the inside, and that fucking scared me. There was too much I didn't want to be seen so clearly. That the Zen thing I tried to go for, the slow movements and the soft voice, were just my way of keeping the almost overpowering frustration I constantly felt from spilling out.

Easton was so lighthearted, like he'd never known pain. The guy's job was to prosecute SVU cases. I knew he saw heinous shit day in and day out, and yet his face was always as open as a blue sky. No hurt, no bitterness. Such certainty everything would be all right. That if you fought the good fight you'd take the day. Like he could show what he felt and didn't fear anyone would come back later and use it against him.

I didn't know what to do with that.

Me, I was painfully aware of what it took for me to get the job I had. What I'd had to do, ignore, let go of, overlook or just bury down until it burned out in my gut. I could work ten times as hard as anyone else, get as far ahead as possible, and the feeling like it could all be taken away was ever present.

That was something I never seemed to shake off. Closeness was not something I could do easily. I'd practically given up on getting it from anyone other than my best friends and the family members who continued to speak to me after I came out.

That was until last summer and Easton. As soon as I set eyes on him walking toward Nesto's truck, those impish green eyes and that perfect smile lured me in. I was still trying to let go. With Easton it was like my heart and my body were working together to override my entire approach to life.

Nesto just shook his head like I confused the fuck out of him. "So?" he said, circling a hand in the air to get me to come out with whatever I was not saying. "How's he?"

I knew the smile on Nesto's face when I mentioned Easton was genuine. Easton had been a good friend to Nesto since he'd arrived in Ithaca. My friend looked out the window, his eyes trained in the direction of the county courthouse where the District Attorney's office was. "He's been busy since he started the interim DA gig. Hasn't stopped by as often. He usually comes here for lunch a few times a week."

I nodded, thinking about what Easton had said last

night. "He mentioned that. Said he's not sure about the politics." Easton's answer had been ambivalent, which was different for him, at least when it came to his job. "Sounds like he's thinking about it though."

Nesto nodded, eyes interested. "He'd be good for this town."

I blinked at that, because Nesto was not one to get political, ever. Jude on the other hand did not mince words when it came to opinions about bullshit happening in town. Once again, I smiled at all the changes love had made in my friend, but before I had a chance to detract the conversation, Nesto called me out.

"Yeah, you're not getting me off your run-in with Easton to talk about politics. Spit it out."

I shrugged, feeling stupid, because I *wanted* to spill my feelings all over this floor and that was so not the norm for me.

"He was fine. It's not like we had a heart-to-heart," I said, lifting a shoulder like an asshole. "I was getting some snacks to bring to the office and ran into him. We only talked for like five minutes."

Nesto just stared at me, waiting for whatever else I was going to say to come out of my mouth. After fidgeting with my pocket square and generally acting like a preschooler, I finally said it. "He said his building had some vacancies when I told him my apartment might not work out."

Nesto's eyes widened at that. "I actually thought about him, he told me he'd been fixing up those two units after the tenants left. He wanted to do something to the floors."

He must have noticed the confused look on my face,

because he angled his head before asking cautiously, "He didn't tell you he owns the building?"

"No, he sure as fuck did not tell me he'd be my land-lord!" I said, annoyed. "You know what, forget it."

Nesto was not done though, he flipped his hand and pointed two fingers at me. "He probably didn't men-tion it because you would have told him no and pulled that judgmental stank face you're rocking right now." He twisted his mouth to the side before really going in.

"P, what the fuck is your deal, my dude? I mean, I know why you may be all cagey with *him*, but why are you doing this shit with me?" He gripped the edge of the bar he was standing behind, as if it would somehow help him get ahold of his patience. "Come on, son. Even if you won't admit it to your damn self, I know your ass is up here at least partly because you're thirsting after his dick. Don't deny, because I know the jobs you turned down to take this one. Not that I'm not fucking elated to have you here, because you know I am."

I frowned as he spoke because he was telling the ab-solute truth, but still the frustration bubbled up. "Okay, let's say it's true. Let's say I do like him, what am I going to do with that, Nesto? I have literally spent the last ten years of my life studying and writing about how the system that Easton works every day to uphold is weaponized to keep people like me in chains. How do I reconcile that?" I gripped my hands together and pressed them to my chest, my voice strained when I fi-nally spoke. "I mean really, I'm asking, because I have no fucking clue how to do that."

Nesto sighed and looked at me like I was too fucking difficult to deal with this early on a Monday.

"I don't know, pa." Nesto exhaled, deflated, because

in the end he knew my struggle all too well. When he spoke, the frustration was all gone, and all that was left was a kindness and understanding that was somehow even harder to hear. "I got no pearls of wisdom to bestow upon you. All I know is, life is too fucking short—and frankly fucked up—to dismiss someone who makes you happy out of hand, just because your jobs put you at odds. I mean what do you really even know about Easton? Other than he's fine as fuck and a generally pleasant guy." He was ticking his fingers at this point. "And that he can obviously work his dick in a way that totally does it for you."

I rolled my eyes at that and Nesto chuckled, holding up his hands to concede some kind of point.

"I know you're gonna keep agonizing over this, and I understand it's more than your jobs being *at odds*. Being with a man like Easton feels like compromising. *I get that*. I know it's not anything to take lightly. So take your time and do what you need to. But just chill out a little, okay? Let your guard down for once. Some people are worth sacrificing certain things for."

The beatific look on his face let me know Nesto was probably talking about Jude again. They'd worked hard at their relationship and their devotion for each other was plain to see. Getting together hadn't been easy for them either. Jude had a hard past, which had made the early stages in their relationship complicated, and Nesto almost let his workaholic ways ruin things for them, but they'd powered through it. Nesto had the life he always dreamed of.

He knew what he was talking about.

I dipped my head, acknowledging he had a point. "I know certain people are. I appreciate you understanding that things are complicated and I will try to take your advice and let my guard down a bit." I shoved my hands into the pockets of my slacks, still conflicted. "At the moment, I'm not feeling ready though. I need more time to get my bearings here, get a feel for my department and the fuckery I'm sure is happening there. So Easton will just have to be on hold for now."

He threw his hands up again, like he knew I wasn't going to budge another inch.

"You do you, P. We here if you need us. Let me throw you a bone by changing the subject."

I laughed helplessly at Nesto's usual directness. "Sure."

He looked back toward the kitchen to where Ari—one of Nesto's original two employees when he first got to Ithaca, and who was now an assistant manager at the restaurant—was standing.

"Ari wants to ask you if you would be his mentor. Nothing too deep, just some advice on school, for now. He's working on getting fully matriculated and wants advice on classes and such."

The warmth in my chest at what Nesto said was a surprise.

"Really? I thought he wanted to be a lawyer? I'm an economics and public policy guy."

Nesto shook his head, glancing over his shoulder, before leaning in close. "That's the thing, he's getting interested in the stuff you do. He read your dissertation paper on distributive justice and he's been all over it. Also he's obsessed with your Twitter game." He shook his head with a baffled look on his face, like he was talking about a deep and dark world that he had no clue why anyone wanted any part of.

"Ari's deep into Black Twitter now, follows all the

dudes you're on there pontificating with. It doesn't matter though." He lifted a shoulder and smiled wide. "Whatever he ends up doing, I think it'll be good for him to have someone he can talk about stuff with." He flattened his lips, worry furrowing his brow. "He's on his own out here. All his family is still in Congo, other than his uncle, who as far as I can tell is a raging homophobe. And that's a problem, since Ari's been making noise about coming out to him."

He looked toward the kitchen again. "No pressure man, of course."

I shook my head, already feeling really compelled to do this for Ari. He was such an impressive young man, and had overcome so much. He'd come to the States on his own as a refugee from Congo when he was a teen and ended up in an immigrant detention center for almost two years before they let him go without ever giving him a reason for why they detained him in the first place. I nodded at Nesto and lifted my hand toward where Ari was busy checking things off from a clipboard.

"I would be happy to. I'm not sure how useful I'll be, but I'm willing to give it a shot."

I noticed that Yin, who like Ari had been one of Nesto's original employees, was standing a lot closer to Ari than a coworker would. Yin was petite, his delicate features serious as he worked with Ari, who towered over him. Ari was a lot taller and bulkier than Yin. His ebony skin a contrast to Yin's milky complexion. Their bodies were comfortable next to each other though.

Like lovers.

Nesto must have been able to tell what I was thinking because he just glanced at them and shook his head with a fond smile on his face. After a moment he hollered for

Ari. As soon as he was within reach Nesto slapped him on the back. Ari looked at Nesto like he was his hero.

"Ari, come and talk to Patrice. He's down with mentoring you."

The young man's face lit up before looking even as he appeared a little embarrassed.

"Boss man, I asked you not to say anything."

Nesto shook his head and laughed. "Why, man? How's he going to know you want him to mentor you if we never say anything?"

I intervened before Nesto embarrassed the kid any more. "I'd be honored to, Ari. I'm not sure how much I can actually mentor you on, you seem to have your shit more than together. But whatever you need, let me know."

"Thank you, Patrice. That would be great. I have a lot of questions."

I pointed at my jacket pocket, where my phone was. "Sure. I have to get going, but Nesto has my number. Send me a text and we can set up a time to talk. I'm interested in hearing your plans. Nesto said you're taking classes at Cornell this semester. Good for you."

He nodded enthusiastically at that. "Yes, I'm only taking two of them, but it's going well."

"Great." I waved at Nesto, who had gone behind the counter again to do some work. "Catch you at home, Nes." He muttered a "yes" with his eyes focused on the screen as he waved his hand over his head. I moved in to give Ari dap and then made my way out onto the street.

I walked to my car feeling lighter than I'd been a half hour before, Nesto's words about giving things with Easton a chance still floating in my head.

Chapter Two

Easton

I tried not to stare too hard as I watched Patrice walk out of Nesto's restaurant and get into a black SUV before driving up the hill to campus. He'd been wearing gray slacks and a navy jacket with some navy and gray oxfords. He even had a dark brown bowtie on. His locs in a half-knot. He looked dapper and professorial, and it suited him. As his car disappeared from my line of sight I thought about how there was something almost regal about the way Patrice carried himself. Like we were all supposed to bow when he walked by.

"*He* certainly has your attention." My boss Cindy's voice ripped me out of my musings, the amused tone in her voice promising questions about my staring. "I don't think I've ever seen that particular puppy face on you before. It takes *a lot* for me to notice a man, but even I have to admit, he's gorgeous. Did you hit it and quit it or was he too smart to fall for your bullshit?"

I rolled my eyes at Cindy because she thought she was hilarious. "First of all, please stop using expressions like 'hit and quit it.' You're my mom's age and that just creeps me out. Second, I'm not talking about it." I forced myself to make eye contact and smiled. Totally casual. "He's a friend of Nesto's. OuNYe's owner."

Cindy threw up her arms while rolling her eyes at me. "Like I don't know who Nesto is. He and Jude are the Gay Power Couple in town these days. I must say it's nice to see that us old Ithaca gays will be passing the torch to such good young people. Present company excluded of course."

"I'm not good at being part of cabals. I tend to get twitchy."

She shook her head like I was hopeless, then pointed in the direction Patrice had driven off. "Don't change the subject. What's up with you and that beautiful man you were just staring at?"

Cindy and I weren't new at this game. I'd known her since she came to work for my father over twenty years ago. Teasing me about my love life was one of her favorite past times.

I looked at her more closely and saw that she was wearing jeans and a flannel shirt, her usual "out in town" look, but she was carrying something that looked suspiciously like a laptop bag. I pointed at it with as disapproving a look as I could manage.

"A better question, Cindy Brooks, is what are you doing *here*?"

Cindy was probably my closest friend in Ithaca other than Priscilla, Nesto's cousin. She was also my boss, and was supposed to be on leave recovering from major heart surgery right now. I shook my head thinking that her wife, also a dear friend, would not be happy to know I was letting Cindy sneak into the office.

"Lorraine would skin me if she finds out you're coming here to work when you should be at home resting."

Cindy and Lorraine had kept me sane through a lot of ups and downs with my parents over the years, including when I came out. My parents hadn't been awful, but they hadn't been the most supportive either, and Cindy and Lorraine became confidantes over the years. That's why when I finished law school, instead of going with the family business, I joined Cindy in the DA's office. That still didn't mean that she got to pry into every inch of my sex life.

After engaging in a stare-off Cindy shook her head and grinned as she patted her bag. "I'm just dropping this off. I'll leave…as soon as you tell me who that was."

I sighed as we walked into the county courthouse where our offices were located, resigned to the fact I was not going to get her to go home. "We had a thing last summer when he was out here helping Nesto with the truck. We just hooked up a few times, which was nowhere near enough for me." I was very focused on not making eye contact with Cindy as I spoke. "He took a faculty job at Cornell. I was hoping we could pick up where we'd left off."

I lifted a shoulder, trying for a lightness I did not feel. "I ran into him last night and he didn't seem interested in me in the slightest."

She clicked her tongue, genuinely sad my hopes for a booty call had gone up in flames. "That's too bad, hon. I've never seen you look at someone like that. You know you're the kid Lorraine and I never got around to having." She paused, holding up a finger and winking at me. "Actually, no, more like you're the kid Lorraine always wanted, but you grew on me." I laughed as she came closer to squeeze my arm. When she spoke she sounded wistful though. "We'd like to see you happy, with someone that can appreciate that big heart of yours, no matter how hard you work to keep it hidden underneath the 'too busy for love' facade. I think I failed you as a mentor in the work and life balance department."

I gave her a rueful smile and turned around. "Now I really am worried you need to be in bed," I teased. "You were an excellent mentor. As for Patrice, it doesn't matter, because he's just not that into me." I hoped that my comment didn't get her thinking of some scheme to get Patrice and me together. Cindy had a tendency of pushing me when she thought I needed a nudge. I knew it came from a good place, but it got old fast.

She opened her mouth with what I was sure was another question when Ron Vogler, our investigator, walked up to us. "Did you hear about last night?" he asked, and I noticed his usually relaxed demeanor was replaced with a somber expression.

Ron had been with the Ithaca Police Department for over twenty years before coming to work with us, and he was in the know about everything happening in the county when it came to law enforcement. He usually wasn't the type to gossip, so whatever this was, it wasn't good.

I shook my head at his question, already pulling my phone out of my pocket to see if there was anything I'd missed. "Amber was on last night, so I didn't hear." The ADAs took turns being on call, so that there would always be someone available to handle whatever came up in the middle of the night or the weekends. I'd been off, so had no idea about whatever fresh hell had Ron brooding.

He pursed his lips before answering as I braced myself. "One of the new deputies from the sheriff's department stopped two Ithaca College students on Route 79. They were black, of course. Going maybe five miles over the limit. One of them recorded the whole thing and posted it on Facebook and it does not look good. The deputy was so fucking overzealous and his tone was, frankly, offensive."

I bit out a curse as I walked through the metal detector, Ron on my heels, continuing his recount of the incident. "Neither of them got hurt, but he did make them get out of the car and made a big show of patting them down. I saw in the *Ithaca Star* that they're filing a complaint claiming he was excessively aggressive."

I heard Cindy sigh heavily from behind me as we made our way to the elevator. "Cindy you really need to go home, this is going to get you worked up, seriously." She waved me off as I turned to Ron, who was looking more pissed by the second.

"Which deputy was it?"

Ron just shook his head, his face grim. "Chief Cooker's youngest." My heart sank.

"Fuck." Cindy's curse rang out in the hallway outside the DA's office.

Cooker had been the head of the Ithaca Police Department for almost twenty years, and had only recently retired. For the most part he had run his department well, and was respected… Unfortunately, his children seemed to only be interested in ruining their father's legacy.

I shook my head in disgust as we walked into my office, because no matter what, this was going to be a shit show. "Awesome," I said, my voice heavy with sarcasm. "I went to elementary school with his brothers and they were assholes even back then. Seems like the youngest one is trying to emulate his older siblings. I'm going to call Sheriff Day."

Cindy's eyes widened at that and I held up my hand. "Cindy, I know that it's hard for you to be hands off, but I am interim DA and you need to be resting. I will handle this." I took my phone out and sighed.

Ron scoffed as I fiddled with it. "Cooker's kids are not the only ones that could use a talking to in that department," Ron said, frustrated.

Ron's wife was black and they were raising two biracial teenage boys. Of course this type of bullshit was going to rattle him. "Nothing is going to change until people start being held accountable and there's an honest conversation about biases in that department."

"Agreed," I said, wondering how Day was taking this. He was a friend, but since he'd barely secured his last run for sheriff after coming out as gay during the campaign, I knew he'd been walking a very thin line. "Day's a reasonable guy, we can talk to him about this frankly, but we need to know how to approach it."

Ron shoved his hands in his pockets and looked between Cindy and me. "I want to burn shit down." Cindy balked at that and Ron shook his head. "But I know my role here, and I will defer to you." His conciliatory tone did little to mask how distressed he was. "Stuff like this is becoming a common occurrence again, and I don't like it."

Cindy groaned as I called Day's personal number. This was not the first time I'd checked in with him about issues happening in our jurisdiction, so when he practically barked that he couldn't talk right, I was taken aback.

I was still trying to figure out how to respond, when

he exhaled, and spoke again, this time not as aggressive, but no less distressed. "I know why you're calling and I'm going to take care of it."

I was about to ask how exactly he'd deal with it, but before I had a chance he ended the call.

When I glanced up, Cindy was looking at me expectantly. "Day said he would 'handle it,'" I used air quotes, unimpressed by my exchange with the sheriff. "He sounded pretty panicked, so I hope that means he's taking it seriously."

Ron shook his head and pressed his back against the wall. "I hope it means they're not just going to yell at the deputy and call it a day."

At this Cindy's face hardened. "It is not our job to tell the sheriff's department how to deal with an isolated issue." She really stressed the word *isolated*, as she looked between Ron and me. "I am telling you, *as your boss* that you need to let Day do his job and when it's appropriate for us to get involved, we will. I am not looking to piss off Day. His special crimes investigators are some of our best partners in the highly sensitive cases."

Like Ron and I didn't know that.

I stood there with the tension suddenly heavy and uncomfortable, taking in what Cindy was saying.

Ron spoke first. "So this office's position is that we wait until there's a crime to prosecute?"

Once again, Cindy spoke over me. "No, this office's position is that we're not going to overstep and possibly burn a bridge with a department that we have worked hard to build a relationship with, unless we absolutely have to. We are *not* there yet."

I was in no uncertain terms being told to mind my business. "Whatever you say, boss." I tried to sound cordial, because in the end, she had the last word. If I was being honest with myself, I had no idea how to deal with any of it either.

Cindy left without responding to what I'd said, which was probably something I'd have to deal with later. The frustration was rolling off Ron, but we'd gotten our marching orders. I sighed and sat down at my desk, closing my eyes for a moment. "Cindy's right. At this point there isn't much we can do other than keep an eye on it."

Ron opened his mouth and then closed it, as if he knew he'd just hit a wall. "These things escalate and they are never *ever* a one-time thing. You know that, Easton. I mean you watch the news, you read. You pay attention."

I glanced at the pile of folders I needed to review for court later and wanted to curse. None of us needed this shit right now. "I do, I also know, as you do, that we can't just make demands from the sheriff's department, especially when not much has happened."

As soon as I said it, Ron's face went stony. Then I realized how flippant I'd just sounded.

Fuck.

"I know this is not *nothing*, and that it's going to scare a lot of people in the community, Ron. *I know that*. I'm not saying we should ignore it. I'm saying you and I can't take this on, no matter how much we'd like to."

I kept the "not that I have any ideas" part to myself and thought of Patrice.

This was the kind of thing he would pick up on and go off on Twitter about. Just one more reason for him to not want to have anything to do with me. And that unhelpful and self-involved line of thinking needed to be cut off immediately anyway, because I was a lot of things, but I would not be fucking callous.

Ron's silence told me that he was probably stuck too, or at least giving up for now. I gestured to the untouched files on my desk and looked up. "Sorry, man, I need to be in court in an hour, let's talk about this later. Can you check in to ask exactly what happened and if this was the same officer who's been getting other complaints?"

Ron looked annoyed but seemed to be on the same page as me. "I'll see what I can find out. Not that the boss is going to let us move on any of it."

I had a sinking feeling he was not far off. Cindy liked to keep all her ducks in a row when it came to our community and law enforcement partnerships. But this was not exactly something we could ignore. At least I wanted to believe we wouldn't.

When I looked at Ron his expression told me he was probably onto what I was thinking. "We'll figure it out. I'm not going to let you down on this." Ron looked about as confident as I felt about my statement, but it seemed like for now he was letting it go.

I took a few deep breaths and tried to push away the stress of the past half hour. There was nothing more I could do with this, and I had cases to work on. Just as I was settling down to look at the docket for the day, I saw my phone buzz with a message. I smiled when I saw it was from Nesto.

Hey, man. Jude and I are having a little thing at our place on Friday, sevenish.

I'm making a Dominican Sancocho (it's a stew thing with mad meat in it) because only for Jude would I cook on my day off. Come thru, if you're free.

The way the heaviness from moments before seemed to lift—at least in part—when I thought about running into Patrice was pretty pathetic. Before I talked myself out of it, I picked up the phone and texted back.

I'll be there. Should I bring anything?

He replied almost immediately.

Nah man, just yourself. See you then.

Great. Thanks for the invite.

I got a fist emoji as a response.

The prospect of seeing Patrice was exciting and unnerving. This was all new territory for me, this level of anticipation to see someone… I wasn't sure what to do with any of it, especially since Patrice was clearly not in the same place as me, but I didn't succeed at my job by taking things sitting down. I wasn't going to push if Patrice didn't want to play, but I wasn't going to hide away either.

Patrice

I was still digesting the conversation I'd had with Nesto about Easton when I walked into my office. I didn't expect much human interaction until I headed to class later in the morning, and was checking my email when Brad Gunham, one of the associate professors in the economics department walked into the office.

"Professor Denis."

Brad was the reason people thought all academics

were insufferable assholes. He went out of his way to let people know all the ways in which he was smarter than them, and could not have a conversation without repeatedly attempting to throw shade or just outright offend. The first time he ever talked to me, he let me know we needed to "band together" since we were the only two minorities in the department.

Brad was white and both his parents were world-famous economists. I came to the States with my mom as a refugee from Haiti in the nineties, and she literally had to work three jobs to support us. But to Brad the fact that we were both gay apparently made us homies, and brothers in the "the struggle." It would've been funny if he wasn't literally the master of micro-aggressions. I sighed internally and tried my best not to sound as weary as I felt when I finally answered.

"Hey, Brad."

He had his usual sneer in place, indicating he was on that bullshit again, and I had literally zero patience for it right now. I had to play nice though. Brad had just gotten tenure and would most likely be on the committee that decided on mine when it came up. The chair of the department was also, from what I'd seen at least, very much a Brad fan, so I had to keep it polite, no matter how much this dude annoyed me.

He raked his eyes over me as he leaned against the door. "Patrice, you're on brand, as always."

What the fuck did that mean?

He waved a hand in my general direction, which I guess was his way of presenting me with the evidence. "You've got the dapper thing down to a T." His eyes were literally glomming me, and I tried my best to suppress the shudder coursing through my body.

He was so fucking greasy.

"Can I help you with anything, Brad? I'm in the middle of office hours right now, and may have a couple of students coming by to talk about the midterm assignment."

He ignored my attempt to get him out of my office, and walked in, parking his skinny ass in one of the chairs. "Oh I won't take long, just wanted to check in how you're getting on. I know that your research topics can be a little controversial and was wondering how it had gone over in your sessions."

This was one hundred percent not his business, and the controversy he was talking about was my research focusing on how people of color experienced discrimination through government sanctioned public policy. It was apparently a little too real for Brad's brand of academia. He also knew I was teaching Statistics 101 like the fucking grunt I was, and that my research was not likely to come up in those classes. He still had to ask, to be an asshole.

"They're handling the class fine, thanks."

"Oh good," he said, sounding fake as hell, and shifted on the seat like he was getting comfy for a long chat.

Fuck. My. Life.

"Have you had time to get around town, get to know some folks?" He stressed the word *folks*, and it was very hard to control the eye roll itching to come out.

"Actually yes, my best friend lives here. He's one of the owners of OuNYe, the new restaurant downtown, and his partner has been here for a few years. We hang out a lot."

He nodded with interest, crossing his arms over his usual cardigan and button-down combo.

"Oh nice, I love that place. It's very popular." He cocked his head to the side, and gave me another assessing look. At this point I couldn't even guess what was going through Brad's head. "I've seen the owner, he's very handsome. Are you sure you're not up here because there's a little more than friendship going on there?"

Of course he'd go there. For Brad nothing was ever lacking nefariousness.

How did this person think it was okay to ask that when I'd just mentioned Nesto had a partner, and why did he think I was interested in having a conversation with him about *anything*?

"Nesto and I have been friends since we were like eight years old, Brad. Also like I said, he has a partner. They live together and are in a committed *monogamous* relationship."

Not that it's any of your motherfucking business, my guy.

He didn't respond and took his time running a hand over his heather-gray sweater, as I sat there fidgeting. "So, I actually stopped by to let you know that you were being 'discussed' at a dinner I was at yesterday, with some of the more senior faculty." The smug-ass look on his face told me this was probably the reason why he'd come in here in the first place.

"Okay." It was hard not to glare.

"They were talking about your social media persona." I would've loved to wipe that shit-eating grin off his face. "Departments have to pay attention to that sort of thing, in case a faculty member says something inappropriate that could hurt the school." He was loving this little bullshit power play, but I would not give him the satisfaction of seeing my even slightly fazed.

When he realized I was not going to respond, he opened his mouth again. "You certainly have a following and seem very focused on hot-button issues."

I tried not to cut my eyes at him, but it was so fucking hard. "I'm not sure I follow."

He lifted a shoulder, and I could tell he was about to say something that would infuriate me and for the millionth time I asked myself why I was willing to work in a field that was full of people like this.

"Well social justice is important and certainly something this department aims to look at closely. It just seems like you're so heated in your tweets."

This time I really did have to school my expression.

"I *am* 'heated' in my tweets, Brad." I actually made air quotes. "I tweet about angering things. I also make it very clear in my account that all my opinions are my own and nothing to do with my employer. Which I don't even mention in my bio, by the way. I know the department is well aware of my Twitter presence, it came up in my interviews."

He just stared at me with that self-satisfied look on his face, like he was super happy he'd pissed me off.

I was getting very close to leaning into my general annoyance with this guy when Ted, another faculty, popped his head in my office and saved me from myself.

I stood up and walked over to the door, feeling deeply grateful for Ted's timing. "Hey man. Good to see you."

Ted was in the sociology department. He'd gotten tenured a few years back, but unlike Brad he was the opposite of pretentious. He was also Jude's friend and an all-around good guy.

"Hey, I was about to go to the coffee shop downstairs." He cast an icy look in Brad's direction and then turned his attention back to me. "I was wondering if you wanted to walk down together."

I was not one to show emotion, but at the moment I hoped the expression on my face could convey just how grateful I was to be rescued from this shit show of a conversation.

"Sure. I could use some caffeinating."

Brad got a clue for once and stood up. But not without adding, "Coffee break already, it must be nice to be in a field where the pressure to publish isn't as rigorous."

Ted only nodded and kept talking to me. His wife Carmen's salt must've been rubbing off on him. "The barista that makes the good lattes is there today, Patrice."

Yeah, that ice he was sending Brad's way was all Carmen.

Brad made a big show of shoving the chair back and popping up. "I should get going, I'm almost done with that revision I've been working on." I loved how all of a sudden Brad was Mr. Hustle when he'd been sitting in my office like he had nothing but time for the last ten minutes.

Ted shook his head as we started for the stairs. "That dude is a fucking pill. I can't stand him. I wasn't even going to get coffee, but when I walked by and saw his ass parked in your office, I figured you needed some rescuing."

I just nodded, not wanting to get into how the conversation with Brad had annoyed the hell out of me. One of the reasons why I liked Ted was that I didn't need to explain to him why certain things people said landed poorly with me. He was a good ally and a mindful listener, and I appreciated having him around.

As we walked to get our coffee Ted didn't push me to talk, which I respected "Speaking of infuriating things, did you see the story of the two students that got stopped by the police yesterday?"

I shook my head, already dreading whatever he was about to say.

"From what I read about it, it sounds like they were barely going five miles over the speed limit. They're filing a complaint for harassment. Of course, nothing so far about accountability for the officers who're doing this shit."

I exhaled at the same time I felt the muscles in my shoulders tense again. "I didn't hear." I sighed, weary as fuck already, and it was barely 10:00 a.m. "I mean it's not like I expected this kind of thing only happened in the city, but it's never not disappointing." Ted only nodded, his handsome face thunderous, as I pulled out my phone. I opened my Twitter app and noticed a tweet from earlier this morning, where I'd dragged some DC flunkie for some mess brewing down there, had blown up. I started tapping out a new one.

Nice to know the move from NYC to Upstate is not going to let me get rusty. Driving While Black seems to be enough to get hassled up here too. Any students getting stopped for going five miles over the limit? @ me if you are.

I hit send and put my phone back in my pocket and when I looked up at Ted he was grinning at me.

"You're going to be good for this town."

Chapter Three

Easton

I'd never been the jealous type, but whatever was happening had turned me into a possessive asshole when I was around Patrice. I'd been seething in silence for the past twenty minutes, watching him get chatted up by some guy at Nesto and Jude's party. I had no clue who he was, but he'd been stuck to Patrice like a fucking shadow since I'd gotten here thirty minutes ago.

"You can't actually burn a hole through a person by staring, Easton."

I turned around and saw Jude standing behind me with an amused look on his face.

"I don't know," I said through gritted teeth. "I feel like I was making progress. Who is that anyway?"

He used his glass of rosé to point in the direction of Patrice and his new chat buddy. "That's Peter. He's a mathematics professor from somewhere on the West Coast. He knows Ted from undergrad and was here for the week doing something up at Cornell. They brought him along since he's not leaving until the morning. No need to worry, he will be on his way out of town soon." Jude was having a little too much fun at my expense.

I kept looking in Patrice's direction, but turned my head slightly to continue talking with Jude. It seemed my desperation was showing.

"Am I that obvious?"

Jude chuckled and took a sip of his wine before answering. "It wouldn't say *super* obvious, but I may be hyperaware of people pining in silence. It was kind of my thing for a while."

In that moment Patrice turned his head and finally looked my way. When his eyes landed on me, the intensity in them heated my skin. For a second he looked at me like he was reaching across the room to touch me. It was gone in a flash though, and then he was back to aloof Patrice, but it was too late. I'd felt the heat of his stare on me.

I pointed at the sideboard where they'd set up the bar. Which was conveniently located next to Patrice. "I'm going to get myself another drink."

This dynamic was becoming a pattern for us: Patrice momentarily letting his guard down and me pouncing.

Carmen scoffed, "We can tell you're thirsty, Easton. You go and get yourself that drink."

I started walking and turned to respond to Carmen, "You're hilarious."

I heard Jude and Carmen laugh as I made my way to Patrice.

When I got to him, he had an amused look on his face, obviously entertained by whatever those two were doing behind me.

I pointed my thumb in their direction as I stood next to Patrice. "Are they making fun of me?"

Patrice shook his head, and the sides of his mouth lifted enough that it could almost be considered a smile.

Almost.

"I wouldn't call it making fun, but they seem to find whatever you said pretty entertaining."

I looked over at the guy who'd been talking to Patrice and held my hand out.

"Easton Archer."

"Peter Black. Nice to meet you." I shook his hand with more force than necessary as Patrice stood there placidly, unaware that I was basically ready to challenge the guy to a duel over him.

The handshake went on a little longer than was reasonable and I barely refrained from grabbing my dick and posturing, all while Patrice looked at me like he was not sure what was wrong with me. But I'd seen that smile when he spotted me across the room a moment ago, so I was staying strong.

Fuck Pete and his sweater vest.

My death stare must have worked because after a quick goodbye Peter made his way over to another cluster of people on the other side of the room.

"Patrice," I said smugly now that I'd successfully managed to get Peter to move on.

He looked me up and down. His eyes landing for just a bit too long on my mouth. I ran my tongue over my upper lip, which I hoped would earn me a reaction.

When we'd been together he nipped at my mouth all the time. Teasing me about how red my lips were. I was hoping, like me, he'd remember those moments. How good they were. I'd felt so close to Patrice on those nights last summer. Like he understood something essential about me and I'd felt like I did the same for him.

Right now, Patrice's body language was mystifying me though. His shoulders were tight and tense and yet his eyes kept coming back to my face and my body. They were almost…needy. Like a kid who's in a candy store without a cent to buy himself any of the treats he's looking at. I brought my glass up to my lips and took a sip of my wine, looking straight at him. Letting him see in my eyes that everything he saw he could have, anytime.

All he had to do was ask.

We stood there, our bodies pulling closer with every breath, in heavy silence. Neither of us wanting to be the one to break first, and it was taking everything I had not to cave. I was trained in this, I did *not* show my cards. I did not reveal my position until I was sure I had the opportunity to take it all.

In the end he spoke first. "It's good to see you again, Easton."

I was going to ask him straight out why he was being so standoffish, but decided to change tactics. What always worked between us was keeping things light. I had a feeling if I got intense on him, I'd send him running in the other direction.

"I came to rescue you from boring mathematicians." I dipped my head in a little curtesy. "You're welcome."

He shook his head, his eyes crinkling with amusement.

"Who says I wasn't enjoying the conversation?" He slid his hands in his pockets and lifted his shoulder a fraction of a centimeter. Unbothered. "I like math. I do a lot of it for a living."

This was us flirting. Patrice barely moving a body part and me practically doing cartwheels.

But as it always worked between us, it wasn't long before our focus on each other built, and I felt the air change around us. After so many months of him act-ing like he barely knew me, I'd started to wonder if I'd made it all up. If I'd imagined this connection so strong it was almost palpable. There relief of seeing in his eyes the same intensity I was feeling made me weak.

Which gave me just enough of a nudge to push his buttons a little. "I know you do. I also know a whole lot of other things you like." I didn't even try to rein in the suggestiveness.

I was going to make my move.

I looked around, to see just how handsy I could get. We were tucked away in the corner now, everyone had moved to the patio where Nesto and Jude were break-ing in their new fire pit. So we were alone.

I had no problem with being shameless. I moved for-ward, my eyes zeroed in on those lips I'd been dream-ing about for months.

"You're pretty sure of yourself, Mr. Archer," he said, straightening as I got nearer. We were barely two inches apart and his lips twitched, like he was getting ready for my kiss. But I made him wait. I could play this game too.

Before I moved in on that mouth I couldn't stop thinking about I put mine close to his ear.

"I'm sure about fuck all when it comes to most things about me and you, but I *do* know you like my kisses." He sucked his teeth and his head tilted, making my lips brush against his cheek.

I turned my head to kiss him, but before I could, he moved in first. Our mouths touched, and the floor tilted under me. I was not a man to lose my footing over a kiss, but Patrice's lips pressed to mine made the room spin.

I didn't care we were in a place where anyone could walk in at any time. *I did not care.* All I wanted was to get closer.

I reached out and placed my glass on the sideboard, put both my hands on his neck, and moved in so we were pressed together.

He licked into my mouth and it felt so fucking *good*, like everything made sense again. We stayed there just for a few seconds, and I let myself go, tasting and licking, remembering his taste. The warmth of him. I could have stood there for hours, but after a moment Patrice moved away. I balked, wanting to keep him close.

He just smiled and picked up my glass and took a sip of wine, but I saw the slightest tremor in his hand. No matter what he said, that kiss had gotten to him. "You're a bad influence."

I was feeling a little surer of myself, my confidence bolstered by Patrice's flustered state.

"I think I'm a great influence. I'm just trying to figure out how to convince *you* of that."

He laughed and I wondered what had changed since last weekend when I'd seen him at the store. I decided not to dwell on it and capitalize on the fact that we seemed to be on the same page, for once.

I moved closer again and said in a low voice. "I was wondering if you'd be up for a drink at my place later."

This time he did laugh, shaking his head, and his eyes sparkling as he looked at me.

"Drink at your place huh? Do people actually fall for this shit in court?"

I laughed at his teasing, but the confidence of just a few seconds ago was starting to slip. "I have my moments."

Patrice reached over and took my glass out of my hand again. He drank as he looked me up and down. It was sort of unreal how the tiniest bit of attention or show of interest from Patrice made me want to drop to my knees and beg him to like me.

Unnerving, really.

I was about to make a joke, anything, to break the tension. But before I could come up with something to say, his eyes widened like he remembered something. He pointed in my direction, my glass still in his hand. I was wondering how much of a twelve-year-old I would be if I took it back and tried to sip from the same spot he'd drunk from. Because that's where things were with me at the moment.

Desperate.

Just when I thought I was going to be cut loose, Patrice roped me back in. "Hey so, I was going to ask if you still had that vacancy in your building. Which, by the way, Nesto said you actually own. Funny that slipped your mind when you told me about it." His tone was a bit reprimanding, but he was smiling wide and I was too busy basking in it to care.

I cleared my throat, trying to think on my feet— which usually was not an issue for me. My entire career was built on rolling with the punches, showing people whatever they wanted to see, but with Patrice my play-book didn't work most of the times. I had to let the mask fall off for Patrice, he could always tell when it was on. I pasted a smile on my face like I did when I felt cornered and tried to keep my voice at human decibels.

"I'm not sure why I didn't say anything. I always feel weird about that sort of stuff. I didn't have to do any-

thing to get the money to buy that building and sometimes I just avoid it."

I cringed because Patrice was looking at me like he
was not sure what to do with my sudden overshare. I
ended by mumbling awkwardly, "Sorry."

He waved my apology off. "You don't need to explain yourself to me. I was teasing. I'm not entitled to
the details of your life. I barely know you."

Ouch.

I was so stunned by how hard his words hit me that I
literally had no comeback. He must've realized the effect what he said had on me, because his eyes softened
and he moved closer.

"Sorry, that was rude. I meant, I don't know you
that well *yet*."

"Right." I nodded, still feeling out of sorts.

Patrice made me so messy.

He was still looking contrite, but I needed to get out
of my feelings ASAP, so I decided to go with the safe
option and discuss the apartment. "There's still a two-
bedroom apartment open. If you want to come and see
it tomorrow that should be fine. Why don't you stop by
after 2:00 p.m.? Just text me when you get there and I'll
have someone come and show it to you."

He nodded and was about to say something when
Nesto barreled in from the patio, his loud voice booming in the small living room.

"There you are! P, you gotta come and tell Jude about
the time Juanpa and Milo dressed up as Salt-N-Pepa for
Halloween. He doesn't believe me."

Patrice's eyes twinkled when he answered Nesto.
"Man I wish we'd had smartphones back then because
that night was epic."

Nesto laughed again and pointed toward the patio. "I'm saying. I'm going back out there, but you have to settle this."

"All right, all right," Patrice said, his voice full of an easy humor he rarely showed. After a moment he nodded and started to follow. When he got to the door he stopped, like he realized I was still standing there.

He looked over at me again and tilted his head toward the patio. "I'm going to go settle this argument." His voice was friendly, but it was no longer the intimate feel from before. The wall was up again.

Immediately I felt slighted that he hadn't asked me to come with him, which was ridiculous. I needed to go home and regroup.

I tilted my own head in the direction of the front door. "I'm going to head home. I was at the office at 4:00 a.m. preparing for court and I'm exhausted. Tell Nesto and Jude thanks for me, okay?"

He seemed surprised at the shift in my mood. I'd gone from flirtatious to exhausted and grumpy in a second.

"Okay. It was good seeing you, Easton. Thanks for helping me out with the apartment thing. I appreciate it." I waved him off and after holding my gaze for a moment he walked out through the sliding doors and left me there looking after him. Wondering once again, if all the things that I'd felt those few nights we had together last summer were only lust and desperation.

Chapter Four

Patrice

I had a feeling I was being set up.

Except that was bullshit, because once I found out that the building belonged to Easton I could've just opted out and tried to find something else, but here I was right on time and ready to look at the vacant apartment in his building.

I got my phone out of my pocket to double check the door code he'd sent me. He said someone would be waiting for me right outside the apartment which was conveniently located on the fifth floor directly below his own top-floor penthouse.

Just as I was about to walk in my phone rang. I saw Camilo's number and immediately felt in a better mood.

"Milo."

"Oh my god. I am so hungover." The amount of drama he could work into seven words was always impressive.

I tried not to laugh at his moaning. "I thought you were at a work thing last night."

"I was! I didn't even drink that much but you know I'm trash for free champagne."

He *was* a whore for an open bar.

"How was it?" I asked, already grinning at the earful of foolishness I was about to get.

Instead there was a heavy silence that could've meant anything. One never knew with Camilo.

"It was good, great butternut squash soup. I gave a super tall, hot as fuck guy a blow job in a sitting room, and then Ayako and I went home. You know, average Friday."

I barked out a laugh. "Oh my god, Camilo. The shit you say. At least the soup was good."

He snickered at my side-step of the blow job. "What are you up to? Are you an Easton going steady already or are you just still acting like you didn't move up there for his dick?"

I sighed out loud, because I did not want to get into any of this with Camilo. He'd push me until I ended up saying more than I was ready to deal with at the moment. I also wasn't sure how to even talk about the apartment. If I mentioned Easton, Camilo would get on his nosy bullshit and I did not want to get into the reasons why I was even contemplating renting the place.

"Oh, I'm just looking at an apartment. The one I got is still not ready for me to move in and even though staying with Nes and Jude has been great, I need my own space."

"I can't believe they're still dicking you around with that."

After punching the code for the front door I stepped into the vestibule and pressed the up button for the elevator with one hand as I held my phone with the other.

"Yeah, it's a problem. Listen, I'll call you back, okay? I'm about to get into the elevator."

"Let me know how it goes. And don't think I didn't notice how you avoided my question about Easton. We'll get back to that next time we talk."

I rolled my eyes and muttered, "Awesome."

Which just got me a wicked laugh from Camilo.

I ended the call just as the elevator doors opened and looked up to see Easton Archer looking fucking edible in jeans and a white T-shirt.

I didn't know what I was doing with Easton, but I could not deny he was the most beautiful guy I'd ever been with. He was just a bit under six feet tall, so I had to slightly turn my head down to talk to him…to kiss him. I exhaled, trying to tamp down the memories of that lithe body under me last summer, and the way he moaned and moved when we'd been together.

Fuck, I was getting hard.

He extended his hand, and if he was aware of my hard-on, he was not going to make a thing about it. He just smiled and beckoned me into the elevator.

I stepped in feeling a little suspicious. Was he going to show me the place himself?

He must've guessed what I'd been thinking because he lifted a shoulder and flashed me those perfect teeth.

"I told my Realtor I could show you the place since I'm already here."

I was about to ask if he always did that, but decided to let it go. So, I just nodded and stepped in.

He was looking at me like he was trying to read my mind. I kept a neutral expression on my face and tried to roll with it. Keep it casual. I was here to see an apartment. Not to flirt.

He didn't say whatever he was thinking and instead looked down at my feet and smiled. "Nice, I like your

Jordans, are those the new Flyknits? I hadn't seen them yet."

I snapped my head up to look at him with what I knew was disbelief on my face. I was wearing the bright red pair of Js I'd bought as a graduation/new job treat to myself. They were the most expensive shoes I'd ever bought by a few hundred dollars and I still checked the weather forecast before wearing them out. I fucking loved them, but of all the people I thought would appreciate how dope these were, Easton Archer, who dressed like a preppy poster boy—all the fucking time—was not one of them.

"Uh, thanks."

He laughed, probably guessing what I'd been thinking. "What, you didn't think I'd be able to appreciate your kicks?"

I was going to go with something PC but decided to say what I was really thinking, "Umm no, not really, since you're usually wearing Gucci loafers."

At this point the elevator stopped on the fifth floor and Easton extended his hand to me so I could get out. He followed right behind.

We stood in front of the apartment for a moment as he talked. "My mentee, Tyren, is a Jordans fanatic." The smile on his face was a new one; there was some protectiveness and clear affection there.

"Well, he's technically not my mentee anymore, although we're still close. I was his Big Brother when he was a high school student and he's at Ithaca College now." His eyes shone with pride when he said that. "Anyway, Ty has like twenty pairs." His tone was indulgent when he talked about his mentee, and it really fucking warmed my heart.

This guy had me bugging, for real.

Easton tipped his head down, his eyes back on my feet. "Ty was talking about those." He rolled his eyes and chuckled, his hands deep in his pants pockets. "He actually convinced me to get a pair a while ago. I have some pretty boring gray ones. Retros of course."

He looked a little self-conscious, like he was waiting for me to mock him or something, but I was still stuck on the fact that he had been mentoring a young man for years, and they were still close. That he clearly cared for the kid. That piece of information, more than anything I knew so far about Easton, broke something open in me.

I was humbled, because I'd made too many assumptions about this man. Nesto was right—I didn't really know very much at all about Easton Archer, other than the way we could make each other feel.

I tipped my head to the side and pointed at the closed door behind him. "I'd like to see you rocking your Jordans some time." He beamed at me, as if he hadn't expected that response. "*But* for now, can I see this place you're supposed to be showing me?"

He really was a beautiful man and with that little bit of red on his cheeks, I was having a hard time not reaching out and touching.

We walked into the apartment and immediately I knew I was going to take it.

Everything looked pristine. It was a loft, open floor plan with high ceilings. There was one bedroom in one corner of the floor and another one in a mezzanine up a spiral metal staircase. The kitchen was completely done in stainless steel, even the countertops, and the dark hardwood floors gleamed.

Easton pointed at the space upstairs. "The mezzanine is deceptively large and it has a bathroom en suite. The one down here is just a shower, but that one has a pretty nice tub." There was that dirty smile again. "I don't know if you remember, but I have the same one at my place."

An image flashed through my head of Easton on his knees inside the enormous tub, hands gripping my ass as I stood with my hands against the wall, looking down as his lips stretched around my cock. I felt heat rise in my face at that memory. When I looked at Easton the flush on his cheeks told me he was probably thinking of the exact same thing.

I cleared my throat, definitely not ready to go down memory lane, and started climbing the stairs. When I got up there I instantly noticed the huge bay windows. We were high enough that I could see the Cornell grounds, the top of the famous clock tower in the West part of campus visible right at the center of the window.

Easton came up beside me as I took in the view. "I have the same view at my place." He shrugged. "Well, mine is slightly higher up." He waved his arm toward the bathroom. "You want to see?"

I nodded, brushing past him and into the bathroom, still not saying much. It was huge, all done in slate-colored tiles. The tub and shower also done in a dark gray. It was spacious and comfortable and right then it hit me. Being here, looking at this place started to feel monumental.

I could afford this place.

This luxurious apartment, with everything spotless and beautiful, was something I could easily pay for. I made enough money now to rent it and not have to worry about whether I could afford heat or food with my meager grad student stipend. All those years of wondering if I was doing the right thing by trying it in a world where people like me didn't just have a hard time of it, but were practically nonexistent. Even though I still had tenure to worry about, I felt...proud of myself.

Right there and now for the first time since graduation and the grueling stress of the job market, it finally felt like this was real. I'd done this, I had finished a PhD in Economics from Columbia University. A kid who came as a refugee from Haiti as a six-year-old, had done that. Against all the fucking odds.

I glanced over at Easton, who was looking at me like he realized there was something going on with me. Then a *really* strange thing happened—I wanted to tell him about it.

I didn't even know why. With Easton's background I wasn't sure if he could get the magnitude of this moment, but I decided not to make assumptions. I wanted to share this with him. Not because he was the only person with me right then, but because I wanted *Easton* to know how much this mattered.

He stood there patiently waiting for me to speak. "Sorry I'm acting so weird. It just hit me that I can actually afford this place." I sounded astonished, and the way his eyes softened made me feel seen. Like he got it. "I guess I hadn't really let it sink yet that I'm not on a graduate student budget anymore."

Easton shifted like he was going to move closer, and I almost moved to meet him halfway, but in the end he stayed where he was. He smiled wide at me though.

"You should be proud of yourself, it's an amazing accomplishment. I've lived in Ithaca almost my whole life and it's not like I know everyone who gets hired up there, but I *do* know getting a tenure track position at Cornell is a huge deal."

Those green eyes on me were like truth serum, because I just kept talking.

"Nesto and I shared a place with another guy in Harlem for the five years before he moved here. The rent was decent, but it wasn't the nicest." I shrugged feeling embarrassed about what I was thinking, but also like I really needed to share this. It was such a strange feeling for me to want to be vulnerable like this. "I've never lived alone. I'm not sure what I'd do with myself in a place this big on my own. It's kind of crazy that you own it actually."

The bright smile faded, and I hated myself a little bit for saying the words that made it happen. "I didn't work for this. I bought it with money I got from my grandmother. *Your* job is an actual accomplishment." He waved his hand around the bathroom. "*This* is just old money begetting more money with very little effort from any of the parties involved."

The tone of his voice was so self-deprecating. I usually wasn't full of sympathy for trust fund babies but I also knew that Easton had a hard job. One that he opted into when he could've been coasting on his family's money. Even though I had a lot of opinions on the criminal justice system and prosecutors, I knew he was out there trying to put away the bad guys.

"Don't be so down on yourself, man. Some people do a lot worse with the money they inherit than putting it into something that is a legit source of income. Also it's not like you're sitting at home waiting for rent checks. You're not exactly doing light work at the DA's office."

He just shrugged and moved toward the bedroom.

I wanted to stop him, say more until that smile he'd been giving me since I walked into the elevator came back out. I had no idea why I was so invested in seeing Easton looking happy again, but I was ready to take the apartment just to do something that might bring some light back to his eyes. Before I knew it I was talking again.

"It's not like I didn't want to have my own place. I just couldn't afford it." I lifted a hand in the direction of the bay windows. "I'm not going to be mad to have a place like this."

His lips twitched at that and my dumbass heart pounded in my chest, because that fucker never learned.

"I actually didn't have an apartment like this in undergrad. I went to school in Buffalo, and my place was not nearly as nice, much to parents' chagrin."

I worked extremely hard to keep my eyebrows in place.

"Oh?"

I'd always assumed he'd gone to an Ivy League school. I never asked, because I was a callous asshole, but the way he was holding himself right now, shoulders back, chin up, told me there was a story there. "Buffalo, then." I pointed at myself, ready to launch into another overshare. "I started at City College and then transferred to Columbia sophomore year, I was working full time and living at home to help my mom out, in the first years at least. It took me about six years to get my bachelor's."

He didn't look at me when he talked, running a hand over the metal banister that led downstairs. "That's incredible, Patrice. I liked SUNY Buffalo. It was the right place for me. I wasn't the best student in high school.

I partied a lot and generally didn't take myself very seriously. It was pretty much a done deal that I would just work for my family's winery, and I can't say that I cared too much about my career."

He laughed, and it was a very tired sound.

"It's so frivolous to even say it, but I knew I'd never have to worry about money or finding work, so I just sort of coasted. It wasn't until senior year when I let Cindy convince me to volunteer for the local domestic violence agency. They had a program for high schoolers where we learned to do peer-to-peer outreach. I'd just come out and was figuring myself out—" He closed his eyes, his lips flattening. He waved a hand, dismissing whatever that brought up, and looked at me. "Anyway. That year was life changing for me, I decided I wanted to work helping survivors. Cindy advocated hard for law school and I knew how much she loved her job."

"I didn't know that," I said, more than a little ashamed by all the ways I'd written Easton off. He lifted a shoulder, as if he was used to that, people making assumptions. "You're a fighter, Easton."

"I wasn't struggling with money, believe me."

Every conversation with Easton drove home more and more that the easygoing, light and breezy rich boy thing Easton had going was either just an act or his way of protecting himself from people and their shitty judgements.

When he spoke again, he sounded more certain. The confidence that I'd gotten used to coming back. "For law school it was the same, I went to the school *I* got into. I ended up at Fordham Law in the city and honestly, I loved it. Then I came back here to the DA's office." He stepped closer to me, as I was still looking for how to respond. With every step he took the need to grab him, pull him to me. Kiss that mouth that seemed to have an uncanny ability to undo me. When he came closer, he didn't look sad anymore. Just like that, his smile was back.

I wondered what it cost Easton every time he did that. "So is this place worthy of your first post-grad-school home, professor?" The way he looked at me, with hopeful eyes, like he needed me to play along, was enough to disarm me.

"I don't know, Mr. Archer. Are you going to be a good landlord?"

Was I flirting? Trying to impress? I wasn't even sure what kind of life I was living anymore. But it was all worth it when I saw that smile.

"Well I usually have a property management company take care of stuff for my tenants, but for you I might want to take care of things myself."

Why was him talking about repairing shit in my apartment making me want to fuck him over the staircase railing?

And why had I even gone there?

Once again I had an image come to mind. This time Easton writhing under me as I spread him open with one hand while I worked an enormous dildo into his ass with the other. Pushing it in as he undulated under me, trying to make it go deeper, while I leaned in to lick at his stretched out rim and he begged me to fuck him harder.

This time I really did have to adjust my pants and Easton started moving closer like he knew exactly what was going through my head. Before I knew what was happening he grabbed my shirt, pulling me down to him. I moved fast and grabbed the back of his neck to pull his face to mine. Like it was the most natural thing in the world. No hesitation, not a shred of reluctance.

I had a couple of inches and about thirty pounds on him. I was a big guy, people usually approached with caution, but Easton came to me like he was coming home.

Like there was nothing he could see that he didn't want to get closer to. I was thinking about what part of him I wanted to get at first when I remembered why I was here, to rent this apartment that he *owned*. If I got mixed up with Easton, it would get messy.

Messy was one thing I did not do.

I released the hand that I had clasped on the back of his neck and stepped back with a heavy exhale. "Easton."

He immediately pulled back and glanced up at me, looking dazed. Once again I wished I could just let myself go. Get what we both wanted.

I looked at him trying to figure out how much my hot and cold shit had pissed him off, and he did look pissed, but apparently not for the reason I thought.

"Oh no. Stop that shit."

I laughed because he was fucking ridiculous.

"Stop what? You're a mind reader now?"

He lifted a shoulder, but I could tell he was embarrassed about the kiss and I felt like shit. I had to give it to Easton, he could handle discomfort. He powered on, and cleared the air. "As a matter of fact, I *am* a bit of a reader, not minds, but certainly body language." He exhaled and waved in my direction. "Looks like once again I pushed you too far too quickly. My bad."

I shook my head and smiled at him because no matter how crazy he made me, I really fucking liked Easton Archer. In fact the more I knew, the more I wanted him. There was no telling myself any different on that.

"Easton, I'm just trying to get into this building without starting some fuckboy drama with you. I want this place and I—"

This I wasn't sure how to say without going into weirdness territory.

"I like you. Like as a friend, and I'm going to be here for a while." I sagged after getting the words out, and he looked at me like he knew what was coming.

"I get it. If you want this place, it's yours, and I will keep my thirsty ass in shape."

I shook my head at him, biting back a smile, wanting to also say my piece. The thought of Easton walking away from this feeling hurt was not sitting right with me.

"Listen, you're obviously not the only thirsty one in this situation." I glanced up to the steel beams in the ceiling, hoping to word this right and not offend him because he had been nothing but decent to me. "I just don't want to ruin the chances for us actually being friends. I don't do very well as a lover in the long term, but I *am* a decent friend. Hearing about your college experience, I don't know, it makes me want to get to know you better, without our dicks being involved."

Easton deflated like I was making too much sense and he might have to agree with me, but he didn't have to like it. "You might have gone with the wrong career, because I'm thinking you would have made a hell of a lawyer."

An unexpected bark of laughter came out of me, a regular occurrence whenever Easton was around, but

I was grateful for the shift in the conversation. "Pssh, being an economist is much better. We don't even try to argue, we just manipulate the data until we can tell everyone how to think. So…"

Easton extended a hand to me as if to seal the deal. "Welcome to 611Cayuga, Professor Denis."

I smiled wide as we shook on it. "Thank you, Mr. Archer."

Easton

Patrice wanted to be friends? Fine, I could do friends.

I was sitting at my desk Monday morning thinking about Saturday and how easy it was to be with Patrice. How wanting him was all I could think about when he was close. But it wasn't just that. I wanted to know about Patrice, about the reasons why he was so careful.

"What are you frowning about now? That's your permanent expression these days."

Cindy.

I lifted my eyes from the monitor I'd been blankly staring at for the last twenty minutes and tried my best to smile for her.

She wasn't buying it.

"Hey. What are you doing here so early? Aren't you supposed to be on medical leave? It's not even 7:00 a.m."

Cindy waved me off as she sat in one of the chairs across from my desk. "I wanted to check in, and I needed to get out of the house." Things were still tense from the stop last week, and as far as Ron and I could tell not much had happened in the way of addressing it. Day had been evasive as hell and Cindy had stayed away.

"I'm so fucking tired of being cooped up. You'd think

recovering from heart surgery wouldn't make you homicidal, but I'm getting there."

I shook my head at her, trying to keep a straight face. Her humor had always been pretty dark, but after her heart attack, it was getting grimmer. Still she was pushing it, and I wasn't sure her checking in was going to help matters.

"I'm calling Lorraine and letting her know you came here instead of going to the rehab place which is what you probably told her, again."

She looked down at herself and her workout clothes, then back at me. "You wouldn't."

I scoffed and gestured toward my phone. "Oh yeah, I would."

She'd scared the shit out of all of us in the summer when she collapsed walking out of court, and there was no way I would enable her to go right back to not taking proper care of herself.

I pointed at the clock on the wall. "Thirty minutes. We can talk about what's been going on and then you are going to your PT. You need to take care of yourself, Cin. We need you back." I lamented. "I'm not built for all this administrative bullshit. I'm court guy, trial guy. Not a paperwork guy, and I'm starting to confirm I'm definitely not a politics guy. This sitting on my hands bullshit is not pleasant for me."

I looked toward the hallway where the investigators usually worked. "Ron says that traffic stop was barely a bleep at the Sheriff's department, meanwhile social media was on fire for days with community members demanding a response. This is going to escalate."

Cindy's shook her head, that stubborn set to her chin telling me she had not changed her mind. "First of all, you would be an outstanding DA and I really want that for this county and for you."

I sighed, too frustrated to argue about this with her, or entertain the run-for-DA conversation.

"About the stop, I understand it's not ideal, Easton, but we need to give it time. So far nothing else has happened, and we have to work with these people. Overzealousness won't work in our favor in the long run. How are things going with the Suarez case? Are you going over all the stuff from his previous arrest?" She could not have been more obvious about changing the subject. I would let it go, for now.

I gestured at the enormous pile of papers accumulating on my desk and sighed. "Yes, I am and it's already a mess." She made a face at that. "His family already started a smear campaign on her and the grand jury barely gave the indictment. They're going to drag her through the mud. After what that motherfucker did to her."

Cindy shook her head in disgust. "I heard his mom remortgaged her house to pay for a defense attorney from Rochester. Like that's going to help him. You have to nail him to the wall, Easton."

I slumped against my chair, thinking about the horrific details of that case and how even with all the evidence it was still going to be precarious, because the perp was a "nice guy, who grew up in town," and the woman was young and Latina and had only been in Ithaca for few months when he broke into her home and brutally assaulted her.

This case was going to be awful for everyone involved, but I would do whatever I needed to in order to get that asshole behind bars, even though there were people in town still defending him.

Sometimes it amazed me that things seemed so black and white to me were all gray for some people. That just made me go back to thinking about the stops. The niggling feeling that we were not doing nearly enough eating at me. This was new territory for me, feeling like my hands were tied.

"What?" Cindy's voice snapped me out of my fretting.

"Other than the various fires actively burning in town, you mean?"

Cindy's eyebrows dipped and she leaned in, trying to figure me out. "No. There is always a lot of shit going on. This place is a madhouse on a good day." That was true, but this felt different. "There's something up with you and it's not just the work." She attempted to scrutinize my face for another minute while I tried to keep cool under her stare and then her whole body perked up.

"Oh my god." She gasped, looking genuinely contrite. "How could I forget to ask? How's your stunner? Is he still giving you the runaround?" I could tell she was worried about me. Probably because she'd never seen me actually thinking about anything or anyone in the romance department for more than a second, and I was now closing in on fifteen months of pining for Patrice Denis.

"Nope, we're just friends, and I wasn't just thinking about that," I said as I started grabbing folders from the mountain of shit I had piled over my desk.

"Easton."

I sighed and looked up at Cindy, annoyed at myself

for wanting to talk about this when I'd told Patrice that I was done with lusting after him.

"It's stupid, okay? He said he's a better friend than a lover and since we'll be neighbors—"

"Wait. Neighbors?" She tipped her head to the side, confused. "When did that happen?"

I looked up, because this was another new symptom of my Patrice "ailment." Everything felt monumental, like it needed to be dissected and analyzed and it was fucking exhausting.

"I saw him at Nesto and Jude's last week and he mentioned he was having trouble with the place he rented, so I let him know I had two units at 611 Cayuga. He came to see the place with two bedrooms, he liked it and he's moving in a couple of days."

Cindy was shaking her head, a big grin on her face.

I held up my hand, annoyed. "Why does everyone think I'm a manipulative asshole who only does shit to further my getting laid agenda?"

She balked at that. "I never said that."

"You're right, you didn't. I don't know." I sagged. "He's a nice guy and this job is a big deal for him. You should've seen his face when he told me he still couldn't believe that he could afford the rent. Like it was the most amazing thing in the world for him to be able to live in that apartment. He doesn't want drama, Cindy. He wants to do his job, which he worked his ass off to get, and enjoy this new place, without his landlord trying to get into his bed."

Cindy was now fully in Mama Bear mode and I was about to crawl out of my skin.

"Easton. Why do you put yourself down like that? I get that he's not looking to get involved, but you're not drama. You're not some guy. You *are* a good man. If he can't see it then that's one thing, but anyone would be lucky to have you."

"It's not that simple, Cindy. I get why Patrice wants to keep things friendly, and I have enough going on here. I shouldn't be getting distracted with a love life that's going nowhere and focus on my damn job," I said, feeling guilty that my need to talk about Patrice detracted me from the conversation about the stops. I stood up from my desk and was about to suggest we go out for coffee so I could clear my head a bit when Ron walked into the office looking pissed.

Before he even opened his mouth, my heart sank.

"It happened again. This time it was two kids driving home after a late shift at the French bistro in town." He shook his head and started tapping something on his phone and then handed it to me to look at. The headline said it all.

Sheriff's Department's Racially Biased Traffic Stops: New Ithaca Trend?

"I knew it. I fucking knew this would happen," I said through gritted teeth. Cindy looked at the phone and sighed.

Ron gave her a hard look and took his phone back. "We need to do something. Day clearly has not dealt with this at all if it happened again in less than two weeks."

I ran my hands over my head, intensely aware that Cindy had so far not said a word.

"Cin, go to the gym. I'll deal with this." My tone was sharp, but I was starting to run out of patience at how nonchalant she was being. Were we supposed to just let this escalate and do nothing?

"Do not do anything impulsive, Easton."

That one hurt, because even if in my personal life I was a bit reactive, I never *ever* did anything that could hurt my work. But again, she was the boss, not me. "I will be cautious of how I approach this, but I need to sit down with Day." By this point I was mostly talking to Ron. "I'm still convinced there is a way to address this without blowing everything up."

She looked from me to Ron, who seemed like he was actively trying not to punch a wall. "Fine. I need to get out of there before I break all the promises I made to Lorainne about taking it easy. Please do not make any statements on behalf of this office until we've spoken with Day. Again, these are routine traffic stops."

Ron scoffed at that, earning an unfriendly look from Cindy. "You're entitled to your opinion, Ron, but while you are speaking for this office you will refrain from making statements about the sheriff's department actions." I squeezed the back of my neck hard, hoping this didn't turn into a shouting match, but after a moment Ron nodded.

"Yes ma'am, but it's not my imagination that this sudden hike in stops of black and brown kids is a very concerning trend."

Cindy stopped at the door and sighed again. "We agree on that." She turned to me. "Easton, set up a meeting with Day. We need to at least hear from him about what the fuck he's planning to do with these assholes in his department."

Ron cracked a smile at that, and I waved her off. "I'll call Day, and this time he's going to have to talk to me." With that Cindy walked out. I turned to look at Ron who had his phone screen practically pressed to his face.

"Oh shit."

"What?" I asked, as I moved over to see what he was looking at with a weird mix of dread and delight.

"Look at this."

He handed me his phone. I wasn't really on social media, so when I saw Patrice's face in the tiny circle on the left side of the screen my heart started pounding. His handle was @AyitienProf and his tweet with a timestamp from ten minutes ago was incendiary.

Fuck.

Young black and brown men continue to be harassed on the roads of this county as they try to work and study.

Those of you who are responsible for putting a stop to this: do your jobs. We're waiting.

"What is this?"

Ron looked at me like I needed to get with the program.

"That's Patrice Denis, he's—"

"I know who he is, Ron! I'm just asking what that tweet is about. I mean obviously it's about the stops, but— You know what? Never mind. I get it."

Ron seemed a bit put off by my outburst, but he just talked over me.

"You need to get on Twitter. Denis is pretty well known on Black Twitter."

"What?"

Ron sighed and I couldn't tell if he was losing his patience or just felt sorry for my lack of social media prowess.

"It is not a separate Twitter, it's just there are a lot of writers, journalists, academics or just people who tweet about racial justice and Denis has been pretty active in the past couple of years. He has a big following, and he does not mince words. He was pretty vocal about some of the stuff happening in New York City when he was down there, and it looks like he's not shutting down his account now that he's up here." He sounded a little bit too giddy at that prospect as my own mood sank some more.

Excellent.

Looked like this would put even the possibility of friendship out the window.

And how unprofessional was that? I needed to be thinking about how to deal with a situation that was escalating, not how I would stay friends with Patrice.

I handed Ron his phone back and went to my desk. "If Day doesn't take my call I'm going to go see him. I'm not impressed at all with his ghosting us." Day and I had worked together for years and he was usually a reliable guy, or at least honest about what he could and could not do. This disappearing act was extremely concerning and not a good look.

Ron nodded as he moved to the door. "I'll do a little more digging around and ask the IPD guys what they've heard of who's being problematic. I'll call up Tony too."

Tony was a deputy sheriff we worked closely with on our sexual abuse cases and he was definitely going to have some insight on what was going on.

"That sounds good. Thanks. I hope we can deal with this before it happens again."

The look he gave me clearly said, "You and me both."

Chapter Five

Patrice

"Bruh, the school's paying for the movers? Damn. You stuntin' for real."

I smiled at Nesto as we stood in my apartment watching two guys place my new couch in the middle of the living room. It was Wednesday afternoon and I'd been dealing with movers since I'd finished my morning class.

"They told me a set amount I can spend. They don't give me cash, just reimburse receipts. So, I figured I might as well spend it and get some professionals instead of trying to bribe you, Jude and Ari with beer and pizza," I said after I handed one of them a tip and thanked them for hauling all my stuff for the last couple of hours.

Nesto chuckled and looked over at Ari and Yin, who were in my kitchen unpacking plates and glasses. My mom had gone a little overboard with getting me stuff for the apartment once I got the job, and before I left New York I had boxes of housewares from her. Not that I was complaining—I hated shopping and she had great taste.

Nesto must have guessed what I was thinking because he grinned at me and started for the kitchen. "Odette really did the most, damn," he said, as he peered into one of the boxes on the kitchen island. "Are those champagne flutes?"

I nodded as he gently picked up one of my twelve brand-new glasses. "Yep, she got me a dozen. You know how she is."

My mother. I loved her, but she was a lot. She was always so preoccupied with appearances. I knew it was her way of showing people that she was worthy of respect, that she wasn't relying on the government or whatever. Her way of making people think twice before they made assumptions about her or me.

It was endless though. The house had to look perfect, she had to look perfect, son had to be perfect. She made sure that there was never a reason for someone to look down on her, if she could help it. Before they could focus on her black skin and make judgements, they'd see her lovely clothes and perfect makeup. They'd hear about her son the Cornell professor and her thriving business.

They'd see her immaculate home.

It was how she coped with everything we'd been through when we first got here. As long as she could shut people up by *showing* them who she was, she would do it. It was an exhausting way to live and one I still struggled not to fall into.

"Yo, where did you go to, man?"

I snapped my head back and saw Nesto, Ari and Yin looking at me.

"Sorry, Nes. I just started thinking. My mom did get me a lot of stuff," I said, running my hands over my head.

Nesto, whose own mom was not subtle in her protectiveness of her son, was unfazed. "She's just trying to take care of her baby. So speaking of people that do too much. How's it going with your landlord?"

I knew *that* was coming. Nesto was still pretty invested in being matchmaker and it was still annoying.

"If you mean Easton, he's fine."

Yin nodded from the kitchen, an impish look on his face. "He sure is."

Both Nesto and I busted up at that while Yin looked over at Ari with a sassy grin on his face. Ari was trying hard to scowl, but he couldn't resist for long and after a second bent down to give Yin a quick kiss on the lips. Yin didn't waste any time and wrapped his skinny arms around Ari's neck.

They were fucking adorable, and so into each other. Nesto said they'd only started dating over the summer after a year of walking around each other like love-sick puppies. Nesto looked at them, and then at me and smiled.

Were we ever that young?

It made my heart happy to see those two able to kiss and show their affection for each other freely. Here, at least. Things were not easy at home for Ari, his uncle was very traditional and would not be ok with Ari having a boyfriend. Yin, whose sisters were fiercely protective, thankfully didn't have the same problem. They had people who were supportive of them and their relationship.

Nesto came over to stand by me and help get books into shelves as Ari and Yin resumed unpacking boxes in the kitchen.

"Should we wipe these down before we put them up?"

I grabbed a couple of old T-shirts I'd been using for cleaning and handed him one.

"Yeah, please. All the boxes are labeled by category. Fiction, nonfiction, poetry and all my work and school books?" I pointed at the two bookcases on the wall behind the couch. "Bookshelf on the right has all the stuff that's not school or work related and the other one has everything else."

Nesto nodded and started pulling books out. I had a couple dozen boxes full of them. Some I'd kept in my mother's house, but most of them I'd just had in stacks all over my tiny apartment. The thrill of finally having space to display my things hit me by moments. I'd be unpacking something and it would come to me again that this place was mine.

"Man you look so fucking happy right now," Nesto said, from where he was shelving books. "I'm so glad it worked out for you to get this place. It is so much nicer than the first one. How is it going with Easton by the way? Don't think I'm gonna let you get away with not answering."

I cut open another box of books and made a show of getting a few out and wiped down before I said anything. I looked up after a minute and Nesto was still there, staring at me, waiting for an answer.

"There's nothing going on, so there's not much to say."

"Bullshit."

I lifted a shoulder and kept working. Nesto was like a dog with a bone with shit like this, but I was just as stubborn.

He of course was not done. "I saw the way you were looking at each other the day of the sancocho. There's something up with you two, it's only a matter of time."

There was more than something. Easton and the way he made me feel sometimes felt like this gigantic piece of a puzzle I didn't even know was missing, but I was not going to get into it right now. "It's not like that. I mean yeah, I want him and he's made it pretty clear that he's down for whatever, but we decided to keep it at just friends."

Nesto was about to say something, but I held up my hand.

"You're right. There is something there, but now I'm living in his building and honestly, it's too messy. And with all this shit happening with the police stops and all that, I won't be able to look the other way and let things go, so—" There was just too much in the way. "Nah man, it's better like this."

Nesto twisted his mouth to the side, like he was literally forcing himself to stay quiet. After a second he sagged and exhaled. "I'm not sure why everything needs to be life or death with you, but all right. It's your life."

"Everything isn't life or death, but this specific thing that's been happening here potentially could be. You know that. I don't need to start rattling off names of people who have lost their lives to get my point across. I'm not saying that Easton is responsible to stop it, because it's not that simple. But it's going to cause tension and I got enough on my plate right now."

I had no idea how Easton was handling any of this and to a degree I almost didn't want to know. If I began to let things slide because I was involved with Easton, I'd eventually hate myself *and* him.

It frightened me more that despite knowing all of that, I wanted him anyways.

"This lone wolf shit is a whole lot, P." Nesto's exhausted tone made me shake off the overthinking, but I seriously didn't want to talk about it anymore. The more I did, the less my reasons seemed strong enough to hold me back from getting involved with Easton.

I looked over at Ari and Yin who were now making out more than actually unpacking, then gestured for Nesto to come closer, hoping to get the conversation off me for a minute.

"So how are things going at Ari's? He said his uncle was still angry about the texts from Yin he saw on his phone."

Nesto's face turned sour at the mention of Ari's uncle. "He's still giving him a hard time. I don't want to push him to move out, because the only way he can pay for school is by saving on rent, but at this point I'm almost ready to have him come live with Jude and me for a while." He sucked his teeth, clearly upset by the situation. "It's fucking ridiculous, but he can't burn that bridge because the uncle is helping him with his green card shit." Nesto's face hardened at that. "The guy is an asshole and so manipulative."

I thought about the green card thing for a second. "I wonder if I can help out with that. I mean I can sponsor him, if that's the issue. We made tentative plans to finally get together this weekend." Between the move and Ari's two jobs and school, we hadn't been able to lock down a time, but we'd settled on dinner Saturday.

Nesto was pleased with that. "Good, I was hoping you could get that going." He looked over again at the two young men and turned back to me. "I don't know if you can just switch since his uncle started the process. It's better for us to talk to him about it." Nesto squeezed my shoulder. "I'm glad that you're doing this. The more people he has in his corner the better."

"He's a good kid."

Nesto nodded again. "They both are, and they deserve to be fucking carefree and happy after all the shit they've lived through. At least Yin's started going to therapy. Ari needs it too."

I almost wanted to go back to talking about Easton, because all of this stuff was heavy and too close to home. As if I conjured him up, I heard a knock on my open apartment door and turned around to see him standing in the hallway outside, holding a bottle of something.

Nesto just chuckled beside me. "What were you saying about the 'just friends' plan, P?"

I wasn't going to answer.

I stood up from the stool I was sitting on and walked over to the door. I probably looked like a slob in cutoff sweats and an old Yankees tank top.

He, on the other hand, looked perfect.

He still had on his work clothes. Gray slacks that fit him like a glove with a green-and-blue gingham shirt. No tie. When I looked down, he was barefoot, which for some reason only made him look hotter. Everything about Easton turned me on so fucking much.

I waved him in from his perch on my door. "Hey. Come in. We're just unpacking. These guys have been helping, but they need to go soon. Nesto has to go back to the restaurant and these two have school tomorrow." I turned to Yin and Ari who were standing close and holding hands.

Ari kissed Yin's head and nodded. "Yeah, this one has classes at SUNY Cortland, so he needs to be up early. We should be heading out." They got moving as I pointed at the bottle and raised my eyebrow in question.

"Oh, just some bubbly to toast your moving day."

Easton handed it to me and walked inside to say hello to the guys. I went to the fridge and put the bottle in to chill. By the time I got back, Nesto was unsurprisingly pushing Ari and Yin out the door.

"I need to be in by 6:30, so I can be there for the rest of dinner service." He looked at his watch. "If you guys need a ride back we gotta go now."

He talked while looking at me, a shit-eating grin on his face.

I mouthed, *I know what you're doing* as I worked very hard at keeping a straight face.

Ari and Yin were ready to go in seconds and within a minute I was walking them to the door. Easton was sitting on my couch watching it all unfold, that placid expression he almost always wore on his face.

Before finally getting the hell out of my apartment, Nesto waved at Easton. "See you later, man. Take care of this guy for me. Feed him too, we haven't even had time to order food."

Easton's smile was a little leery, like he wasn't sure what reception he would get. But he still nodded, and with his eyes fixed on me, he assured Nesto I was in good hands.

I closed the door to the apartment and walked to the couch and sat on the coffee table across from him. I could tell myself all kinds of things, but it was going to be very hard to ignore the effect that Easton's mere presence had on me.

"Thanks for the champagne. I'd offer you some, but

I haven't had food since like 11:00 a.m. this morning, and I'm a lightweight when it comes to alcohol."

He shook his head and leaned in a little, trying to move closer.

"I didn't bring it for you to open it for me. You can do it later, drink it with whomever you want."

I gestured to the stainless steel refrigerator which now held the bottle of champagne and nothing else. "I'd love to drink it with you, after I have something to eat. I'm sure there's something we could order. I haven't had time to go food shopping yet." I grimaced, pointing at the takeout bag Nesto had brought from the restaurant. "I love Ernesto like a brother, but I can't eat another burrito." Easton cracked a sympathetic smile at that and stood up suddenly.

"If you're up for it, I can make something at my place." He said it tentatively, like he was pretty sure he was getting a yes, but didn't want to seem too cocky either.

i wasn't sure what I was doing with Easton. I really didn't. It seemed like my ability to follow through on boundaries just didn't work when it came to him.

"That sounds great." There was that smile. Like the fucking sun.

"Good." The way he said that, like I'd just offered him the exact thing he needed, made my gut tighten with want. "Is there anything you don't like?"

"Nah man, I'm good with everything, as long as I don't have to cook it."

He laughed, and looked so pleased. And if I was being honest, I felt good too. I wanted to keep that going. Always see Easton smiling.

"Well, I love to cook. I love feeding people too. Now

I'll know who to call when I make too much food." My stupid heart lurched at that.

"I'm always up for getting spoiled a little." That wasn't a lie, between my mom and the guys' mothers, we were always getting fed.

"I'll keep that in mind." Suddenly something changed and Easton's eyes were smoldering. What had I said? Who the fuck cared?

I ran my eyes over him, and he stood there for a moment letting me take him in. After a while he exhaled and gestured toward the ceiling, but made no move to get any closer, respecting the boundary I'd set.

"I'll go and get things started. It'll take me like thirty minutes. Come up whenever you want okay?"

"Okay, I'll just wash up and come up. Thanks."

It was starting to become startlingly clear for me that when Easton called, I would have a very hard time not running.

Easton

"I brought the champagne to have with dinner. It smells great in here." I looked up and saw Patrice walking into my apartment. He had the bottle of Veuve I brought him in one hand, and it looked like he'd showered before coming up. He had another pair of those fitted sweats he wore that molded to his thighs, and a long-sleeved Cornell T-shirt. He looked edible. His big body filling up the room and robbing me of oxygen.

"Hey, come in. I'm just finishing up the vegetables. Do you like green beans?"

"Sure." Patrice came up to the kitchen and I pointed at one of the stools on the counter. "Take a seat. I'll open this." I took the bottle from him and went to open it as Patrice's eyes followed my movements.

I poured us each some bubbly and handed him the glass, then lifted mine. "To all your accomplishments this year. May it only be the beginning."

Patrice made a sound between a grunt and a "thank-you" and we both took a sip. I turned around to start plating the salmon fillet, green beans and curried pearl couscous I'd made us for dinner. As he sat there quietly watching me move around the kitchen.

I'd changed too, and was in an old pair of jeans and sweatshirt, but the way his eyes kept landing on my ass told me that he was not as unfazed as he'd like to pretend he was.

"That looks amazing, Easton." He sounded pleased. Patrice's voice was deep and he always spoke carefully, every word measured. Whenever he said my name it seemed to sound different to how everyone else said it. I didn't know if it was because from the start I never knew where I stood with Patrice that made me pounce on every morsel of attention I got from him.

"Thanks. We can eat over here." I gestured with my head, walking out of the kitchen with the two plates in my hands and set them down on the dining table. I felt such a thrill from the simple act of preparing this food for Patrice. Taking care of him like this. I was not a nurturer, but I suspected he was not one to let people who weren't his friends or his mother do for him, and that made it even more significant.

I gestured for him to come over as I finished setting the food down, and was about to go back to the kitchen for my glass when Patrice gracefully reached over and grabbed it then stood up to join me.

He was such a big man. His size was intimidating, but he moved like a dancer. He took very good care of his body and he was careful with his gestures. I could watch him for hours. In a few strides he got to me and handed me my glass.

"Here you go." He smelled crisp and like the ocean, and I wanted to run my nose up his neck.

"Still using the same cologne?"

My voice sounded just on this side of breathless, because that scent, of the cologne and his skin, brought me right back to some of those nights we had together last summer. Me slowly roaming over his body, then straddling him to take him inside me. My nose buried in his neck, his arms tight around me as we moved together. No one had ever made me feel like Patrice did.

"Yeah, same one." His voice pulled me out of the incendiary image and when I looked up, the heat in his eyes said he at least suspected where my mind had gone.

"It still smells amazing on you." We stood there, bodies tight and alert, from the proximity as we both looked at our plates set on the table. I remembered that first night we were together, how he'd picked me up and laid me out right on this table and fucked me within an inch of my life. Patrice could make me feel so good, it was hard not to go back to wanting that when he was this close.

After another second of hard staring, Patrice pulled out a chair and gestured for me to sit. This was another thing about Patrice that always charmed me. He was so courteous.

I bit back a smile as I sat. "You're always such a gentleman."

He lifted a shoulder and took the seat across from

mine. "My mom was pretty intense about manners. She had this thing about needing to show 'the kind of people' we were. When we moved here we had a hard time. We were black and refugees. There wasn't exactly a welcome wagon if you know what I mean. So we needed to always be beyond reproach." He laughed, but there was no lightness to the sound. I put my fork down and tried to stay as still as possible because I knew in my gut that this, Patrice talking about his past, did not happen very often.

He shook his head and looked at me as he gently placed his fork and knife on either edge of his plate. Just like my mother had always pestered me to do when I was a kid. I held back the barrage of questions that were on the tip of my tongue and let him take his time.

"We had to leave Haiti in '91 after the coup." He ran a hand over his face as he said that. Like whatever he was remembering was almost overwhelming. "A military junta took over and the country was in chaos. My mom was an administrative assistant at the French Embassy in Port-au-Prince, which back then was a really good job." He looked almost startled as he spoke, like he couldn't believe he was telling me all this stuff.

"Was your mom able to get out because of her job?"

He lowered his gaze then and picked up his fork. His movements careful and slow as though he was figuring out how to answer my question. "No. My father helped us."

"Oh," I said quietly, unsure how to respond.

The way he said "father" made me think there was a lot more to that story. I waited to see if he was going to say something else, but then he scooped up some of the couscous and took a bite.

I guess we were done talking.

We ate in silence for a few minutes. I glanced at Patrice every few seconds, observing him. He moved like a prince. His back straight, those big hands holding the flatware delicately, placing small bites of food in his mouth and chewing slowly and deliberately. There was nothing that, in my eyes, Patrice Denis couldn't turn into an erotic experience.

"This is really good. Thank you," he said with appreciation.

"Anytime. Seriously, I always make too much and I'm not a fan of leftovers. I end up just throwing stuff out." I smiled at him. "Now I'll know what to do when I make too much."

He lifted a shoulder and went in for another bite. "It's nice to not have to eat alone. That's one of the things I'll miss about having roommates. I like my space, but living with Nesto all those years I got used to sitting around a table." There was a real wistfulness in his face and I wondered how much he was missing New York.

"Do you miss the city?"

Another shrug. "I do, but having Nesto here is great." He picked up the napkin and wiped his mouth. "And living in New York on a graduate stipend isn't the easiest. So the job and better income goes a long way in helping with the homesickness."

I nodded, not sure what to say. No matter how much I tried to claim some independence and step out on my own, I always had a pretty massive safety net. Going to Buffalo instead of letting my parents pay for me to get into Cornell was more symbolic than anything. I still had full access to my trust fund, if I ever decided I wanted to stop working.

I was still thinking about what to say when he smiled at me. "Besides it's not too bad in Ithaca." He paused then, and the smile evaporated from this lips. "For now, at least." He looked like he wanted to say more, instead he grabbed his glass and took a long drink.

I wondered if he was thinking about the stops. If he wanted to say something, but wasn't, because of how I might react. I wanted to know though. I wanted to hear his thoughts.

I knew I was probably playing with fire, but I asked anyway.

"I saw your tweet about the traffic stops."

He put his glass down as I said that, his attention fully on me and I could almost see his hackles go up.

"You mean the sheriff department's practice of stopping young men for essentially driving while black?"

There was not much I could say to that, other than agree.

"You're right. It's a problem." I wanted to say more, tell him I was feeling like my hands were tied. That I thought we were not doing enough to address the incidents that had already happened and nothing to prevent new ones. Instead I just looked down at my plate.

Patrice's face turned thunderous, like he couldn't believe this was my explanation. He put down his fork and pushed his plate forward, half of the food still on the plate.

"If you know it's a problem then why hasn't the DA's office made a public statement? Why has there not been a single word on this in the media? Because so far it's just been black and brown boys getting hassled a little bit, and that doesn't even escalate to the level where anyone in law enforcement even deems to talk about it?"

He looked disgusted and it took everything I had not to get defensive. To start parroting out excuses.

Patrice's words brought home once again that we weren't doing nearly enough. I pushed my plate away, practically squirming under Patrice's stare. I debated with what to say next. There were so many ways I could go here, but I would not bullshit him on this.

"Honestly, I'm out of my depth here."

Patrice looked at me like he was trying to figure me out.

"No one's saying dealing with any of this is easy, but acting helpless or like acting it's out of your hands is not it. It's irresponsible."

I ran a hand over my face and sighed again. "I'm realizing I know a lot less about dealing with this situation than I thought I did." I let out a tired laugh at that. "I'm not even sure why I would think I was equipped for any of it. It's not like I've had to deal with this particular issue before."

Patrice raised an eyebrow, but he was not giving me anything.

As I started coming up with a response, things became clearer for me too. "Domestic violence, sexual assault…those are black-and-white things. It's not hard to go on a righteous rant about someone hurting their loved ones. As far as I'm concerned anyone who's out there defending rapists can fuck right off. With this, every step of the way I feel like I am fucking it up, or worse, trying to get people I thought shared my views to admit that there's even an issue."

Patrice looked at me for a few moments as if calculating what I wasn't saying, but when he spoke the understanding in his voice felt like grace I didn't deserve. "Not ignoring it, letting the public know you're addressing it, *is* a first step."

I made a noise between resignation and frustration.

"I'm going to talk to Sheriff Day. I'm not anywhere near done with this." I sounded more sure than I felt and Patrice looked like he was reading right through me.

"So are you going to ask him to hold the deputies pulling that shit accountable?"

"That's exactly what I'm going to do."

Patrice just picked up his fork and kept eating. After a minute he spoke again. "I'm glad you're talking to the sheriff but, I'm just going to give you this to think about, and then I'd like to get off this topic. It's never been 'a couple of bad apples' issue. Removing one or two guys may be a temporary solution or appease a few people, but it's not what will fix things in the long run. That fix involves a lot more discomfort and painful conversations than getting the two guys who can't keep their shit in check in trouble."

He was right and yet, I knew that it was probably as much as I would get from Day. It was hard to hear, and even harder to acknowledge, that the best solution I could come up with was not going to fix anything.

"I don't want to fuck this up, or make it worse by trying to help."

Patrice stared at me so intensely, as if trying to figure if I could really be trusted. "This sort of thing always gets to a place where you need to pick a side." He laughed humorlessly as he played with the stem of the wineglass. "And the side I'm on, the one you have to pick if you're going to really make a change here—it doesn't get a lot of wins."

I groaned feeling that truth sink into my bones like lead.

He raised his gaze from the table up to me, his eyes less hard now. "I'm glad you're not acting like you have an easy fix for this, or that you even have any answers. Honestly it's a relief to hear it because at least that means that you see it for what it is. Hard work."

"Thank you for saying that, and for understanding. I can't imagine how frustrating this all must be for you." This time his lips turned up and it was almost a smile.

"Frustrating is a mild way to put, but again, hearing you say that you get none of this is simple helps."

I kind of marveled at the fact that we were able to talk like this. That he wasn't making demands or ultimatums. Before I knew it I was blurting it out.

"Why aren't you pissed at me right now?"

He really took his time on that and I found that I wasn't nervous about his answer.

"If changing things was up to just you, up to any one of us, I wouldn't be sitting here. I'd be fixing it." He let that last part sit there between us, what else was there to say?

After a moment, he glanced around the room, his eyes landing on my enormous wine rack, which was mostly filled with bottles from my family's vineyard. "Are you going to the Fall Wine Festival this weekend?"

I almost got whiplash from that sudden shift in conversation, but I went with it.

I'd promised my mother I'd take her for a little bit, since she felt compelled to attend any event Archer Vineyards, my family's business, was sponsoring. She had no interest in the business, never had, and my father barely let her in on anything going on. But he did require that she make an appearance and perform her duties as the Mistress Archer, and I usually let her drag me along when I could. I sighed and looked over at Patrice, who was still waiting for my answer.

"I will probably stop by, I usually go with my mom for a little bit. Are you going?"

He looked like he wanted to ask something, but after a moment he took a sip of champagne and shook his head. "No, I'm driving down to the city tomorrow, since I don't have more classes for the rest of the week. My mom always makes this traditional Haitian dish called Soup Joumou this time of the year to mark the start of the Holiday season. Soup Joumou is traditionally made on New Year's Day to celebrate Haitian Independence Day, but at some point in college my mom started making it in the fall. All the guys and their families go."

I assumed by *guys* he meant his three best friends, Nesto, Camilo and Juan Pablo. They'd all grown up together in the Bronx and now Patrice and Nesto had coincidentally ended up here, but the other two were still in New York.

I looked over at him and smiled, noticing that his expression lightened just from the mention of his friends. "Sounds like fun. Are you staying for the whole weekend?"

He stood up and grabbed this plate as he answered me. I guess we were wrapping up the evening. "I'll be back Saturday." He extended the hand with which he held the plate. "This was great. Thanks for the food and the wine. I would've probably just caved in and had a burrito for dinner." He made a face and winked at me, and my dumb heart wanted to burst just from that.

I stood with my plate and walked with him to the kitchen. "It was nothing. I was glad to have someone to eat with. Most nights I just eat standing up in the kitchen. It was nice to set the table."

He leaned against the kitchen counter, once we'd cleaned up and I sat down on the island right across from him. I was intensely aware of his body. Then again, I was always hyperaware of Patrice whenever he was in the room.

We were so close, but I could not touch. I was practically vibrating with the need to run my hands over his chest. To kiss and nip at his skin like I'd done before. I had to close my hands into fists, because the temptation was almost overwhelming. After a moment I cleared my throat to say something, *anything*, to break this tension.

"So will you stay with your parents when you go to the city?"

He gave me a look like he wasn't sure if I was being serious or not in my sudden interest of his family. "It's just my mom. Well, she's married now, but that happened only a few years ago, so it's not like I call him dad or anything. They got together after I started college. He's a nice guy and he treats her well." He did that shrug thing I'd noticed he did when he was trying to convey indifference. "My dad was never really in the picture."

Now I felt like an asshole, because from what my friend Priscilla had told me I should've assumed that his family history would be complicated, and probably not in my WASPy, everyone hates each other but pretends everything is fine kind of way. I was about to try to pivot away from a topic that clearly was going to be problematic, when Patrice moved to pour some more champagne in my glass and topped himself off.

"My mother was my father's mistress in Haiti." He looked right at me, head back and shoulders straight.

Like he wanted to make it very clear that he was not ashamed.

"He came by every day for a few hours, but he was never a parent." He made a dismissive hand gesture as he spoke. "He said hello and asked me how I was doing or whatever, but he wasn't my *dad*."

He chuckled, but again there was no humor in it. "I didn't realize not everyone's dad came over from six to eight at night Monday to Friday, until I was like eight."

I tried to say something because I felt like him sharing this was some kind of self-punishment. "Patrice you don't—"

He shook his head and kept talking. "My dad had money and he wanted to take his family to France when things got bad after the coup. He told my mom he couldn't take us with him. His wife wouldn't tolerate that, but he did help her get visas for us to come here." There was an edge to his voice. Whatever else happened between Patrice and his father, none of it seemed like it had been good.

"He gave her money too. We left Haiti by car and drove to the DR, then flew out of Santo Domingo to come here." I noticed he was no longer glaring, just talking. Telling me his story. Opening up to me.

"That must've been so hard, Patrice."

He lifted both shoulders and shook his head, clearly not as unaffected as he wanted to appear. "I was six, so I don't remember a lot. I do remember feeling afraid. I'll never forget my mom's face when we left our little house and got in the car to leave. She looked so scared. We only had two suitcases and left everything else to my mom's family. When we got on the plane to Miami, my mom doubled over." The edges of his mouth were tight, his handsome face pinched with the images from those times. "I remember she shoved a handkerchief she always carried around into her mouth, and sobbed so hard her shoulders shook."

A breath shuddered out of me picturing him as a little boy, his entire life changing.

"I'd never seen her like that. I remember I needed to go to the bathroom, but I didn't tell her. I was so worried about making her more upset. She'd always been a rock you know? Calm," he said, holding out a steady hand. "When I was little if I fell and showed up at the house with the bone sticking out of my leg, she just turned around to get her purse, and said, 'You'll be fine. We can take care of that in the ER.' But that day, she was inconsolable. But she was just a kid herself, she was only twenty-seven."

I shook my head as he talked. I could not imagine what it was like to leave everything behind like that. Not knowing when or if you'd come back, if your family would be okay.

I couldn't not touch him.

I got closer and ran my hand over his face. "Patrice."

He shook his head then looked at me like he forgot I'd been there the whole time, and then laughed. "I don't know what it is about being around you, but I just want to spill my guts." He sounded embarrassed and a little bewildered.

I was going to make a joke or say something to make thing less serious, like I usually did, but I stopped myself. Patrice didn't need me to make this funny or light. He had opened up to me for a reason. Even if neither of us could admit what that reason was yet.

"I'm always in awe of people that do what you and

your mom did. Pick up and start over in a new place, with a new language and which honestly isn't always very welcoming. And to achieve everything you have. It's amazing." The awe in my voice was one hundred percent sincere.

That was the last straw apparently, because he stood up from the counter so he was facing me, our bodies only inches apart. "Why can't I stay away?"

He didn't need to say from what or who.

"I'm right here." I was going to say something else about how I was happy to be his friend, but I left it at that. Because I *was* here. I could rein it in, I could be respectful, but if he wanted more...

I was here.

He moved his body closer, his feet planted on the floor, but his torso swaying in my direction and I didn't move, too turned-on and overwhelmed by the feel of him. I stood there, barely breathing and hoping he lost it first, my heart pounding in my ears.

I could almost taste him again, but when I tipped my head up, hoping for a kiss, he closed his eyes and stepped back instead.

"I'm going to head out." He smiled, friendly, but the moment was over. "Thanks again for dinner."

Point taken.

I walked him out of my apartment and watched as he took the stairs. I weakly reminded myself that friendship was better than nothing. I could at least build something with him, but I was not going to lie to myself. What I wanted was Patrice Denis in my bed, and I was certain that's what he wanted too.

Chapter Six

Patrice

"What is this? A college professor wearing sweats and basketball shoes. How was your night with Juan Pablo and Camilo?" my mother said, giving me her usual commentary on my clothes with a grin as I stepped into her house. I'd been home for a couple of days but had barely had a chance to see her.

I bypassed her comment about my clothing and distracted her by giving her a tight hug and a double kiss hello.

"Sa'k Pase, Manman?" I kissed both her cheeks and went into my mother's picture-perfect living room.

She gave a knowing look as she went in for another hug. "I'm good, but I was talking about your clothes."

I pointed at the couch, grinning. "Is this new?" I asked as she went into the kitchen. She'd moved out of the Bronx to Mt. Vernon a few years ago when she got married, after she and my stepdad bought a house. She had such a different life now than the one we'd started out with in this country. But I worried sometimes the need to make sure she had financial security didn't let her enjoy what she'd achieved. I also knew she had never quite gotten over some of the stresses of those first few years. At least she'd been working on some of it. In the past year she'd started seeing a therapist to sort out some of her anxiety about her business, and she did seem more relaxed.

"It's new. I got it for Oriol, for our anniversary." I had to laugh, it was just like my mother to get my stepfather a couch she wanted for his birthday. "But tell me what you were up to today, I've barely seen you," she said as she walked over to her open-plan kitchen.

I sat on the new couch as my mom came out from the kitchen with glasses of fresh juice. "Here. Have some carrot and ananas." She sat down next to me on her gorgeous brown leather sectional, wearing her "at home" clothes. Which usually consisted of jeans and a nice sweater. The braids in her hair coiled into an intricate design. She looked young and lovely, like the successful businesswoman she was. She'd had me when she was just twenty-one, so she was only fifty-six and did not look a day over forty.

She clicked her tongue at whatever she saw on my face, patted my leg with a perfectly manicured hand. "So tell me, how is it? I want to hear more about your new place and job."

I sipped from the juice and sighed, so good.

"I sent you the photos," I teased, knowing that would not be nearly enough. She'd asked for pictures the day I moved in, and I made sure to send a few featuring some of the kitchen cabinets which were laden with the dishes and glasses she'd gotten me. "It's very nice, almost brand new, and the guy who owns the building is—"

I cleared my throat and looked down, annoyed that

after just a few words I was already bringing up Easton. I'd been thinking about him nonstop. Since that dinner, we'd texted a couple of times. Just silly shit about books we'd been reading or we'd send each other pictures of something we saw or were doing. I'd even promised him a photo of the soup.

I looked over at my mom and she gave me a weird look, probably because I was smirking and staring into space like an idiot.

"Pardon, Manman." I squeezed her knee and she waved in my direction indicating I needed to keep talking.

"I have a guest bedroom for when you and Oriol come and visit. I'm starting to feel comfortable there."

She smiled and kissed my cheek. "Good, you deserve it. You worked so long and so hard for that. I'm proud of you, bébé. But we need to talk about these clothes. I thought we agreed you needed to dress more formally."

I rolled my eyes because I knew she'd get on my case about it. "Odette, *we* would mean *you* and *I* both decided on something, not you telling me what to do." She gave me her patented unbothered look, and raised as eyebrow as to say, *and your point is?*

"I spent the day running errands," I said, peering down at my sweatshirt, jeans and J's combo. "This is perfectly fine."

She shook her head like I was a very lovable but completely lost cause. "But you're a professor now. Why spend hundreds of dollars on tennis shoes? If you're going to spend your money, buy something nice."

I threw my hands up, laughing. "These shoes are nice and I don't need to wear suits all the time! I promise I don't teach in these clothes."

She adopted the mischievous look that in my childhood had always been the prelude to something that would either mortify me or delight me. I could never tell.

"Maybe I should start asking for OOTD selfies."

I did bust up at that. "Manman, where did you hear about that?" I said, grinning at how pleased with herself she looked for throwing "outfit of the day" at me.

"You know I got my fashion sense from you. I'm not showing up in class looking like a scrub." She gave me a look like she wasn't convinced in the slightest that I wasn't going to show up to class in some Tims.

I had to distract her with something, or this was going to end with her forcing me to go shopping with her. "How's business? You said you're expanding?"

She immediately perked up at that. My mom was the OG hustler. She'd started her own business when I was finishing high school and was always on the move trying to take it to the next level.

She looked over at me, her face open and smiling, and I could tell she had a lot of updates. "Your Manman is now officially working in the Westchester courts," she said, snapping her finger. "So far we've gotten a lot of business, there are lots of Caribbean people moving up here, so our court interpreters are getting a lot of work."

"Of course you are." I grinned, so proud of her. She'd worked on that expansion for two years. "You always know when to make your next move. Did you hire more people?"

"Yes, of course. I've been working with Camilo's agency. Training some of the women in their economic mobility program." Soon she was launching into a detailed explanation of the expansion. My mom had started working as court interpreter in New York City when I was finishing middle school, after years of night school and working minimum wage jobs to support us. Once she'd been in it for a while she noticed there was a lack of interpreters from Haiti, Cuba, Puerto Rico and Dominican Republic who could better accommodate people from those countries when they needed to testify in court or to be deposed. So she decided to start a business that specialized in court interpreters from the islands. After only a few years, business was booming. She had over fifty interpreters now. She favored women in her hiring, because she wanted to help those who, like her, were trying to make it here.

"You are killing the game, Odette." That made her preen, and she had plenty of reason to. She had put her all into that business, and I was so damn proud of my mother.

I always had an amazing example to follow. My mother paid a steep price to be able to start her business, but she'd made sure she never had to ask for help again. That was something I never ever forgot.

We both looked at each other as if we were thinking the same thing. But before we could go down memory lane we heard the doorbell and I stood up to get the door, and could already hear my two best friends arguing on the other side of the door.

"Juan Pablo, just *call her*." I found Camilo giving Juanpa epic stank face, while J just stood there unresponsive.

"Do I even want to know?" I asked, as I ushered them inside.

"Just trying to talk some sense into him." I raised an eyebrow, because with Camilo that could mean anything, since he freely told us what to do about pretty much every aspect of our lives.

He rolled his eyes at the puzzled look on my face. "Priscilla." Oh. No wonder Juan Pablo wasn't talking.

I was going to tell Camilo to leave him alone when the doorbell rang again. I opened the door and found Camilo's mom, Dinorah, and Juanpa's parents, each holding a dish of something. My mom jumped up as soon as she saw them.

"Finally, I thought I was going to have to sit and hear these three fight all night," she said as she passed Camilo, Juanpa and I, delivering double kisses to them as she went.

After the routine hellos, which with a mix of Caribbean people and J's Italian mom, took some time, we all went in and started helping get dinner on the table.

"Odette, this smells amazing," Camilo exclaimed as he brought out the gigantic bowl of soup. I was just remembering I'd promised Easton a photo when my pocket buzzed.

I still haven't gotten any feast photos. You already forget about me, professor?

Why did my stomach have to dip like that whenever I saw a text from Easton?

I saw Camilo looking at me from the other side of the table and quickly shoved the phone in my pocket. I'd gotten enough from him about Easton last night when we had dinner at Juanpa's.

We got our bowls of soup and sat around my mom's dining table. It felt so good to be with my people. Nesto was missing though, and that hurt a little bit. Now that I was up in Ithaca, we'd reconnected again and it made me miss the times when it was the four of us against the world. When I'd finally found friends who looked at me and truly saw me.

I thought about Easton and the ease with which I could talk to him about my life. I couldn't believe I told him about my dad. That was something I rarely ever discussed.

"Damn bruh, where's your head right now?" I snapped my head up to see J looking at me with bemusement.

"Nothing. Just thinking about all the shit I need to do for my class."

Neither of them looked like they believed me, but I didn't want to get into Easton right now. I was still trying to figure out how I felt about him. I'd been struck by his honesty of being unsure of what to do about the stops and his desire to help. Of course it could all be lip service, but it seemed like he was at least trying.

Thankfully Camilo changed the subject.

"How's it going with Ari? I forgot to ask about it when I saw you before. I'm so glad you're going to be his mentor, P." I smiled at that, because I was glad too.

"Honestly, I still haven't gotten a chance to really sit down and talk with him." I lifted a hand to appease Camilo's stank face. "Chill, I made plans to meet him as soon as I get back to town." I wasn't going to drag my feet on this. I couldn't control or fix some of the shit that was going on in Ithaca, but I could step up and support Ari.

"Between the move and his schedule, we haven't been able to make time." I sighed, remembering what Nesto told me the night I moved in. "It seems like his uncle's making trouble for him about his immigration and—" I cringed thinking of his plans to come out

"—things are getting pretty serious with him and Yin. Nesto's worried if he comes out that will make things much worse."

Camilo and J both looked horrified. Milo was the first one to talk. "Oh my god. That is not okay. After poor Ari spent all that time in an immigration detention center. You'd think he'd earned his chance to fall in love and act like a normal twenty-two-year-old."

"I know that's right." It was rare to hear Juanpa give an opinion about things or people he didn't know too well, but Ari had grown on all of us. He certainly deserved some peace.

"I hope that between Nesto, Jude and I, we can make sure he at least feels more supported. It's not like he's not trying either. I've never seen anyone with more hustle."

Camilo put a hand on my shoulder, his gray eyes a little sad. "You'll be good for him, you get where he's at." I nodded, remembering the tension of those first few months in the US when my mom and I had no idea how we were going to stay here. The desperation of not knowing. So many nights I'd up and find my mom crying in bed.

Our first year here we'd lived with friends or friends of friends as our asylum case was evaluated. On people's foldout couches or on a mattress on the floor. The money my dad had given her to come to the States kept in a secret place for when we landed somewhere that felt safe to put down roots.

It wasn't until we finally got to New York and my mom connected with an old friend of my grandmother's that things started looking better. But that first year in Florida almost broke her. I wondered what Easton would think about if I told him everything. All the things my mother had to do to make sure we didn't end up on the street.

"Dude, you wild intense tonight. More than usual, and that's saying a lot." Juanpa again.

Camilo smirked as he picked up a spoonful of soup. "He's thinking about his man."

I thoroughly ignored that and changed the subject. "You assholes still want to see a movie afterwards?"

Juanpa nodded and gave me a thumbs-up. "Yeah man. We'll go to the place by me. It's got a full bar and kitchen, bruh. We can order beer."

"Ignoring my true statement doesn't make you less thirsty for Easton," Camilo muttered, at least he was considerate enough to not get my mother's attention.

I shamelessly ignored Camilo again and turned to Juanpa. "Sounds good man."

I was about to ask what movie he'd decided on when Dinorah looked over at us. Like usual the "kids" had been talking with each other while the "grownups" did their own thing.

"Patrice, m'ijo, tell us about your new job. We want to know how it's going over there."

That got the conversation off in another direction, and as I talked, I tried to make myself forget that all I wanted to do was take my phone out and message Easton.

Easton

I was in the Bad Place.

Patrice hadn't answered the text I'd sent over two hours ago. So I walked out of my office at 9:00 p.m.

on Friday, feeling the weight of my phone like an anvil in my pocket.

I would have to sit and think about what was going on with me. My desperation for Patrice had reached the point where not getting a response from a text sent me into a tailspin of self-doubt. Every few minutes I was caught in a cycle of wanting to delete it, feeling stupid for sending it and ultimately hating him for ignoring me.

"Man you look like you need a drink," Ron said as he walked to the elevator where I was standing. "Did Sherriff Day cancel on you or something?"

I shook my head and sighed. "No, the meeting is still on. I know Cindy won't like that I called this meeting without asking her."

The look Ron gave me told me that he didn't care about feelings if it meant getting a handle on what was going on with these stops.

"I hope that Day can be reasonable. I'm not trying to tell anyone how to do their job, but this approach of waiting until shit explodes to do anything seems reckless."

Ron grunted as we got into the elevator. He was a big guy, Patrice's size. Because everything these days ultimately led to Patrice.

"It's not about you telling him how to do his job, it's about you having a conversation with him about problematic shit that's happening on his watch. Day's a good guy and I respect him. But waiting until something worse happens is not how you protect a community."

"I can't argue with that," I said, shoving my hands into my pockets.

Ron's scowl deepened as he went on. "The DA's office and local law enforcement should be on the same page. They bring us the cases to prosecute, and if we can't trust their judgement, it's going to be a problem."

We walked out of the elevator into a crisp Ithaca fall evening, as I mulled over Ron's words. "I've always respected Day too. I hope he can hear what we have to say."

Ron clapped me on the back, a smile appearing on his face. "For what it's worth, everyone in town respects you too. Day won't ignore something you bring to him."

I didn't know how to react to that. I worked my ass off and I'd proven myself in the courtroom in the years since I started as a prosecutor many times over. But that niggling doubt that people saw me as just a rich kid rebelling against his parents was ever present.

"Thanks for saying that, Ron."

He nodded as we reached the parking lot. "Don't thank me, it's the truth. You're too hard on yourself. So you want to go for that beer? Corinne's out of town with the kids seeing her sister in Syracuse." He waggled his eyebrows.

"Nice, nothing but beer and wings for the next two days, huh?" Ron's deep laugh was something.

"You know it."

Just as I was going to ask him where to meet him my phone buzzed. I held up a finger and quickly got the phone out of my jacket pocket. As soon as I saw the screen I felt a shiver run through my body.

Patrice.

I opened the message app and saw two photos: one of an enormous bowl of pumpkin and beef soup that looked delicious and the other of the Manhattan skyline.

Soup was good then went to the movies with C and J. Driving back up to Juanpa's place, I'm staying with him tonight. Got this shot when we were driving over the Whitestone Bridge. If you're up for it, hit me up later. I'll be around…

My stomach did an actual flip.

I had no idea my body could do the things it had done in the last two minutes. What did the text mean? Did he want me to call him?

Ron cleared his throat, reminding me he was waiting for an answer about going for a drink. I slowly lifted my head and found him smirking at me. "I assume that text changed your plans for the evening."

I blushed and, like a complete tool, pressed the screen against my chest.

He laughed, clapping my shoulder. "I gotta go, Mike's already there and he eats all the good wings if I'm late, leaves all the sweet ones." He made a hilarious face of disgust and I chuckled.

"All right, Ron. Have a good weekend. See you Monday."

He waved as he got in his car. "I hope whoever made you smile like that treats you right, Easton. You deserve it."

Now I was really fucking blushing.

I waved at Ron as he got in his truck and immediately started the three blocks to my building. I kept thinking of ways to respond. *What should I say? Should I send a photo?*

By the time I got to my apartment, I'd made up my mind.

I started undressing as I moved through the loft, the

feel of air against my skin was almost too much. I felt like my body was on fire...over a text. I toed off my shoes by the stairs going up to the bedroom, and took off my shirt as I went.

I got to the room and turned on the lamp by my bed then with my back to the window took a selfie. I sent Patrice the image of me, shirtless with rumpled hair, before I talked myself out of it.

Just the clock tower view for me tonight, and bed soon...

I knew I was starting something, but I was loathe to stop whatever this was.

Chapter Seven

Patrice

I was in bed already when I felt my phone buzz with a message containing a selfie from Easton. My heart raced from just seeing his face. He was standing in his room, and there was enough of his bare chest in the picture that I could see a little bit of the patch of hair he had between his pecs. The same patch of hair that I'd run my lips over almost obsessively last summer. Seeing it now made me recall exactly how warm his skin always felt, the way he was always eager for my touch.

I was really tripping.

I'd felt too wired all day, wishing I was in Ithaca and could show up at Easton's door and end this game we'd been playing for weeks now. I ran my fingers over the screen of my phone, considering my next move.

I was always overthinking, calculating the many pitfalls that could come with being impulsive, of letting my feelings get the best of me. That's why dating had always been on the backburner, something I couldn't afford to throw myself into. There was too much at stake for distractions.

But now, with tenure looming further in the distance,

life didn't feel like an obstacle course. I felt like I could look around, like I could relax, and the only thing I wanted was more of Easton.

I opened my texting app and typed the words before I reconsidered.

FaceTime me when you're in bed, so I can say goodnight.

Regret hit me almost as soon as I sent the message, but I wasn't taking it back. Still, I quickly dropped the phone on the table next to the bed and grabbed my e-reader, pretending to read while I waited to hear the buzz of a message or a call coming in.

I was reading the same sentence for the fifth time when the phone started skittering on the wooded surface. Instead of taking it, like a complete asshole, I got out of bed and ignored it. I listened to the phone vibrating as I slowly turned off my e-reader, then walked to the bathroom and wrapped my locs. I let myself feel the craving to see him, the butterflies in my stomach when the phone stopped buzzing. I thought about Easton sitting there confused, wondering why I'd told him to call just so I could ignore his call, and hated myself a little.

Mind games, fuckboy shit…and why? Because I knew the moment I grabbed that phone it was all over.

After I took my time with my locs and brushing my teeth, I walked back to the bedroom and picked up the phone as I got back in bed. When I touched the screen I saw he left a message to call when I was ready. Just like that. The tightness I'd been feeling all day started to loosen as I tapped my phone to call him back.

Inevitable.

I held the screen up to my face and waited, after only a few rings Easton's face filled it. His expression a mirror image of mine. Head propped on a pillow, his bare neck and chest visible on the screen.

He looked tired and so fucking beautiful, and the smile he gave me felt like what I'd been needing all day.

"Hey."

I smiled back and greeted him. "Hey yourself, long day?"

He lifted a shoulder before answering, the weariness obvious in his expression. "It wasn't particularly longer than any other day. We're preparing for that case of the community college student who was assaulted by a classmate last year."

I grimaced, remembering I'd seen the story about the upcoming trial a few days ago. "That must be intense."

He nodded and ran his hand over his hair. When he did, I could see the little mole right below his hairline. It was funny, my friends always teased me about how casual, almost dismissive I was with the people I dated. Not really paying attention to details, but with Easton, I'd memorized every centimeter of his body. Each freckle and scar seared in my mind forever.

After a moment he answered with a tired smile still on his lips. "Yeah, gearing up for a trial is always kind of grueling, but we have it mostly under control." I could tell he wasn't up to talking about his job anymore. Easton did not like talking about his stress, or troubles. He didn't like talking about himself too much either.

Sunny, all the time.

It stung that I was yet one more person in his life he felt needed that from him.

I tried to focus on him and what he was saying, and

not get caught up in regretful thoughts for once. "We decided to take the weekend off to get some rest since the next two weeks are going to be hectic." He tilted his head, eyebrows raised in question.

"How are the guys? Was soup night good?" Work talk was over then. Now it was my turn to fill the space. Tell him about my things, my people.

I exhaled, trying to remember the last time I'd been this intimate with someone I'd been dating.

I could not recall.

"Soup was good. My mother likes to monitor my wardrobe choices, which gets old, but I let her get away with it. It was great seeing everybody though. I went to see the latest superhero movie with Juanpa and Camilo after."

"Nice," he said with a bit more wistfulness than I'd expect. Easton seemed like the kind of guy who never wanted for social engagements or people to see. I always envisioned him surrounded by people wanting to be with him, but maybe that was just me projecting.

We were silent for a moment and I ran my eyes over the little bit of his body I could see. He looked sleepy and soft and I wanted to be in that bed with him. Make him feel good, lose myself in his body. That was something that I'd only known with Easton, a chemistry and pull so powerful I'd forgotten everything else when we were together. It had been a heady thing to feel. Desire so strong it drove me literally out of my head.

I noticed a little black satin pouch by his pillow and before I even opened my mouth, my heart started racing. "What is that?"

He turned his head in the direction I was pointing and looked at it, like he'd forgotten it was there, then his eyes widened in surprise. But when he turned his attention back to me the wicked smile, which usually meant dirty delicious things were about to happen, made an appearance.

"It was a gift from Priscilla, she brought it when she was in town last week."

"Oh?" I asked in a voice that was more growl than anything else.

Nesto's cousin and Easton's best friend, Priscilla, was a police detective whose side hustle was an online sex-positive toy shop. She loved giving all of us freebies.

I smiled at the lascivious expression on his face. "So you're one of the lucky recipients of Pris's freebies."

"Her deciding to open Come as You Are has been a boon for me. I've been really wanting to try this one."

And that was all I needed to hear for my dick to get fully in the game.

I groaned, shifting in the bed, my legs falling open to give myself more room. My pulse quickened with every lusty look Easton was flashing at me on that screen.

Fuck it. I was doing this.

"What is it?" I asked, committed to taking this shit wherever it needed to go, and Easton was loving it, if that smirk on his face was any indication.

He took his time to answer, looking at me with just a hint of doubt in his eyes, as if asking, "Are you sure you want to do this?"

I pushed the sheets off me and doubled down because as a matter of fact, I really fucking *did* want to do this.

"I want to see it. Right now."

I wanted to push and prod until I had Easton panting. It felt like the only thing in the world that mattered in this moment. That dirty smile came back out and I pushed down the elastic band of my shorts so I could stroke my cock. Already desperate to get this thing we were doing, whatever it was, started.

I shuddered out a breath as I saw Easton reach over and grab the pouch with his thumb and index finger, delicately placing it on his chest, his eyes locked on mine the whole time.

He blinked twice, the corners of his mouth pulling up as he fingered whatever was inside.

"This?"

I chuckled at his teasing, gripping my dick, and praying I didn't come before I got to see his.

He was going to stretch this out, make me wait. Force me to be patient and to ask for what I wanted each step of the way.

I'd always been one for furtive encounters. Quick and impersonal. Not with Easton, every night I'd spent with him had been intense and unhurried. He'd refused to let me run out after a quick fuck. Sure, I'd resisted, wanting to keep to my usual MO, but Easton wanted what he wanted, and in the end I'd stayed.

Hell, I'd come running back for more.

I would never admit it, but I was hooked on the way he *made me* tell him what I wanted. He never let me hide behind my mask.

I had to tear it off for Easton.

Name each and every one of the things I wanted from him. I could drown in the things Easton made me feel. I could barely keep my head above water now.

Still holding the phone up to his face, he took the toy out of the bag. It was a black curved silicone vibrator, the head a lot thicker than the base. I could already picture the look of ecstasy when he worked it inside himself.

"I want to watch your face when you fuck yourself with it." I stroked my cock again as a shiver ran up my spine.

He sucked his teeth in response, while a flush worked itself up his neck, his eyes fixed on what I was doing. "Let me see it." I didn't have to ask what he meant. "I've been dreaming about it for months."

The way his breath caught on the last word told me that like me, he was touching himself, too turned on to stay still.

The wickedness that only showed up when Easton was in the picture bubbled up and suddenly I wanted to play. "What? This?" I moved the phone up so he could only see my chest, and over the speaker I heard a frustrated groan.

"Two can play at this game, Professor Denis." That last word was more a gasp, and just the sound of him getting revved up made my balls tighten. I tipped the phone up so I could see what he was doing. His face was totally out of the frame. I heard him though, and with the way he was humming, my own breathing started coming faster. By the time I raised the phone to my eyes all I saw was Easton's ceiling.

"I thought you were waiting to see something?" I asked, feigning confusion, and after a moment he was back on the screen.

"Show me." His voice was tight, like he wasn't sure he'd get what he was asking for. What he didn't know, what I wasn't sure I could ever say, was that in that moment I would have given him anything.

I licked my lips as I lowered the phone to where my

other hand was busy stroking my dick. For a second I felt foolish, my dick in my hand while I FaceTimed a guy I should probably stay away from. But the flames fanning this fire were more than I could contain.

The pained groan from my tortured audience of one made me grin as I lifted the phone back up to my face.

"I cannot tell you to the degree that my mouth waters whenever I see your cock." He sounded just a little resentful. "It's Pavlovian at this point."

I laughed as he winked and started moving his hand down his chest until I couldn't see it anymore. He jerked after a moment, a moan escaping his lips.

"Are you touching yourself?" I asked, just so that I could do something if I couldn't be there to touch him. He nodded frantically and looked up at me.

"Yeah, I just brushed my finger over my hole. It feels so good." He closed his eyes like the feeling was too intense, and I had to pull hard on my balls to get myself under control again, and practically barked the next words out. "Get some lube."

He moved so fast he dropped the phone, but within seconds his face was back on the screen. Those green eyes barely visible around his blown-out pupils. That flush of red kept creeping further up his neck, and I wanted to be there. Run my teeth over that blushing skin and make him fall apart.

I must've been showing a lot more than I thought I was because for a moment he closed his eyes again and took a deep breath. He shook his head once and a smile crept over his lips. When he spoke, it was so low I could barely hear him.

"When you look at me like that, I can't breathe."

I heard myself say it before I had a chance to think about my words. "Look at you how?"

"Like that." He lifted his finger and pointed in the direction of his phone, his eyes still closed.

"Open your eyes, Easton, I want you to look at me when I tell you what I want."

He snapped them open and the hunger there matched mine exactly.

Ravenous.

"Get the lube on the vibrator."

"But I'll need both hands for that." His chest was moving up and down like he'd been running.

"Do it." I growled again, just to keep from laughing at how conflicted he looked.

"God, why do I find your toppy bullshit so hot?" he asked, flustered, as I lay there grinning.

That was the thing about Easton, I was different with him. Careless and careful at the same time. More focused on all the things that were going right, and not so worried about what could go wrong. I could be like that for hours, lost in Easton. He put the phone on speaker and set it down somewhere.

He came back, his face still flushed. "What do I do?"

"Let me see it." Apparently I no longer spoke, I just growled.

He raised the hand with the toy up to the screen and the head was glistening with lube. My hands shook, wanting so badly to be the one putting it inside him.

"Let me see how hard you are? But don't touch yourself yet." I stroked my cock again, running my thumb over the head of my dick. I was so turned on I knew I wouldn't last much longer.

Easton shuddered out another breath and shook his

head. "I'm so hard right now, baby, let me touch myself, please."

His words were like lightning crackling through me. I was never one for endearments, and neither was Easton, but when we were like this, delirious from wanting each other, all the rules went out the window.

"No cheri mwen, don't touch."

He turned the phone and I could see the vee of his legs, his knees drawn up, thighs spread and his cock sticking straight up. The force of how much I wanted him was almost overwhelming.

"Tell me what to do, baby." His voice shook when he spoke, and I could barely keep it together.

"Fuck yourself with the vibrator. Turn it on and put it in slowly."

He moved the phone back so I could see his face and nodded frantically. He squirmed as he held the phone with one hand and himself with the other. The cords of his neck were tight and his mouth went slack as he worked it in.

At this point I was just gripping the base of my dick, just so I wouldn't blow before he even got the vibrator in all the way.

"Tell me how it feels."

His face was pure ecstasy. "So good."

"Does it feel like when I'm inside you?"

He shook his head hard, the phone shaking as he did. "Nothing feels like you. No one feels like you."

His words hit me hard. I was writhing from how turned on I was and how much I wanted to respond in kind, tell him that nothing felt like this for me either.

Easton could just say things like that. Tell me exactly what I was to him. No reservations, and it was fucking terrifying. I was so close to saying reckless shit to Easton, but the way he was moaning as he played with himself got me back in the game.

"Those sounds you make. Are you hitting your spot? I know how hard you can come when I hit you just right."

"Uh huh," he said, completely lost in what he was doing. "Ungh, the tip is tapping right against it. I'm so close." He gasped and tightened his jaw.

I was stroking myself just enough, but I knew one hard and fast stroke would set me off.

"Turn it up, I want to see your face when that thing really starts drilling you hard. Are you leaking baby?"

After a second he let out a long, husky moan and started muttering a long string of "Oh fuck, oh fuuuuuck."

"Oh shit." I was rambling right along with him, barely hanging on until he came. "Jesus, you look hot," I said, already feeling my orgasm build, that tight heat in my groin making my ass clench.

"Shit." I shuddered. "I'm coming."

Just as I sped my hand up, I saw Easton push his head hard into the pillow and his mouth open in a silent moan, eyes tightly shut. He looked so beautiful like that. Lost in chasing his orgasm at all costs.

I dropped my phone and ran my hand over my chest until I found a nipple, twisting it just enough to take me over the edge. My vision whited out and in the distance I heard Easton swearing through his own orgasm. Long ropes of come spurted out, hitting my stomach and neck. As I came out of from the fog of my orgasm, for a second the sated bliss was edged out by a hint of regret.

But as I picked up my phone again and found Easton

on the screen, looking like the very picture of pliable contented man, I pushed my worrying out, and decided to enjoy this moment.

I was about to speak, but Easton beat me to it. "I'd act like this was unexpected, but I've been hoping for you to do this with me since the moment you got to Ithaca."

Easton

I was sitting up against the headboard and Patrice was doing the same, somewhere in Yonkers. His big body at rest, the tattoo on his chest—the one with the Haitian and American flags in the shape of human heart—moving as he took deep breaths. He had that secret smile I'd noticed only happened when I was being a particular brand of bratty.

"So this was all planned. You got that toy to tempt me."

I put a finger under my chin as if considering his question. "Maybe."

He laughed and shook his head, but didn't have a retort. Things felt comfortable between us, no stalled conversation or weird silences.

I watched him as he ran a hand over his collarbone, where he had another tattoo. This one just two words, *Ayiti Cheri*, which he'd told me meant, *Beloved Haiti* in creole.

The skin where the tattoos were was a bit bumpy in places from keloid scarring. When I'd first asked him about it he just said his skin scarred easily, and it was why he didn't have more tattoos. I'd run my fingers over those spots so many times when we'd been together. Never getting anywhere near my fill when it came to Patrice. Which only made me remember what he'd called me while we were messing around.

"What's *cheri mwen*?"

He smiled, a little embarrassed, but I could see he was determined to say whatever it was. "It means *my darling*."

Oh, there went those butterflies again.

I was so tempted to ask more questions. *Was* I his darling or was it just something he'd said in the heat of the moment?

I'd never heard him use it before with me, I would've remembered.

Did I want to know?

I didn't want to lose the feeling those words had brought. I wanted to keep him open to me. Looking like I was a place of comfort.

But my insecurity won out and I asked the other thing I'd been wondering. "Why are you not freaking out right now?"

He lifted an eyebrow, looking a bit amused but mostly surprised at my question. Like he couldn't believe I'd actually asked. He stared at me for what seemed like a very long time, his eyes not angry, but very intense as he considered his answer.

He turned onto his side, his face pillowed on his strong arms.

I did the same and it felt so intimate, like we were face-to-face.

"I'm tired of not letting myself have the things that I want."

It took him so long to respond I was momentarily confused by what he said. Then it sunk in.

I was what he wanted.

I chose not to dwell on the fact that doing this with me had come as the result of some sort of battle he'd won against his common sense.

Again against my better judgement I opened my mouth. "Hearing you call me an object of your desire is doing things to me, Professor Denis."

That look on his face, like he was caught between finding me utterly fuckable and somewhat obnoxious, made the butterflies in my stomach come out to play once again. But he didn't answer, just let the information he'd volunteered sit there between us.

I decided to retreat then, feeling scared of pushing him to a place where he would pull up his defenses again.

I wanted this Patrice, *my Patrice*, around just a little longer, so I went back to safer waters.

"So dinner was uneventful, then?" He lifted a shoulder and then brought his arm under his head, making those big muscles shift and flex when he moved.

"Yeah, my mom's husband is out of town this week at a conference, so I missed him." He chuckled at that for a second and then dipped his head.

"He helps run interference with my mom whenever she gets militant about my locs or tattoos, going to church, my nose ring, wearing sweats or whatever thing I'm doing that drives her crazy."

His tone was light but there was a tightness in his jaw, which told me that maybe it bothered him more than he'd like to admit.

"She doesn't like your tattoos?"

Another shrug. "She thinks they give people the wrong idea of the kind of person I am. Like they're going to make assumptions based on that."

My gut instinct was to make a joke. Whenever anything came a little too close to heaviness or baggage between me and Patrice, I quickly lightened the mood. Never giving him a reason to feel weighed down when he was with me. I didn't want to now. I wanted to know.

"Do they?"

He scoffed then and his eyes, which could be serious, or disinterested at times, but never unkind, turned cold. "Of course they do. But no matter how my hair is or what I'm wearing, people will always make assumptions." His voice was strained like talking about this took him back to a place of endless frustration. He stopped and looked away for a second and when his eyes landed on me, they were soft again, the frustration back wherever he usually kept it under the surface. "People will always think they know who I am, and almost always they will be wrong."

"People suck." It was such a dumbass response and not nearly enough, but Patrice chuckled, and a real smile tipped up those lush lips.

"They do."

I wanted to ask more, about how that was for him. How he handled it without being angry all the time. But I didn't. Wanting to stretch out this moment, I asked something trivial.

"So what are you doing tomorrow?"

I thought I saw a glimpse of disappointment in his eyes at my obvious attempt to change the subject. It stung, but it felt like it was too late to take it back.

He must've caught something in my face. "Are you okay?"

I smiled at him tempted to reach out and touch the screen, wanting to feel closer.

"I'm fine. You didn't say what you're doing tomorrow?" I asked again. Not even sure why I insisted on asking the question.

He shook his head gently and sighed. "Driving back afternoonish actually. I need to get some stuff done for my classes next week and I won't get anything done here. I also told Ari I'd meet him for an early dinner. So I'll be around." There was too much promise in that answer for me not to pounce on it.

"You want to come over for a drink after, maybe some dessert?"

That sounded a lot more salacious than I'd intended, but he didn't exactly look put off, and I went with it. "I promise I won't jump you, I mean unless you really want me to."

He laughed at that, and I lit up inside. "I told you I will always be down for someone else making me food, and I have a wicked sweet tooth. I'll bring some wine."

I shook my head at his answer. "You don't need to."

"I want to. I'll text you when I get back. I should be back in town by 5:00 p.m. or so."

"Okay," I said, trying very hard not to grin.

After that Patrice's eyes got droopy like he was going to doze off. "I think I need to get to bed. I'll see you tomorrow."

That wasn't a question or a maybe, it was a statement of fact, and it was hard to contain myself. "Okay."

We signed off and I lay in bed thinking about the call, the intensity of the phone sex. The way my body responded to Patrice even when he wasn't in the room. How much I wanted him *all the time*.

If it were up to me we would've burned the candle at both ends long ago. But Patrice didn't operate like that, he was methodical and careful and I couldn't blame him.

I thought about seeing him the next day and right under the want and need, there was fear. I was scared, of whether in the end, no matter how hot were together, Patrice didn't want me like I wanted him.

Chapter Eight

Patrice

Resisting Easton had started to feel like a full-time job, and I had plenty of work already.

That was the line I was feeding myself as I drove into Ithaca. I'd left earlier than I anticipated from the city, so I'd get there before 5:00 p.m. My mom had been disappointed, but when I told her it was because I needed to make sure I planned my lessons, she immediately backed off. I felt guilty about it, but my thirst for Easton had been in overdrive since last night. It was like once the dam broke, I couldn't think of anything other than getting my hands on him.

I was sitting there mulling all this when a call from Ari came in. I picked up, wondering if he needed to reschedule for dinner, and spoke before he had a chance to talk. "I'm pretty close. I should be in town soon." The long silence on his end gave me pause, and when he finally spoke I immediately knew something was very wrong.

"I'm sorry to bother you." His usual elegant and lilting accent sounded thicker in his distressed state.

"Aristide, est-ce que tout va bien?" Since I'd met him

while helping Nesto with the truck we'd fallen into the habit of speaking in French, both of our native tongues. He usually teased me about me losing my accent, but the long pause after my greeting started to worry me.

"Non. I am not good."

My heart sank at the finality. "Did something happen with Nesto?"

He answered quickly, as if just realizing that I would think that. "No, he's fine. Everyone is fine. I just." He let out a long shuddering breath. "The police stopped me."

I hit the brakes then, trying to find a place to stop. I needed to be still while I listened to Ari. I looked around, disoriented as panic took over.

I was on a small county road still about ten miles outside of Ithaca and it was deserted, so I pulled to a stop and after a deep breath I spoke again. "When?"

"Like twenty minutes ago." It was almost 5:00 p.m. and had just started to get dark in the last few minutes.

"What happened?"

"I was coming back from dropping Yin at his house. We worked at the restaurant this morning. Since we have brunch now on weekends, we were there early and finished around 4:00 p.m. I stayed at his house for a bit longer than I should have." He cleared his throat then, and even in the midst of this shitty moment I smiled hearing how his voice filled with affection whenever his spoke of his boyfriend. "I was rushing to make sure I could stop home before meeting you. I told my uncle I would bring him some dinner from work. I was going faster than I usually drive. They pulled me over right outside of Trumansburg."

"Did anything bad happen during the stop?" I waited in silence, dreading what he'd say next.

"They were rude, and asked me to get out of the car, but they didn't hurt me. I did everything you and Nesto told me."

When they'd been over helping with the move, Ari shared he was scared of driving on his own. He'd bought Nesto's old Prius when Nes upgraded to an SUV some months back, but was still very careful on the road. Nesto and I had talked to him about what he should do if he ever got stopped, told him about the videos he could watch.

"I was just scared." His voice sounded small and I felt so damn sorry he'd had to go through that. "When they asked for my ID, I almost panicked. I have my license, but I heard they've been asking for papers. All I have is my work authorization. I was worried they'd see it and ask me about Batavia." His voice shook when he mentioned the detention center he'd been held in for over a year. I closed my eyes as my own heartbeat throbbed in my ears. It made me sick to my stomach to hear that he'd gone through that.

I didn't want this for him.

When he spoke again, his voice, which was usually so strong and jovial, sounded tiny and terrified. "I thought they would call my uncle and you know how he is. He would've been furious to know I was driving back from Yin's house. He keeps threatening me that he won't help me with my Green Card if I don't stop being friends with him."

My mood sank even further at the mention of Ari's uncle. I knew the man wasn't evil, but he was certainly going out of his way to be an asshole. I had a feeling his uncle was using this to scare him and that he was not necessarily able to do all the shit he was threatening Ari with.

"Where are you now?"

"I'm at the employee parking lot of OuNYe. I didn't know where to go and didn't want to scare Yin."

Poor kid.

I did some quick mental math on what the best course of action was. I didn't want him to get on the road again if he was still freaked out. "I'm only like ten minutes out of town, why don't you call Yin and tell him I'll pick him up. You can walk over to my place. We'll order some Thai food and watch a movie. Is that okay or do you need to be home for anything?"

"No, I can tell my uncle I'm sleeping at a friend's house." He didn't sound like he was thrilled about that conversation. But he seemed to be happy with the dinner and movie at my place idea, so I went with it.

"Thanks, Patrice. I am so embarrassed to call you like this, but I didn't want to bother Nesto and Jude on Nesto's night off. They had plans to go to that new place on Seneca Lake and I know they would've cancelled if I told them what happened. They've already done too much for me."

I shook my head as though he could see me still struggling to keep the sharp anger that was bubbling up from coming through in my voice. "I'm glad you called. I'll see you soon."

As I powered up the SUV again and got on the road to go pick up Yin, I tried hard to calm myself. I didn't need to put my own shit on Ari, but someone was going to have to put the sheriff's department on blast about this nonsense. Because the longer this went on unchecked… It was only a matter of time before a tragedy happened.

Of course my mind went straight to Easton, and his job in particular. When we'd talked about it before, we'd both tiptoed around the topic and eventually fully dropped it when it was obvious it would ruin our conversation. I compromised because I wanted to spend time with him. Because I let my own wants become more important than my values. I knew this was all bigger than the both of us, but unlike Easton, for me it wasn't about a cause or a job. This was about my community, my purpose. I could not get involved with someone who would muddy the waters of what was important to me.

I needed to focus on my work, on my activism. Easton was not the person for me. There were things I needed to do that would get too messy if I pursued a relationship with him.

So what if I wanted Easton. So what if he made me feel good. I was still me and he was still him. Our worlds were still at odds, and that was not something I could ignore, no matter how much I wanted to.

I pulled up to Yin's apartment building where I knew from dropping him off a couple of times, he lived with his two older sisters. I had barely brought the SUV to a full stop when Yin ran up and yanked the car door open. He got in the car with a backpack on this shoulder, his usually sunny face drawn and worried. "You have everything you need for a sleepover?" I asked with a hell of a lot more lightness than I felt.

He looked like he was about to cry. "Yes," he said, pointing at a small leather backpack. "Thank you for picking me up. I didn't want Ari coming to get me. He might get into an accident," he said as he wiped his eyes. "He's too upset. My sister was going to drive me on her way to work, but she doesn't leave for another hour."

"No problem. You want to call in the order for dinner? Thai?" He nodded and pulled out his phone.

We spent the last few minutes of the drive in the negotiations of placing a dinner order and by the time I drove my SUV into the underground parking of my building, we were both feeling a little less on edge.

Ari was waiting for us when we walked up to the building. He and Yin embraced, hard. I imagined with what they've both gone through just to get to the States that they were deeply aware of how fragile life could be. They'd been apart for maybe an hour, but they were touching as if it'd been years. It was a relief to see them be a comfort for each other.

As we reached my door I noticed a note taped to my door. I knew who it was from before I even read it. My heart sank and my stomach flipped before I could make out the words. It was only a couple of lines, letting me know he was home and I could come up whenever I got in. But the frustration and fear of the last hour were more than I could ignore. I ushered Yin and Ari into my apartment then pulled out my phone. I quickly tapped out a text, ruthlessly ignoring the ache in my chest as I did so.

Sorry to tell you last minute, but I won't make it tonight. Have a good rest of your weekend.

After that I turned off my phone.

I looked at the couch where Ari and Yin were sitting. They were talking quietly, their heads so close together their foreheads touched, and I decided this would be where I'd place my energy for now. I needed to focus on the places where I was needed.

"What would you guys like to watch? There's a bunch of new stuff on Netflix or we can buy something?"

Yin perked up and Ari shook his head. "Bébé, I'm not watching *To All the Boys I've Loved Before* again."

Yin scrunched his face like he couldn't understand how a person could be that heartless. "But we haven't seen it in a really long time."

Ari rolled his eyes and put his arm around his boyfriend. "Three weeks is not a long time. We saw it when we babysat your niece."

Yin huffed again and I couldn't help but laugh, despite the hole in my stomach.

"How about *Black Panther*?" They both seemed pleased with that answer, and before they changed their mind, I fired up the movie.

"We can pause it when the food comes." I turned around and noticed they were already settled in on the sofa with a throw over them. Comfortable in my house, and I felt glad that at least I could provide Ari a space where he could be himself while he figured things out.

I couldn't use my attraction for Easton as a distraction anymore. No matter how much I ached to run upstairs and apologize for leaving him hanging, for hurting him. It was better to do this now than later, before we were both too emotionally invested. It felt like a betrayal to even think like this, but my own wants could not take precedence this time.

Easton

I didn't see his face, but I didn't need to. I would recognize those shoulders anywhere. Patrice was embracing another man outside of the building at 10:00 a.m. the morning after cancelling on our plans with zero explanation. From my living room window I had a front-row seat of the unfolding scene. He stood there, his face serious, both hands in his pockets as he watched the man drive off, and then went back inside. I felt like the skin on my face was burning, jealousy and humiliation coursing through me.

I was a fucking fool.

Patrice wasn't busy working like I told myself when I got his text last night as I frantically ran around preparing the elaborate dessert I'd ended up shoving into the fridge untouched.

He was with *someone else*.

All that shit he said on the phone the other night was just that…shit he'd said. I had to finally get it through my stupid fucking head that Patrice and I weren't doing the same thing. We were nowhere near the same page, and I need to leave this alone.

And yet, before I knew it I was running down the two flights of stairs to his place and knocking on his door. I didn't even have the excuse of being drunk. Gearing up for a big case in less than two weeks meant I couldn't afford to kill my productivity with hangovers.

So within seconds I was in front of Patrice's apartment door, knocking on it like I had a right to, with all of one mimosa in my system. I had no idea what I thought I was doing, but I felt so hurt.

I needed to hear from him why he'd strung me along like that.

When he finally opened the door, I saw a blend of surprise and weariness on his face. Not exactly what I was hoping for, but not exactly unexpected either. Besides I didn't come expecting a warm welcome, I'd come to give Dr. Denis a piece of my mind. Before he said anything he brought up his arm so he could look at the watch on his wrist. When he saw the time he raised an eyebrow in question. Like that was supposed to embarrass me.

"How can I help you, Easton?"

That aloofness cut deep, and for a moment I hesitated. I'd wanted to believe there was something between us, but when I saw him shut down like this, I faltered. His cool eyes made me wonder made me feel so pathetic. I breathed through the heat I knew would probably creep up on my face if I didn't calm down.

"Just wanted to say I hoped you had a nice date." I was practically spitting out the words, but the look of confusion on his face mollified me a bit. Once I was done, I didn't even give him a chance to respond and before I humiliated myself more, I started turning away.

But like it always had the power to do, Patrice's deep voice brought me to a dead stop. "That wasn't a date, Easton. That was *Ari*. He and Yin stayed over last night." He sighed wearily and I stood there, with my back to him waiting to hear more. "Ari got stopped by the police yesterday afternoon driving back from Yin's place."

I spun around to look at him. Worry for Ari stamping out my pity party. "Is he okay? Did they do anything to him?" My mouth felt wooden when I talked, dreading all the possible terrible answers to that question.

Patrice's face was thunderous, but he shook his head before he spoke. "They were rude and stopped him for going eight miles over the speed limit, but they let him go." The "fucking ridiculous" in his tone did not go unnoticed, and I couldn't disagree.

"He was a little freaked out and I invited him and Yin over to hang out and watch a movie. His home situation is not the best right now and I wanted him to have a place to calm down and talk about it before going back there."

His perfectly reasonable answer made me feel even worse, instead of relieved. He was helping out a friend and I made the whole thing about me. I nodded and was about to apologize for my incredibly inappropriate behavior when his voice pulled me out of my brooding.

"No. Don't do that," he said as he gently tugged on my arm and pulled me inside.

"Do what?" I sounded surly and unhappy, but still let him guide me into his place. He was probably trying to not give our neighbors a front-row seat to whatever it was that we were doing.

"I didn't cancel with you because you weren't important." He closed the door and leaned against it, his arms crossed tightly against his chest. He was wearing his Cornell sweatshirt and loose jeans that looked soft and worn. His locs were hanging halfway down his torso.

His hair always smelled like peppermint and coconut, and more than anything I wanted to get closer, press my nose against his neck.

Instead I stood there, my own arms a mirror image of his.

I'd made a career and a reputation out of being a guy who could own a courtroom, no matter how stressful the situation. Not today. I was sweating, nervous that Patrice would see right through me.

"You could've told me you had an emergency. I'm not that fucking self-centered, Patrice."

He pursed his lips at my words, like he'd bitten into something sour.

"Stop saying shit like that about yourself, Easton," he said, softer than the words warranted.

His face relaxed and he pushed off the door. My entire body thrummed with the need to take the three steps to where he was. Still I didn't move. I didn't want to do anything that would get me on the other side of the door.

Patrice was the only person in my life who constantly made me feel like I was looking in from the outside.

I'd always been an insider; very few doors had ever been closed for me. If there was an insiders club, a VIP section, I always had full access. Not with him. What I got, he allowed; there was not trampling in and assuming I would be welcome.

"I cancelled because i wanted to see you too much." He shook his head and laughed, but there wasn't very much humor in it. "I felt guilty that I'd been hurrying home to see you and—"

Waiting for him to cross those few feet between us felt like I was watching him cross an ocean. Once he was there, so close I could lift my hand and tug on his locs, bring him down for a kiss, I still didn't move.

I wanted him to tell me why.

Why he'd left me hanging after what we'd shared last night.

"Why, Patrice?" I could see the muscle in his jaw twitch, a gesture of frustration, but I knew there was also uncertainty there. I'd seen him do that before, when he was figuring out how to proceed.

Without another word he closed those last few inches between us and grabbed my face.

His hands felt hot, and I almost flinched from the shock of it. It seemed like I hadn't felt them on my skin for ages. As his fingers grazed my cheek, I recalled how rough his hands were. Calloused. So unexpected for a man who worked with his mind.

I knew it was from many summers working on construction sites for a family friend, but it still made something tight unfurl in my chest to feel those hands on me again.

My professor, a man who earned his livelihood from his intellect, had hardened hands. I shivered as his lips touched mine, that mouth which had ruined me for any other, so close to giving me what I'd been dreaming of for months.

I don't know how I managed it, but I stepped back, because I wasn't playing this game anymore. He was going to have to tell me.

"Why?"

He sighed and closed his eyes like it was really costing him to have to say it. "Because I fucking *want* you. Because when I'm with you, you're the only thing that matters and I never lose my focus, Easton." He exhaled again, and it was a helpless, astonished sound. "You make me reckless."

Those words, that confirmation that I wasn't the only one who was far gone and in too deep. It was like a dam broke and I wanted, no, I *needed* to kiss him.

Our lips touched and it was…absolutely everything. Patrice blindly walked us back until we hit the couch, as I scrambled to get my hands on more of him. Without even coming up for air, I started pulling at his jeans, tugging them down. We were both barefoot and pretty soon, we were down to our briefs and panting. Breaths short as if I'd run for miles. Our tongues tangled as our hands grabbed and scratched with barely refrained desperation.

I let go of him for a moment and leaned back, needing some distance. I wanted to tell him that I was pissed that he'd deprived us both of this. Of all the time we'd lost in this stupid game.

But when I looked at him, he was shaking. His face was tight with the need to get closer, and it finally dawned on me.

Staying away had cost Patrice too.

"You know what I thought the first time I saw you like this?" I asked, my hands under his sweatshirt right above the raised skin on the tattoo on his chest. He was always so hot, like he had a fire roaring inside him.

He shook his head, jaw tight.

"I thought, 'I've never really wanted before.' Because the way I want you, it's more powerful than pretty much anything else." I leaned closer, and this time he didn't try to move, just let me run hands over him. All that dark brown skin, sinew and muscle.

Patrice's body was like carved ebony. Every inch of him was perfect. I took care of myself, worked out. But Patrice was pure beauty.

I ran my palm lazily down his chest, the sparse wiry hair tickling my hands. I stopped just above his cock and looked up at him.

I turned my hand and possessively ran it over his erection. I gripped him hard like I knew he liked, still looking at him. My mouth watered as I felt him pulse against my palm.

"I dream about touching you like this."

He shuddered out a breath, still not saying a word, and pulled me in for another kiss, his tongue licked at the seam of my lips, and I opened for him again. I lifted my hands and put them on either side of his face. Wanting to stay like this, locked with him. He sucked on my tongue hard and I whimpered, his hands making their way down my back until he was at my hips. My awareness of him suddenly overwhelming. I froze for a second and he pulled back, looking at me with that barely restrained intensity.

"Easton. I don't know if we can do more than this." He didn't say anything else, but I understood what he meant. He wasn't sure he could give me more than this one time, and it hurt to hear it, but there was no stopping this.

"I know." I nodded and grabbed his hand, pulling him toward the coiled metal staircase that led to his bed. I hadn't seen it after he'd moved in, and as I led him up I didn't look behind me, scared that he might change his mind.

I would have to think about this more closely some time. Patrice was right, we couldn't keep doing this. I would end up resenting him for how little he could give, and he would grow tired of keeping me at a distance. But did that knowledge stop me? No.

When we got to his bedroom he pulled me toward him, looked at me for what felt like minutes, and then very gently pressed our mouths together. It felt so intimate, as if he wanted to mark this moment.

As he kissed me, I skinned out of my briefs, my hands trembling from anticipation. This had been a long time coming. So long I'd almost given up hope that it would happen again. After I was naked I pulled back, breaking the contact just to get my bearings. I closed my eyes and swayed, standing there for just a breath, until I felt strong hands pull me in.

"Come here." I didn't think I was imagining the shakiness in his voice.

We tumbled onto the bed and I let myself sink into the mattress with his body covering mine. This feeling. The way he covered me completely, how his hard body felt on mine. I'd missed it so much.

I opened my mouth to say something, anything, but all I could do was breathe out his name. He shook his head as he lowered himself over me. He went in for kisses and nips of my neck, my lips. His tongue lashing at my skin, making me shiver.

"Patrice. Please."

"Now that we're here, I'm not sure how I held out this long," he said almost grudgingly as he made his way down my body. Within a moment he was busy worrying my nipple between his teeth, making my entire body feel like it was on fire. I was torn between asking for more and not wanting to break the spell with words. Even lost in the moment, in the way Patrice made me feel, I knew it could be taken away.

I grabbed his head as he brushed his lips against my cock and made him look at me.

He looked hungry, like he could devour me. He hiked

an eyebrow as if to ask why I was interrupting, his loose locs tickling my skin as he moved.

"What?" His voice was rough, guttural almost.

I placed my hand at the nape of his neck, thinking of what to say. "Just wanted to look at you I guess."

Our eyes locked and held for a couple of breaths, like we were both letting the moment sink in before really going for this. After a second he brought a hand up again then took my cock in his mouth without hesitation. That was another thing about Patrice, no matter how much he wavered, once we were together, he was all mine. Every ounce of his focus solely concentrated on me. It was addictive.

As he bottomed out on my dick, I fisted the sheets, breathing through my mouth, flooded with the things that Patrice's tight hot mouth on my cock was doing to me.

"Ahhh, Patrice." I wanted him inside, now, now, now. "Please, I'm gonna come, and I want…"

He lifted his head and started moving before I could even finish. He sat up on the bed and pushed my legs apart and then ran his big hand over the inside of my thigh, spreading me open. I held my breath, trying to hold myself together, to not fly apart, from everything happening in my body and in my head.

He bent down, flicking his tongue along my neck, and moving up until our mouths met for more messy, fevered kisses. Like nothing could be held back anymore.

He breathed against my ear, his hands still playing with my ass.

"You didn't finish what you were saying, counselor. You want?"

I leaned my head back, trying to get some air. "I want your cock."

He pulled back to a kneeling position and grabbed his dick. It was uncut and that pink head glistened. I lifted on an elbow, my mouth watering to taste him, but he shook his head.

"Stay right there, because I'm about to come just from the faces you keep making at my dick."

He tipped his head toward the bedside table as I laughed at how annoyed he looked at my "making faces."

"Grab the condoms and lube in there."

I reached over and pulled them out as he alternated between stroking his cock and playing with my balls and hole. By the time I handed them to him I was panting again.

He rolled that Magnum on in record time and it was all I could do to not whimper, remembering what it was like to have him inside me. The way he'd grind his hips, relentlessly, until he was all the way in.

"You already rolling your eyes?" he asked, not even trying to mask the smugness in his voice as he bent over me to grab a pillow and kiss me in the process. He stuffed it under my hips and pushed our groins together.

"You're so full of yourself."

"No, that'll be you in like a minute." I balked at that and the bastard just laughed. "Hold your leg up, baby." He grunted and I instantly obliged, his sure hands already busy opening me up. His locs brushed my thighs as he bent his head, focused on getting me ready, while my heart raced, waiting for what was coming next.

Patrice was the very embodiment of control and restraint, but whenever we were together like this there was always a moment when something snapped and he turned into the dirtiest fucker in the entire world. And it revved me up like nothing else.

"What's got you so serious?" I could hear the mischief in his voice, and I braced for it. His tone placid, as if he wasn't two lubed fingers inside. "You thinking about the dicking you're about to get? Hmmm?"

I gasped, my back arching off the mattress when he brushed right against my prostate. "As far as I can tell the dick in question is still MIA."

I knew I was playing with fire, but I was here to get burned to the ground.

He lifted an eyebrow and grabbed his cock, getting it right up against my entrance. "Oh. You want me to give you a better view." He pushed in just a bit and I started shaking, desperate for it.

"No." The word was one long moan. "I want to feel it. I want you to *fuck* me, Patrice."

I brought my legs back, opening myself up to him.

He sucked in a breath and glided a shaky hand over my thighs. "Fuck. I've dreamed of this. This. How tight you are, how fucking good you feel."

"Do it," I said, thrusting to meet him as he worked himself inside.

He did.

Worked that cock in until I was so full I could only take short, sharp breaths. Once he was all the way in, he leaned over me and started moving.

"Easton." He was panting in my ear as he moved, his hips circling in and out in a way that made me feel every inch of him.

"God, why is your dick so fucking amazing?"

He laughed and panted out, "You feel pretty damn

good too, come on, make it tighter, baby." I clenched around him and he rolled his eyes. "Awww, that's so good. I swear, I could spend days fucking you."

I knew this was just the moment, the pleasure, but I wanted to say things. Instead I clenched my teeth and let myself sink into how good he felt.

After a moment his thrusts redoubled and I felt that flooding in my groin when I was about to come.

I unhooked one of my arms from around his neck and starting stroking my cock. After just a few I felt myself going over. "I'm coming," I muttered through gritted teeth.

Patrice nodded, slamming into me. "Good. Come on, cheri mwen, let me feel you." His breaths were getting shorter and shorter, sweat dripping off his skin.

I gasped as my vision whited out, and in the distance I could hear Patrice moan as shudders coursed through him.

After a moment he let himself fall on top of me, slick with sweat.

His voice was muffled, but I heard him clearly when he said—with just enough remorse to make me cringe—*shit*.

If I'd had any sense of self-preservation at all when it came to Patrice Denis I would've gotten up then and walked out, but instead I lay there with my eyes closed, letting the exhaustion of the sleepless night and the afterglows of the mind-blowing sex take over.

Chapter Nine

Easton

I woke up, unsure of how long I'd been asleep, and found Patrice sitting in bed reading from what looked like a pile of papers. I shifted onto my side, and he turned to look at me. He was wearing those reading glasses I'd seen on him a couple of times, bare chested and so handsome it took enormous restraint to keep from sighing. The rain must've stopped while I was asleep, since a couple of slivers of sunshine were peeking in through his window curtains. He put down the papers and placed them at the top of the pile sitting on his bedside table and ran a hand down my naked flank.

For a moment I lay there, blissfully imagining that he was mine and I was his. That he hadn't told me we were over before we really started. We stayed like that for a few minutes, me pretending to be asleep and him quietly stroking my back.

I was almost drifting back to sleep when my phone, which he apparently got out of my short pockets and placed on the little table next to the bed, started buzzing. When I opened my eyes, I found his trained on me, and then he smiled. That smile I rarely saw which was pure and unguarded. I was about to say something, but reached for my phone instead.

It was a message from my dad.

If you have time to spare from the temper tantrum you call a career, your grandfather would like to see you at his birthday brunch today. You're already an hour late.

It was like someone had dumped a bucket of cold water on me. My father never failed to let me know that to him I was nothing but a selfish self-satisfied brat. Most days I blew him off and ignored him. But something about being back here again a year later, still feeling unsure and somewhat pathetic for throwing myself at Patrice, made the whole thing sting. Without responding, I sighed and put the phone down, trying to figure out what to do about Patrice. I wasn't sure what I was supposed to do now.

Did he want me to get dressed and leave?

Since I'd barged into his house in a fit of rage, fucked him and then took a nap in his bed without asking, I'd probably worn out my welcome.

I turned around, trying to get myself out of the bed, and spoke while I still had my back turned to him, not wanting to see the relief in his face when I told him I was leaving.

"I'm going to head out now. Sorry I fell asleep." I tried to laugh but gave up. This could just be awkward and weird. I didn't fucking care. But as I was about to stand, Patrice touched my shoulder.

"Why don't you try to go back to sleep? You looked so tired."

Pity. My favorite thing to hear from a lover after sex.

I shook my head, still not looking at him. "I'm fine. I'll let you get back to your Sunday." This time I did turn around, wanting him to see that I wouldn't cross that line in the future. He was my tenant for fuck's sake, I shouldn't have done this. "It won't happen again."

"Don't go, Easton." There was just a hint of urgency in his voice. Knowing that Patrice was just as fucked up about whatever we were doing as I was only made me more tired.

I sighed as I looked around for my clothes and then remembered I'd left them downstairs.

"What am I going to stay for, Patrice? So you can fuck me again and then let me know immediately after you regret doing it? No thanks."

To his credit he looked contrite. I wasn't even sure why I was blowing up at him. It's not like he'd asked me here. I'd showed up at his door after making all kinds of assumptions. I deflated, remembering who it was that I'd seen him with. Patrice was right about us. There was too much stacked against us.

"I'm going to go, Patrice. I'm sorry about Ari. If there's any way I can help let me know. I have a good friend from law school that does immigration law in Rochester. I can get in touch with him. He does a lot of pro bono work." Patrice looked surprised and I thought he was going to say something, but he just nodded.

"All right. I'll walk you down."

I started for the stairs before I humiliated myself any further. "Don't worry about it. I have to run anyway. I'm supposed to be at a family event and I am ridiculously late, I should've been headed there instead of barging into your house, coming on to you—"

Patrice made an exasperated sound as he moved to

follow me downstairs. "You didn't come on to me. I was right there with you and wanting the same things you wanted."

When I looked around his living room trying to find my shoes I recalled that I'd come to his house in nothing but gym shorts and a T-shirt. Embarrassed by just how fucking ridiculous I'd been, I finished getting dressed as fast as I could and was heading to the door within seconds. Patrice stood in his living room watching.

"Easton, don't leave angry. Things don't have to be like this between us. I want us to be friends. I—"

He fidgeted as I stared at him, for once forcing myself not to make the moment easier for Patrice, not to let him off the hook. It was what I'd been doing from the first moment we met. Diffusing and putting him at ease so he wouldn't run off on me. I was done with that.

"Have a good day, Patrice."

I walked out of his place, determined to stay away. I wanted him, and judging by the sex we'd had and what he'd made me feel, I probably would always want him. But there was nothing I could do to keep Patrice from running, because no matter what it was, he'd always find a reason to.

I'd grabbed the phone out of my pocket to send a quick message to my dad when I saw a new text from Ron.

There was another one. We need to figure something out.

I felt a shiver run through my body. I wondered if he was referring to Ari or if someone else had been stopped. I quickly tapped a message telling him I'd call him in a few minutes.

I texted my dad as I walked into my apartment.

I'll be there.

I had obligations, I had work to do.

My needs would have to take a back seat for once.

Patrice

I could've handled that better.

I was still standing by the door a long time after Easton left. Hating myself for once again making him feel like shit for something I wanted just as much as he did.

There was no question about that. Half of the time I felt like I had no idea what I was doing whenever Easton was involved. Except that was a lie. I knew I wanted him, that whenever I was with him I felt free and at ease. That he always left me wanting more. I just didn't want to admit it to myself for much longer than it took to make us both come, and in the process, I kept hurting Easton.

I was about to go back to grading papers, which was what I'd been trying to do all morning, when a knock on my door shifted my attention off my fuckboy nonsense. I glanced at the clock on the mantel and realized it was past noon already. It had to be Ari. He'd gone to take Yin home, and he told me he'd be back so we could talk since we never got the chance yesterday.

As I moved to the door I felt glad that I'd at least showered while Easton napped and wasn't going to meet with my mentee after the weekend he'd had smelling like come.

I opened the door and found Ari looking better than he had last night. I went in to clap him on the back, feeling just a bit protective of him still. There was so much about how Ari carried himself that reminded me of myself. His stoic approach to things, his drive to "make things work" no matter what.

"Thanks for last night. Yin would've been up all night if I'd been at my uncle's."

It didn't escape me that even after years living there, Ari still didn't call his uncle's place *home*. One more red flag to add to the pile when it came to that situation.

I sat on one end of my couch and looked at Ari as he typed out a text before pocketing his phone. "I stopped by OuNYe to tell Nesto. I didn't want him to hear it from someone else." He grimaced and fidgeted with the laces of his Adidas and when he looked up, he seemed a little embarrassed. "He said that maybe you could help me figure out the immigration thing now. Things with my uncle are not going well, and I want to have a plan."

And of course I was right back to Easton. I leaned against the cushions we'd been pressed against before making our way upstairs and, like an idiot, wondered if they still smelled like him.

I coughed a few times, trying to buy myself a moment, because I'd apparently lost the ability to even *talk* about Easton. "So I know Easton has a friend that does immigration work." Now I felt like an ass for blabbing about Ari's situation, but when I looked at him he seemed to have perked up at the prospect of Easton getting involved.

"I trust Easton, he will find someone good." I took

a moment to let that sink in, to take in Ari's faith in people's goodness. His ability to give people a chance.

I nodded, holding in all the shit that was trying to spill out. "Okay, that's good, I know he'd like to help." I rubbed the back of my neck, feeling like I needed to be honest. "He was over here this morning and I was still feeling a little heated about what happened to you last night. I told him."

Ari dipped his head in acknowledgment, but did not seem bothered at all.

"You don't mind that I told him?"

He shrugged and then smiled. "I trust you and Easton." I wasn't sure he was intentionally pairing us together or if he was just talking, but it seemed like my new thing was to read too much into everything whenever Easton was involved.

It felt weird bringing Easton into this—his job was already featuring in more than one unhealthy way in our relationship—but he also had offered and he would know what he could and could not do. I could let him know Ari was interested and let him decide what was the next step. Not that I even knew if he was still talking to me after I'd fucked him and then acted like an asshole.

My face felt hot, remembering how mortified Easton looked walking out of my house, but if I had to grovel to get him to help Ari, I would. Although that was bullshit too. I could not say much for sure, but I knew Easton would not go back on an offer to help Ari because he and I had a falling out. Between the two of us, the only fickle one was me.

"I just don't want you to feel like I'm telling your stuff to people." I really meant that too.

Ari's shrugged lightly but I could tell he was thinking hard on what I'd said. "Easton is a good guy, and if he wants to help me, I won't say no. After that time at the detention facility I learned that if there were people wanting to help me out, that I would never let my pride get in the way. I can't deal with all of this on my own." He lifted a hand in a gesture of that seemed to say, "What can you do?"

"If I could, I would've been out of my uncle's house a long time ago, but I can't. If Easton can help out, then I'm glad for it."

Ari's matter-of-fact tone made him sound much older than his twenty-one years. I thought that even though our stories were similar, in some fundamental ways we were very different. Ari had made his passage to the States alone and had faced trials I never had to. He took the help that was offered to him gladly, learned to trust even when he had very little reason to do so. Which brought me back to Easton and how I kept pushing him away.

Ari's soft laugh got my attention back to our conversation; he looked amused at whatever he saw on my face. "You look like I did all of last year when Yin was trying to convince me we should date and I kept telling myself it would never work. Are you and Easton having troubles?"

That brought me up short. "Easton and I aren't dating."

Another laugh and this one has a definite "bitch, please" ring to it.

"The way you look at each other certainly seems like you could be. Yin would be very unimpressed by you blowing a chance to date Easton."

I laughed at that, remembering Yin's very vocal opinions on Easton's hotness. I could barely believe that I was so messed up about Easton that I was coming to my own mentee for dating advice, and yet here I was poised to spill my guts again.

"It feels too complicated with Easton's job. I mean look at what happened with you yesterday, I can't be with someone who is so connected to the system that allows these things to go unchecked."

Ari ran a hand over his face as he considered what I'd said. After a long moment he looked at me and asked, "Is Easton okay with the stops?"

The intense "no" that bubbled up in my chest surprised me. "No. He's not okay with it."

Ari sighed and I could tell he was trying to figure out how to say what he was thinking. He was always cautious with his words. In part because he was still self-conscious about his English, but also because he wasn't a careless person. I wondered if he'd always been like this or if the things he'd been through had changed him.

"One of the best things about being with Yin—" I'd been so in my head that his voice startled me, and it took me a moment to digest what he'd said. "—is that he's taught me that I need to imagine a future that is just for me. My parents sacrificed so much to send me here, I still can't believe they were able to, honestly. All that time I had to sit in that detention center not knowing if I would be able to stay, or if I'd have to go back." He shook his head as if still hardly believing he'd managed to get out of there. "All I could think was 'I need to make all this worth it. If I ever get out of here I will work until I can bring them over, until I can show them I deserved their sacrifice.'"

I was trying to figure out what words to use to convince Ari that of course it had been worth it, when he continued this time, sounding too wise for his years. "Being with Yin, I realized, that aiming for my own happiness made it worth it. We need to have some dreams that are just for us." He laughed, with his hands up. "I know it is not easy what I am suggesting you do, but don't cheat yourself out of the happy future you're fighting for."

I felt utterly unprepared to really dig into most of what Ari had said, so I went with something to lighten the mood of the conversation. "I don't think you're getting much out of this mentoring deal. All you do is give me advice." Ari grinned knowingly at my attempt to change the subject.

When he finally spoke, he dropped another truth bomb right on top of the others he'd detonated in the last few minutes. "You were never on the hook for all of it, Patrice." He waved his hand in the empty space between us. "We're both supposed to be getting something out of this. You learn from me and I learn from you. Reciprocal, that's how all relationships should be. I like to hang out with you because you want me to do well and you take my dreams seriously, even if they may not make total sense to you. That's all I need." After that, he stretched and looked over at the kitchen.

"I'll go make us some tea, and I'll give you the details about my case so you can tell Easton." I just nodded woodenly at him while his words were wreaking havoc in my head.

I thought of my mom, and how I had always felt like a burden to her even though she never once made me feel that way. How my father's absolute disinterest puzzled and humiliated me. How I never felt like I quite gave as much to my friends as they did to me. Then thought of the joy I felt seeing Easton light up with my touch. The ways that the heat is his eyes when he told me how much he wanted me felt like it would burn me. I wondered what it would be like to let down my walls and just own that despite all the reasons why it was complicated to want Easton, I still did.

I'd never know until I did and there was no denying that I desperately wanted to try.

Chapter Ten

Easton

I drove up to my parent's house in Cayuga Heights and as soon as I got there I remembered why I hated coming to these parties. There was valet parking, of course. I sighed as I passed the long line of luxury cars parked along the street, because heaven forbid any of these people should walk the four-hundred yards from their cars to my parents' door.

I noticed the valet was our old housekeeper's grandson, Martin. I went in for a one-armed hug instead of handing him my keys. "Hey man, making some extra cash for college?"

The kid grinned at me and gave me a back slap as he passed me a ticket. "Yeah, it's coming up soon."

I smiled at his sunny face; he'd always been such a happy kid. "Dude, you're miles ahead of most high school kids. I didn't pull in a steady paycheck until it was absolutely necessary," I said jokingly.

Martin looked at me with a funny expression on his face, like he wasn't sure what I was talking about. "*Dude,* you never had to work. Believe me, if I didn't have to do this, I'd be home playing video games. Besides, you more than make up for it now. Grandma's always talking about how proud she is of you, how her 'baby boy' is out there fighting the good fight." I'd always loved Alfreda, she'd been good to us. She'd see my mom, sister and me smarting from whatever scathing comments my father had directed at us, and feed us, or give us an excuse to smile.

"Thanks for saying that. Is Alfie in there? I'll go say hi." He nodded distractedly and pointed to the house, already busy taking keys from another customer.

I braced myself as I walked into my parents' place. It was my grandfather's eighty-fifth birthday and he'd asked for something with close family. My mother interpreted his request as a themed party with a hundred guests and high-end catering.

I made my way through the crowd, dreading the inevitable clash with my father. I was so not up for the usual passive-aggressive jabs he used as a way to communicate with his children. I think my mother sided with him just from sheer exhaustion.

I spotted my grandpa hiding in a corner with my sister and smiled as I walked over to them. These days my grandfather had no filter and a hilarious low tolerance for what he called "blue-blood bullshit." My sister, Emma, I actually enjoyed spending time with. She worked for the family as the winery's marketing director, but she did not take any crap from my dad. She was brilliant at marketing and had done amazing things for the business since she'd taken over. He needed her, and they both knew it.

I bent down to give my grandfather a hug as soon as I got to them. "Hey, old man. You're looking fancy." He was dressed in a burgundy cashmere sweater and slacks. His feet ensconced in the handmade house shoes I'd gotten him for Christmas.

He held on to me for a few seconds longer than usual and let me go with a sigh. "How are you, son? How's the business of putting bad guys away going?" I smiled, touched by the pride in his voice. When I told my family I'd be joining the district attorney's office after I finished law school my parents weren't exactly thrilled. My grandpa, on the other hand, thought it was fantastic, and he'd been supportive ever since.

"It's all right. Some troubles with the sheriff's department." My sister, who had been talking to someone else, turned back to us as I said that.

"Hey bro, I was going to text you about that," she said, leaning in to give me a kiss on the cheek. "What's going on? Looks like every story I see involves a black or Latinx student." Her expression looked a lot like I felt, tight and unimpressed. "Not a good look. It's frankly super disturbing, and not a trend I want to see picked up here."

I shook my head as I pulled back from kissing her. "Believe me, I am not thrilled about any of it, and I'm still not sure how I'm going to deal with it." I thought about the meeting with Day in the morning and whether that would bear any results. I doubted it. In some ways I felt like I was infringing, that I shouldn't interfere, but I also couldn't just let these stops continue to happen without saying anything. I remembered Patrice's face when he'd told me about Ari, and felt sick to my stomach.

"You don't look so great, is this getting to you?" She gave me a concerned look and my grandfather looked up from whatever game he was playing on his iPad.

I lifted a shoulder as I made a move to grab a mimosa from a tray one of the servers was passing around. "Of course I'm worried about it. I'm also frustrated because Cindy wants to be extra cautious about not stepping on toes, and I want to go in guns blazing and tell the sheriff to tell his people to cut it out."

Emma's brows furrowed and she moved in to squeeze my shoulder. "You know I love Cindy, and the joy it gives me to have an out and proud District Attorney who is the boss of my brilliant and out and proud big brother—"

I knew a "but" was coming.

"*But*, Cindy fought long and hard for that office, I mean she was in the trenches for years." She frowned, and I could tell sharing this was not easy for her. "I don't know if she's going to take up arms for this too. And someone has to, East. No matter how many good people we have in this town, and we have plenty, problematic things will continue to happen until they are dealt with head-on. That's why you need to think about running for DA. You're ready and this town needs some shaking up."

I looked at her for a moment, really looked at her, and felt so much pride in my litter sister, always the truth teller. And because my brain could not help itself, the thought just appeared, *she'd get along great with the other truth-teller in my life.*

I ruthlessly stamped that foolishness out of my head and wondered how to respond to the advice my sister was giving me. Even when at the same time I felt totally unprepared to take it. The more time that passed without any real action from anyone in town, the more it seemed like it might come down to me. I also had the sinking feeling that my best would not come close to enough.

People like Patrice and Ari were looking to me to find the answers and all I had were bad questions.

Still, Emma was right. "I'm going to see Day tomorrow, and I won't leave until he gives me a better answer than 'I'll deal with it.' Because clearly he hasn't. As far as running for DA, I'm considering it. I know you think I'm ready, but I'm still wondering about the politics side of it." Cindy's waffling in this situation had been disappointing in ways I hadn't wanted to explore too closely, and I was not going to willingly go into a job where I had to choose "saving face" to acting on something.

Emma came in for a hug as she snagged the glass of champagne from my hand and took a sip. "I'm not going to get pushy, but I know you can handle this. Now let's talk about your hot professor moving into the building." Emma had a little house in town, but that did not keep her from being in my business.

But she and I were not new at this and I could hold her off for days. "You look great, sis, that green suits you." Her expression at my comment said, "I know what you're doing," but she still looked down at herself, feigning like she didn't even realize what she was wearing.

Emma was petite like my mom, but after years of struggling with never living up to my father's exacting standards, she'd finally arrived at a place where she loved herself exactly like she was. She ran a hand over the front of her dress and smiled. "Thanks, bro, grandpa helped me pick it out."

I cracked up at that image, as Emma and my grandfather looked very pleased with themselves. "You let her convince you to go shopping?"

This time it was grandpa who was a loss for words, then shook his head and pointed at the iPad I'd gotten him for Father's Day. "We did it all on the tablet. She got me this sweater too."

My chest warmed looking at them, preening for compliments. "You both look great," I said with a smile, as the thought from earlier flooded my mind again.

Would I ever get a chance to introduce Patrice to Emma and Grandpa? Probably not. Not by how things went this morning.

"Boy trouble?" my grandpa asked, completely serious.

Emma and I both laughed at his question. But he didn't look like he was letting it go. My grandfather, unlike my father, hadn't batted an eye when I came out in high school. He'd also proved to be a surprisingly good relationship advisor on the rare occasion when it had come to that.

I played with some kind of salmon mousse and toast canapé I'd snagged from a tray, as I came up with an answer. "I wouldn't say *trouble*, more like self-imposed angst. I've been trying too hard with someone who doesn't seem to be very interested in me."

Despite the pile of evidence I had to support my statement, the words sounded like lies. I thought about this morning and the intensity with which Patrice had touched me. His eyes and hands so focused on my body. It hadn't felt like disinterest. It felt like *need*.

I turned to Emma, who was examining my face as if figuring out a math problem. "What's with the face?" I asked.

"I just haven't seen you this wistful in a long time. Now I really do need to meet him." Emma and I were only two years apart, so we had a lot of the same friends and knew *a lot*, too much really, of each other's dating history.

I lifted a shoulder and was about to say something to redirect the conversation when I saw my mother headed for us. She was looking picture-perfect in a navy knit dress and Gucci boots, her hair and make-up immaculate. We exchanged air kisses and she did the compulsory rundown of what I was wearing, in case I had missed the mark on the dress code indicated in her invitation. She seemed to approve of my semi-formal ensemble.

"Easton, darling. Your dad didn't say if you confirmed. I was so busy this morning with last-minute fires to put out I didn't have time to check. And yesterday we barely had any chance to talk." I'd ended up bailing on her after only thirty minutes at the Fall Wine Festival. I'd felt bad, but left after some work stuff came up. My mother didn't have the same degree of loathing for my job my father did, but she wasn't throwing the DA's office any fundraisers either. The only time she'd come to my office, the seventies wall paper and bad carpeting had her practically in tears.

"Sorry I left you hanging, Mom." She gave me a tight smile, then looked down at my grandpa with a fond one. "I made do. I only stayed for a few more minutes and came home and watched a movie with Grandpa. Your dad is always so busy at those things, it's best to let him work without interfering."

I swallowed hard on the words that wanted to come out of my mouth about my dad making it his life mission to ignore all of us whenever possible. I was about to comment on her outfit to just find something to say when my father walked up.

"Glad you could join us, Easton. I can't imagine they make you work on Sundays at that place." You'd think I was working for the mob, the way my father talked about my job.

"No, they don't." I kept my answers short with my father. With him anything you said, *could* be (and usually was) used against you.

I'd also been with the DA's office for years, so nothing about my job or my schedule was news. That didn't stop him from acting like it was some random thing that I'd started doing overnight just to piss them off. It always caught me by surprise that my father's unrelenting disapproval of everything I did still managed to hurt. I should be used to it by now, since my entire life he'd acted like everything about me from my sexuality to my job were somehow personal affronts.

My mother's face had that tight expression she usually sported whenever my father was being particularly assholic, but I knew she wouldn't challenge him. That would just give him a reason to say something shitty to her too. My grandfather, on the other hand, had no such qualms.

"Leave him alone, Junior. He works too hard to have to put up with your bullshit whenever he's here." The way he said "Junior" made my dad squirm, and it almost made putting up with his shit worth it.

The gasp from my mom at my grandfather's language was almost comical. "Father! Language."

My dad just huffed and turned to talk to someone else. It seemed he was done being an ass, at least for now.

Grandpa just rolled his eyes and turned to me again

while Emma distracted my mother with some questions about the catering.

"What's going on, son? You don't seem like yourself," he asked me, concern clear in his eyes.

I hesitated, trying to find the words. I wasn't so sure even I knew what was happening with me. Other than I was beginning to realize some of the things that Patrice had been saying. What Emma had been trying to tell me. That to be a good guy, it wasn't enough to not be bad. I couldn't take shortcuts with that if I wanted a real shot at being with Patrice.

I remembered my grandfather was waiting for an answer and I sat in a chair next to his wheeled one so we could be eye to eye, taking the hand he gave me. His skin felt papery and delicate these days, a little more frail each time, but those eyes told me he was well aware there was something I needed to get off my chest.

"I'm just asking more questions, I guess. Not taking things as a given, making myself see what I don't want to see." I tried to pull the words out, because that was sort of the rub of it all, not voicing the things that bothered me. "It's new for me to feel like I'm inconvenient."

Grandpa made a sound of understanding and gripped my hand tighter. "You really are tangled up. You're usually on the other side of this conundrum and you certainly don't pine."

My grandfather, as always, saw too much, and soon I had Emma as an audience too. What he said was true: I was so past my usual playbook when it came to Patrice I had no clue where I was. If I had any sense, I'd just give up on things.

Except I hadn't imagined how his hands trembled on my face as he kissed me.

"I'm not sure if this is the right person for me. Being with me is complicated for him. I think it feels like he's compromising his ideals."

"Are these ideals worth sacrificing yourself for?"

"Yes." I thought about Tyren, Ari, Ron and the fact that, to me, what was happening in town was a concern, even an inconvenience, but to them it was a real threat. No, Patrice's inner struggle about us was not completely unwarranted. Still, I looked at my grandfather, hoping he had some magical solution to my problem.

"Then don't make him." The tightening in my gut at the finality in his words confirmed I'd been lying to myself all morning. I had not given up on having something with Patrice.

My grandpa's strong grip snatched me back to his attention. "It's not about giving up, son, it's about you letting him know that his ideals are valuable to you too." He held up a hand as I was about to refute his solution. "I know that you've probably said so to him, but you can't just say it, you need to figure out a way to actually let him see it. Meet him halfway, just make sure he and you both know that keeping *you* is worthwhile too."

Emma chimed in, of course. "I wish you could see what we see, East. You're not just good at your job, you're an amazing guy and I'm sure Professor Hottie knows that too. He keeps coming back, doesn't he?" I smiled at her nickname for Patrice, but stayed quiet, figuring myself out.

The truth was, no matter how much I wanted to take what they were saying and run with it, things kept getting more complicated, and this morning hurt. If there really was any chance of us moving forward, I couldn't keep making the first move, or letting Patrice act like whatever happened was him not thinking. No, I agreed with Grandpa. I could meet Patrice halfway, but for any of this to work, he would have to step up too.

Chapter Eleven

Patrice

I walked up to Easton's apartment feeling all kinds of inadequate. He'd left my house this morning looking defeated and shamed. I'd done that with my shitty behavior, and I had to fix it, or I could at least try to make amends. I knocked on the door twice and then remembered there was a buzzer. But before I could press the button, the door opened.

I'd been prepared for pajamas or sweats, but Easton in denim cutoffs and an oversized University of Buffalo sweatshirt, wearing adorable woolly socks, had an intense effect on me.

I sucked in a breath as I held up the bag of Vietnamese takeout I'd picked up from a place Nesto kept raving about. There was a bite in the air, and I thought some pho might be a decent peace offering.

"I brought you dinner." I shuffled my feet some, and felt awkward as hell as I made myself say the rest of what I'd come here to do. "And an apology."

For a second Easton hesitated, his eyebrows furrowed like this turn of events had completely thrown him off. He turned his head to the side and looked behind himself, as if the food had to be for an imaginary roommate, then he stepped out into the hallway.

I was not being invited in. Okay, I deserved that.

I backed up to give him space and his eyes were giving me no quarter. "You don't owe me anything." The finality in his tone was not easy to hear.

I hoped he could see how fucked up I felt about how things had ended with us this morning. I hoped he knew what to do about this, about us, because I was lost.

I was about to try and tell him that when he sighed and closed his eyes. When he opened them again, he looked tired. "I'm really tired, Patrice."

I didn't know how the rest of his day had gone, but I sure as shit knew I had not made it any better. Groveling or apologizing for fuckboy behavior was not exactly in my wheelhouse either. I usually got out before shit got anywhere near complicated. But I was doing this, because if anything I wasn't going to let Easton think that he deserved to be treated like he didn't matter.

"I'm not sure why I thought showing up at your house with two tubs full of soup was a great idea, but I figured I at least owed you some dinner," I said in a friendly tone that didn't get me more of a reaction. If his intention was to make me squirm, things were certainly going as planned.

His expression still gave me nothing, and the desperation I felt made me think of something Nesto told me. I had to stop pretending, because right now, all I could think of was that I would do *anything* to make him smile again. To have him talk to me like he wanted me here. The urge to plead for another chance was on the tip of my tongue, I didn't even know what I'd ask for. I just knew I wanted more time with him.

We stood there in silence. Easton's eyes on me, and his gaze completely serious. "Why are you really here, Patrice?"

I squirmed under his scrutiny, the way his entire body seemed to be asking the question.

Tonight I was getting the full treatment from Assistant District Attorney Easton Archer. He just stood there, his arms crossed over his chest, leaning against the wall by his door, patiently waiting for me to crumble under his stare.

He didn't have to make this easier for me. So far, he'd spent every minute we'd been together accommodating my hang-ups. Smiling through all the mixed signals I kept sending his way, unrelenting in his honesty about how he felt about me. He told me again and again that he wanted me. That the rest we could figure out as we went. Not tonight.

He was going to make me say it, and really I owed both of us that much. If I'd gotten anything from Ari's words today, it was that I needed to stop acting like what I felt for Easton was something that was just happening to me.

I opened my mouth to say some other asinine reason for why I was standing here, but before I started I closed my mouth. He deserved better than this, than me making shit up just to keep from admitting to why I was here. I was deliberate in every other part of my life. I had to stop acting like my heart didn't deserve the same intention.

"That's not true." I shook my head as he stared at me. "I mean, it's true I thought you might be hungry. I'm not here just because of that though. I wanted to see you. And apologize for acting like an asshole...again."

This finally got me a reaction in the form or a slightly raised eyebrow, but still his lips were sealed. But now I was committed, so I finally told the truth.

"I always want to see you. I always want *you*." Admitting it was like a dam broke inside me because suddenly I could not stop talking. "It sort of freaks me out how much." Easton parted his lips like he was about to say something, but I had to get all of this out. No matter what happened between the two of us, I needed to make sure that Easton heard this. "I'm tired of fighting myself about wanting you, Easton."

He gave an exasperated sigh as he peeled his back off the wall and moved toward me, one hand raised, palm up, as if to stop me from talking.

Resigned to the fact that I had fucked this up, feeling like there was a hole in my chest, I handed him the food.

"Have a good night, Easton."

I was about to turn around and walk down to my apartment when he grabbed my wrist with his other hand.

"Oh no, no, no." When I turned to look at him, those green eyes were blazing, but there was just a little bit of humor in his voice. "No, Professor Denis, you're not leaving now. I was going to say that it sounded like a conversation you'd rather have inside my place."

The relief at those words was enough to make me lightheaded, and when I looked at him, a much smaller but no less heartening version of the smile I'd been desperate to see was firmly in place.

"Come on." He ushered me in and I didn't give him a chance to change his mind, quickly stepping into his penthouse. I pointed at the glass of wine on the coffee table next to a mountain of papers.

"You were working."

He waved at the pile of papers dismissively. "I was supposed to be working, but I was sulking instead," he said matter-of-factly as he took the food to the kitchen.

I never again wanted to be the reason for Easton to feel unimportant. Because even if I wasn't ready to say that out loud, with every passing day he was becoming almost essential for me. If I'd been brave enough, I'd tell him exactly that. Instead I walked over to where he'd been pulling takeout containers out of the bag.

I came to where he was, just inches away. We were so close I felt his heat, I wanted to wrap my arms around him, envelop him with my body, but I knew there was more I needed to say. I whispered into the space between us. "I'm sorry," I said as I ran my thumb over his lips. They were perfect, red and fleshy.

Easton swallowed hard and I could almost see his pulse racing. There it was again, that pull. In so many ways I felt like with Easton and I, words sometimes were unnecessary. I bent my head and he lifted up to meet me. He clasped both hands behind my neck and kissed me like his life depended on it.

But after a few seconds he shook his head and pulled back just as I was making my way down his neck.

"No." He just had to say it once, and I stepped back, wondering what had happened.

When I saw him, with his bruised lips and mussed hair, I had to fist my hands to keep from grabbing him again.

His chest was heaving, but when he spoke his tone brooked no argument. "Nope. We are not doing this again."

He waved a finger between us. "*This* is our problem, as soon as we're together we end up fucking." He held up a hand, those whiskey and moss eyes thunderous. "We're going to act like whatever is happening here is worth working on. We clearly can't stay away from each other, so let's start acting like we mean it." The exasperation in his voice—there was something else there. Determination.

Easton was done letting me run the show, and seeing him calling the shots was fucking sexy. "We're talking about important things happening in our lives right now, and trying to understand each other. You say you want my friendship, then that means actually getting to know me. This hot and cold shit ends now."

He looked mad salty and I wanted to wreck him. This Easton was somehow even more irresistible.

I felt my body relaxing and the intensity of the evening, of the whole weekend started to diffuse a little. I smiled at him then. "All right, counselor, so you're feeling some type of way. I hear that," I said as I grabbed the big tubs of broth. "Why don't I warm up this food for us." I waved a hand around his kitchen. "I think I can figure out where to find stuff. You go relax and we can talk while we eat."

He looked genuinely bemused by my sudden surge of domesticity, but he didn't argue, just nodded and went back to the couch. I fussed around the kitchen for a few minutes while he put away his papers, and sipped from his wineglass.

When I walked out of the kitchen with two steaming bowls of soup, he got up to help me. "Here, I'll get spoons and chopsticks. I also have a bottle of Sriracha around here. Let's eat in the living room."

He came back with all the stuff we needed and a glass of wine for me. After a moment we both sat down, holding our bowls, alternating between bites and slurps. The soup was flavorful and fragrant, and delicious, and as soon as I tasted it, I remembered I hadn't eaten since my post-workout breakfast early this morning. We both ate in silence for a couple of minutes before Easton spoke.

"Thank you for this. All I've had all day were a few canapés, and until now had not realized I was starving."

I angled my head, confused. "I thought you were eating with your mentee."

He frowned at that and went in for another mouthful of noodles. He shook his head as he chewed. "I had to cancel. It was my grandpa's birthday today and my mother had a luncheon thing, so I went there this afternoon."

From the way he spoke about his parents I knew Easton wasn't exactly close to them, but he did seem to see a lot of his family. There always seemed to be an event he had to make an appearance at.

"How was the party?"

He lifted a shoulder with a resigned expression on his face. "My mother's parties are always flawless and a little boring." He gave me a lopsided smile, but it wasn't totally unhappy. "My dad's an ass and not really interested in any of us, but my mom tries to at least get the family together. It was good to see my grandpa and my sister too." I realized it was maybe the most he'd said about himself or his family that didn't include some self-deprecating comment and I wondered if part of all that was about me.

"You almost never talk about your family. Is it because you think that I'm not interested?"

He widened his eyes like he was thinking about it for the first time. "Honestly? My family in some ways feel parallel to my life. I'm in town working this job and that is sort of foreign to them, even to my grandpa, who's so supportive. It's almost like my real life is one thing and I dip into this other world I belong to too." He looked closely at me for a moment, a vulnerability there that I was loathe to betray, and as if he was reading my mind, said, "You are always firmly in the 'real' part of my life, Professor Denis."

Before I even had a chance to react, he flashed me another one of those smiles and totally changed the subject. "Did you talk to Ari today?" he asked, brows furrowed, obviously worried about the answer. I found that I wanted to tell him everything Ari and I had talked about, the things I'd been thinking about, but I needed more time to figure myself out.

"I did talk to Ari. He's doing okay, and there are actually a couple of things I want to ask you about, but we were talking about you." I ran my hand over his bare calf and he shivered from my touch. "Tell me about your dad. Did he give you a hard time?"

He gave me a doubtful look, then put his own bowl down. He brought his legs up onto the couch and hugged his knees as he looked at me. "I just don't know if I have a right to complain when my 'family issues' seem so minimal in the grand scheme of things." He placed his chin on his knees. The need to close the space between us and engulf him in my arms was powerful, but I held back, because I wanted to hear him, and he was right about things getting derailed whenever we were touching. "I mean, sure, my parents are not very warm, but my life has been very easy."

"It's not all black and white, Easton." I laughed at his astonished expression.

I probably was the last person he'd expect to hear this from. "The things that hurt you still hurt *you*. Just because you were born into wealth doesn't mean that you can't be hurt by your dad's shitty behavior." I shook my head, not wanting to launch into a rant.

"Privilege doesn't mean that you can't be sad, or that you don't have the right to complain about it. You also deserve people in your life who can see that pain and tell you that you didn't deserve to be hurt like that. The people in your life, me included, need to do better at showing you how dope you are." He busted up at that while I reached out for him, deciding enough was enough. If we were going to go into our feelings like this, then I wanted to be fucking holding him.

"I'm glad you approve of my person."

We maneuvered around until he was lying between my legs, his back pressed tight to my chest. "You know I do," I said with feigned annoyance as I ran my hands over his arms. I pressed my nose into his hair which always smelled like the beach for some reason. But I stopped before pressing a kiss to his ear, which with our track record would most likely fully derail the heart to heart.

Easton sighed as he laid his head back on my chest, sounding so exhausted I almost wanted to let it go. To just let him relax after what had been a stressful day for both of us, but I couldn't. I came here to make things right, and I was going to see that through.

"Baby, I—"

Easton's back straightened and he turned around to look at me, his eye twinkling. "I think I like where this conversation is going already."

I tightened my arms around him and pressed my mouth to his ears. "Stop, this is serious." I was not going to apologize for calling him baby either. I was here with him, and it felt good, and I would be a hypocrite to tell him he deserved to get what he needed, when I kept denying myself the same thing.

"I don't want to get too deep, because we've both had long ass weekends. But I really meant what I said before. We're all figuring out how to show up for the shit we believe in, and privilege doesn't mean you can't get hurt."

He ran a hand over my cheek, his skin brushing the stubble there. It felt so natural, so right to be with him like this.

When he spoke, he still sounded unsure. "I get what you're saying, but look at this shit going on in town. Compared to what happened to Ari yesterday, my problems just seem so trivial."

I sighed at that. "It's not a competition, Easton. At least it shouldn't be. My struggle shouldn't minimize or dismiss yours, no matter how different they are." I took a moment to take stock of what I was feeling and I really felt no contradictions, not turmoil, about telling him that. "I think that's at the heart of so much of what's made us all so disconnected from each other. This fear of naming people's pain, the energy and the destruction that has been sown just to keep up this farce that we've 'moved on.' How can we be over what we don't get to mourn? Isn't it better to just say, 'I can see your pain and you can see mine. Let's find ways to fix both.'"

That was heavy, but it felt good to be able to say it to Easton and to have him hold my words. After a few moments he spoke again, his voice soft and low.

"Thank you."

I didn't have to ask why, because I felt the same gratitude. To be here with him, with all the different things happening around us that would deny us this moment.

I turned my head so I could reach his cheek and pressed a kiss there. I let my lips linger, grazing his stubbly chin. He felt so good, always. "You're welcome. Maybe we can call this a truce?"

Easton sat up then and pulled away from me, and quickly turned around so we were face-to-face. The smile that was beginning to feel like one of my biggest accomplishments made an appearance again. "Maybe we can call it a start."

Easton's optimism, his faith in things working out sort of bowled me over. "All right."

He came in for a kiss, his tongue stealing into my mouth, igniting feelings in my body that I could not even really name.

When we broke apart, his face looked all business, but there was a spark in his eyes that hadn't been there before. "Okay," he said, suddenly serious. "Tell me what you wanted to discuss about Ari."

For a moment, I felt that pang, the one that chastised me for forgetting what was important. I tamped it down and remembered Ari's words. I would not write myself out of the future I was working for. "I wanted to ask you about your friend who does immigration law."

He nodded, immediately grabbing his phone from the table. "Of course, I'll reach out to him tonight."

I bit back a smile, because for all he could be so laid back, there was intensity to Easton when it came to his work that I really admired. "Thanks, but come here first," I said, my voice suddenly husky and low.

He lifted his eyes from what he was doing on his phone. I grabbed his hand to bring him in against my chest again, and as always, he came.

Chapter Twelve

Easton

"Are you going to take that?" I asked, barely able to contain the grin that had been pasted on my face for the past hour. Patrice and I had finished our enormous bowls of soup and instead of running home like I would have expected, he'd cleaned up and then gotten back on the couch with me.

I'd been too scared to ask if he was staying, but eventually he just grabbed the control and turned on the TV. We'd been dozing while an episode of a superhero show droned on when his phone rang.

I handed him the phone, which had Nesto's face flashing on the screen.

I tried to get up to give him space, but he just pulled me back to him. I had no idea what was happening, but when he put that big arm across my chest as he answered the call, I let myself melt into him. I was not going to stress and I was not going to question anything happening between us tonight.

"What's up, brother?" Patrice's soft voice brimmed with affection when he spoke to his friend.

"Where are you, man? I'm at your place." Nesto was

pretty loud, so it wasn't very hard to listen in on the conversation.

I looked at him for a moment and then stood up, signaling with my hands that he could go back to his place. But he didn't move, he just brought the phone down from his ear and tapped on the screen. Speaking as he did.

"Nes, I'm just putting you on speaker. I'm actually up at Easton's." He cleared his throat as I stood there wondering what happened with the skittish Patrice I knew.

He leaned over and pulled on my hand, while Nesto's amused voice filled the living room. "Oh? You visiting your neighbor then." There was a whole lot that was not being said in that answer, but Patrice wasn't giving him anything.

"That's right. I brought over some dinner, to pay Easton back for the one he made the other night."

"Right." The tone of Nesto's voice evoked a clear, "More like you went up there with a peace offering for being an asshole."

If there was one thing I knew, it was that Patrice and his friends told each other *everything*.

After a few seconds of Patrice glaring at his phone, I broke and spoke in its direction. "Nesto, you can come up if you want."

I mean we hadn't been fucking or anything, everyone was fully clothed and there had clearly been a meal happening. Nesto didn't need to know the details about the last hour of true confessions and cuddling by the fireplace.

Nesto's friendly laugh snapped Patrice into action. "I'm already here, my dude." The knock had us both standing up and walking to the door.

I waved my hand to indicate Patrice could let his friend in. As he walked I stayed behind to watch his ass in one of his seemingly endless supply of fitted sweats. By the time he got there and started opening the door I forced my eyes to move up to where Nesto was standing, a shit-eating grin on his face.

After giving each other a hard pat on the back, Nesto sauntered into my place, taking in the scene, which even I had to admit was pretty cozy.

He walked up to me and gave me one of his strong hugs. "What's up, man?"

I smiled at the way his eyes moved around the room. "Not much, we were just hanging out a bit. Patrice was nice enough to bring me dinner."

Nesto just winked and sat on the couch smiling. "Looks like you guys were enjoying a night in. Sorry to disturb." That last part he said while innocently blinking at Patrice, who ignored him. "Anyways, I don't have a lot of time. I have to go pick up my man at Carmen's." It was always amazing to me how Nesto used such a tone of complete adoration whenever he spoke about his partner. "He still eats dinner with them on Sundays when he's not at the restaurant. But I wanted your help with something, P."

Patrice seemed to relax when it was clear Nesto was not going to pry about why he was hanging out at my house on Sunday night, lounging by a fire. He walked over to his friend and sat next to him on the couch while I took a seat on the chair across from them.

"What do you need?"

The way he said that, it was so obvious that there was nothing his friend could ask that Patrice wouldn't try his best to make happen.

Nesto turned to me, his face serious again.

"Did P tell you about what happened yesterday" His grim expression told me he could only be talking about Ari's traffic stop.

I nodded, my face burning with shame that I had nothing better to offer than a nod and a shrug. "I know."

Nesto nodded once and turned his mouth to the side, clearly refraining from whatever he wanted to say.

"P, I want to do something at OuNYe. Sheridan and I have that fundraiser in a couple of weeks. We were going to give all the proceeds to the agency that helps immigrants and refugees. The one that got me connected with Ari and Yin when I first got here. We still are, but I want to do something more."

Nesto ran his hands over his head, he looked shaken, which was such a departure from the no-nonsense businessman I usually saw around town. He spoke to Patrice whose eyes widened at Nesto's serious expression. "You know I like to keep my head down with this kind of stuff. I'm not political like you and Milo. I stay in my hustle and I know I do my part by creating jobs and shit." He paused then and his generous lips pursed. He looked at us both before he spoke again. "The way that Ari looked this morning when he was telling me about that bullshit that went down last night. I can't look the other way, bruh."

Patrice gripped his friend's knee. From the look they shared, I knew these two men had seen each other through everything. "What'd you have in mind?" Patrice's tone clearly said, whatever it was, Nesto could count on him one hundred percent.

Nesto turned to look at me then and smiled. "I actually want your opinion too, Easton. You've been in this town your whole life and people trust you. I talked to Harold about it and he wants to do a match giving, or some shit. Whatever we raise that night, he's going to match it and give the same amount to that place that works with black and Latinx kids teaching them about their rights, the Ithaca Justice Project."

He lifted a shoulder then and looked back to Patrice. "I'm not worried about people getting pissed and losing business. I just need to do *something*."

Patrice dipped his head in agreement with Nesto's words.

"I think that's great, Nesto." I glanced up at Patrice and saw that he was completely focused on me, clearly waiting to hear what I was going to say. "As a matter of fact, I'll go in on that. Whatever you raise that night, I'll match the amount for each agency." I put my hands up, needing to make it clear I didn't want cookies for this. "I'll be an anonymous donor. I don't need to sidle into your event."

Nesto smiled wide then and sent Patrice a look that was very much in the vein of "I told you so."

"That's great, man. Thank you. We're going to start promoting the event more aggressively since it's in a couple of weeks."

He sighed and looked over to Patrice who was still focused on me. "What do you think, P?"

He didn't hesitate, nodding enthusiastically as he answered Nesto. "I think that's great, Nes, when local businesses do this type of thing it really gets communities more engaged. OuNYe's a new place, but it's already well-respected, and so are you for that matter. Harold Sheridan is a big fish here. People will pay attention to the fact that *you're* giving to the Justice Project. I'll make sure to go in hard on my Twitter account promoting it over the next two weeks."

He looked over to me and then he did something that had Nesto and me almost dropping our jaws. He walked over and bent down to kiss me. Not just a peck either, he braced himself on the arms of the chair and licked into my mouth.

My heart actually skipped and by the time he pulled back I was lightheaded. "Thanks for offering to help."

"Of course." I was breathless, and would've gone back for another kiss, but Nesto cleared his throat reminding us he was still there. Patrice and I both turned to find him grinning at us, like we'd just made his entire week.

"Okay, I'm going to go get Jude, since you two seem like you need some privacy," he teased and made a show of putting a hand over his eyes as he stood up.

"Thanks for the help, guys. I feel better about this now that I know you have my back."

I nodded as we got to the door. "Just let me know any other way I can help."

After Nesto left, I leaned against the door, looking at Patrice who was walking up to me with a predatory look in his eyes, seemingly unbothered by the events of the last few minutes.

He did that thing where he braced his arms on top of my head, so that I was ensconced by him. I looked up and my field of vision was all Patrice. When he spoke, it was low and so close to my ear, I felt his breath fluttering my hair. "That was really nice of you to do."

I swallowed, feeling way too many things, to be able to give a proper answer. "It's the least that I can do."

He nodded, his face serious, but his eyes were still

soft and completely focused on my mouth. "Still you didn't have to and you did."

"We'll see how things go with Sheriff Day tomorrow. That will have to do a lot with whether I actually can help put a stop to all this."

Patrice's face turned sober then, and for a moment I thought I'd lose him again. I could tell he was looking for the right words. I counted one, two, three breaths before he spoke.

"I know you'll try."

I exhaled and tipped my head up to look at him, a little bit scared of Patrice's vote of confidence. Something had shifted today, but Patrice's faith in me scared me, because I was still not sure what I did would change a thing. Still I told him the truth. "I will do my best."

I didn't say the words that were almost crawling out of my throat. *I don't want to let you down.*

He was still leaning in to me, and it was overwhelming in the best way possible. I pushed up to kiss him and he responded without hesitation, his tongue stealing into my mouth, hot and hungry. I let that take me my mind off the things I needed to do. The trial that was starting in two days, the meeting with the sheriff, the things I knew were on my shoulders to fix and I wasn't sure if I could.

After a moment Patrice pulled back and brought his hand to my mouth. He brushed my top lip as he looked at me, with an expression of complete befuddlement.

"I thought once I'd let myself go with you." He dropped his other arm to grip my hip hard on that last word. "That the crazy lust that seems to fill my head whenever you're around would die down some." He shook his head as if genuinely confused. "But it hasn't. I still can barely think from wanting you."

I almost laughed, because if he only knew.

"I can assure you that you're not the only one with that problem." I pushed off from the door and grabbed his hand as I moved back to the couch. "What are we going to do about this, professor?"

Patrice's face was serious as we got back on the couch, he sat back as I straddled his hips, my arms around his neck. He grabbed my ass and pressed me to him so that I could feel his hard cock against me. Like always with Patrice, everything else seemed to shrink to nothing if he was around.

I waited for his answer, as we rocked against each other, the need building with every movement, and still Patrice didn't speak.

Finally he pressed his face to my neck, and let out a long, weary breath. When he looked up his eyes looked scared, but determined.

"I want to be here, so I'm going to stay." He didn't say more, his body relaxing as he ran his hand over my back. I wanted to say so many things I knew I shouldn't. In the end I told him the one thing I was more certain of than anything else.

"I want you here, for as long as you do."

Patrice

I walked into the kitchen of Nesto's restaurant, completely certain the conversation was going to revolve around me and Easton. It's not like I hadn't gotten a warning; he'd texted me last night after he left the penthouse, telling me to be ready for questions. I was feeling so fucking good after last night that I might just answer them too. Easton filled places in me that I didn't even know were empty, and now that I'd let myself actually feel that I was loathe to let it go without a fight.

Before I left this morning we'd talked about his meeting with the sheriff's department. I didn't push him on what he would say; after all, Easton's job was his job. So I'd wished him good luck on the trial preparations and went on my way.

Now I was here, certain that Nesto would not be happy until I spilled my guts about what I'd been doing at Easton's last night. But I wanted check in about Ari and talk about the fundraiser a little more, so Nesto would have to deal. I tried to focus on where I was going and said hello to Nesto's staff as I passed. I noticed Yin was standing by a ton of boxes, checking something off from a clipboard.

"Yin."

He turned around and pushed up to give me a double kiss on the cheeks. I smiled as I obliged, thinking he must've picked that up from Ari. "How's our boy doing?"

"He's running some errands for Nesto, but he's doing better. Talking to you really helped."

Funny, because during that talk, the one that had dropped life-altering knowledge had definitely not been me.

Yin, looked more relaxed though, so it seemed we'd all been able to move past the scare and stress from Saturday. He lifted his pen to the doors that led to the dining area, without me having to ask. "The boss is out there."

I nodded in the direction he pointed and saw Nesto

sitting at a table working on his computer. As soon as he saw me, he stood to give me dap.

"What's good, P?" The mischievous smile on his face told me I was not getting away with not talking about Easton. "You looking fly, man. *Relaxed.*"

He snapped that last word. This motherfucker really thought he was hilarious.

"You're a lot less funny than you think you are," I said, somehow managing to keep a straight face as I pulled a chair to sit across from him. "If you must know. I *am* feeling pretty good considering how fucking stressful shit got this weekend."

Nesto's expression sobered as soon as I said that. He rubbed his hand over his face before he answered. "Tell me about it, man. I swear I'm this close from getting in my truck and moving Ari out that fucking house. His uncle is up his ass constantly."

I sighed, feeling tired already. "Easton got in touch with his friend who does immigration law and the guy got back to him last night. Ari told me I could give Easton the case details. The lawyer comes to Ithaca every week to work with a few clients and will set up a time to meet with Ari. So that's handled." I felt a surge of pride then that Easton had followed through.

Nesto nodded at that. "I knew it. If anyone can get that worked out, it'll be Easton. But seriously, tell me what was up with you guys last night." His tone clearly stating that he knew what we'd been up to.

I ran my hand over my mouth, not wanting to say too much. This shit with Easton was way too different and I didn't feel like sharing. Not in my usual, "There's nothing to say, because I don't care" type of way either. I felt a little freaked out. Like I was so new at this, so bad at being with someone like I'd been with Easton last night that somehow I'd ruin it.

"Yo, what's up with you?"

I snapped my head up to find Nesto staring at me with a concerned expression. Something about the way he was looking at me, made me voice my worries out loud.

"Nes, I'm afraid I'm gonna fuck it up. I'm too closed off and Easton is so pure." I closed my eyes, knowing I sounded ridiculous. "He doesn't hide anything. He looks at me and I can *see* how bad I could hurt him. I don't know if I'm built for this."

Nesto's hand slid across the table and he gripped my wrist hard. His face as serious as I'd ever seen it. "Get the fuck out of here with that bullshit, about you not knowing how to be a good man to the people that love you," he said through gritted teeth. "I swear to God, Patrice. I hear you on being afraid, all of this is scary as fuck." He laughed then and looked around the dining area of his restaurant, taking it in as I noticed he did sometimes.

"We're our ancestors' wildest dreams, mi hermano," he said, waving a hand between us. "You and I, we came here from both sides of that island with *nothing*. Not even the language. Our mothers and us, we busted our asses to have the lives we dreamed we could have."

He was right, it had been a long hard road. Remembering those first years in school when I could barely understand what the teacher was saying, and I begged my mom to just let me stay home, still made me shudder. But I'd done it, *we'd* done it. I was a college professor at an Ivy League school, for fuck's sake. It wasn't that I thought I couldn't do what was hard, it's that I didn't know if I had it in me to be the lover Easton deserved.

I pursed my lips, trying to find a way to explain. "Yeah, but *that* we knew how to do, Nes, hustling is in our DNA. That was the plan from the moment we hit the ground here. Work, school, that was the script." I pointed to the courthouse where I knew Easton must be preparing for his trial. "I have no game plan for this. My mom was my father's *mistress*, Nesto. I only saw that man on his way in and out my mother's bedroom a few times a week, for the little bit of time he was even around."

Nesto's eyes darkened at my words and leaned in closer, his hand still tight around my forearm. "You have nothing to be ashamed of, and neither does Odette for that matter. And I'm not here for any bullshit moralistic standards set by people who have no idea what our lives are like." He lifted a shoulder, as if to concede a point. "It's true, we didn't see that at home, the parents loving on each other and all that shit. Odette, Dinorah, my mom, it's sad that they didn't have more of that. But they *deserved it*, and *so do we*. Now chill the fuck out before I call Milo and tell on you."

Fucker had to make me laugh when I was confessing my deepest and darkest fears.

"Ice cold, Ernesto. Ice cold."

He stood up then and I did the same, knowing my friend would probably want to hug it out. I pulled him to me and tightened my arms around his shoulders.

"You'll be fine, P." Nesto's voice was so certain when he said that, I almost believed him. I would never stop being grateful for the people I had in my life, who never failed to show me the kindness it was sometimes so hard for me to show myself.

One thing was certain. I may not have seen many examples of couples growing up, but I could not say I didn't have men around me who knew how to show love.

Chapter Thirteen

Easton

"We are not here to start a fight with the sheriff, Ron," I said in the sternest voice I could manage.

"Dialogue. Starting *a dialogue*." That was Cindy; she'd shown up at the parking lot this morning, pissed that we hadn't consulted with her about the meeting. Now she was in my car after refusing to go home, and according to her, she was here to make sure we "kept it cordial." I'd never thought of Cindy as anything other than a fighter. When it came to domestic violence and sexual assault cases she'd always been fearless. I'd seen her call up the chief of police in the middle of the night to yell at him for not making an arrest fast enough. And yet, with this she seemed almost tentative. My sister's words kept ringing in my head.

Was Cindy's plan really to wash her hands, and by association the DA's office, from this? I wasn't sure what to even do with that if it was the case.

As we all got out of the car I saw Ron pursing his mouth before answering Cindy's admonishment. He looked a lot like I felt.

"Cin," Ron said tiredly. "Believe me, I don't want to

start a thing with Day, you know he and I go way back. I was his mentor when he started at IPD for fuck's sake, but I am not going to sit there and let him feed me excuses about what some of his deputies have been up to." He looked over to me, barely restrained frustration all over his face. "He's been ghosting Easton, and from the looks of it, has done nothing to deal with any of it."

I looked over at Cindy who was definitely still not up to high-stress meetings yet, and bit back the curse that was on the tip of my tongue. "Cindy, we are not here for a social call. Day has to give us some straight answers about what's been happening on his watch."

Cindy whispered to me as we walked and headed to the front desk area. "I just don't want us to get into a place where we can't work together."

I looked around and spoke to her in a low voice as Ron let the deputy in the front know what we needed. "I'm aware. Corey and Tony are invaluable in the sexual abuse cases, hell they're two of my strongest witnesses for the trial going on now. We still need to have a word about these bullshit stops on county roads." I ran my hand over my head as I followed Ron to Day's office, trying to control my annoyance. I was getting tired of Cindy implying that us asking Day to do something about these stops was equivalent with declaring war. "I don't want this to become a public pissing match any more than you do, but I don't think I need to tell you that if Day can't hear our concerns about this, then we *really* need to be worried."

I almost told her about Ari, because I needed her to understand, to hear, that this was something happening to real people. Our work sometimes got so stressful and there was so much of it that we forgot we were not just responsible for what escalated to crimes. It was our duty to respond to situations like this, especially when it was becoming clear that these stops were not just random. Before Cindy could get a word in, Day came out of his office to greet us.

If you could use a word for Whitney Day, it would be "strapping." He gave off a no-nonsense vibe that kept people on their toes. He was tall and strong, with piercing blue eyes that could make you squirm if directed at you for too long. His blond hair was getting lighter as some grays came in, but still…he was a very handsome man.

Day had been a notorious bachelor, but no one knew much about his personal life until he'd unexpectedly come out during his run for sheriff. It almost cost him the election too. Regardless, he was so well liked he'd been re-elected. At thirty-five he'd been the youngest and first openly gay sheriff ever elected in Tompkins County, and until this bullshit started it seemed like he was running his department well.

"Archer." I stretched my hand to Day after he'd gone in for a backslap with Ron and kissed Cindy hello.

"You've been a hard man to pin down lately," I said as we followed him to his office.

Like my own, it was sort of an ode to the seventies. Lots of wood paneling and bright carpeting, but it was large enough to accommodate us. Unlike mine, Day's office was scrupulously tidy, everything in its place.

He sat down on the small round table in his office and leaned in the chair with his arms crossed over his chest. I wasn't sure what vibe he was giving off, and I didn't want to start on the wrong foot, so I thought about how to best get the conversation going.

This type of situation was always tricky for me. In a courtroom, there were no holds barred. I would come in guns blazing and do what I needed to do. But when it was colleagues, I had the tendency to let myself get mowed down. I didn't want to hedge on this though, but before I could speak Ron did.

"So how are we going to get these little fuckers to realize they're too stupid to know their implicit bias is making their decisions for them?"

"Ron!" That was Cindy.

Day's face barely moved, but his neck was getting redder by the second. I put up my hands out trying to get people to calm down, knowing I couldn't afford this meeting to go off the rails before we even started.

"Whitney, there's a problem," I said with the most conciliatory tone I could come up with after Ron's outburst.

Day just looked at us, his expression inscrutable. I was starting to get a bit on edge from the stare down he was aiming at me when he finally opened his mouth. "I got a couple of young deputies who are a little overzealous and obviously need a little more training, but I'm not ready to call this a problem." He looked genuinely puzzled, and even a little hurt. "I don't recruit racists. The minute I hear anyone's been using slurs or anything like that, there will be consequences."

Ron's mouth flattened at that and Cindy looked like she was really close to having another cardiac episode.

I suppressed a sigh before I spoke again. "Whitney, we can't just ignore the fact that the stops in the last few months have increased and that the drivers were overwhelmingly men of color, mostly Black and Latinx.

Just because people are not using hate speech doesn't mean there's not an issue."

Day leaned in then and his face did not seem to be indicating that we were going to make any progress on getting him to at least admit that this was in any way related to race.

"I have things under control, the guys will be disciplined. They don't need to be putting people in the community on edge because they can't keep their shit together on a shift. But things are way too heated right now. Some local activists have been up in arms about this and I just don't think me getting in there is going to do anything." Him using the word "activist" brought me up short, because he wasn't just talking about an anonymous person, he was talking about Patrice. This was not just some people trying to start trouble, it was people in our community who were fearful for their safety asking us to do our jobs. I was going to say exactly that when Ron spoke again.

"Activists are up in arms because people are scared, Whit. Actually stepping up and saying this is an issue could show the parents of black kids who can't sleep at night since this shit started that this community cares about their kids." Ron's angry voice boomed in the room.

If possible, Day tightened his arms even more tightly against his chest, and he did not look like he was going to budge much from his position. "It's not the right time."

Ron scoffed, angling his head toward the sheriff. "What would be the right time for you, Whit? After one of these kids gets shot on their way home from school?"

Cindy looked like she finally realized that she'd

made a bad call by coming to this and stood up. "I'm going to get some fresh air."

Sheriff Day's eyes widened as if just now realizing that Cindy was only a few weeks out of surgery. "If Lorraine knows you're out here, she's going to have all our heads." Cindy's partner had been a teacher in the Ithaca school district for twenty years and most of us knew her well and respected her. We also knew she was not anyone to mess with, especially when it came to Cindy.

Cindy glared at all of us as she walked to the door. When she had her hand on the doorknob, she turned around. To my surprise, she finally seemed to have lost her patience.

"Whitney, I'm old and don't want to have another heart attack. Can you please stop acting like there's not a problem? Fix this for fuck's sake. Do we want all your hard work blowing up because a kid gets shot?" With that she left, leaving us all in tense silence.

"If it were a matter of one person fixing this it would already be over. I know you can't fix all of it," Ron said exhaustedly. "But you need to do better than a slap on the hand."

Day twisted his mouth to the side, and when he spoke I had to refrain from sitting on Ron. "It took a year to get this department back on track after I came out. Easton, you know that. It seemed like half the county was suspicious of me. If I take sides on this…" He trailed off, but his meaning was crystal clear.

Ron leaned in then and the menacing look in his eyes made me think that we'd be lucky if this thing didn't end up in a brawl. "Please tell me this isn't about your fucking popularity, Whitney. Do you know what it's like to have two black teens about to get licenses with this mess going on?"

Ron's emotional words seem to finally sink in. Day's usually unaffected face went from realization, to concern, to what finally looked like genuine empathy for Ron's distress. He uncrossed his arms and clapped Ron's shoulder, before he spoke. "Ron, I'm not trying to say this is simple, I just don't seem to have any good solutions for this."

Ron's shoulders relaxed a fraction, but he looked to me to respond.

"I'm not saying any of us have all the answers here, but we need to find them. This is our fucking job. We promised to do this. If people are scared for their kids we are failing at our jobs. To start, we need to let this community know, in no uncertain terms, that we do not think what is happening is acceptable."

Day let out a long breath and turned to look at me. "I've made an active effort to recruit more minorities." I sighed at his words because he just wasn't getting it. "You know I even had that LGBT training last year, and how much shit I got for it. We've got a lot going on, with opiates addiction wreaking havoc in the rural areas."

I sighed, well aware of all the shit he was dealing with, because our office had to deal with all those drug charges, but it irked me the way he was talking like he wanted us to commend him for doing the bare minimum. "But hiring minorities is not exactly groundbreaking." He flinched at that, but I needed to make it clear that I was not patting him on the back for doing what labor laws required him to do. "I know you have your hands full, Whitney." I leaned in, looking straight at him. "But we cannot just kick the can down the road on this. If something terrible happens, what are we going to tell ourselves then?"

He nodded and let out another long suffering breath. "Fine, I will make sure this is dealt with, but I will appreciate it if I'm given some time to handle this internally. I'm not ready to crack heads just yet."

It wasn't exactly what I wanted to hear. I wanted Day to push for an anti-racism training for recruits. I wanted him to publicly talk about implicit bias training, to say that we didn't want to become another town where young black and brown men had to be scared for their lives just because of the color of their skin. But I knew I couldn't make Day do it, and now he was asking me to keep my mouth shut too. I looked over my shoulder at Ron, who'd been standing since Cindy had left the room. He twisted his mouth to the side, and I knew, like me, he wasn't impressed by Day's answer, but also knew it was probably all we were going to get.

I spoke up before Ron could. "We can give you time, but I can't promise we won't have to respond to this at some point. I will not let this county be another one in the long list of towns in this country that sweeps shit like this under the rug."

Chapter Fourteen

Easton

"Where are you running off to?"

I looked over my shoulder and saw Cindy coming after me as I tried to make my escape out of the courthouse. Things between us had been a little awkward since the meeting with Day, but I'd been too busy to give too much thought to it.

It was Friday, the end of the first week of the Suarez trail, and it was almost 7:30 p.m. We'd been debriefing for the three hours since the judge rested for the weekend. I was ready to call it a day. As always, in cases like this, it had been emotionally draining and combined with the stress of the fuckery happening with the sheriff's department, I needed a break.

"I'm not running," I answered Cindy as we made our way down the steps leading out of the courthouse.

Cindy had been coming to the see the trial, which meant she probably wanted to talk about it with me. Our side was done with witnesses and the defense was bringing in their first one on Monday. That meant we'd work all weekend figuring out what they would try to bamboozle us with. I wanted a night off before the two straight days of work I was sure were ahead of me.

Especially because I was supposed to see Patrice tonight. We were actually going out for dinner, which was different. We'd been doing this thing where he'd show up around dinnertime, either with some takeout in hand or with a bottle of wine. I wasn't exactly sure what any of it meant, but I wasn't in a place to deny him. I'd gladly have Patrice Denis in my bed as long as he wanted to be there.

Although that wasn't fair. We'd been getting to know each other. My biggest problem at the moment was the fact that the more I got to know Patrice Denis the more I wanted him, all of him. Even after all the time we'd spent together, I wasn't sure if I'd ever get that.

"Oohhhh, this is about the stunner," Cindy said, her distant expression changing for the usual impish one she sported whenever we talked about my dating life. A knot I didn't even know I had in my stomach loosened a bit and I smiled back.

"His name is Patrice Denis, and yes, we're having dinner together. I'm meeting him at that brewery that has the good pumpkin beer."

Cindy balked at that. "Ugh, I don't know how you drink that stuff," she said, shuddering.

I looked around at the trees, which were half bare already. Early October had a bite here in Ithaca. "I embrace the fall weather and all it has to offer."

"Ummhmm." Cindy did not look convinced. "So things are going well, then?"

It felt good to just chat normally with Cindy after the tension of the last few weeks. It was such a relief that I went along with the line of questioning, instead of my usual deflections when she got too nosy about my love life.

"So far things are going cautiously well."

That was an understatement. I knew, and Cindy knew it, but that was all I was willing to say at the moment.

"Good. I'm cautiously happy for you, then." She winked, and for the first time since I could remember she left me off the hook without a full interrogation.

"Thank you." I could tell she wanted to hear more, but she didn't push. She did reach out for my arm then, wanting to keep me there a bit longer, and I knew she'd followed me for a reason. "So have you given more thought to the DA's race?"

I looked around the deserted sidewalk and focused back on her. "Cin, is this really the best time to talk about this?"

She gave me that stubborn look I'd seen her use in court hundreds of times. It said, "I'm here to do a job, you're not getting me off track."

"This is the perfect time, since you hedged when I tried to talk to you about it after the meeting with Day." Her expression got a little grim when she mentioned the meeting. It had not been anyone's finest moment. For all my mouthing off, we walked out of there with very little to show for it.

Cindy's insistent tone jerked me back to the conversation. "The deadline for submitting the papers to run is in a few weeks. You'd be a good DA. People trust you and respect you, Easton." There was a lot that was feeling fraught with Cindy these days, but I knew she believed what she was telling me.

"I don't know, Cin," I said, hesitantly. My parents talked about my job like it was a strange hobby they didn't get, but I loved it, and I was good at it. If I was honest with myself, I wanted the DA position, not just to show my parents that this was not some kind of whim, but because I thought I could make a difference. I complained about the paperwork and the administrative piece, but I wondered if I could be a good leader if I just had more leeway. It had become abundantly clear dealing with these stops that when it came to speaking for the DA's office my hands were tied.

I looked over at Cindy who was still waiting for my answer. "I'll think about it, okay?"

She nodded, seemingly satisfied for now. "I'll hold you to that." She then moved in to give me a peck on the cheek and shooed me away.

"Okay, go see your stunner, but I'll be back on Monday to make sure you put the paperwork in."

"Okay," I said, walking off with a nod, and setting aside my complicated feelings about Cindy and the DA position for now.

As I walked the few blocks to the brewery, I considered the past week with Patrice. No matter how much I got from him, it felt like only a taste, when I wanted mouthfuls.

A buzz in my pocket broke up my musings. I grabbed the phone, expecting to see a message from Amber, my co-counsel on the trial, but instead I saw it was from Patrice. I had to press a hand to my chest, at the throb there from just seeing his name on the screen.

I see you, counselor. How are you not wearing a coat?!!!!

I laughed at his alarmed message and looked up. I spotted him leaning against the brick wall next to the brewery.

God, he was beautiful.

When I lifted my hand in greeting, he did the same, and that unguarded smile I sometimes got glimpses of made an appearance. His face was open, obviously glad to see me, and I wanted to do something ridiculous like wolf-whistle. The weight of the week, the pressure of knowing that getting justice for that young woman rested on my shoulders…all of that lightened a bit now that I'd seen him.

I stood at the corner, waiting for the light to change, focused on him. There was so much to take in. His locs were coiled on top of his head today, giving me a clear view of his face. He was wearing dark jeans and black Chelsea boots, his gloved hands in his navy pea coat, a bright yellow scarf wrapped around his neck. That big body at rest, waiting for me. It was all I could not to run to him.

When the light changed I started walking, and he pushed off the wall to meet me. My heart pounded as I got close, and I took a moment to revel in the fact that I had butterflies in my stomach. I got to him and stopped just a couple of feet short of where he stood. "Hi."

"How are you not freezing?" he asked, his lips turned up in a tiny smile. I lifted a shoulder and looked down at myself.

"I guess I'm not that cold," I said distractedly, too focused on how close we were and that I wasn't kissing him.

I wasn't sure how to greet him. I *wanted* to kiss him, but I didn't know how that would be received. I could see in his face that he was debating something too.

After a moment, his expression grew determined, then he moved closer and pressed his lips to mine, putting the question to rest. I immediately put my hand behind his head to bring him closer to me. I pressed my palm to the back of his neck, my eyes closed as I kissed him, feeling the warm skin of his neck, face and shoulders.

Our breaths mingled and I marveled at what was happening, I was kissing Patrice on a street corner and he was kissing me back, his arms tight around me. I should've been terrified, because this feeling, this would hurt whenever it went away. Instead I licked into his mouth, just once, to taste. When we pulled back I had my eyes closed, still reveling in the feeling, and when I finally opened them, the way Patrice was looking at me almost made me swoon.

He held my hand as he angled his head to the bar door. "Shall we?"

The urge to say, "I'd go anywhere with you by the hand," was on the tip on my tongue.

But I kept it short, cautious not to break the spell by, as Tyren would say, "doing the most."

"Let's go."

The usual Friday crowd of townspeople and students were scattered all over the popular brewery when we walked in. We spotted two stools at the end of the bar and headed over. As we dodged bodies on our way to the empty seats Patrice leaned over and spoke into my ear.

"How did today end? I saw on my news feed that you guys finished with your witnesses."

I settled in my seat and looked around to see who was within earshot. A habit of being a small town prosecutor. "It's going well, there is a lot of evidence," I said with more confidence than I felt. "The issue will be whether a jury will actually choose to believe that any of what happened was consensual." I grimaced, thinking about the pile of photographs from the victim's medical exam after the assault. "It's not likely." I lifted a shoulder. "But you never know."

He dipped his head and I could tell he was thinking hard about something. Before he answered, the bartender came to take our drink orders, and distracted us for a moment. When he walked away Patrice picked up the conversation again, his face serious. "That is a huge amount of pressure on you."

I ran a hand over my forehead, ready to give an answer along the lines of "well I'm just doing my job" and then thought about the way he'd said it: "is" not "must be." That distinction rocked me for a moment, because it was not very often that people in my life acknowledged that the pressure of this job sometimes could be paralyzing. For once I didn't try to alleviate the other person's worry, I just said it.

"It *is* a lot of pressure. We've worked our asses off, and prepared as much as we possibly can, but the jury ultimately decides. We have good witnesses, and the sheriff's department did a really good job with the investigation part. So we'll see."

He ran his hand over mine before speaking, "I can't imagine what having so much hanging on me would be like. No matter how I feel about the justice system, it is not an easy job that you have." He then moved closer and asked in a low voice. "Any news about the sheriff?"

I shook my head and tried not to show the frustration I felt. After the meeting with Day he'd followed up to let us know he'd "made it clear" to the deputies that they needed to be more careful, but there didn't seem to be any real sign he was taking things further than that, at least for now.

There was only so much I could tell Patrice anyway, so I just shook my head. "No, not really. I'm sorry." I meant that sincerely.

I worried that my answer would shift the mood of the evening but Patrice just nodded and ran his hand over mine again. He gave me a tiny smile and when he spoke his tone was intentionally gentle. "I know this stuff is not all on you. I just want you to know that I've been working with some of the groups in town and people are organizing for whenever it happens again."

My heart sped up then, worried for him, and once again feeling like we were making a huge mistake with our silence.

"Patrice." I wasn't even sure what I wanted to say, but he lifted his gaze to mine as if he was also thinking of how to say what was on his mind. I leaned closer, waiting for his answer, when a voice from behind startled me.

"Well, well, well and here I was thinking that I'd have to show my new colleague around. I guess he's doing just fine."

I pulled back to see who the voice belonged to, and when I glanced at Patrice he was barely containing his annoyance. I didn't blame him, Brad Gunham was a piece of work. We'd known each other since we were kids, and had had one very underwhelming date when I was trying and failing to get Patrice out of my system, so I couldn't exactly pretend I was blanking on who he was.

"Brad." Patrice's flat tone made it clear that though they might be colleagues, they were not friends.

While I was still trying to figure out where this was going Brad leaned in and spoke very close to my ear, completely violating all personal space rules. "I haven't heard from you in a while, Easton."

I sat there wondering what exactly this guy thought he was doing. We'd gone on one bad date that ended up in mediocre sex before we went our separate ways. Why he thought he needed to come and talk to me when I was obviously with someone else was a mystery to me, especially given our history. Which I really hoped did not come up tonight.

I leaned further back from him until I was flush against the bar before I spoke. "Brad, I'd make introductions, but you know Patrice." I extended my hand, intentionally ignoring his comment.

When I turned, Patrice was sitting upright and sending a very unfriendly look in his colleague's direction, then trained his eyes on the spot on my arm Brad was touching.

When he spoke his voice was a barely restrained growl. "We work together."

Brad's smirk was condescending enough to make me want to smack it off. He gave his back to Patrice as he spoke.

"Oh Dr. Denis and I go way back, I was on his hiring committee. There was a lot of talk before we hired him, as there usually is when the department takes a big chance on a candidate."

Before Patrice could answer I stood up, grabbing our drinks. I was not going to let Brad get up to his usual shit stirring and ruin the dinner with Patrice that I'd been looking forward to all week.

I glared at him, my tone chilly. "I'm sure the pressure was high to make the best offer possible to Patrice, considering all the options he had." I looked over to the man in question and he was standing with his back against the wall, his face completely closed off. Then I turned back to Brad. "We're headed to our table, have a good evening."

I handed Patrice his drink and we started walking. Patrice muttered something that sounded a lot like a curse word and was at the table before I had taken two steps there.

When we sat down, his face showed the frustration that I was sure he'd held back at the bar.

"I'm sorry about that," I said as I glanced in the direction of the bar and saw that Brad had already left, probably looking for someone else he could fuck with. "Brad is an ass."

Patrice watched him walk away, his gaze icy. "Brad thinks he can talk to people however he wants." He paused then and I could tell he was working on letting go of the annoyance of the last few minutes. He took one breath, then another and lifted both shoulders as if to shed some of the tension there, the whole time his eyes trained on mine.

He opened his mouth to say something, but instead of saying whatever was on his mind, he reached across the table and grabbed my hands possessively. His eyes locked with mine. "What bothers people like Brad is that I don't take his bait. He wants to get a rise out of me, so when I curse him out he can point at me and say I'm trash and that I don't know how to act. He knows I don't give a fuck about him getting off on talking to me like I'm the help, and that just makes *him* look bad." It was clear he was not done talking about all the ways

Brad pissed him off, and the way he was looking at me made me hold my breath. "But if I see him pawing or talking to you like that again, I'm going to pop him in the mouth. I don't care what kind of influence he has in the department."

Oh wow what was even happening in my chest right now. I breathed through my nose until I found words. Patrice Denis was going to ruin me. "I didn't know you had such a possessive side, Professor Denis."

He dipped his chin, and his expression turned just a tiny bit bashful, but he answered with a flustered laugh. "I didn't either."

I couldn't help the smug smile that was probably pasted on my face. "Brad and I go way back. His parents were a power couple at Cornell, and my parents loved to have the local academia luminaries at their dinner parties."

Patrice twisted his mouth to the side at that. "I don't like the way he talked to you."

I lifted a shoulder, aware of what he meant, the dismissive way in which Brad had talked about my job. "For my parents, and some of their friends, my entire career choice is mystifying." I made air quotes as I said the next part. "Apparently, spending five years working on some of the toughest cases in the region is my cute way of getting people to 'take me seriously.' Even my mom, who at least tries to be supportive, just can't see why I would do this instead of work for the winery."

His face became thunderous then. "Well that's just bullshit. Don't they read the news and see the cases you're dealing with?"

He shook his head and there was a fluttering happening in my chest that I'd never particularly felt be-

fore. "That shit's not happening again on my watch."
He looked so serious, and he sat there with his mouth
closed, running his tongue over his teeth, as he came up
with whatever he wanted to say. But after a few breaths
he relaxed his shoulders and let go of my hand to grab
a drink of his beer.

He'd said his piece.

Something I was learning about Patrice was that he
never said more than he had to, but whatever did come
out his mouth was good as gold.

What he said, how incensed he was on my behalf, it
made me want things that I knew very well I should not
ask for. But I was still me. "Are you going to be my de-
fender?" I was trying for humor, but even I could hear
the yearning in my voice.

Patrice's eyes took me in. Inch by inch, they moved
over me with such intensity that I could swear my
clothes were at risk of igniting. "I'm going to tell you
what I see, if other people in your life can't or won't."

There was danger for me here, I knew that. This was
not territory I could tread into without serious risk of
injury, but I never was one to heed trouble. "And what
exactly do you see?"

"Someone worth me getting my shit together for."
It came out in grumble, like he wasn't even sure how
he'd gotten there himself.

I laughed then and leaned over, deciding to kiss him
after all. When I pulled back I smiled at his serious expression. "You sound so agonized about it."

He lifted a shoulder and looked at me, and I felt
scared for a minute that what he would say next would
hurt me. That he would blow off this moment and make
it something less than what it had meant to me.

"I can be conflicted and still know I am where I'm supposed to be. I'm trying to learn how to make that work."

They weren't exactly lines from *Romeo and Juliet*, but they didn't have to be, because I knew that Patrice Denis was braving unchartered territory, and he was doing it for me.

Chapter Fifteen

Patrice

The knock on the door came a second before the holler from the hallway.

"Are you ready, professor?"

I just laughed, because for a guy who looked like he'd be right at home at the Cornell Club, Easton Archer could holler. I grimaced at the racket he was making then remembered he owned the fucking building, so we were probably okay.

"I'm coming." I could barely keep the humor out my voice, because that was my permanent state these days.

I walked around happy as hell, smiling at people and asking about their dogs and shit. It was like fucking with Easton Archer had turned me into a…happy person. I opened the door, digesting that new development with a grin on my face, knowing what my current state of nothing but sweats on would have on Easton.

He didn't even say hello, he just got a look at my chest and jumped me.

I stumbled backward, laughing my ass off as he did his best to get this tongue down my throat.

"This is not right." Those eyes looked up at me like I was everything he'd ever wished for.

I exhaled and nuzzled his neck. "Your eyes make me think of the semester I spent in Edinburgh. Whiskey and moss."

He groaned as he backed me up against the nearest wall. "Why do you hate me? Here I am trying to be suave. Trying to *woo* you, so that you don't think I'm just after your dick, and you start telling me my eyes are like all Scottish and drugging?"

I couldn't help it, I busted up and tightened my arms around his waist. "You trying to woo me, counselor?"

He ran his hands over my bare shoulders and the possessiveness there made me grin again. When he answered his voice was strong.

"Yes, and we're going someplace we can't run into anyone. Last time I thought you were going to rip Brad's head off." He tried to make it humorous, but I seriously wanted to pop that fucker on the mouth. It really pissed me off that Easton was so used to people talking to him like Brad did. I could only imagine the type of shit he dealt with from his father for him to be practically unbothered by a prick like Brad talking down to him. I vowed right there and then that I would never be one more person in Easton's life who didn't let him know what he was worth.

Easton's tongue clicking brought me back and his face was a mix of serious and horny. "You feeling some type of way, professor?"

He thrust his hips toward me and I could feel his hard cock brushing against me.

"You letting Tyren teach you words again?"

He laughed and pressed closer. "No. You just looked

really serious. But I'm having trouble staying on task right now. It's hard not to get hot and bothered when you make that face. I'm only human, how can I be expected to resist six feet four inches and two hundred plus pounds of—"

"Pissed-off Haitian?" I asked, biting the inside of my cheek to keep from smiling.

"I was going to say of gorgeous broody man." He wrapped his arms around my neck and looked up. "I almost want to cancel this outing. It's too cold today anyway." His tone told me that he was a lot less concerned with the temperature outside and lot more with getting into my bed. He was also bundled up in jeans, snow boots and what looked like a few layers under his parka. I shook my head as I dislodged his arms from my neck. "Nuh uh, we said we were going to do stuff together," I said as I went to grab my socks.

"Fine." His pout was too fucking cute. "But I think not staying indoors while you're so close to being fully naked is a really wasted opportunity."

I dipped my head once, biting back the smile that seemed to be permanently ready to come out whenever Easton was around. Despite the tension that had been going on with the stops, things seemed to have calmed down. Easton had said his meeting with the sheriff hadn't been terrible, but not great either. He didn't elaborate other than to say he expected things to quiet down for now. I was still working with some groups organizing a "Know Your Rights" teach-in in town, and that was a priority. But I was trying to make a go of things with Easton and I could not put every shitty thing that happened in town on him to solve.

"Okay, what are you thinking about?"

I shook my head, trying to focus on the moment. "I was thinking I need to put on at least four more layers so we can begin our romantic adventure."

He rolled his eyes at my obvious lie. "Are you still worried about the meeting with the dean?"

That reminder I could've done without. I'd been called in for a meeting, which coincidentally came the Monday after Easton and I had our run-in with Brad. It was supposed to be a "check in" but when I asked Ted, he'd told me that was unusual. So I was expecting to be called out on the carpet for something that had nothing to do with the job I was actually hired for. But that was another thing I didn't want to get into right now.

"Nah, I'm trying not to worry about it until it happens. There's nothing I can do about it at this point." I lifted a shoulder before turning around and going up the stairs to finish getting dressed with Easton right behind me.

"I hope this isn't Brad being a petty asshole, but this would be very in line with his MO. Fucking with people because he can't deal with rejection." I stopped as I got to the mezzanine and looked over my shoulder at him. His angry expression made me wonder what that little prick had done to fuck with *him*. But before I could even answer he just shook his head and waved his hand as if asking me to forget about it.

"That was a long time ago. I don't indulge in grudges about petty shit people do." The way his mouth flattened and his face blanched made it pretty obvious it was not just some petty thing. Easton liked to maintain that un-affected facade. Except I could tell he minimized how things that people said and did hurt him. He acted like his dad's slights didn't affect him. How much it hurt him to be dismissed. But I'd seen it when I'd done it to him.

I pulled a T-shirt and then a sweater over my head, trying to figure out how to let him know he could trust me, while Easton acted like a fool, fake swooning and fanning himself. He was so extra, but fuck if I could stay mad with him around.

I walked up to where he was leaning against the dresser and tightened my arms around his waist. Again taken aback by the way he just made me forget to be pissed at shit that usually infuriated me. "You're a clown."

He preened like I'd given him the best compliment of his life. "I think you like it though."

I shook my head, my mouth itching to break out into a grin. "I've had to learn to live with the constant bullshit you're on. I'm also curious about this romantic date." My voice was serious but that little flame of excitement in my belly came back to life. No matter how much of a grumpy bastard I pretended to be, being the object of Easton Archer's attention was apparently one of my new life goals.

He pushed up to kiss me and then pulled my hand as he started going down the metal spiral staircase. Once we were downstairs, he started wiggling like he was so excited about this date, he could barely contain himself. "Well, I don't want to brag, but it's pretty amazing."

I went to grab my coat as he flashed me those perfect teeth. "I don't even know when you would've had time. You're in the middle of a trial." As soon as I said it I regretted it because the light in his eyes went out completely.

"We're trying to take one day in the week to recharge."

Fuck, now I'd made him feel guilty. I hurried over to him as it sunk in that seeing Easton unhappy even for a second had now become unbearable for me.

"Of course you should take a day. I've seen all the late nights you've been pulling." I bent down to kiss him, sliding my tongue with his, that immediate and complete connection powerful as always. Sometimes it felt like we'd been giving each other comfort forever.

When he pulled back he had that addled look he got sometimes, the one that made me feel ten feet tall, and I decided to say exactly what was on my mind. "I'm honored you'd want to spend your day off with me."

He lifted a shoulder then, a cheeky smile on his lips. "Well, everyone else was busy, so I figured I'd take you."

I walked by him to the door and smacked his ass. "Come on, let's go get your plan to sweep me off my feet on the road, Mr. Archer."

Easton

"So what other books have you been reading? What Chris Hayes is breaking down isn't exactly light reading," Patrice asked, as we drove to the stable where I'd arranged our date. The closer we got, the more concerned I got that the frigid weather was going to mess up my plans. So I turned my attention to Patrice's questions.

He'd been surprised a few minutes earlier when he tried to put on some music and ended up hitting play on *A Colony in A Nation*, which I'd been listening to. I kept my eyes on the road, not sure I wanted to see his reaction to my reading choices. I didn't want him to think I was only doing it to impress him or something.

"I've just been thinking there are things I need to get some perspective on, so I asked Pri to recommend some books. You know she has every opinion on everything."

I looked over and saw him nod. "I was just surprised. I mean clearly these are topics that are important to me. I'm happy to talk about them with you anytime."

I thought about that for a moment as I drove up to the turn for the stable. I didn't want him to think I didn't value his thoughts on this, but I wanted him to know I didn't feel like it was his job to enlighten me on things that it was my job to be aware of. "I want to come to you when I feel like I have more knowledge about the things I need to understand." I looked at him then. "The more I'm with you the more it's sinking in that I could've lived my whole life being a quote unquote good guy, without ever having to think about the true history of my own country, or my privilege," I scoffed, feeling embarrassed, but compelled to continue. "If you don't have that luxury, then neither should I."

He swallowed hard and then in a very quiet voice said, "I think you're a good prosecutor, Easton, and I'm glad you're doing this. It's necessary."

I did turn to look at him for what I wanted to say next. "There is too much I've not thought about enough and it embarrasses me because I wonder how it's impacted my ability to do my job."

"You're doing it now, and that matters." That was all he said, but there was a relief in his voice, like this had reassured him of something.

I didn't quite know what that meant, but thankfully our arrival at the stable put the conversation to rest.

"We're here."

Patrice still had a faraway expression as I powered off the car. As soon as we stepped out I knew that my big plan was going to be a bust. I looked over at Patrice, whose teeth were chattering despite being bundled up in a heavy coat, gloves, scarf and hat.

"Shit, I think it's too cold," I said, looking around at the stable parking lot and noticing that other than the owner's truck it seemed no one else was here.

Patrice, who was now shivering so hard he was vibrating, raised an eyebrow while taking in his surroundings. "So I take it that part of our romantic date involved the outdoors." I groaned and he pointed at the barn longingly. "Maybe it's warmer in there?"

I sighed and nodded as I grabbed the saddlebags I'd prepared with some snacks and spiked hot cocoa for us to drink at some point during our snowy trail ride.

"Yeah, but it's going to be a challenge being on a horse in this weather." I grimaced again as we stepped into the less cold, but not nearly warm enough barn. The weather outlook had been good, but around here a squall could hit at any time.

"Horse?" Patrice asked, sounding more than a little freaked out.

Fuck, maybe Patrice didn't like horses.

I put down the bags on the floor and turned to find him looking a little spooked and still shivering. It was still freezing even inside the barn and he was looking around the stable like he expected a wild horse to break free from one of the stalls and trample us to death.

"So I take it you're not a fan of horseback riding?" I asked, and watched him stiffen with every word.

"I've never ridden a horse before." He shrugged and

tried to smile, but I could tell he was embarrassed. "It's not like there's a big riding scene in the South Bronx you know?"

I couldn't tell if the humor in his voice was real or if it was just his way of trying to not make me feel like a jackass. Why did I assume that Patrice would be up to gallivanting on a horse in the snow like we were in a fucking Disney movie?

"Hey, what's all that glaring about?" Patrice's light tone went a long way to make me feel less like a clueless moron. "It's a little cold, but we can still have a good afternoon." Now he was talking to me like I was a hurt kitten.

I exhaled through my nose as I stiffly returned his embrace. The only thing that was keeping me from being completely flustered was the fact that Patrice seemed to think that my utter failure was adorably funny.

I looked up at him and saw that he was smiling so big his eyes were crinkling, and I could see his molars. "Why are you smiling? You're usually somewhere between solemn and full-on annoyed. But me bringing you out here to freeze your balls off on my pretentious faux date has you downright giddy." I huffed as he laughed again. "What the fuck, Patrice?" I could not for the life of me avoid sounding like a whiny baby.

Patrice gave me a rueful smile and tightened his arms around me, his mouth so close to my ear his warm breath made me shiver. "I kind of like this pissed-off you. It's nice not to be the moody asshole for once. Besides we can still have a nice time, we can eat in the car, there's heating in there."

I rolled my eyes, but it was hard to stay mad when he was like this.

"Well, for the record, it stinks to know that my idea to sweep you of your feet was stupid and poorly executed, even if you seem to be weirdly happy about my fail."

More smiling and acting delighted. "We don't have to give up on this totally, and knowing how busy you are right now I do appreciate that you went to the trouble of planning something. Besides, it's not your fault it's unseasonably cold today. I'd still like to see the horses. I haven't really been to a horse farm before."

He was beaming.

I angled my head and tried not to sound too annoyed when I spoke again. "So wait, you can barely muster up a smirk ninety percent of the time, but this utter fiasco is somehow the most fun thing ever for you?"

Again with the smiling, but his eyes were telling me that there was a lot more to his mood. He was *seeing* something. The way he was looking at me, holding me, it felt different. It was like he was fully there with me for the first time.

"I'm not sure what's happening right now," I said, genuinely puzzled.

He took my hand and, without answering, started moving to the stalls. The smell of hay, manure and horseflesh was overpowering with all the ventilation pretty much closed because of the cold. I found the smell comforting, since horses had been one of the few things I'd had growing up that my parents actually approved of. But I knew it wasn't something most people found pleasant. He seemed fine though, looking around, taking everything in, a contented smile on his lips. When we got to the bay he asked in a low voice, like he was afraid of disturbing the animals, "Which one is yours?"

"How do you know I have one?" was my evasive answer.

His exaggerated eye roll was almost comical.

I pointed at my guy, who had been fretting since he'd heard my voice. "That's him," I said, pointing at my black Percheron that was now openly demanding my attention, snorting and bumping his nose on the door of his stall. I walked over and gave him some love while Patrice watched from a distance. "This is Justice."

He laughed and shook his head at that. "Subtle."

I dipped my head, sure I was blushing at his teasing tone. "So much about me is understated."

I actually got a snort out of Patrice Denis.

"He's beautiful." He inched toward where I was standing petting Justice's big head. "And large."

I smiled at Patrice's very cautious tone and movements. "You can move closer, he thinks he's a dog. He'll probably try to lick you, but other than that, you're pretty safe."

We stood there for a few moments petting Justice and feeding him an apple I'd brought for him, while I thought of how to salvage this afternoon. I was running scenarios through my head when Patrice tugged on my scarf.

"Hey, no fretting. We're having a nice a time." He hiked his thumb in the direction of the parking lot. "Let's finish visiting with Justice then go warm up a little in the car. We can drive back home after." The word "home" was uttered in a very suggestive tone. The way he was looking at me made me feel like my clothes were going to disintegrate from my body.

After giving a last pat to a very unhappy Justice, I let him pull me out of the barn and we walked to my SUV. I said in genuine amazement, "This Zen thing you've got going is quite remarkable. I'm not sure I can handle it."

He laughed again as we got into my frigid car and I immediately blasted the heat and turned on the seat warmers. As we sat there thawing out, I saw Patrice was mulling over what I'd said.

He leaned down to get the thermos I'd brought with me and opened it. When he sniffed it he raised both eyebrows. "Is there liquor in here?"

I grinned at his surprised expression. "Just a touch of bourbon."

He shook his head and closed it up. "Maybe just water, then."

I just nodded, still waiting for his answer about my previous comment. After taking a long drink of what had to be icy water, he looked at me and I could tell he was still considering how to approach the conversation I'd just reopened.

"It's not Zen." He shook his head as he bit the side of his mouth. "My utter lack of chill doesn't exactly allow for that," he said ruefully, then let out a long breath and pressed his head to the back of the seat and turned those almost-black eyes on me. I couldn't stay away when he was this close, so I leaned in and pressed a kiss to his mouth.

When I pulled back he put his hand on the back of my head and pulled me in for another, licking into my mouth with gentle brushes of his tongue. Making me feel his kiss all the way down to my toes.

Only after did he start to talk again. "I just like that you're able to lose it a little bit with me. That you don't feel like you need to do that Mr. Sunshine thing all the time."

Mr. Sunshine?

He leaned in and kissed me again. "It's just nice to see that you can be real with me. I want to reciprocate, babe."

Babe?

I was literally stunned into silence, but apparently the new Patrice was chatty. "I want to make this work, and to do that I need to let go a bit, be a little sunnier, so you can feel free…not to be. Balance."

I pursed my lips and could almost see my eyebrows with how much I'd furrowed them. "So you *like* that I threw a fit?"

He actually cackled at my bafflement. "I like that we can be ourselves with each other. I like being with you in the car right now, and not freezing my ass off while I try to ride a gigantic horse that could crush me. I like *you*, Easton."

My heart was beating that way it had started doing whenever Patrice was around. "I like you too."

He nodded and then thrust his chin out in the direction of the steering wheel. "Let's go back to your place. Maybe we can put the rest of this afternoon to good use."

I pulled out of the stable and onto the road back to Ithaca, thinking about what had just happened. My romantic afternoon had been an utter fail and somehow things between Patrice and me felt more solid now than they ever had. Before I knew it, I was talking about something I hadn't said to anyone else before.

"Brad outed me to my dad."

I briefly glanced at Patrice's face, which had lost all semblance of relaxation. "He did what?" he asked, his voice barely contained fury.

"It was a long time ago, we were still in high school. I actually went to the public high school, because they had better AP classes. Brad did too. He was a year behind me. Anyway, junior year, I wasn't out, but I'd been seeing this senior."

"Okay." That was the only thing that Patrice could manage to say.

I cleared my throat and thought of Justin. "His mom was a professor too, but his dad was a local artist, they didn't run with my and Brad's parents' circle. He was out to his family, and they were so great. I loved going to his house." I sighed thinking how weird it was to be in a house where the adults actually seemed to get along.

"Anyway, Brad was obsessed with Justin, and did everything he could to get his attention. When he realized we were dating, he made it his mission to fuck with me."

"What did he do?" Patrice's voice was heavy with dread.

"Typical Brad, he 'accidentally' asked in front of my parents if I was bringing my boyfriend to my family's annual holiday party." I shook my head. "Needless to say it did not go over well with my dad. He acted like it was no big deal and then as soon as everyone left, my dad iced me out and didn't talk to me for months. When I confronted Brad he just said he didn't realize it was a big deal. He's always been like that. A vicious little prick."

"Your dad didn't speak to you for months?" He shook

his head, confused. "I can't say things were perfect for me coming out, but I at least was able to tell my mother on my own terms. That motherfucker, no wonder you can't stand him."

I lifted a shoulder, surprised at how little I felt about Brad. "My mom was better about it. It's hard for her to go against my dad, but she did her best to be supportive. Brad's like that. Sneaky and mean. That's why I was worried about that meeting with your chair. I would not be surprised if he's behind it."

He sucked his teeth and looked out the window at that. "I'll be fine. I figured it was because I've been making noise with all the stuff I'm doing in town."

I almost didn't say anything to that, but then I figured fuck it. "I hope they don't interfere with that. What you're doing with Justice Center is great."

He eyes softened at my words and something in my chest cracked just a little. "I'll be fine. I also won't put up with bullshit. They knew exactly who I was when they hired me. If they thought they were going to do a 'diversity hire' and then make me invisible they have another thing coming. And Brad better not try me. I didn't like him before, but after hearing what he did to you, I don't give a fuck if he was fifteen, that shit's just evil. Why are you grinning?"

"You're really pissed," I said in an amused voice.

He just shook his head and grabbed the hand I had resting on my thigh and kissed it. He didn't say anything, but he didn't have to.

Chapter Sixteen

Patrice

We got back to Easton's after a reasonably stressful drive in the snow, and I was still processing all that had happened on our non-date. We walked into his penthouse, and Easton went over to the fireplace while I ruminated about the conversations we'd had this afternoon. The new sides to Easton I'd seen. That shitty story about Brad outing him, and what he'd said when I'd asked about what he was reading. I was still thinking over the words he'd used and must've been pulling a face because I heard a scoff from somewhere in the big room.

"Wow, I know I messed up the date, but I didn't know you'd be that upset." He was trying to be funny, but I could tell he was also wondering if my mood had shifted somehow. I was being weird, standing by the door with my coat still on. I shook of my brooding and went to hang my stuff by the door, then walked up to him. He was standing by the fireplace, looking unsure and like he was regretting all the things he'd shared today.

When I finally got to him I wrapped an arm around his waist and used my other hand to smooth out the worry lines in his face. "Your romantic date planning is…interesting." He huffed even as he pressed closer to me. He loved getting close enough that he had to tilt his head up to look at me. I twisted my mouth to the side, trying not to grin at the redness creeping up his neck. "You do have me feeling some type of way, Mr. Archer."

"Oh. What way is that, then?" he asked, hooking his leg with mine. The utter delight in his voice made me shake my head. I didn't know how Easton could stay like this, like he was untouched by the shit I knew very well he came in contact with constantly. The things that I now knew had been done to him. He was resilient and strong, so fucking strong. He kept opening his heart, even when he knew it could be trampled.

I placed my hand under his chin and I brought his face up for a kiss. As we grazed our tongues together, the thought that kept trying to edge out my usual doom and gloom creeped in again.

Maybe this could work.

Maybe we had enough here to go on, to build something. I took both his hands in mine as we kissed, our fingers intertwined between us as we tasted each other. Moments like this with Easton shut the world out, and that would never stop being a revelation for me.

I was so lost to kissing him that I almost didn't hear my phone going off. The only person who ever called me was my mother and the guys, but they all had ringtones I recognized, so I figured it was the wrong number. I almost just let it ring, but Easton pulled apart, his face adorably annoyed.

"What if it's something important?"

I bit my lip, trying not to laugh. "More important than this?"

An eye roll was his response as I got my phone out of my pocket. When I saw Ari's number my heart immediately started pounding, remembering the last time he'd called me. I instantly dismissed the thought, he couldn't have been stopped again.

I lifted a shoulder at Easton who noticed my concerned expression. As soon as I took the call I knew something was wrong. "It's Ari."

"What's going on?" I asked, my heart pounding already. There was some shuffling on the phone and when Ari spoke it was obvious he was trying not to cry.

"I'm so sorry to bother you again, Patrice."

I closed my eyes, glad to hear that he at least did not seem to be physically in distress, but still concerned about how upset he sounded. "You don't have to apologize, I'm glad you called."

I looked at Easton who was standing right next to me, his shoulders tensing at my words.

There was more sniffling and I heard muffled yelling in the background.

Ari sighed heavily then spoke. "My uncle does not want me to stay with him anymore." He could barely talk at this point. "Yin was over here, and he, and we—"

He started crying then, and he didn't need to say what happened for me to figure out what was going on. I felt the skin tighten on my face, so fucking angry for Ari, as I felt the humiliation in the agonized cries over the phone.

When he spoke again he sounded completely miserable. "We were just kissing. Now he's saying I can't take the car because he helped me pay for it and with the insurance."

That motherfucker.

"Ari, I'm coming to pick you up. You can stay with me until we figure something out, okay?"

There was more breathing on the line, but this time it sounded a lot like relief. "Yes, please."

I turned around and started walking to the door, Easton right behind me. When I shook my head at him, he mouthed "I'm coming with you" with a very stubborn set to his jaw.

I nodded, unable to deny my own relief at not having to deal with this on my own. "We're leaving now, be there in fifteen minutes."

I was about to hang up when Ari spoke again, his voice strained again.

"Can you look out for Yin? He ran out of the house when my uncle started threatening us and told him to leave or he was going to call the police. He left his phone here. So he may just be walking home, and it's freezing outside. It was snowing before." He sniffled again. "He was so freaked out when he left, I'm scared he'll get hurt."

Fuck.

"Okay. We'll keep an eye out for him. See you soon."

Only after ending the call with Ari did I realize that I'd said *we*. I quickly tried to think of a time that I'd used a plural pronoun to refer to someone other than the guys or my mom. I could not come up with a single one.

"What happened?" Easton asked, his voice alert and worried.

When I turned, I saw him standing there ready to go, coat, hat and scarf already on. His keys and my gear in his hand.

My instinct very much called for me to handle this myself, but I pushed it down and let myself be glad that

Easton was here right now. I took my coat from him and explained as I quickly shrugged it on.

"His uncle caught him and Yin, and apparently kicked him out of the house," I said, my voice tight with frustration.

"Shit. Is there anyone you want me to call? How can I help?"

There it was, no hesitation. Something was happening and he was here to help.

"Thanks," I said, gripping his hand for a second as we walked to the elevator. "Actually, could we go in separate cars?"

He tensed at my words and I could tell he thought I didn't want him with me. "It's just, Ari's worried about Yin. He ran off so fast when the uncle came that he left his phone. There's no bus route or anything around there and Yin doesn't drive."

I could see the tension around his eyes ease as I told him the reason. A look of determination replacing the doubt that had been there a second ago.

"Of course. I'll follow you, but I'll go a bit slower so I can look out for him," he answered as the elevator's doors opened. "If anything comes up, just call me."

As we got to the garage and we were about to head to our cars, I had to stop and grab his hand. "Thank you."

He gave me a look that said, "What did you expect, asshole?" and didn't give me time to respond as we quickly got into our cars. I pulled out into the snowy afternoon, the roads slippery and messy, starting to panic that something terrible would happen between Ari and his uncle before I got there. I tried not to let anger and frustration at Ari's uncle take hold and focused on getting there as quickly and safely as possible. I could only imagine the things that the man had said to him, the humiliation of having that done to him in front of Yin. And poor Yin must've been terrified.

I sighed as I turned onto the road to the house and decided to call Ari again to let him know I was on my way. He answered after one ring.

"I should be there in a few minutes, Ari."

"Merci, Patrice. I'm waiting at the post office that's down the street from my uncle's house." He could barely talk from how hard his teeth were chattering. How could that man do this to him? After everything he'd already gone through.

"Did you see Yin? I'm scared that he'll get lost, the snow is so heavy. I can't see anything."

I hesitated then, only realizing now that maybe Ari wouldn't like Easton being involved in this.

"Actually, I was at Easton's place when you called and he's right behind me in his car trying to look for Yin."

"Good." The sigh of relief on the line was unexpected, but not a surprise once I thought about it. Easton had been in touch with Ari since arranging things with the lawyer. Of course Ari trusted him. It also wasn't exactly like he didn't know about us either, not after that big pep talk he'd given me.

Before Ari could respond I spotted him standing in the snow-filled entrance to the small post office. "Can you see my car, Ari?"

I saw him end the call and come out to the side of the road. He had his backpack and a fairly large suitcase with him. Which must've been hell to drag through the snow. I jumped out to help him get his stuff in the trunk and noticed he was soaked through and I was glad for the towels that Easton had run to get before we headed outside.

Even though it was a mess with the snow, I had to pull Ari into a hug. As soon as I did I heard a strangled sob escape his throat.

"We'll take care of you," I promised, feeling fiercely protective of him. Needing him to know he was not on his own. "You're not alone." He nodded as he sniffled on my shoulder. I pulled back and started moving to the driver's side door. "Now let's move, this snow is getting heavier."

As soon as we got in the car a call came in from Easton. I turned to Ari, who was looking at the Bluetooth screen like it was about to blow up.

"Hey." I heard some rustling before Easton's came in through the speakers. "I got Yin. He's a little wet, but doing okay." I turned to Ari, who looked like he was going to start crying again.

"Thank you," I said, relieved they were both fine. "I have Ari here. I'm sure they want to check on each other."

I raised an eyebrow in question at Ari who immediately opened his mouth to say something when Yin's low voice came over the speakers.

"I'm sorry." He burst into tears then and my heart broke for how distraught he sounded. Damn Ari's uncle for doing this shit.

These were good kids. They did not deserve to be going through this. I was once again so fucking grateful for Easton, who made sure that Yin was at least out of the snow, if more than a little bit distressed.

"You didn't do anything, bébé." Ari's voice, for the first time, sounded back to normal. Clearly trying to be strong for Yin. "You were kissing me. That's all. My uncle is the one who did this. You and I didn't do anything wrong. I have your phone, cher. I will keep it safe for you."

"I love you." Yin's quiet but unafraid, unashamed words made me feel like an intruder. It made me wonder if I'd ever be that brave, to tell Easton how I felt no matter who was watching. I glanced over at Ari and how hard he was working at keeping himself together, but still fearlessly responded to Yin's words. "Je t'aime aussi."

I cleared my throat, feeling out of sorts from the last few minutes. "Easton, why don't we all meet at my place?" I looked to Ari, who was now staring out the window, his hand gripping a phone I assumed was Yin's. "Ari, you okay with that plan?"

He nodded but didn't look at me. It seemed almost like now that he'd heard his love was safe, he went into himself. His body there, but his mind had retreated somewhere else. I heard Easton whisper something, and then his clear strong voice came on the phone.

"We'll see you there. Ari, did you get a chance to get all your immigration paperwork before you left? If not we can come with you to get them once things are calmer."

I hadn't even thought of that. Ari nodded, pointing as his backpack. "I got them."

"Great. I'll take a look at them when we get to the house, and don't worry. I texted Jim and he said he's got everything he needs to formally take your case. We don't need your uncle for this."

Ari's lip trembled again. "Okay. Thank you, Easton."

For the second time in the last hour I felt immensely

grateful for Easton Archer. "Thank you," I said, my own voice quavering with emotion.

"Of course. I'll see you at home."

I was not going to question the ball of fire that the word "home" from Easton lips set off in my chest. I had things to take care of, and it seemed like I wouldn't have to do any of it alone.

Easton

"How's he doing?" I asked Patrice when he walked into my kitchen, looking completely worn out.

He sighed as he wrapped his arms around my waist, tired eyes flickering shut. When he opened them I could see the toll the last few hours had taken on him. "I don't know honestly. Yin's sister agreed that it was better for him to stay here until the storm calmed down. There's no way she's getting here from Trumansburg to get him in this weather, anyway. I gave them some space and said I'd be up here if they need anything. If that's all right with you, of course."

This night had turned out very different than I had planned, but having Patrice here, coming to me for a little comfort… I wouldn't change that for anything. I turned around and tightened my arms around his neck, locking us together in the warmth of my kitchen. "Of course it's fine," I said, rolling my eyes. "Like you don't know I'd happily have you here all day every day. Is Ari still eerily quiet?"

Another tired sigh. "Yeah, he's in worry overdrive. Worried about what's going to happen, worried about what Yin's sisters are going to think, worried about his papers…just worried about everything."

"I just talked to May again and they're just as worried about *him*, they're not angry. They see how Ari's with Yin." I smiled remembering May's words. "She said, 'he treats Yin like a precious snowflake.' That, if anything, he needs to spoil him less." That pulled out a small smile from Patrice's lips. "They know no one is more upset about this than Ari."

Patrice gave me that puzzled look he got sometimes and I thought he was going to tease me about OD-ing on my own positivity, but instead he bent down to kiss me. He pressed his lips against mine. It was such a slow and chaste kiss compared to how we usually came together. But the way his fingers dug into my back made the stress of the day start to feel a bit less oppressive. I placed my hand at the nape of his neck and felt the prickle of his locs brushing against the back of my hand.

I groaned, wanting more, but Patrice wasn't letting us get revved up. He was giving me this slow, gentle kiss and I was going to have to take it.

When we pulled apart, he had that same look from earlier, like things were getting too deep too fast and he wasn't sure if it was good or a bad thing. "How do you know Yin's sisters?"

He asked the question like he already knew, or suspected the answer. I turned back around and fussed a bit with what I was doing. I picked up a piece of pumpkin, wondering when Patrice would notice the ingredients that were scattered all over the kitchen counter.

"I just helped her out when they first came," I said, peeling another chunk of pumpkin. "I can't give too many details, but it was a tough situation. I'm glad she was able to walk away from it." I was not going to disclose about the violent boyfriend who threatened her and her siblings for months.

He ran a hand over my shoulder and said, "I can respect that." He sounded curious, but I knew he'd leave it at that.

After another moment, he gasped and came to stand right next to me. "What are you making?" he asked, as if he could not quite believe what he was seeing.

I looked up, feeling really awkward now, wondering if the second part of my failed romantic date would also be a bust. I put down the vegetable and lifted my eyes to him.

"I'm making Soup Joumou?" It wasn't a question, it was what I was making, but now I felt like an idiot for trying to make his traditional dish as a surprise. He was still saying nothing, his eyes assessing the ingredients scattered all over the counter.

"I thought it would be nice since it's—"

He moved so fast that I had to lift my arms to the sides so I didn't stain him with my hands. This kiss was one of *our* kisses. Teeth, tongue and fire. He sucked on my lip as he dug his hands into me. I felt like I was sinking and he kept lifting me up.

I pulled back, gasping for air, and the way he was looking at me was going to make it very hard for me to get back to soup making. "You're making Joumou from scratch?"

"Yes?"

He laughed then and held my face in his hands, kissing me hard again. "Stop answering everything like you're asking a question."

I laughed, feeling flustered, but so glad that I'd made him laugh in the middle of all this stress. "I *am* asking, because I'm pretty sure I'm going to mess it up. I looked for recipes, and it all seemed so straightforward, but now I'm kind of lost and there's a large amount of pumpkin to peel." I looked around at all the stuff I needed to get done for this soup and felt my earlier enthusiasm starting to wilt. "I could not find the Scotch Bonnet peppers that go in the soup anywhere and this might end up being more of a breakfast type of thing."

He rolled the sleeves of his sweatshirt back and stood next to me, extending his hand. "I'll peel. I have years of experience, you get the other stuff ready. With the two of us we'll have it ready before Ari and Yin come downstairs asking for dinner." His smile faltered a little bit when he mentioned Ari, but he seemed in better spirits.

I nodded and reached for the limes and oranges I needed to juice for the marinade. "You peel and I cook."

When I looked over my shoulder I caught him giving my ass a very thorough assessment.

"See something you like, professor?" I asked, certain that the response would probably derail our food preparations.

He leaned down and nibbled my ear, making me run the risk of severing a finger. "I'm gonna rail you tonight, you know that right?"

I chuckled as I halved limes and tried to talk without sounding completely breathless. "That was the only part of my failed seduction attempt I was pretty sure I could count on."

Patrice's laugh rang all over my kitchen as we worked together and I felt so happy it almost scared me.

Chapter Seventeen

Patrice

It had been the longest week in fucking history, but somehow Nesto had managed to stay on track and Ou-NYe's first annual fundraiser for local social services agencies was happening tonight. I was meeting Easton at the courthouse, and we were supposed to walk there together.

Things with Ari had calmed down. He was still staying with me, but the plan was to find him a place. Harold Sheridan, Nesto's business partner, was making noise about helping him with school and Easton had offered him a studio in our building for almost nothing. The lawyer he'd gotten for him was great and Ari seemed to be slowly getting out of the funk he'd been in after that mess with his uncle. The man had made no attempt to get in touch with him in the week since he'd been staying with me, which told me him getting out of there had been the right move.

I'd seen again and again how people had come out to take care of Ari. The community that Nesto had found here in Ithaca had supported Ari in every way he needed. Despite the issues in town, and there were many, this place had come through in a big way for one of its own. I also felt like I'd been a part of that effort, that I was already part of the tapestry here somehow. Like I could make a place for myself here.

I should've known that the warm and fuzzy feeling wouldn't last long. While I was trying to get into the courthouse, I stopped in my tracks as the bailiff looked me up and down a few times while I tried not to suck my teeth.

"Can I help you, sir?"

"I'm here for the trial." Polite, calm. I didn't need to get heated.

He gave me another thorough once-over as I put my wallet and watch into a little bin on the conveyor belt. I was still not sure what was happening, because the guy was certainly interested in me. I was not looking for a reason to get mad today, so I kept it moving. When I got to the other side, he stared at me like he was going to say something, but at the last minute just waved me through.

When I started heading for the elevators he pointed to the marble staircase at the center of the courthouse. "Courtroom is on the second floor. I think they're wrapping up."

I thanked him and took the stairs. Once I found the courtroom I quietly walked to the back. It was a huge space with dizzyingly high ceilings, and still the air was crackling with tension.

As I sat down on of the wooden benches, I tuned into Easton's booming voice. I didn't really look up until I'd settled into my seat, but when I zeroed in on him, he seemed to be in complete control of the room. He was in one of his Tom Ford suits, hair, shoes, tie, everything perfectly in place as he addressed the jury. Hands in his pockets, body relaxed and casual, but his words were strident. He was talking about the victim, about what her life had been like before she was assaulted, what her life was like now. The strength it took for her to seek justice. After a breath, his relaxed pose turned more commanding. As if to say, "I'm done taking it easy on you."

When he spoke again, every word was an edict. "I ask today that you take the duty this court gives you and deliver the justice Ms. Suarez deserves."

With that, he ended his summation and in two long strides was back at his table. Every person in the room seemed to cut off the imaginary strings he'd kept us on as he talked. Easton had completely commanded our attention and now that the moment ended, we could all take a breath.

That's when I realized it. This is where it all went. The fierceness, the fury, the intensity, he put it all into this. His work was where Easton unleashed all that passion I got to see, but that he rarely showed elsewhere. I finally realized that, like me, Easton kept his true self tightly under wraps, only a precious few got to ever see who he really was.

I sat there letting it sink in as the judge gave the jury their instructions for deliberation, before concluding for the day. As people started gathering their things and the twelve tasked with delivering justice were ushered away, I moved up the aisle to go talk to Easton. As I got to him I saw an older black woman, come to give him a hug, which he returned. There were people walking around him but it was like he didn't even realize they were there, his attention completely on her. They stepped out of the room, talking quietly, not noticing my approach.

By the time I caught up with him, she was giving him another hug and openly crying. He tightened his arm around her, and I could see he was working hard not to cry too. He watched her walk away, his shoulders tense, like the weight of the world was settled right between them.

I wasn't sure what I thought Easton did in this building every day. But right then was when it sunk in. People counted on him to right wrongs every single day and he stepped up to that challenge. He somehow handled it all and still managed to be how he was, who he was.

I touched his arm lightly and he startled at the touch. "Hey."

As soon as he saw me his eyes lit up and he almost pushed up for a kiss, but at the last moment just tapped me on the shoulder.

"You were something in there." I pointed my chin in the direction I'd seen the woman go. "Was that lady related to Ms. Suarez?"

He nodded with a sigh as he lifted a hand, indicating we head up the stairs. "That's her mom." He spoke so low I had to bend down to hear him. "She's pretty amazing, put herself through nursing school while taking care of three kids on her own." His eyes softened as he talked about the woman. "I hope we did what we needed to do in there," he said, shaking his head.

As we got to the landing he pointed at a door that read District Attorney's Office.

"I just have to grab my stuff. Everyone in the office is headed to Nesto's thing, so we all agreed that we'll reconvene some time tomorrow. The jury is not deliberating until Monday morning. It's a waiting game for a few days."

He sounded tired, and I knew he was probably exhausted. I'd slept at his place for the last few nights, and every morning he'd been up and out by 4:30 a.m. He'd go for a quick workout at the gym in the building and would be in his office by 5:30 a.m. I was pretty intense about my gym time, but even I couldn't keep up with Easton's hours.

"You're exhausted," I said as we walked through a cluttered mess of cubicles and offices.

He lifted a shoulder, the smudges under his eyes more noticeable in the bad fluorescent lighting. "I'll just be a minute. I'd give you a tour of the office, but all we have is piles of paper and bad carpeting."

He wasn't lying.

I thought my small office in the economics building was a blast from the past, but this made my office-in-a-box seem sleek and modern in comparison.

The entire space looked like it hadn't been renovated since the seventies. Clearly a place where people were too busy to think about décor.

It was not how I'd envisioned where Easton spent his days.

I'm not sure why I thought that someone who worked for the county would have an office that looked like a Wall Street law firm, but that's what I'd imagined. Now, walking into his small and cluttered office, painted in a very non-pleasing bright blue, the reality of who Easton Archer was hit me. He had opted into this. Knowing the family he came from, I was almost certain there was an empty office somewhere decorated in sleek leather, hardwood and chrome he could've claimed. That he walked away from, to do this.

"Why are you looking at me like that?" Easton's puzzled tone snapped me back from my errant thoughts.

"Like what?" I asked, perfectly aware that I'd been staring.

"Like you're trying to crack a code," he said as he got his coat on. His brow furrowed at whatever face I'd been pulling.

"Not a code. I was trying to figure *you* out."

"Me?" he asked, as if I'd said something terrifying.

"Yes. You." I lifted my shoulders as I leaned on the wall waiting for him, and decided to say something that I'd needed to say for a long time. "I was just thinking that you're sort of an outlier. The more I know, the more I like you. Which is generally not the case."

"Well thank goodness for that," he joked, and stepped up to me and smoothly closed the door to his office. His eyes looked tired, but that ever-present playfulness was there. When he leaned in to kiss me he ran his hand behind my neck. I sighed into his mouth, tongues caressing, a reconnection after a long day.

When he pulled back he seemed normal again.

My sunny man.

"I needed that." He sounded like he'd just taken a bite of the most decadent dessert. "Now let's go to this fundraiser."

He looked a little hesitant when he said it, and that surprised me. "You don't want to go?"

He sighed as we made our way to the elevator, then turned to me, speaking quietly. "Of course I want to be there. I wouldn't let Nesto down." His gaze dipped and when he looked up he had the unhappy expression that appeared anytime a particular subject came up.

"Are you parents going to be there?"

He lifted a shoulder in response and we moved to get into the elevator. "I'm not sure, I haven't talked to them, but my sister will be there. She heads all the philanthropic efforts for the winery, so they may not come. But OuNYe's is the new hot place in town and knowing them, I wouldn't be surprised if they're there."

I was expecting to feel freaked out or uneasy about meeting Easton's parents, but as we waved at the bailiffs who greeted Easton as if he were their favorite person that feeling of protectiveness took over again. I grabbed his hand as we walked onto the rainy sidewalk and hurried along the two blocks to Nesto's restaurant. The temperatures had risen since the snowstorm the week before, but the rain still felt like ice on my skin.

Easton didn't say anything but tightened his hand around mine. "You're so quiet tonight."

He looked at me and I could see again just how tired he was. "It's not because of my parents. I'm always like this after we wrap up a trial. I sort of run through everything in my head a dozen times, trying to figure out where we fucked up. It's how I keep my expectations in check. I need to be prepared for disappointment because I have to face the families after and I can't go to them feeling like the outcome came out of nowhere."

"I get that, I hope that jury does right by her."

After a second Easton lifted his head and glanced up at me. "How are things at work? Are things still good?"

I nodded, glad to see the restaurant was near. "Yeah." The meeting with the dean had gone a lot better than I'd thought. He'd basically called me in to ask if I wanted to be involved in a task force looking at implicit bias in the faculty, which I did not expect. "Task force thing is moving surprisingly fast."

"Good," Easton said, as we arrived.

Nesto, as expected, had drawn a crowd. I knew Jude and his best friend Carmen had been helping him with the planning and the place looked great. The usual crowd of college students and young professionals that frequented OuNYe had been replaced by very wealthy-looking and older people. As we walked in, I once again took a moment to look around my friend's restaurant. The place was lit by vintage lamps hanging from the high ceilings. On the red walls were enormous aerial photos of the islands Nesto, Camilo, Juanpa and I came from. I glanced over at the gigantic photo of one of my favorite places in Haiti, the old fort on the northern tip of the island called Cap Haitien.

I was still bowled over by what Nesto had done and how he was honoring all our roots with this place. Nesto had built all this with his hard work and being tenacious. Like he always said, we really were our ancestor's wildest dreams.

Easton let go of my hand as he took his own look around and pointed his chin in the direction where Nesto had placed a coat checker. We spotted my best friend too, and as soon as he saw us, he grabbed Jude's hand and made a beeline toward us, a big grin on his face.

He came in close to give me dap as Jude smiled at us, waiting for his turn to say hello. Nesto gave Easton a pat on the shoulder and angled his head in the direction of the courthouse. "I heard you kicked ass in court today. Cindy's around here somewhere, she came in buzzing about how she's going to make you run for DA." Easton groaned as Nesto and Jude both grinned.

"If you're not up for it, you better let Cindy know now, Easton, because she looked like she was going to make the official announcement," Jude said with humor. "I feel your pain too. Cindy's like an older version of Carmen, pushy and selectively hard of hearing when people don't want to do what she says." Jude's commiserative tone pulled a smile out of Easton, who lifted a shoulder before answering.

"I've been handling Cindy since I was fifteen. The key is waiting her out," Easton said with a grin, but the way he looked, I knew he wasn't amused about Cindy talking about it publicly. Before I could ask, Nesto pointed the drink he was holding toward me.

"You haven't met Cindy yet, P?" he asked with a glint in his eye that made me think that was probably a good thing.

"Not yet," I said as I bumped Easton's shoulder. "But I've heard a lot about her."

"I'm not even going to ask if any of it was good, because I know how this demon likes to slander me." The voice came from somewhere behind me, and when I turned around I saw a tall and slender middle-aged woman with a crew cut and no-nonsense pantsuit giving me an impish smile. She extended a hand to me at the same time that she put her arm around Easton's shoulders.

"You must be the man that's brought my best prosecutor to distraction. Cindy Grey." I almost laughed at Easton's pained groan and extended my hand to her, unsure of how to respond.

"Patrice Denis."

Cindy rolled her eyes at Jude and Nesto, who were standing there looking incredibly entertained. "Oh, I know who you are. Believe me," she said, giving Easton, who was beet red, some side eye.

Easton exhaled and looked at her with an equal mixture of fondness and frustration. "Cindy, why?" I actually cracked a smile at his exasperation. "Also, what are you doing out, aren't you supposed to be resting?"

That got him another look of fond exasperation. "I'm here with Lorraine. We wanted to stop by, and support this wonderful event," she said as Nesto preened. "We're heading out soon."

She leaned in closer to me, as if to share a secret, but when she spoke everyone could hear her. "I don't know what you've been doing lately, but keep it up. This one's practically skipping into the office these days. I might actually get him to agree to run for DA."

This elicited another groan from Easton and a laugh from the rest of us. "I'll try."

Before she could embarrass Easton any more she waved goodbye and walked off toward the door where a short woman with white curly hair was waiting for her.

Jude shook his head and smiled, watching them leave the restaurant. "She's playing hardball with the DA thing, Easton. She might wear you down."

I looked over to see his reaction and noticed he seemed uneasy. I wasn't sure if it was about Cindy, the DA thing or about his parents. "She's been on me about it for weeks." He lifted a shoulder then and gave me a look I was not entirely sure I understood. "We'll see."

When we'd talked about it weeks ago he didn't seem very into the idea and the way he was still looking at Cindy made me think he still felt the same way. I wondered if he hadn't talked more about it with me because he thought I'd be put off by it. If I was honest, I wasn't sure how I felt about it. Thankfully, before I could go down a rabbit hole of worry over something I had no control over, Nesto spoke up.

"P, did you talk to Ari today?" Nesto's face had the concerned parent look he got anytime we discussed Ari.

I shook my head as I glanced around the room, trying to spot my mentee. "No, I left early for campus and didn't see him." I wasn't going to say that I'd stayed at Easton's for the fourth night in six days, and that I didn't even make it to my place this morning.

"That's cool, man," Nesto said. "No big, he's just staying with Jude and me this weekend. Last weekend at the Farmer's Market for the season and he wants to be close to the kitchen since he's in charge of the truck now." Nesto always talked about Ari like a proud dad.

I nodded and looked at Easton, who still seemed a bit flustered from Cindy's teasing. "Sounds good, man."

Nesto angled his head in the direction of the kitchen. "I gotta go check on the food." He turned to Jude then. "Baby, can you go take one last look around to see that everything's set to go for the silent action?"

Jude nodded and pushed up to give Nesto a kiss on the mouth. "Sure." Those two had been together for almost two years, and still could barely stand to go for a few minutes without touching. I turned to look at Easton and tried not to read too much into the wistful expression on his face.

"Thanks for coming, brother," Nesto said, pulling me in for dap.

"Like you would let my ass stay home," I grumbled.

He laughed as he clapped his palm against Easton's. "True. Easton, you know you're in your house, man."

Jude waved at us too as he and his man walked off.

Easton and I stood there in a corner of the crowded restaurant, too close to not be together, but not close enough that people would label us as a couple offhand like they would with Jude and Nesto. Those two could be on opposite sides of the room and you could see they were a unit. It was like they had an invisible thread that tied them together.

I thought about how it would be to get there with Easton. It's not as if I didn't feel that drawn to him. The issue was letting it show. To let the whole world know he was mine. I wasn't exactly surprised to notice that between reluctance and yearning to have that, the latter feeling won out.

"You're certainly deep in thought." Easton's voice was curious and when I glanced at him I found him looking at me as if he knew what I'd been thinking.

"Nah, just taking everything in." He didn't look very convinced about my answer.

I was about to deviate the subject to Cindy's comment about him running for DA when I saw Easton's eyes widen and then heard him groan as an older couple headed in our direction. The woman had platinum-blond hair coiffed to perfection. She was dressed expensively, almost but not quite too formal for the occasion, and was very petite. I'd recognize those green eyes anywhere though. Easton took after his father, because the man walking toward us could've been my lover in thirty years.

Easton's entire demeanor changed by the time they reached us. His mother spoke first, as she leaned in to air kiss him hello. "We weren't sure you'd make it, darling."

"We thought you'd have to stay late at that place with everything you seem to have going on this week." That was his dad, voice heavy with disapproval. I assumed he was talking about the trial Easton had been killing himself over for months now, but from his tone you'd think he was running heroin up and down the Eastern corridor. He just bent down and kissed his mother's cheek, then responded in a jovial tone.

"I was able to slip away," he informed his father, who'd been giving me a long look. "Father."

"And who's this?" Easton's eyes widened when his father asked the question and then turned his head so he was fully facing me. When Easton turned around, his expression was completely blank, like he barely could recall who I was. I had yet to see that expression on his face. I was sure that for him to do his job he'd probably learned to master not showing his emotions, but he'd never done that with me. From the first moment I'd met him I'd always been able to see exactly how he felt about me. Now, with his eyes seeming to go right through me, it was like a gut punch.

Before he spoke, he moved so that there was some distance between us. He extended a hand toward me and kept his eyes on his parents. "This is Dr. Denis, he's one of the new faculty at the Cornell economics department. He's also best friends with Ernesto, OuNYe's owner." He blankly glanced at me for a second before speaking. "These are my parents, Anne and Easton Archer Jr."

I shook their hands, still not sure what was going on with Easton. I knew things with his parents were strained, but he seemed to have morphed into a different person. It was like he could barely stand to look at me.

I was about to excuse myself when Anne spoke, her tone pleasant while her eyes did a very thorough assessment of me. "Dr. Denis, how are you finding our little town? Must be a shift from urban life." Her tone was pleasant enough, but *urban life*? What the fuck was that supposed to mean?

My back almost went up at that, but years in the Ivy League meant I'd had many a run-in with Anne Archer types, nice ladies who had a very interesting idea of how a black man got to be in places where they didn't "usually belong." Easton, on the other hand, seemed to get tenser with every word exchanged.

"It's Patrice, and Ithaca has been fine so far, ma'am. Thank you for asking." Again I kept my tone polite. Odette had not raised me to be anything other than painfully polite to women like Anne. Not a word, not a look, not a *hair* out of place.

Easton Archer Jr. spoke next, and he didn't bother to pretend he was doing anything other than sizing me up. "Where are you from, Dr. Denis?"

I wasn't exactly sure what he wanted to hear, but I was not in the mood to make people comfortable today. "I'm Haitian, sir. I came to the US with my mother when I was young." I turned my eyes to see what Easton was doing and he looked like he was going to be sick.

Did he think I was going to embarrass him or something?

I gave myself and internal nudge, to finish answering Easton dad's question. "We came seeking asylum in '91 when I was about six years old. I'm fortunate I came at a time when refugees were still welcome."

I got two variations of those kinds of smiles people give you when they're not really sure what you are, while Easton made a sound like he was in pain.

Easton's mom gave him another look and it seemed like she was finally putting two and two together, and the way her face changed told me she wasn't really happy with the information. "Your parents must be really proud of you." She said it in a way that made it clear she was not feeling the same way about her own offspring.

Easton's dad jumped in then, to continue the Twenty Questions game. He eyed me up and down before speaking. "It must've been quite a change for you to come to the US."

I nodded at his comment and tried to come up with something to say, feeling like wherever this conversation was going was not a place I wanted to be. "Well I've lived here most of my life," I said, working very hard not to roll my eyes. "It is different, better in many ways, but I missed Haiti, I still do. We left a lot behind."

"Oh?"

I almost laughed at the surprised expression on both their faces when I said that. Like the fact that I would miss my homeland was completely crazy.

Easton started fidgeting then. "I'm sure Dr. Denis has other people to talk to."

Like I was going to leave him alone with these two.

"I'm not in a rush. Everyone will be here for a while," I said, noticing Easton did not seem relieved at all by my response, but before I could process his reaction, his mom took another turn.

"Well, but look at you now. Having achieved so much. I'm sure it's nice to be able to help your family with all your education." She sounded genuinely glad for me when she said it, but there was something in the way she talked to me, like she could not quite figure out how I was here.

"Well, like I said, it's just me and my mother here, and she was an amazing role model. I had a lot to look up to at home."

"No father in the picture, then." This was Easton's dad. I'd always thought the expression "doing a double take" was a figure of speech, but my head actually swiveled.

Anne made a sound almost like a protest, but didn't call her husband on his rude fucking comment.

At least it got Easton to finally look at me like he knew who I was. He seemed like he was about to say something to his father, but I didn't let him speak. I was perfectly capable of dealing with this particular type of bullshit.

"No, Mr. Archer, there was no father in the picture. He was busy taking care of his wife and kids, so my mother and I had to come here on our own." I looked at Easton then, locking eyes with him and in this place packed with people I voiced something I rarely said out loud. I never took my eyes off him, making sure he knew that I was not ashamed of where I came from. "My mother was my father's mistress, so when things got dicey, he decided we were not a priority." I lifted a shoulder, trying hard for an unbothered air that did not match up with the pounding in my chest. "We did just fine without him."

Easton's eyes were wide, like he had no idea what to do, but I wasn't going to wait around to hear whatever scathing comment his parents would come up with next. "Excuse me."

I moved past, without looking at any of them, and went to find the nearest exit. I walked out into the frigid November night and tried to take a deep breath.

I felt small. Not because of whatever had come out of Easton's parents' mouths. That shit I was used to. People looking at me and making assumptions. Going on whatever headline they've read about my country and using that to tell me who I was.

People sometimes commented about how I always had this air of disinterest, aloofness. I wished I could just tell them how much it took to let people talk to me like this, the anger and humiliation I constantly had to snuff out.

I kept replaying how Easton had acted. Like he wanted to put as much distance between us as possible. Like he didn't want them to know we were together.

That had hurt.

I didn't even know why I was surprised. I knew this was bound to happen. No matter how much Easton wanted to act all woke and shit, he was from one place and I was from another. The minute his family showed up, he iced me out and acted like he barely knew me.

I wanted to leave. Go back to my place, lick my wounds, but I stood there on that cold sidewalk shivering. I almost considered walking home like this, until the biting cold reminded me that no matter how upset I was, my ass was going to freeze out here without a coat. But when I turned to do the walk of shame back to the crowded restaurant to get it, I almost crashed into Easton. He was standing there with my coat, scarf and hat in his hand.

He stepped up to me and when I saw his face, he looked wrecked.

"I'm sorry."

I wanted to be able to push him away, to act like I didn't give a shit about whatever it was that had happened in there. But instead I did the one thing that I swore I'd never do ever again. I let Easton know how much he'd hurt me.

"So, you know me now?" I asked, shoving my arms into my coat, and feeling so fucked up I could barely untangle what was going on with me.

"Patrice, just let me explain—"

I shook my head, and tried hard not to raise my voice. "I don't need you to explain to me what I already saw. It's all well and good until the disapproving parents are around, huh?" I said, snapping my head up and down. "Good to know."

I walked away leaving him there. I had turned the corner to head home, to the building Easton fucking owned, when I heard him yelling after me. "Patrice, wait. Fuck."

Instead of ignoring him like I wanted to, my fucking feet would not move, so I stood there, waiting for him. I opened my mouth to let him know again that I wasn't doing this with him. But as soon as he got within a few feet from me he started talking.

"Let me talk. Please." He was begging me, and fuck if I could do anything other than stand there quietly, hoping that whatever he said gave me enough of an excuse not to give him up.

He raised a hand toward the restaurant, an agonized expression on his face. "You saw how they are. That's how my father talks to people. Like he's entitled to say whatever he wants. And my mother's—" His face twisted in a distasteful expression. "If I would've said you and I were together it would've been worse." He exhaled in frustration, and when I looked closely I saw how embarrassed and hurt he looked. "This is how they are. My father lives to disapprove of everything I do, and my mother never calls him on any of it." He ran his fingers over his eyes and answered before I could ask what that meant.

"I don't know why he's like that, I've sure as fuck never asked. Maybe it's the gay thing, or the fact that I have no interest in being part of the 'Archer Dynasty,'" he said, using air quotes for the last two words.

"I don't know, but whenever he sees I've found something that makes me happy, that I care about, he wants to ruin it. That whole time they were talking I realized I was afraid that they'd say something that would taint things between us. That if spoke I'd make it worse. I don't want to hurt you with my words *or* with my silence, Patrice, and I'm still working on that." His eyes pleaded with me as I stood there trying to process what he'd said.

I went from annoyed, to mad, to feeling like all the anger had seeped out of me in the span of a few seconds. When I locked eyes with Easton I felt that once again he was letting me see everything. That I was being given something that I should not squander. He looked alone and miserable, and I could either let his father's disgusting behavior be an excuse for letting him down, or I could step up.

"All I've ever wanted was for you to *see me*, just me. The thing is that I come with a history that I can't, that I won't shed." I pointed to the restaurant. "Your parents are not the only people that see me and create some story in their heads of how I got here, like something from a movie. And honestly I don't care if they do, but with you, I need you to see all of it, and fuck, sometimes wish it didn't even matter, but it does."

"Of course it matters. I don't want pieces of you, I want all of it and it should not be on you to have to spoon feed it all to me. I have to learn so that when I come to you, I have clarity of exactly how fucking lucky I am to be with a man like you."

I pulled him to me until I had him up against the icy side of the building.

"You can't just let me be mad for a minute can you? I'm sorry that your parents make you feel like that. It's not fair that you need to run interference for their rudeness," I said with my mouth so close to his ear my lips kept pushing into it. "And don't think I don't have reason to feel lucky too."

He scoffed at that and looked at me with a flinty expression. "I wasn't going to let you think that I was embarrassed of you or didn't want them to know we were together. That what my parents thought had any bearing on what I want with you."

The shit that came out of Easton's mouth, like he wasn't putting my entire life on a different course with every word.

"What you want with me." It was more of a question than a statement, but at times like this it almost felt easier just to let the tide of Easton's faith in whatever it was we were doing pull me in. I'd gasp my way back to shore later...or not. "I'm not sure how Anne and Easton Archer Jr. would feel about having me at their Thanksgiving table."

"I don't give a fuck about my parents' opinion on this. I just need to stop trying to overcompensate for their piss-poor behavior with fake politeness." He lifted an ungloved hand and gripped the back of my coat, bringing us closer. "As for what I want with you. You know perfectly well that nothing would make happier than all of fucking Ithaca knowing that you're mine. But I know how you are."

He huffed the words out as he pulled me down for a kiss, and his tongue was like a fucking drug. Everything just dulled around me when he was kissing me like this, dirty and so fucking slow. Sucking on my lips, running his tongue down my neck until my dick was so hard I felt it would pop out of my trousers.

My breath hitched, as he bit on my earlobe his hand rubbing my cock, hard. "Why don't you tell me how I am Easton, because I swear I thought I did before I met you."

"Stubborn and in denial." That was said with his hot mouth against my ear.

We should've gone inside and joined the party again. But by the time Easton ran a hand up my chest and sucked on my lip, I knew the only thing happening next was fucking.

Easton really did test every single of one of my limits until they broke. Because I was out here on the damn street as close to public indecency as I'd ever been. And yet the only thing running through my head was how many more minutes it would be before I had him naked and panting on my bed.

Out of nowhere, he started talking again. That hot tongue like a fucking fire iron on my skin. "You're defensive, assume the worst and don't give people the benefit of the doubt. Still I hate that I had to be a reason for you to go to a bad place, or to think for even a second, I'm not crazy about you." I tried to pull back, but that dirty low-down playing fucker literally grabbed me by the balls.

I gasped, as he lifted onto his tiptoes, so that we were eye to eye. "Yeah, I said it. What are you going to do about it?"

I had my arms stretched over him, covering him completely, and feeling wild. "I don't know, Easton. You're the one with my dick in your hand."

He sucked on my lip, bringing my head down. His filthy chuckle rumbling between us.

"I think we need to continue this in private. There's too much hate-fuck energy happening here, and I don't want to get arrested when I have a jury out deliberating."

I had to laugh, because this motherfucker really had my number. "So is this how you do it? Get people so addled that they do what you want."

That feline smile he gave me was new and completely devastating, and fuck if I could walk away.

"You tell me. *Are* we good?"

"Like I can stay mad with you sucking on my lip and working my dick like that." He gave me that shameless laugh that kept me all tripped up on him. Without saying a word, I pushed off the wall and pulled him up the street to our building.

Chapter Eighteen

Patrice

We walked into Easton's house in silence, but the tension from the last hour had turned into something else. That conversation with his parents had made me feel exposed in ways that I had to take time to process. But when Easton wrapped one arm around my neck and slid the other one into my briefs, all thought flew out of my mind, and my life's purpose became how fast I could get him out of all these fucking clothes.

"Ungh, I want it." He moaned into my ear, as he wrapped his hand around my dick.

I had to take a couple of deep breaths, before I could even respond. "Baby, the sounds you make."

He gasped again, his eyelids flickering open. His pupils were blown out and he looked starved. "Why is it that I go a little crazy when you call me baby?" he asked, sounding legitimately surprised. "I usually hate endearments or cute nicknames. But whenever that comes out of your mouth, I'm caught hedging between melting into a puddle and begging you to fuck me."

I shook my head and laughed, as puzzled as he was.

I brought his mouth to mine again and let the bruising kiss be my answer.

He pulled back after a while, panting for breath, and walked me back to the couch, licking his lips as if he was trying to figure out where he was going to take the first bite from.

"Where are we going?"

He raised an eyebrow as he pushed me down. As soon as my ass hit the cushion he went down on his knees, every ounce of his focus on me.

I was *not* a romantic, but when Easton Archer looked at me like that I felt like I could invent a whole new life. Just so I could get to have him without conflicts or guilt, without the world getting in the way of this joy.

I'd always liked sex, and took pride in being a good sexual partner, but it had never been a place of joy for me. My chest tightened at the unbridled want I saw in his eyes, the urgency of his hands tightening around my thighs as he ran them over me, like he could barely hold himself back.

I placed one hand on his cheek. I needed to touch him. Easton was vibrating, and without saying a word dove for my cock. He took the head in his mouth, sucking it hard, just like I liked it, making my eyes roll.

When he pulled off he nosed at my crotch with his eyes closed, complete bliss on his face. "I'm shamelessly obsessed with your cock." He said it so matter-of-fact as he pulled on the waistband of my pants and briefs.

I laughed as I sank into the couch, throwing my head backward, already so close to losing it with Easton's hand and tongue on me. "I'm pretty into that mouth of yours—"

My words got cut short by the mind-melting sensation of Easton taking me to the hilt.

"Fuck you can suck dick," I said, thrusting into his mouth as he circled the base of my dick with his index and thumb and sucked me down, the pressure so good, so perfectly tight I had to grip the back of the couch to hold off the orgasm. He worked that mouth up and down, taking me deep, and pulling off so he could tongue the slit.

I gritted my teeth as he did his best to make me lose it. When I got myself back under control, I opened my eyes to find him looking amused. I clicked my tongue, totally taking the bait. I knew how much he loved when I ran my mouth. "Such a whore for a compliment, even with your mouth full of cock."

That made him double down and soon I was gasping for air. He took me down so deep, I could barely hold back from fucking hard into his mouth, but even with the controlled thrusts I was almost coming. When he swallowed around me, I lost it. My entire body went cold and I lost myself to the fireworks going off behind my eyes as Easton took everything I had. I opened my eyes just as he was climbing onto my lap. He looked like a fucking wet dream, wiping the back of his hand over his mouth, lips cherry red and swollen.

"Did my mouth live up to its reputation?"

The fact that he sounded hoarse from taking my dick was almost enough to make me want to try CPR on it so I could move right on to fucking him.

I groaned as I grabbed the back of his neck to get on that tongue. "You are truly gifted."

He gave me that grin that usually meant he was about to say something outrageous. It was almost like he did it so I'd shove my cock or my tongue into him to shut him up. Before he got a word out I pushed off the couch, holding him up with one hand and hiking my pants up with the other.

When I started up the spiral stairs to his room, he bit my ear and I could feel his grin when he grazed my skin. "If it wasn't complete torture for me I'd almost wish we would've run into my parents sooner, because this level of hotness can only mean you're about to fuck me like you mean it."

It was hard to laugh when I trying to carry him up a windy set of stairs. "I always mean it, and are you trying to get us killed? I'm trying to go up these stairs blind."

"Am I wrong though?"

I smacked his ass hard as we reached the landing. "You're a brat," I answered as I watched him skin out of all his clothes in the time it took me to get out of my sweater.

"I'd try to address it, but you seem to enjoy it," he said, as he crawled to the center of the gigantic mattress. I took a moment to look at him, the lightness in his movements, the glint in his eyes. The way he could bounce back from anger or resentment…how being with him was making me that way too.

By the time I was naked, he was sprawled on the bed, one hand stroking his cock and the other one pinching a nipple. I was still recovering from that blow job, but seeing Easton looking like he was more than ready for me to dick him out was making mine want to get back online, fast.

"You better take it slow, I thought you wanted me to fuck you."

He shuddered out a breath as he spread his legs

wider. "But you're taking too long. Come on, touch me." He kept stroking his dick and now had one hand playing with his balls. His teeth biting down hard on his bottom lip.

"Patience, I have plans for you." He shivered again, his eyes glomming me up as I moved around the room.

I kept my eyes on him as I went to the table by his bed where he kept his toys. I stuck my hand in the drawer but kept my eyes on Easton. I leaned down to run my hand up his chest, stopping right at the base of his neck, where I could feel his pulse. I kept it there as his breathing got faster, and started pulling out toys from the drawer one-handed. Every time one dropped on the mattress, the thud made his breath hitch. Still he didn't turn his head to look at what I was doing, eyes locked with mine.

When I opened my mouth to speak what came out was nothing more than a growl. "Are you going to let me use these on you, baby?"

His answer was barely audible. "Please."

I took my eyes off him to pick up a bright blue silicone dildo I'd seen in the drawer. "You want it so bad." He nodded, swallowing hard. "Lift your legs. I want to see that hole, get it ready for me. I'm going work this ass, stretch it out for me, and then I'm going to fuck you, long and slow." I ran a hand over my cock, which was almost ready for a second round. "Make you take all this."

"Fuck, why do I love this toppy bullshit from you so much?"

He actually sounded pissed. I laughed at his frustrated expression. "You sound so aggravated," I said, leaning down again to kiss him. I pried his mouth open with my tongue, licking into it. I wanted to lose myself in Easton, forget every single one of the reasons why we couldn't work out and let this certainty I felt right now tell me what I wanted. I tried to pull off, still sucking on his bottom lip, but his hands were gripping me tight, like he couldn't bear to let me go.

"Patrice." He could barely talk, his voice high and needy.

"I'll take care of you, baby."

I pushed his legs back, exposing him to me, and ran a thumb over his entrance.

He shuddered out a breath and thrashed his head, as he let out a tortured moan. "You need something, baby?" Easton's expression was pure frustration as I pressed my thumb against his rim, not quite pushing in. "Stop teasing me, Patrice. Fuck me."

I laughed as I pumped some lube into my hand. "So greedy, baby. I haven't even started yet."

"It's your fault, I—"

His words go cut off when I pushed a lubed finger in, stretching him, now starting to feel desperate to have him too.

"Yesss, more," he begged, as I pushed in another one, he started those little moans and grunts that made my blood hot; all rational thought flew out of my head.

"I'm going to fuck you with this dildo first. So I can slide in, hit you right in that spot that makes you scream for me."

"Do it now." I propped a pillow under his ass, and without too much ceremony I pushed the lubed toy in, just a half inch, he sucked in a breath and on the exhale I pushed in further, then pulled back. I kept fucking him

with shallow thrusts, watching his face, his mouth slack and his eyes rolling back.

After a few more thrusts I licked my hand before taking his balls in my hands. From the first touch his already impossibly hard dick jumped up, the head leaking as I pushed in further. I leaned so I could lap at the bead of liquid. Making him scream.

"You're leaking for me. Fuck, you make me crazy when you get like this."

The sight of him thrashing on the bed as I fucked him with the dildo was making my own dick so hard, I wasn't sure how much I'd last.

"Patrice. Fuck me, fuck me, fuck me now."

I usually had a cooler head than this, but the way he said my name, like I was the only one who could give him what he needed, had me fumbling. After fucking him a couple more times with the dildo, I pulled it out and quickly got a condom on, my hands shaking as I got some lube on.

I pressed my dick right at his entrance and slid right in, he felt so fucking good. Every time with Easton felt like the first time.

"Fuuuuuuck, nothing has ever felt this good." As always, Easton just said what I was desperately trying to keep inside my mouth.

I watched myself pushing into him, the tight grip he had around me, and felt lightheaded from all the ways I was losing myself right now.

"Fuck me hard, Patrice. Come on, baby." He pressed both hands against the headboard and in one go had me in to the hilt. "Oh, I'm so full," he said as he moved that ass, impaling himself on my cock.

"Easton," I said, breathless. I started moving in earnest and pretty soon we were really fucking. Bodies rocking together in unison, and I felt my orgasm coming fast as Easton grabbed his dick and started working himself hard.

"Oh shit, I'm gonna come so hard," he said, his hand flying over his cock.

Just a few more pumps of his hand and I felt him spasm around me, making my climax barrel into me. I gasped as every nerve in my body seemed to short out at once. I let myself drop on him for a second as I carefully pulled out.

When I turned my head to look at him, I saw in his eyes the same thing I was feeling: totally fucking wrecked.

Easton

Being in Patrice's arms sometimes could feel like the most dangerous and safest place I'd ever been in. Lying here with him now, wrung out and warm, enveloped in his smell, in the sweaty mess we'd made, I felt happy.

I'd been certain that my parents had ruined things with Patrice tonight. When I saw his face after what my father said, I was convinced he would never want to see me again. I watched him walk out of the restaurant and I felt desperate. For the first time ever I'd actually called my parents on their behavior. I felt like I could walk out on them for good and I told them so. When I told my father he'd acted like an asshole he jerked his head back like I'd backhanded him. My mother literally pearl-clutching at my "my language," like she hadn't heard the shit my dad had said.

I walked away without even responding to her, not

sure I could keep from ruining Nesto's event if I did. The thought that my parents could've pushed Patrice away confirmed what he'd been worried about from the first moment. That our worlds were too different to ever work. That's why I'd rushed after him, terrified that if I waited I wouldn't be able to undo the damage my parents had done. That we'd go back to shaky ground if I didn't make it clear that my parents never ever spoke for me.

"Why did you accept my apology?" I asked into the darkness.

He stayed quiet for a long time, his breaths slow, but I knew he was awake. It took him a moment, eventually he answered. "I accepted it, because it wasn't right to punish you for what your father said. You didn't tell him to say any of that to me."

The answer didn't surprise me, Patrice had never been unfair. But there was something there. Tonight had been the second time he'd ever mentioned his father. Once again he'd made it very clear that there was no love lost there. And there was so much hurt in those fierce eyes whenever he looked at me and told me his secrets. The need to show me he wasn't ashamed of who he was. I remained quiet, hoping he'd feel safe enough in this small haven we'd made, to tell me more. To finally let me see some of his scars, like I'd let him see mine.

"I know what it's like to feel responsible for the actions of your father, and yet know you're helpless to make him change."

I moved so I could lay on top of him, my head on his chest and his legs spread wide, holding me between them. I turned so I could kiss him, my lips brushing the spot where his Haitian-American heart tattoo was.

I nodded and tried to respond as honestly as I could. "I wish I could just walk away, but there's my sister, my grandfather, family obligations. I feel like turning my back on them after they gave me so much, would be ungrateful." He brought his hands down then and ran them across my back, and if you took away the fucked-up conversation topic, it was pretty perfect.

"My mother always tells me to be grateful. To think that my father could've been like a lot of other wealthy men who father children they have no intention of taking responsibility for. That at least he helped us get out of Haiti. Helped me with school." His voice was hard and his hands, which had been so gentle on me a moment before, stopped moving. "As if every cent that my father gave us, my mother didn't pay for tenfold. As if she didn't have to humiliate herself many times over."

I tightened my arms around him as much as I could, wanting to let him talk, but also needing to comfort him. Because I *knew* this was not something he shared very often.

He let out a long exhale before he spoke, and when he did his voice was almost detached. "The last time I saw my father I was a junior in high school. He came to New York with his family for Christmas, and somehow sent my mother word of where he was staying."

I tried to use the most soothing voice I could manage when I spoke. "Was that the first time you saw him since you'd left Haiti?"

He let out a long breath, as if just the memory of it exhausted him. "Yeah, it was 2002, so things still felt a little fragile with 9/11 being so recent. Back then my mom was working two jobs so she could pay for her school and our bills. We were struggling big time. I mean we had food and could pay rent, but that was about it."

I didn't know what to say to that, because my family always had a lot of money. I had no idea what it was like to struggle like that. Patrice paused again and bent over to bring me closer to him, his strong arms lifting me effortlessly. When he'd kissed me and I was settled with my back against his chest, he started talking again. "The day we went to see him, my mom and I had gone to Milo and his mom's house so we could borrow money from Dinorah to pay the heating bill." He scoffed then and I felt his body tense. I also noticed that whenever he did that, he'd touch me or kiss me, as if it helped him calm down. It didn't escape me how free he was becoming with his touches and kisses. So far from the man I'd first encountered, who I'd have to coax into even a few words after the sex was over.

"All the way there she kept reassuring me that it would be fine, but I could tell she was nervous. Once we got to the hotel, I realized why. My father was staying at the Waldorf-Astoria. I felt sick when we got there and I realized that while my mom had to borrow money from a friend to keep our heat on, my dad was staying in one of the fanciest hotels in town."

"That's...pretty infuriating," I said, shaking my head.

He kissed my neck in response and my body once again was struggling to filter all the things happening to it. "Are you angry on my behalf, counselor?"

I turned around then so I could see him. "Of course I am. That's so fucked up, Patrice."

He didn't answer and did that silent and intense thing he always did, and sucked my lip into his mouth.

When he let go and I was panting again, I let out a frustrated breath. "It's so fucking hard to be righteously outraged about your father's fucked-up shit when you keep licking and sucking on me." I sounded aggravated and more than a little flustered, because I really was. "I should not be this turned on when you are clearly telling me something that is important to you."

He started shaking and I wondered if he was okay, and when I turned around the asshole was laughing at me.

I knelt in front of him, trying as hard as I could to contain my own smile. "This is serious. You're finally opening up to me, and it is not a laughing matter, Patrice Denis."

"Okay, bébé," he said, and I almost regretted pushing us to get back to the conversation, because he looked so content just then. And I wanted to keep him like that for a little longer.

I turned around again, knowing it'd be easier for him to say the rest if we were like this. "So we got there, and it was so awkward. I didn't know him very much, so the conversation went to what every conversation does with Afro-Latinx males. He commented on my muscles, asked if I had a girl and then ignored me. My um…" His voice changed then and his arms tightened around me, any humor completely gone now.

"He asked my mother to go up with him somewhere."

I wanted to sob for him, because I heard the shame clearly then.

"Baby," I said as I tried to turn, but he kept his arms on me and rested his forehead on the back of my head.

"Let's just stay like this," he pleaded. "She told me before we went there she wanted to ask him for some help with money for college, and knowing her, she would do whatever it took. When she left with him, I sat there feeling like my skin was crawling." His voice was clogged, and the need to turn around and hold him was so intense I shook in his arms. "When she came down, my father made a point of looking straight at me, as if to let me know this was how the world worked. Right as we were about to leave, I saw a woman and two teenage girls coming into the lobby, with a ton of shopping bags. He walked right over to them like we didn't exist. My mom and I just stood there until they went up to their room."

He sighed then, sounding exhausted. "My mom and I didn't say a word on the train, but a few days later she left a bank statement on my bed. He'd wired fifty grand to her, which in the end was not even a third of what we needed." He exhaled, voice strangled again. "As far as I'm concerned, he never gave me anything. My mother paid for every cent we ever got from that man."

"Can I turn around now?" I asked, needing to look at his face. He let go and I turned around so fast I almost elbowed him in the face.

I kissed him and wrapped my arms around his neck. "You're amazing and so is your mother. I can't even imagine. I'm so sorry my father disrespected you and your mother today like that."

"Bébé, don't look so sad. It happened a long time ago. It's done. I just wanted to tell you." He laughed then, and it was surprisingly carefree, lighter than I'd ever heard him before. "I hadn't told that story to anyone, not even Camilo, and that little fucker knows all my secrets."

"Thanks for trusting me with it."

The possessive way he pulled me to him made it so hard to tamp down the urge to tell him everything I was feeling, instead I smiled and nodded and kissed him again. I told him how much it meant to me that he shared that with me.

As we wound down and he fell asleep with his strong chest plastered to my back, my skin seared by the heat from his, I thought about the one thing I didn't say.

Chapter Nineteen

Patrice

"Why does the fucking world insist on cock-blocking my life?"

I bit back a smile as I made my way back up Easton's torso, which I'd been licking and biting on my way down to his dick. "It could be important," I said, trying not to laugh at the annoyed expression on his face.

"But it's not even six and I'm not on call, and you were doing *so well*." He grabbed his cock and stroked it as he looked at me. "I mean your tongue was really building up expectations. So…"

I didn't even answer and leaned down to kiss him again. I covered him with my body, arms on either side of his head, my hips circling in that way that drove him nuts as I licked into his mouth.

"You want me to swallow your cock, is that it, counselor?" He ran his foot over my calf and thigh, as he kissed me.

He pulled back and those green eyes were twinkling with mischief. "Well, I wouldn't turn that down, but you've been so accommodating this morning already."

Saturday I'd woken up expecting to feel stupid or

regretful about telling Easton about the stuff with my
father, or for him to treat me differently. I should've
known he wouldn't. He'd woken up in my arms and
gone straight to kissing and touching and telling me how
much he loved having me in his bed every morning.

Two days later everything still felt solid.

Just as I was about to tell him so, his work phone
went off and I knew whatever it was, it was important. I
sat up to let him get the phone from the table, he groaned
as he looked at the screen, and his face paled as soon as
he said hello. I wondered if it had something to do with
the trial. I knew the jury would not start deliberating
again until this morning, so it couldn't be the verdict.

"When?" he asked, his voice icy. "Fuck."

He turned so that he could get up from the bed. When
he looked at me, the way he could barely make eye
contact, made me grab my own phone from the side of
the table. I heard him hurry downstairs, his voice so
hushed I couldn't hear it. I didn't need to, as soon as I
opened the Twitter app on my phone I knew what the
call was about.

My mentions were out of control with people tweeting at me about another traffic stop. Apparently last
night police had stopped three young men on their way
back from a party, for a broken taillight. During the stop
something happened that resulted in one of them being
hospitalized. It was hard to get the exact details of what
happened, but people were outraged. There were calls
for the sheriff to resign and for charges to be brought
against the deputy involved. My pulse raced as I tapped
on tweets and headlines to get more information.

I got up from the bed, the bliss from the previous half
hour long forgotten, and started putting on my clothes

as I scrolled through my notifications. There was a DM from one of the local community groups asking me to join them in organizing a peaceful protest tomorrow I stood in Easton's bedroom looking out his picture window, it was too dark to see much but in the distance I could almost make out the outline of the clock tower. I held my phone loosely in my hand, and I hesitated. I knew that whatever Easton was talking about downstairs had to do with the reason for the protest I was being asked to help organize. A protest that would demand that the people in Easton's position take some action about what was happening. I almost tapped out a yes, but I hesitated. Instead I shoved my phone in my pocket and made my way downstairs.

I didn't need to know exactly how bad shit was, even though it was written all over Easton's face. He was standing in the middle of his living room with his eyes closed and his hands grasped tightly behind his head, looking spooked. When I got to him, he glanced up at me as I walked over to put my shoes on, his silence more telling than anything he could say.

I took a moment to finish getting dressed and pocket my wallet before I walked over to where he was. He looked like he was about to puke. I knew what he was feeling because I felt it too, the knot in my stomach that told me reality had come knocking.

But I was not one to delay the inevitable, so I said what had to be said.

"They put a kid in the hospital this time. It sounds like whatever your friend the sheriff said to his deputies didn't exactly take." There wasn't even an edge to my voice, I was just tired. I could see the muscles in Easton's jaw moving and I was wondering if he was trying to decide how much of whatever he heard on that call he was going to tell me.

"Patrice—"

I don't know if it was my face or what, but something about the situation made him stop talking and when he spoke again the intimate tone was gone. Still friendly, still warm, but I was no longer talking to my lover.

"I don't know how much you got already," he said, fidgeting with his phone. "But it was a broken taillight. The deputy flagged them down about five miles out of town. It was pretty routine, until for some fucking inexplicable reason the deputy made them get out of the car."

The frustration made his voice tight, and I could tell that it wasn't just about one more incident and optics. Easton was struggling with whatever was happening. I wanted to go to him, I did but I stayed where I was, I could not let this turn into something about me and him.

He glanced skyward then, and I wasn't sure if he was regrouping or if he just didn't want to look at me for the next part. "One of the kids started convulsing and ended up passing out. Apparently he has pretty severe asthma, but didn't want to reach into his coat pocket to get his inhaler."

Because he was afraid he'd get shot.

"He blacked out." Easton's tired exhale said it all. And to think only ten minutes earlier we were ready to start the day playing in bed. "He's at Ithaca General, stable. The other two are fine."

I nodded, because I didn't have to say what we both knew. That things could've been much worse if that kid hadn't been more scared to reach into his pocket than he was of passing out from an asthma attack.

"I'll deal with this, Patrice," he offered, his voice pleading.

I ground my teeth together, my hands fist-deep in my coat pocket, hating this shit. Hating, that once again, something I wanted, something I needed, was being taken away by other people's actions.

"Easton, this is not something you need to resolve to appease me. It's not even on just you to resolve."

He threw his hands up at my words and tried to move closer, then thought better of it and kept himself on the other side of the couch. "Of course it's not about appeasing you, Patrice. I fucking know that." He ran a hand over his face and exhaled before he spoke again. In a weird twisted way, I wished he'd say something terrible, something condescending or flippant, so I could retreat and go back to the more familiar place of expecting the worst.

"I don't do this job to piss off my parents, Patrice. I do it because I believe that I can play a role in seeking justice. I'm not naïve, I understand what it means that that kid risked suffocating to death rather than reach into his pocket. We will address this."

"Will you address it in the press?"

This time he was the one grinding his teeth. "That's not up to me."

My anger at his answer boiled up and then fizzled out just as fast, because I didn't want to be doing this right now. I didn't want to have to turn away from what I'd had just minutes ago with Easton because of something that neither of us had done.

It felt so fucking unfair, but he was who he was, and I was who I was, and if I let what I felt for him change that, we'd be over before we really started.

I walked up to him anyway and did the thing that I

would've never done before Easton Archer came into my life. I compromised *again*. I took his face in my hands and pressed our lips together. He opened up for me like he always did. I licked into his mouth and pressed my fingers into his skin. My hands tightening on him.

Possessive, even when I didn't want to be. That pull that made me want to forget myself. Always one brush of skin away from igniting.

"I know this is not all up to you," I said just as much for myself as for him. We pressed our foreheads together, his hands gripping my wrists. We were there for one, two, three breaths, before pulling apart.

"I'll call you later," I said, pointing down. "I'm going to go get ready for class. I'll keep my eye out for any news on the jury. Good luck."

Easton only nodded, his face subdued and worried, but said nothing and I wondered if like me, he feared that if we started talking about this it would all come tumbling down.

I walked out of his apartment and took the stairs, my phone burning a hole in my pocket. When I drove off to campus a couple of hours later, I responded to the organizers of the peaceful protest in the only way I could.

You can count on me.

* * *

It was past four in the afternoon and already getting dark when Ted barged into my office. "The jury's got a verdict."

I looked up from my monitor and waved him in as I opened the tab to the local newspaper's Twitter. They'd been posting updates.

"Looks like the judge is reading the charges." Ted was now behind my chair reading it too. His mouth twisted to the side when he saw some of the previous tweets about the latest traffic stop. "The silence is deafening on this," he muttered, eyes seemingly regretful, and I assumed it was because he knew about Easton and me. But from the time I'd known Ted, I also knew he was not going to take it easy on me just because I was fucking one of the ADAs.

"They think people won't notice because of the trial. Are you going to help out with the protest?"

"Yeah, the director of the Ithaca Justice Project texted me this morning about it." I was looking at my phone to see if there were any texts from Nesto—he always seemed to know the news before anyone else— when I heard Ted suck his teeth before a pretty astonished, "Holy shit, good for him," came out of his mouth.

When I looked at the monitor, it was there in black and white.

Court Update: Jury convicts on all counts. Interim DA Easton Archer to run for DA in special election.

"What the fuck?" I said in genuine astonishment.

"You didn't know about this?" Ted asked in a tone that brooked a very clear *I'm glad I'm not Easton.*

I lifted a shoulder and was about to say something offhanded when I saw a text come through on my phone.

Easton.

We got him on all counts. BTW Cindy made that announcement without my permission, I had no intention of committing to running. I still don't.

The way my chest caved in with relief shouldn't have

surprised me. This day needed to end because there was just way too much shit happening. Still I was proud of Easton for getting justice for that family, and after seeing him with the survivor's mom on Friday, I knew it wasn't just another win for him. So when I responded, I went with my heart, not my head.

I'm proud of you, we can talk about the other news when I see you.

His response came seconds later.

Tonight?

I looked up and waved at Ted who was back-walking out of my office, pointing at the watch on his wrist, before texting Easton my response.

Tonight.

I thought about heading out, of going to the gym and exerting some of the pent-up anxious energy I was feeling on a grueling workout, but instead I grabbed my phone again and did something I rarely ever did. I called my mom.

She picked up after only two rings, probably freaked out thinking something bad had happened.

"Everything's fine. Just calling to say hello."

The hissing I heard on the line told me my mother was not buying my bald-faced lie. "So you just called your Manman because you miss me?" The snark in her voice made a smile break out on my face, even as I closed my eyes, unsure of how to broach the subject.

"I've been seeing someone."

"Oh?" My mother had a gift for delivering an entire monologue in one syllable.

The unsaid, *you must be real pressed if you're calling me for advice...* came through loud and clear.

"We're too different." My mother made a sound between exhaustion and sympathy at my outburst. But she knew me well enough not interrupt. The next part I knew would get a reaction. "He's rich. His dad's kind of racist," I said, ruthlessly leaving out everything that made Easton the man I was falling in love with.

Because that was it, that's what had me hesitating, trying to figure out how I could hold on to what I had with Easton for a bit longer, when with anyone else I would've walked away long ago. I could hide it from him, and even from my mother, but the weight of trying to hide it from myself was becoming impossibly heavy to carry.

"Uh huh," my mother said knowingly. "So, now that I know all the things that are wrong with him, why don't you tell me the reasons why you're calling me to talk you out of letting him go."

I groaned at her ability to see right through my bullshit. "Manman, he's a prosecutor. It's going to put us at odds, it already has."

I heard tongue clicking and a tired exhale. "Is he a good man?"

"The best," I said without hesitation.

"Patrice, son, why do you look for ways to cheat yourself? Don't let my mistakes cost you your happiness."

I sighed, not sure what to say, but I'd called my mother for a reason. I needed to hear this.

"I want to be happy Manman, but I won't compromise what I believe in."

There was more teeth sucking before she spoke again. "Pitit, for once let yourself fully have something before you start finding ways to push it away. I am sure you have good reasons to hesitate, son, there is just so much that can go wrong when you open yourself up to someone like that. But you actually called me today to talk about him." She laughed, sounding truly astonished. "That's never happened, and that means something. Does he make you happy?"

I shuddered out a breath as I thought of how Easton woke up smiling. Before he even opened his eyes, the sides of his mouth would defiantly turn up, challenging the world to wipe it off his face. I wanted that in my life every day.

I ran a hand over my eyes before I answered, bracing myself for what needed to be said. "I think I love him."

My mom sighed at my revelation and when she spoke I could hear the smile in her voice. "Then you should try to find common ground, Patrice. If he loves you, that is worth fighting for. We have travelled such a long road since that day we left Port-au-Prince. Sometimes I can't believe we've come so far." The wonder in her voice, made my throat close up. "My strong and brilliant son. You make me so proud, Patrice, my chest cannot take it." Her accent thickened the more emotional she got and I knew tears were not far behind.

"I failed you—"

"No, Manman," I protested.

"No, I did. When you told me about yourself, I thought of my own fears and not of yours. I was so worried about the world that I didn't take care of your heart first. But I don't ever want you to think that you don't deserve to fall in love, to be cherished. Let yourself at least try."

I didn't know how much I needed to hear those words from my mother until she said them, and the emotion in her voice made me think she'd needed to say them too. "Okay. I will," I said, wanting to believe I could.

After we ended the call I sat there thinking about my mother's words, how she urged me to give what I had with Easton a try. I looked at my messages again and saw Easton had left one for me.

See you at home.

I could either walk away from that promise or for the first time ever, let my heart override my head.

Chapter Twenty

Patrice

"You sure you don't want a glass of prosecco with your slice, P?" Nesto asked as I took a second piece of the passion fruit silk pie thing he'd made for dessert.

I shook my head as I licked some of the crust and delicious filling off my finger. "Nah, man. I'm driving."

He shook his head like I was the most stubborn motherfucker on earth. "Man, you gotta chill," he teased and turned to Easton, an eyebrow raised and the bottle tipped in the direction of the flute by his place setting.

My boyfriend smirked at me before raising the glass to Nesto. "I'm not nearly as good as Patrice," he said as he leaned in to kiss my cheek.

Nesto scoffed. "Yeah, but you had like one glass of wine and now one of prosecco. That's not exactly getting your drink on." He got up and slapped a hand on my shoulder. "My man has to relax a little more."

From the other end of the table Jude protested, "Leave him alone, Nesto, it's been a bit stressful in this town for the past couple of months. I don't blame him for being careful."

Jude was quiet and very mild mannered, but he did

not pull a punch when it came to shit that he felt strongly about. At his words I saw Easton's back go up. But Jude had those baby blues right on him. It'd been a few days since that last stop. Easton had gone to visit the kid who'd passed out at the hospital. Thankfully he'd made a full recovery, and of course things had quieted down again.

I could see Easton trying to keep his sigh inward instead of responding to Jude.

"I don't blame him either, even if he is a little bit more intense than I am with these things," Nesto said ruefully.

Easton took a small sip then gave Jude a serious look. "Day has finally agreed to take a stronger stance and have some kind of diversity training in the department. Honestly I don't think that's enough. He needs to make a statement, publicly."

He'd been trying to get his boss to say something too, but so far, nothing. I was starting to wonder if that was where it would stay.

Jude nodded and looked straight at me, as if he knew we'd be on the same page. "I know you'll try, Easton. I just hope there's not a tragedy while they're sorting themselves out."

"Me too," Easton said heavily, pushing his barely touched glass of prosecco away. "It's what has me considering this run more seriously, maybe I could do some good. Take a different position as DA." When he looked at me, I reached over and ran a hand over his.

We'd reached a sort of détente since the day Cindy had announced his candidacy; he'd been moving behind the scenes trying to shake things up. I'd ended up participating in the peaceful protest after the last stop, and had been quietly helping some local groups organize. I'd also been intentionally laying off Twitter. I wasn't sure how long it would work to leave things hanging like this. Those parts of our lives were too big to just keep them to ourselves. Eventually we'd either have to bring them together or they would collide on their own. But the struggle and the law could not go to bed every night, without coming to a standoff at some point.

I heard Jude clearing his throat and found him looking at Easton and me like he knew exactly what was going down with us. But when he opened his mouth it mercifully went in another direction. "Did Ari tell you about the moving in date?"

I nodded and smiled over at Easton, who was suddenly super focused on his hands. "Yeah," I said, pointing a fork in my boyfriend's direction. "His new landlord made sure the apartment was ready for him within a week."

Easton rolled his eyes at Nesto, Jude and me like what he had done was no big deal. "It didn't need that much work. It's a studio. Took like two days to get it ready."

"Uh huh," Nesto said, putting his arm around Jude. "You're charging him what he paid his uncle for rent, which I know was not very much, and giving him a brand new place downtown, which happened to be fully furnished. That ain't nothing, my guy."

I could see the color rising on Easton's cheeks like it always did whenever anyone tried to give him a compliment.

After a moment he looked up from whatever he'd been closely inspecting on the table. "He's gone through a lot this past month, so I'm glad that I can help on this one thing. It's not like it comes at big cost to me."

Before I could interject, Nesto voiced what I was thinking. "You also got him the immigration lawyer who took his case pro bono. And you didn't have to do a thing, but you did it anyways. So stop trying to talk yourself out of your cookout invitation, bruh."

That got us all laughing and moving on to discuss the logistics of getting Ari situated in his new place.

After some more talk about what each of us would get for a housewarming I noticed Easton's yawns were coming more and more frequently. I'd been staying at his house pretty much every night for the past month, and knew he was back to leaving for the office before five in the morning, preparing for his next trial. So, when I saw him nod off, I ran a hand over his shoulder.

"Hey, you want to head home?"

The sleepy look he gave me did not match up with the cheeky response or the lopsided smile that appeared on his face when I said the word "home." "Will you tuck me in?"

I could only laugh as I pulled him up with me. "Only if you're good."

"Well that doesn't bode well for me then," he said, feigning annoyance.

All I could do was shake my head. No matter how much I tried to keep my fortress of solitude act up, Easton always found a way to make me take myself a little less seriously.

I liked the person I was with Easton.

I looked over at Jude and Nesto who were getting up too. "We should be heading out. Easton's on a super early wake-up schedule and I've started getting up with him and heading to the gym before class."

We exchanged hugs and goodbyes and soon were walking up the street to our cars. Easton looked at me and pointed at my black SUV that was parked right by his. "Do you want to leave your car here and go in mine? I can drop you off here in the morning."

I laughed at the suggestion, because it made zero sense. "That would mean you driving like forty minutes tomorrow morning for no reason. So, no thank you," I said, unable to keep a straight face at his hurt expression.

I pulled on his scarf so I could give him a kiss and when he pulled back he seemed in much better spirits. "That should tide me over."

I was about to get in my car when he tugged on my hand, not letting go. "Hey." The way he said it, made me turn fully around.

"Hey, yourself."

He put both arms around my neck, and looked up at me, eyes locked with mine. "I could fall in love with you, Professor Denis." His voice was clear and strong.

To my surprise my response to his words seemed just as certain. "I'm pretty sure I'm falling in love with you."

Radiant.

That was the only word for the smile the words got me, and the kiss afterward was so sweet I felt greedy that I got to have all of it.

After a few more kisses, Easton pulled back, biting on his bottom lip. "Does this mean I get, 'we said I love you sex'?"

I shook my head, laughing as I got in my car. "When have you ever not eventually gotten what you want from me?" I waved as he grinned at me in answer. "I'll see you at home."

I saw Easton quickly get in his BMW and drive off while I checked my Twitter account. I had a bunch of stuff in my mentions. People tagging me on different events and posts related to race relations in Ithaca. I responded to some and retweeted the less incendiary ones. Everything else I just let sit there for now, tonight I would be a little selfish, like my mother had said. I felt so good right now, I wanted to hold on just a little longer.

I'd been on the road for about fifteen minutes when my phone rang. I had on those magnetic things where I could mount the phone on the dashboard, so when the screen lit up I saw it was Easton. I smiled and shook my head as I hit the Bluetooth button on the steering wheel to take the call.

"Where are you? I just got into the garage." Of course he had, because he drove like a New York City cabbie.

"Uh I'm still like five miles out of town, Speedy."

I heard him scoff and smiled in anticipation of his response. He had a very inflated sense of his driving skills, which was kind of adorable. "I didn't even drive that fast. There's barely any traffic at this hour."

I nodded in the direction of the phone, like he could see me. "You know I like to go just under the speed limit at night, helps me feel like I'm more in control of the vehicle." I sped up a bit, because it was true that there was no one on the road and I was driving mad slow, not that I would admit that to him.

"Did I accidentally call my grandpa?"

The genuine bafflement in his voice had me busting up. "All right, smart-ass, I'll see you in a few minutes.

I'm really close to town," I said, grinning as I drove down the dark county road.

"Fine, I'll leave the door—"

A siren coming from behind startled me out of the conversation. I tried to slow down in case a first responder needed to get past me, but when I looked in the rearview mirror, there was a patrol car behind me, its flashing lights trained right on my car.

"Patrice?" I heard Easton's voice still full of humor, and for a moment it felt like I was in a dream. Like time had slowed down, and then I realized it was panic. I was scared.

"I think I'm getting pulled over," I said woodenly, my bare hands on the steering wheel suddenly felt like sausages. Still I quickly tapped on my phone screen, and switched the call to FaceTime, as I steered the car over to the side of the road.

When I saw Easton's face he looked terrified. "Where are you? I'm coming over there."

I didn't have time to answer, because I had to deal with the deputy rapping on my car window.

I lowered the window all the way down and made sure I immediately put both hands on the steering wheel where he could see them, and made eye contact when I respectfully addressed him.

"How can I help you, officer?"

Right how I'd learned on those videos.

Easton

The first thing I realized when I heard Patrice say he was being pulled over was that until that moment I'd never truly felt terror. I must've gone through the first thirty-six years of my life without experiencing helpless, debilitating fear before, because what I was feeling was completely new.

I was having hot and cold flashes and my skin felt tight on my face. Even my vision went blurry. I looked at my phone as I powered up my car, frantically trying to think of what to do. How to help him without making things worse. I could only see a side of his face, and one of his hands, which had the steering wheel in a death grip.

After a second, I heard the voice of the officer. "Do you know why I stopped you?" He sounded young and cocky, and I prayed to anything that would listen that he could keep a cool head.

I could see half of Patrice's jaw clenching at the deputy's tone. I knew he was working hard on not mouthing off, and I wanted to scream into my phone, beg him not to do anything to piss the guy off.

"I assume it was because I was speeding."

"You were going sixty, this is a fifty-five speed zone."

Was he really stopping him for going *five* miles over the speed limit? The memory of my teasing from just a few minutes ago soured in my stomach and I had to breathe through the urge to puke.

I wanted to call the sheriff's office and tell them to call this guy off, to tell him to leave Patrice alone. To not hurt him.

Every conversation Patrice I had had about how these things went was flashing before my eyes, and a wave of nausea rolled in my gut.

I didn't know what to do.

I couldn't take the call off because I wanted to see

what was happening, and I had to think fast. Every second that passed had the potential to escalate.

"Sir, where were you coming from?" I stared at the screen, watching the scene unfold, and with growing horror realized this deputy seemed hell-bent on starting something with Patrice.

"I thought this was a speeding stop, can I just get my ticket and go?" Patrice's tone was getting more and more annoyed with every word he said.

The guy spoke again, this time with a definite edge to his voice. "Sir, I asked you where you were coming from."

I saw Patrice hands tighten on the steering wheel, then turn his head fully in the direction of the voice.

"I was driving back from Trumansburg. I was there having dinner with some friends and my boyfriend."

Shit.

"Oh, your boyfriend." The pit in my stomach widened at the cop's snide tone.

"Yes, my *boyfriend*. Look is there a point to this? Are you going to give me a ticket or is this just outright harassment?"

"Did you consume any alcohol this evening?"

The conversation from earlier came back into my head, and the relief of knowing Patrice would have no reason to lie was so powerful, I almost wept.

"No, I did not."

"Where are your license and registration?" This fucking guy was just not going to let up.

"They're on the visor above this seat. I am going to take one hand off the steering wheel to reach for it." Patrice was enunciating every word in a clear calm voice, obviously aware of his every move, something that would've never occurred to me to do.

I saw him reach up and after a moment, the deputy talked again.

"So you're from New York City, what are you doing up here?"

"I work for Cornell. Again, is there a point to this?" Patrice could not keep the annoyance out of his voice when he talked, and before the cop even responded I knew things were about to get a lot worse.

"Get out of the vehicle." The cop's voice all of a sudden shifted, and he sounded pissed.

"What? Why?" If I didn't know him the way that I did. If I hadn't spent the amount of time I had with him in the last few months, I would not have been able to hear the genuine fear in Patrice's voice.

"I said *get out of the car.*"

I sat there frozen in terror, praying to every deity I'd ever heard of to please just make him do whatever the deputy was asking him.

"I'd like for you to tell me the reason why I need to get out my car when you stopped me for going five miles over the limit."

There was muffled sound as though someone was trying to force the car door open, and for what seemed like forever, I could not make out what Patrice was saying. That's when I panicked, because I could already see Patrice on the ground, shot. I immediately put the phone on mute and dove to get my work one out. I didn't know what I was doing, or who I was calling, but I needed to stop this right now. On the screen I saw that Patrice was no longer holding the steering wheel. He must've gotten out of the car.

Completely out of fucks and shaking with fear for what could happen if I didn't do something, I called Day.

He picked up after two rings, even though it felt like a century. I spoke over him as soon as he answered.

"Do you know who's posted on the road to Trumansburg tonight? You have to call him off. He's got my boyfriend on the side of the road, Whitney, and it's escalating."

"What are you talking about?"

"My boyfriend," I screamed into the phone, not caring at all how this looked or what it could mean later. "He's a professor at Cornell, got pulled over and your deputy is being an asshole. He made him get out of his car for no fucking reason. You need to find out who he is, and *call him off*." I was practically barking at him, and I knew this would probably come back to bite me. I did not care.

I could leave my entire career right here, right now, if it got Patrice back in his car and headed home.

Day didn't hesitate. "Let me call in."

I waited on the phone, fearing the worst, because Patrice was still not back in the driver's seat. I thought back to just minutes before when we'd stood on the sidewalk and said I love you. The thought of losing that, of losing him was unbearable.

Finally Day came back on the phone. "It's Deputy Hines. He's fairly new. I'll radio him."

I exhaled, feeling relief beyond anything I'd ever felt in my life. My limbs felt liquid as the tension started to seep out of me. After a few seconds, which felt like hours, Day spoke again and I could hear the tension in his voice.

"I radioed him, he's letting him go."

I nodded, forgetting he couldn't see me, as I stared at my phone screen and finally saw Patrice getting back in his car.

"Thank you."

Day exhaled. "No problem."

I ended the call without saying another word and waited for Patrice to say something, but he must've forgotten that I was still on FaceTime. The next thing I knew, it seemed like the car was moving. When I looked at the length of the call I saw we'd only been talking for six minutes.

The longest of my life.

"How are you doing?" I asked in the most normal voice I could manage. Afraid I'd spook him while he was driving.

But when he spoke his voice was distant. "I'm fine. I'm going to turn this off, while I'm driving. See you in a few."

Chapter Twenty-One

Patrice

The five-minute drive to the building took me fifteen, because I had to stop twice when my hands started shaking so bad I thought I was going to get into an accident. I kept replaying the last ten minutes over and over in my head and I felt sick about all of it. I tried to calm myself and figure out a way to have a conversation with Easton about what he had done without losing it. I hated feeling like I did, humiliated and scared, so fucking scared.

I pulled into my parking spot, feeling like my head could snap right off my neck from the tension. I didn't want to blow up, take things out on Easton. I didn't want to say things that I could never take back. I thought of the sweet moment we'd just had by our cars, and it felt like it had happened to someone else.

I opened the door and saw him getting out of his car, which he parked on the spot nearest the elevator. As he hurried over to me, I took one breath, then another. Looking at him now I had the same thought that I had when that cop made me get out my car, I don't want Easton to feel responsible for me. I didn't want him to have to see me get hurt and then feel like it was his fault. Maybe all this was bigger than the two of us. Maybe this was all hopeless after all.

"Are you all right?"

I turned and leaned against my driver door as he stood just a few feet away. Still trying to breathe through the jumble of emotions of the last few minutes. I decided to stay here, to talk to him while we were out in an open space. A place where I'd have to keep my voice down, where I'd have an easier time walking away.

I looked down at my feet as I thought of what to say. Of how to explain to Easton that what he'd done was not even remotely all right, but that beyond that the reality of where we both stood in life finally sunk in and I was scared for both us. When I looked up I could see the flatness of his mouth, the way his fists were shoved in his coat, that he knew things were not okay.

"You've been telling me for weeks now to be patient, that things are just so slow when it comes to these things. Not a public statement, not a word to the community that this was not okay, that they were right to be scared. Your boss didn't, you didn't." With every word I said Easton got paler, his eyes downcast, and something in me almost *wanted* to hurt him. When I spoke again my voice sounded so fucking tired. "But the minute these stops come to your door, you have it taken care of it in three minutes."

He stepped toward me with a protest in his mouth, but I held up my hand.

"I want you to tell me, Easton. Tell me how it makes sense to let those stops go on for months now without taking any kind of position, when it was other people's lovers, or parents or kids."

My voice broke then, and I had to take a deep breath, to finish saying this shit, because the shock from everything that had gone down in the last hour was starting to wear off and I was shaking again. "I can't be that person, Easton. I can't be the one for whom the rules are broken, while every other fucker that looks like me has to just live with it."

His mouth twisted then and he took a step, closing the space between us. "That is not what that was, Patrice," he said, desperation clear in his voice. "It's not that I don't care about what happened to other people. I know now how wrong it was for us to stay silent, to not reassure the community." He fisted the hand he'd been running through his hair. "I freaked out, okay. I got scared. I get that I may seem hypocritical—"

I scoffed and leaned my head back, starting to feel pissed off. "*May* seem hypocritical, Easton?"

"Patrice—"

"No. That's the kind of energy you need to have for every single person that is stopped in this town, and doesn't have a boyfriend with the pull to help him out. You know what it takes to make this better for everyone? Sacrifices. Your boss won't say anything because she can't piss off the police, the sheriff can't do it because he already lost some votes. Meanwhile black and brown people in this town go on thinking the people who are supposed to keep them safe just don't care. You knew all along that what was happening was dangerous."

I wanted to touch him one last time, to run my fingers over those lips one more time. "You remember when you told me that you could go your whole life without thinking about the real history of this country?"

He gave a sharp nod in response, his arms crossed

tightly against his chest. "We're not just learning history, we're making it too. You can't just be brave when you've secured yourself a soft landing or without making any of your friends uncomfortable."

"Does anyone get a second chance with you? Or is everything black and white, Patrice?"

I laughed again, pushing off the car. "You know what's wild?" I sounded as if something had been turned off inside me, numb. "When I got stopped the first thing I thought was: *if something happens to me, I don't want this on Easton's conscience.*" I let out a choppy breath and could hear Easton's shuddering one. "I also don't have the luxury of navigating in the grays, and I won't be anybody's token, especially not yours. It'll destroy us."

I walked away and headed to the elevators, but before I took two steps he was hot on my heels. "Oh no you fucking don't," he gritted out, getting into the elevator with me. I pushed the button for my floor and put in the special access code for him. And almost laughed about the symbolism in that small detail. The fact that Easton had the kind of life where one needed a special code to get to him.

As the elevator doors closed he got right back in my face. "I'm not going to beg you, Patrice, because I know that there's nothing I can say that you won't turn it into another self-righteous reason to condemn me and then yourself for caring about me."

His eyes were a dark green now and blazing, to anyone else he would've looked angry, but I could see that he was hurting. "I fucked up. I should've done better. I don't have a do-over, and I have to live with that." He shook his head as the elevator stopped on my floor.

"But there was never going to be a way for me to win when it came to us."

I stood there not knowing what to say, too tired to try.

"You can tell yourself that you're just saving us both by doing this." He ran a hand under his nose, but somehow he kept the tears from falling. "Before we even really begun you'd already decided that I was going to disappoint you. Now I have. I hope your sanctimoniousness keeps you warm at night."

With that he pushed past me and walked out of the elevator, but before taking the stairs to his place, he turned back to look at me, and in a strangled voice said, "You're so much stronger than I am, Patrice, because I would never put my convictions ahead of the people I love. If had to do it again, I'd still make that call."

I opened my mouth to tell him he was being unfair, but before I could, he pulled the door open and took the steps up to his place.

When I got to my apartment, I closed my eyes tight and tried to breathe through the tears that were threatening to spill. I kept repeating under my breath, *this is for the best, this is for the best, this is for the best.*

Easton needed someone who could be with him without reservation, who could love him without conflicts or guilt.

Maybe I just wasn't that man.

Easton

"Are you all right?" Pri asked, the naked concern in her voice making me grimace.

I sighed as I tried to sit up on my bed, my muscles achy from lack of use. My head still groggy from all the sleeping I'd done. I debated on what to say but in the end decided I didn't have it in me to act like I wasn't wrecked.

"No," I croaked, glancing up at the clock on the wall, which was telling me I'd been in bed for almost fifteen hours.

"Did something happen with you and Patrice? I called him after I read his thread about the stop, but he didn't pick up. Just texted back 'I'm fine.' Like the broody asshole he is."

She sighed again and I could tell she was trying to gauge how much to push. "I didn't even bother asking him how you were doing, because those tweets about the stop were at an eleven, so I figured at the very least you and him got into something."

I scoffed at that major understatement and slumped against the headboard, completely at a loss about how to make things right with Patrice. Because no matter how much I hedged, he had been right about me. I'd chosen to let an issue that at some point would end in a tragedy slide until it came right to my door. Because it would piss people off.

I swallowed hard thinking about the thread, of what he'd written about the humiliation and fear he felt last night, the things I never got to hear. I opened my photo app and pulled up the screenshot with the tweet that had almost made me weep for him.

That feeling that no matter what I do, how hard I work, how far I climb... It can all be taken away in a moment.

No matter how much I tried to act like Patrice overreacted to my calling Day last night, I understood that it felt like I was adding insult to injury. "He ended things last night. After."

"What? Why?" Pris asked, sounding exasperated.

She let out a long harsh breath. "Patrice cannot be so fucking unreasonable that he's blaming you for this?" I appreciated her outrage, but I didn't have the energy to be mad.

I swallowed past the lump in my throat and confessed to Priscilla. "He got mad because I reached out to Day to call off the deputy who stopped him." Pri gasped at that. "I can see how that could land badly with him."

I ran my palms over my face, feeling exhausted. "Especially when the DA's office and everyone else in town have been tiptoeing around this stop and pretending there's no reason to be concerned."

"But that's not just on you to figure out, Easton," Pri said in my defense, and I smiled at her loyalty.

"It's not to a degree, but it at least warranted some kind of public acknowledgment from us, and I didn't say a word. But when my boyfriend got stopped I literally called on the cavalry, like Patrice said, it's hypocritical."

I could almost hear Pri thinking on the other end of the call. "But things had been going well. Right?"

I wanted to curl under the covers and not come out until I'd literally slept away all my feelings. "We were doing great." I ran my hand over the satin-covered pillow that still had the imprint of Patrice's head. The smell of coconut oil still lingering on the smooth surface. "I don't know how to fix this, Pri. Patrice wants perfection, for every person in his life to interpret things the way he thinks they should and anything beyond that is betrayal. I can't live up to that. I need him to be able to love me with the flaws I have. I can't do with Patrice what I had to with my parents my whole life."

"Fuck no." Pri's outrage, made a tired smile break out on my face. "Patrice needs to get his head out of his ass, for real." She let out a long breath, deflated by the conversation. "Babe, I'm sorry."

"I'm sorry too, but I'm not going to beg Patrice. I own that I fucked up, and I will make it right, but I can't be in a relationship where I'm constantly one mistake from being iced out."

"He'll come around. This time he has something big enough to lose."

I sighed again, getting up to go look down on the sidewalk behind the building.

"I'm not going to pretend I won't open the door if he comes here with an olive branch, but I can't keep bending myself to keep Patrice appeased. I have some things I need to take care of and for now I'll put my energy on that."

"Okay babe, that's good. Put that energy elsewhere. If you do need me to come up there, just call, all right? I'm pretty sure I can still kick his ass like I did when we were kids."

I laughed at that and kept my attention on the sidewalk as I saw a figure that looked a lot like the man I loved coming closer to the building. "Thanks, Pri."

We ended the call as I saw Patrice finally get to the door at the back of the building. Before he went in, he stepped back and looked right up at where I was. Seeing him still made my stomach flip, even as hopeless as things felt right now. He was in a black parka, his locs unbound and hanging down his back. He looked as stark and as lonely as I felt. Our eyes locked for a few breaths, and I saw the same regret in him that I'd been swimming in since last night. I wanted to lift my hand in a wave or call for him, but I just stood there until he finally dipped his head and walked inside.

Chapter Twenty-Two

Patrice

"Can I come in?" I asked after I'd rapped twice on the door of my department's chair office. He looked up from behind his cluttered desk and waved me in. He was the exact type of man you'd expect to find chairing an economics department in an Ivy League school. In his fifties and had the absent-minded professor look down pat, complete with the coffee stain on his shirt.

"Patrice, please take a seat."

I lowered myself onto one of the black leather chairs in front of his desk, unsure of what was about to happen, but almost certain it would not be pleasant. I looked down at myself and realized I'd missed a button on the vest I was wearing, and sighed. It had been two days since the stop and almost by the hour my regret for the way I'd handled things with Easton doubled. But since I was pretty sure I was about to get reamed out, I needed to stay focused on this particular fire and not the others actively burning in my life.

"Thank you for coming on such short notice," he said, snatching me out of my pity party, his voice all awkward, as if we didn't both know I didn't exactly have a choice in the matter.

"Of course," I said, wondering if he was going to straight-up tell me to stop tweeting or if he was going to tiptoe around it for the next hour.

He cleared his throat and looked at me, as if he was trying to figure out how to take the first bite out of me. "I saw that you were involved in a traffic stop this weekend."

Had to give it to him, he could spin.

I dipped my head in a nod as my skin tightened from the mention of the stop. "Yes."

He sighed and shifted in his chair, awkward as fuck.

"First of all I just want to say we're glad that you're all right." He cleared his throat. "I'd also like to reiterate that the department hired you for your innovative research. *And* that your interesting perspective on social justice and activism was also a factor." I could tell the fact that I was looking straight at him was making him uncomfortable, but I did not care. He wanted to shut me up, he could look me in the eye when he told me.

"And." He paused there and I wondered just how bad the next part would be, but when he looked at me again his eyes were friendly. "I can't speak for the school on this, but I can tell you that personally I think what you're doing is great. We need to speak out about what is happening in our community. I will do what I can to support your efforts in town."

I felt like I'd fallen through a hole and ended up in the upside down. I was sure I had not heard him right. "I'm sorry. Could you say that again?" I asked, genuinely baffled. So much so I resisted the urge to cup a hand around my ear the next time he opened his mouth.

"I said that I think what you've been doing is something our community needs and I will gladly support you in any way I can. Mind you, this is just me, not the department." This time I was the one having trouble maintaining eye contact. "It's not easy taking these things on and I know the pressure you're under to get tenure. I just wanted to tell you I see your work and how it goes beyond just publications. You're doing what's right. I see and respect that. A lot of us here do."

This conversation was literally going in the complete opposite direction I expected. I came in to be dressed down and warned, not to be offered support.

I had no game plan for this.

"Umm, thank you, sir. I appreciate it," I said, feeling foolish for doing what I always accused people of doing to me—making assumptions without reason. Which only made me think of Easton. I'd accused *him* so harshly of being a hypocrite and here I was being confronted by my own hypocrisy. "I'm trying to balance what I say and do, I know that I'm a brand-new hire, so I don't want to make any enemies, but I can't not bring attention to this."

Dr. Simons nodded again and leaned in so that his head was only a few feet from mine. "It's a national issue and one that affects our students of color every day, especially our young men." He extended a hand at me. "And our faculty even. We are part of this community and we can't look the other way on this."

I nodded again, not sure how to act. I had no clue what else to say. "Okay, thank you again, sir. I—"

I opened my mouth to say some generic, cordial thing and walk out of the office, but instead decided to say what I was thinking. "I walked in here expecting to be told to shut down my Twitter account or else." I shook my head, needing to get all of this out. "I'm not used to getting this kind of support. I'm not even sure what to say."

He waved me off with a kind smile and for the first time I was really seeing him. "We hired you because you were the best candidate we had on this search, Patrice, but also because you were walking the walk. I am tired of hiring faculty that have no interest of ever being in the world they're trying to figure out." He paused then and I could tell he was debating whether to say more. "The reason I initially asked you to meet me was because another faculty member seems determined to paint your activism in a negative light."

Brad.

He pursed his mouth as if he found whatever he was remembering distasteful. "What good are we if we don't figure out how to use the knowledge we have to challenge ourselves and our communities? Good research is not enough, we have to be good citizens too." The fire in his eyes reminded me of my advisor at Columbia, and I wondered how I hadn't noticed I had an ally in this place all along.

"I couldn't agree with you more," I said sincerely.

I looked at his office and saw photos of him and students at different events. Every single one, some old and some more recent, showed him surrounded by diverse groups of kids. His arms usually around a couple of them. His office wasn't full of fancy leather and wood furniture. It was cluttered and a little dusty. It was a workspace.

I stood up, feeling humbled. It wasn't like every person in the department was going to be like Dr. Simons, or even close, but he and I were here and that mattered.

I extended my hand to him and he gripped it, with that small smile still on his lips. "Just let me know how I can help."

"Will do," I said sincerely. "For now I've been helping to plan another peaceful protest that will go from the clock tower down to the commons. I'd appreciate the school not shutting it down."

"We would never shut down a peaceful protest. The right to gather peacefully by students has a long tradition here." He pointed at his monitor and looked up at me again. "I'll make sure to say something about it in my own Twitter account, and let other faculty know if they want to end class early or let the students who want to participate leave class, that they have my blessing."

"You're on Twitter?" I asked before I could help myself, at which he responded with a hearty laugh. "I have three grandchildren in college. I've been on Twitter for years. I've been following and admiring you for a while now."

Well, I'd be damned.

I walked out of Dr. Simons's office and headed to mine with my head swimming, but one thing kept coming up to the surface.

Easton.

The more I thought about that night, the bigger the hole in my stomach got. Because I knew that, just like with Dr. Simons, my own assumptions and my own fear of not being seen, made me put up walls. It helped me protect myself from getting hurt, but I'd also been keeping out those who could lift me up.

I *needed* to talk to Easton, but first I had to make

sure I hadn't fucked up things beyond repair. I walked into my office, closing the door behind me, and before I could talk myself out of it, I called Priscilla. I considered Camilo, but he would just curse me out, and I needed someone who could keep a cool head and give me some clue on how Easton was doing.

She picked up after one ring, and before I could say a word she let me have it. "I'm driving in to work and have ten minutes. I hope you called ready to be read for filth, because I got no time to play with any of you fuckboys today."

I sighed, but didn't even consider protesting. "How's Easton doing?"

The exhale on the other side was sort of over the top, but I knew what I was getting into when I dialed the number. "How do you think he's doing, Patrice? You've been icing him for two days and letting him feel like he's a fucking monster for acting out of fear that you were going to get hurt."

I could almost see her mouth twisted to the side as she talked. I sighed again, not even sure what I wanted to say. "I was unfair, but I also was hurt, Pris. Easton had been waffling on this shit with the stops for months, yet when it was me, he acted like it was a life-or-death situation."

This time it was her sighing. "Yes, he did that, and he owned it. He's also figuring out how to make it right."

"What does that mean?" I blurted out, interrupting her.

"That's for him to tell you, not me, Patrice. What I do have to tell you is this: you need to learn how to value the people in your life who are willing to put it all on the line for you. You're self-righteous and you're judgmental. You need to let go of some of that anger, P. Open your eyes and see that not everyone is out here trying to let you down. If you need to get some professional help to work some of that out do it, before you lose big."

After my talk with Dr. Simons I felt that in my bones. "I know."

Pri clicked her tongue, and when she spoke again she sounded a lot less pissed. "Patrice, I've known you since we were in elementary school. I have seen you harden, and I know, believe me, I know the world has given you plenty of reasons. I'm a woman of color trying to move up the ranks of the police department in New York. I fucking live in a space of barely contained frustration. But I can tell you this, my struggle will not get any easier by shutting out the people who hold it down when I need it. Are people going to stumble? Fuck yeah they will, there is so much bullshit to unlearn."

The truth in her words were cutting me to the core. "You need to figure out why you believe that you don't deserve to be happy."

"I never said I don't deserve to be happy, I just don't want to betray myself." I wasn't sure that was true, because almost at every opportunity I'd tried to minimize how much I felt for Easton.

"You need to stop seeing your happiness like foreboding."

Did I do that?

"Well that's not a switch I can just turn off, Priscilla." This conversation had me completely out of my depth.

"Do you really think that's what Easton expected? That you would fall in love with his dick and all of a sudden you'd drop the 'I'm an island' flow you've been rocking for the last thirty-four years?"

She had to make me laugh. "I'm not sure why I thought calling you instead of Camilo would somehow mean I didn't get my ass handed to me."

She snorted a laugh and I could almost hear the eye roll. "Because you're a fool." The sigh she let out then, told me that the jokes were over.

"Patrice, if I were you I'd sit with what you want with Easton for a bit, before you go and try to talk to him. Easton deserves someone who can show him that he's worthy of love. There's no one more painfully aware of their privilege than that man. That doesn't mean he won't falter, or that you won't."

I closed my eyes, wondering if there was even a chance this would work out. "I'm going to think on this some. Thanks for listening and going somewhat easy on me."

"You're welcome. Do right by him, P, and by you, you both deserve it."

I ended the call and immediately opened the Twitter app, as I usually did when I felt like I was burning up with something to say. But after a second, I thought about the urgency I was feeling. This wasn't something I wanted to share with the world, it was private and it already belonged to someone.

I tapped my phone until I had the message app open, and hesitated for a second, afraid that I would be rebuffed or ignored. Pri's words started to make sense then. I kept myself so primed for disappointment, for the people who came into my life to hurt me, that I never fully felt anything, not the joy, not the pain. I'd started feeling that with Easton, but I'd pushed him away too. To get what I deserved I needed to start showing all the way up.

I tapped the message like six different times, until I realized that I was trying to text what I *thought* I should say, instead of just saying what I meant.

I should have said thank you.

I put the phone in my breast pocket as I got up from the small love seat in my office and moved to my desk, hoping to get some work done on this eventful morning. But as soon as I opened up the internet browser, I felt my phone buzzing. I pressed my hand over the pocket and took a deep breath, before I dared look at the message. I smiled sadly at Easton's refusal to do anything less than to put his whole self out there.

You being all right is thank you enough.

As I put my phone back into my pocket a small bubble of something that felt dangerously like hope started blossoming in the middle of my chest.

Chapter Twenty-Three

Easton

"You're not going to back out, right?" Cindy asked me for what felt like the hundredth time as I got ready to go give my statement to the press to officially announce my run for DA. This was Tompkins County, so it's not like it was an actual press conference, but there would be a couple of journalists from the local media outlets to ask me some questions.

I looked up from the notes I was pretending to read, and tried not to be too harsh. "Cin, I need you to take a couple of steps back here." Things had been strained between us since I told her I could not keep waiting for this office to put out an official statement about the stop. Days later, I was still waiting for an answer. Like Patrice had told me that night, I'd finally realized that being on the right side of this would mean that I would lose some people I thought I could count on. Cindy's inaction was disappointing but that was her choice. I had my own to make.

Debating on whether I should clue her in on what was going through my head or let her find out what I was actually doing once it came out of my mouth like everyone else, I went with "I'm beginning to feel handled, and I don't like that."

"Easton—" she began, but I held up my hand, not wanting to hear her once again explain why my being the next DA would be the salvation on the entire town. "Cindy, I need to do whatever is best for me, as well as for this office. I will not be the DA so that you can continue to run things by proxy." I ran my hands over my face in frustration when I saw how hurt she seemed by my words. I ran my tongue over my front teeth a few times, trying hard to say what I needed to say in a way that didn't break her heart.

"I need to do this my way. You put me in a terrible position by announcing my candidacy alongside the Suarez conviction."

She sighed, crossing her arms over her chest. "Lorraine is pissed with me, too."

"Of course she is," I protested, unable to muster any humor.

"I just wanted to give you a push. I know how much this town needs you. I was a decent DA, but I'm not even half the trial lawyer you are."

"Cindy, being DA is about a lot more than trials."

She nodded as she tightened an arm around my waist. "You're good with people and I think you have the political courage to do a few things I could not. You'd be an outstanding DA."

I shook my head and lifted my wrist to look at the time. "I need to be in the conference room for this interview, why don't you walk me down."

As we made our way down the stairs I stopped so I could look at Cindy. "It's not that I don't want it, but I need to be in control of my path. If I wanted to be in an environment where someone else held the reins of my life, I would've gone to work for my father."

The color rising on her cheeks told me she'd finally understood just how much she'd fucked up with me. "Don't worry I still like you a lot better than him."

She scoffed. "Glad to hear I still make it above that extremely low bar." She frowned as we made our way down the stairs again. "No matter what you do I'll support you."

I smiled at her as we got to the conference room. "It's killing you not to be able to make me give you a straight answer?"

She pinched my cheek. "You think you're cute."

"Not cute enough to keep a boyfriend though."

She waved her hand around as if I was talking nonsense. "You're a keeper. Never ever doubt that. Let's hope the stunner gets his head out of his ass, and does right by you." She clicked her tongue regretfully, and for a second it felt like it usually was between us. "There's just been a lot of letting you down going around."

I shook my head as she straightened my tie. "You didn't—"

"Yeah I did. I let you down, and we'll need to figure out how to come back from it. Now, go."

This time, I did give her a hug and hoped that we could. I walked into the conference room and quickly went to shake hands with the two journalists from the *Ithaca Star*. I'd done enough of these to know the drill, so within seconds the camera was rolling and a very young-looking Latinx woman was getting on with the interview.

"Thank you for sitting with us today, ADA Archer."

I nodded and gave her the full, veneer smile. "My pleasure, and it's Easton, please."

She gave me a short nod and raised an eyebrow like she was not planning to pull any punches. "You've had an eventful couple of weeks. The jury voted to convict in the assault case of Ms. Suarez, and on that same day your intention to run for district attorney was announced." She said it in a tone I couldn't figure out, but whatever it was there was a lot of sarcasm there.

I nodded in response to her comment, as she launched into the next part of her question. "You've been operating as the interim DA now for a few of months, and know how things work. Can you tell me why you think you should be the next District Attorney?"

I shifted in the chair I was sitting in and angled my head, figuring out how to get out what I needed to say.

"Before I tell you about all the ways that I have been a great ADA, I want to talk about ways in which I need to do much better."

She leaned in closer at my answer, her eyes trained on my face, as if not wanting to miss a single word of whatever was about to come out of my mouth.

"In the past couple of months a concerning trend of incidents have been occurring in our county. Young men of color, especially black men, have been the subject of an unusually high number of traffic stops. Most of those have gone on without incident, but a couple of weeks ago a young man who was stopped with two other friends was hospitalized."

I shook my head, still so shaken by the facts around that incident. "Even though that young man was in the middle of a severe asthma attack triggered by the stress of being stopped, he was too scared to reach into his pocket and get his inhaler." She nodded at my words in encouragement, and I obliged, feeling like it was finally time to be honest.

"I can't imagine what it's like to be so scared you'd rather risk losing consciousness than make a sudden movement and chance getting shot. And what that tells me is that no matter what we may think about the intentions of our law enforcement, we need to face the fact that we are not immune to what has been going on around our country. If we can't take a moment to be honest with ourselves and the biases that exist within our institutions, then we are failing the public we are supposed to be serving."

I shifted again in my seat, and tried to focus on something on the far side of the wall so I could say what I needed to say. "When I say 'we' I want to be clear, I very much mean me. I should've been more vocal when the stops began to happen more frequently. I should've challenged myself and my colleagues to find a way to publicly talk about why they were happening. To deal with the reality that these stops don't feel routine to black and brown young men, they feel like life-or-death situations. That for certain communities in our county, contact with the criminal justice system feels dangerous and at times like the opposite of justice. We have to be courageous enough to say we've failed in this."

"That's a pretty self-recriminating statement. Can you tell me more about that?"

I needed to say this, I could not move forward unless I did.

"It's the truth and I'm disappointed in myself for not opening my eyes to this until it happened to someone I care about."

Her eyes kept getting bigger and I really was starting to worry they'd pop out of her head. But I had to keep talking until I was done. I also wanted Patrice to hear this, to know that I'd finally understood what he'd been trying to tell me, even if his way of relaying the message made it hard for me to hear it.

"Last week someone I love was stopped by the police," I said as my interviewer gasped like she was at the intense part of a movie. "I was talking to him on the phone when it happened. I'd called him to ask why he was so far behind, and teased him about how cautious he was when driving." She grimaced at that, as if she knew what happened next.

I cleared my throat and relaxed my muscles like I did whenever I was in court and I knew I had the last shot at driving my point home. "When he told me he was being stopped by the police I thought to myself, 'I don't think I've ever been this terrified.' The first thing he did was switch our call to FaceTime, and I knew he was scared for what would happen and wanted someone to be able to witness the stop." I shook my head, remembering how frantic those moments felt. When Patrice told me he feared I'd live with the guilt of something happening to him.

"It's so wrong that anyone has to feel like that. I've told myself a million times that the people I know and work alongside every day in this county are good people, and they are. But there is another reality, people of color fear for what could happen to them when they're stopped by police, and you only have to do a quick Google search to find more than enough tragedies all over the country to warrant that fear. Both those things are happening at the same time, and one of those two groups hold a lot of the power to shift that reality."

I tried to keep my face neutral as I always did in crucial moments, but my heart was pounding. I knew that with every word I said I was probably making another enemy. "Denying the reality of what our neighbors experience will not make us safer. We need to do better. *I* need to do better, and there is a lot that I have to learn. I don't think I've done the work yet to be the kind of DA this county needs, so today I'm officially withdrawing my candidacy for District Attorney."

I sat there smiling woodenly and waiting for my very stunned interviewer to react. After a second she blinked and finally got with it. "That is a very bold statement, since so far there had been no mention of these incidents. Is your partner all right?"

I smiled at her genuine concern. "He's not my partner, but yes he is all right." I was certain the wistfulness in my voice had not gone unnoticed.

She extended her hand and for the first time in the meeting she gave me a real smile. "Thank you, Easton, for being so honest today. I hope you reconsider your run, I think your point of view will add a lot to the conversation."

With that the camera was off my face, indicating we were done.

As I thanked her once again she gave me a knowing look. "Was the person you were talking about Patrice Denis?"

"What makes you say that?"

She laughed and shook her head, looking a little embarrassed. "Don't worry, this part is off the record. I've just seen you guys around town together, and since he was just stopped recently and said someone intervened, I put two and two together."

I just nodded, not sure how to respond. "Yeah, I was talking about him. When is this going up?" I asked, wondering how much more time I had before my life got really upended for a few days.

She turned around to look at the kid with the camera. He considered for a moment, his attention still on the laptop in front of him. "It'll be up by the end of the day."

I left it at that and walked out of the room, hoping that if my career in the DA's office went down in flames, that I'd at least done the right thing.

Patrice

I was getting my stuff together to leave my office after a particularly brutal grading session, when I saw my phone screen flashing with Ari's number. So far things had been calm with him. He'd been mostly staying at Yin's house for the past week. The new development to his housing situation was that they'd both be moving to the studio in my building in a couple of days. The levels of excitement they had for this big step in their relationship, at least on Yin's side, were reaching rapture-like intensity. And of course my mind went to Easton's help, which had really been a game-changer for Ari.

I answered the call, thinking once again that I needed to figure out how to reach out to him.

"Hey—"

He didn't let me get the full greeting in before screaming into the phone, "Did you see the video?" He was so hyped up I couldn't tell if the video was supposed to be a bad or a good thing.

I frowned, wondering if there had been another stop. I quickly opened another tab on my browser and went to the *Ithaca Star*'s website since they usually put stuff up really fast, but when I got to the homepage my heart almost beat out of my chest. There was a video up and the face behind the play icon was none other than Easton's.

The headline to the article read, *Easton Archer Withdraws from DA Race and Speaks about Recent Traffic Stops.*

I only realized I'd been holding my breath when I heard Ari's voice calling my name loudly. I shook myself out of the trance I was in and answered, as I tried to read the article at the same time. "Sorry. I was looking at the *Star*'s website. Easton pulled out of the race?"

"Sounds like it, but you should see the video, Patrice. He talks about you, without giving names of course," he said, as if he knew what I'd get hung up on. "You won't believe all the stuff he said, I wonder if it's going to affect his job?" Ari's astonishment made me hit play on the video, my heart racing as the camera zoomed in on Easton's face. He had smudges under his eyes like he did when he was not getting any sleep, and my heart lurched knowing I was at least partly responsible for that.

I spoke into the phone as the woman in the video introduced Easton. "Ari, let me call you back, okay?"

"Sure, P. We'll talk later."

I ended the call and increased the volume as she asked the first questions. With every word he said, the need to go and talk to him, to see him, went from an urge to an absolute need. By the time he told the interviewer that he hadn't done the work to be a DA yet, I had my coat on and was slinging my backpack on my shoulder. When I stepped out into the cold November air, I thought about the things Easton said in that interview, the way he took responsibility for his actions. He had always done that, owned his mistakes.

I got into my car and set up the phone so that I could listen to the interview one more time. As I made the short drive to my building I thought about all the ways that Easton had put himself out on the line in our relationship. How he stayed hopeful and open even when I told him over and over we could never work. What Priscilla told me was true, I'd let the fear of letting someone in shut me off from really leaning in to the things that brought me joy.

Even in the moments where I was fully with Easton I let the dread of wondering when the other shoe would drop steal my happiness. Now here I was, having probably cheated myself out of something amazing. I didn't know if Easton would be up for giving me one more chance. I would not blame him if he didn't. But I swore I would not let him spend one more day thinking that he wasn't enough for me.

By the time I was walking into the elevator I started wondering if Easton even wanted to see me. Still I made myself move. I took a couple of breaths and I tapped in the code to the penthouse floor.

The elevator for Easton's place basically left you at his door, in a small hallway. Stepping out of it, I felt like I was the creepiest fucker on earth. I stood there like an asshole, in front of his door, deciding between calling him or going back to my place and texting him to ask if I was okay for me to come by. I must've been more pressed than I thought, because Easton's voice coming from the end of the hallway made me jump like a foot in the air.

"What are you doing here?" I turned to see him walking toward me carrying some folded up cardboard boxes.

"Are you moving?" As soon as the question came out of my mouth, I realized how fucking stupid it was, and by the incredulous look Easton was giving me, it seemed like he was having the same thought.

He paused just beyond the door, and gave me an assessing look. He ran his eyes all over me, but I noticed it wasn't in the appreciative, flirtatious way he usually did. This was guarded and very far from the warmth I'd become used to. He looked at me like I was someone he had to be careful with, and that, more than anything, finally brought home just how badly I squandered the gifts that Easton had given me.

That stopped now.

"I won't say I'm sorry, because I've already done that and continued to act like a clueless jerk. But I do want to say thank you."

"You don't have to thank me for anything, Patrice, everything that happened between you and me was out of free will and my desire to be with you."

He was still holding himself tightly, the boxes in a death grip in his hands, and I wanted to move closer. To take them out of his hands and hold him, touch him for the first time in so many days. But I didn't want to take anything else from Easton that I was not willing to give right back to him.

I swallowed a couple of times, stuck on the fact that he said "happened." That he was talking about us as if it was all in the past, and I let myself feel that.

It hurt.

"I *do* have to thank you. For what you did today, for what you did for me that night." I shook my head, trying hard to find the right words, the ones Easton needed to hear from *me*. "I was humiliated and scared that night. I felt so fucking angry that I had to be in that situation, that these things keep happening. But it was not right to take all that out on you." I closed my eyes for this last part because I was afraid of what I'd see when I said it. "Because you were right, I would've done the same. If our roles had been reversed I would've done anything I could to get you out of that situation."

When I opened my eyes I saw him dip his head in acknowledgment, but still his lips were sealed. Easton was no longer open to me. I'd lost that.

I needed to pour my soul out right in this hallway, because for some reason Easton was still willing to let my sorry ass waste his time. I took one deep breath and lifted my eyes to his face, and made sure he saw exactly how much I needed to tell him this.

"It's funny. I've spent so much energy keeping myself as far away as I could from love that could wound me." His eyes widened at my words, but still he did not budge. Even with my heart pounding out off my chest. "Except you never hurt me like I've hurt you. I let my fears turn me into someone who's careless with the people he loves." I shook my head when he gasped and made myself say, "No, not people, you, with you, the man I love."

My head and heart were pounding and my mouth was bone-dry, waiting for a reaction from Easton. His throat moved, and he closed his eyes, the boxes still clutched to his chest.

"Patrice, I understand why you were upset that night. I get it. I just," he said, moving a little closer to where I was standing, his eyes sad, but there was still just a glimmer of something there that made me hold on to hope. "I can't keep getting pushed away every time things go awry. My parents have made me feel like I wasn't enough, my whole life. I can't do that with you too, no matter how much I love you. I know that you don't think you and I could ever be on the same side of the things that you fight for—"

"No," I said, shaking my head hard, finally getting closer. "Easton, that's the thing, what's not possible is for me to do any of this *alone*. I'm not in control of any of this. This is not just my fight, to keep doing this I have to be whole. I need a partner and I need an ally." I took a chance and, one by one, placed the boxes on the floor and moved until we were just inches apart, so close I could feel his warmth. "I need you. You're not just enough, you're everything I want." I was gasping for breath at this point. I felt like I'd put everything on the line.

"I can't keep getting gutted, Patrice. I can't." Even as he said it he pushed closer, but this time I would not leave him hanging. Never again would I let him think that he was in this alone.

"I talked to Priscilla." His eyebrows shot up at that, his face completely surprised.

"What, again?"

I almost smiled at the how put off he was that his friend didn't spill the beans.

"Yes, I called her and she told me that I had to stop cheating myself out of joy. That I was letting my baggage not only have my past, but I was letting it rob me now. I don't want to keep cheating myself."

He closed his eyes and I counted, holding my breath, *one, two, three.*

When those green eyes were on me again, they were joined by a hint of a smile.

"You can come inside." I felt a jolt in my chest like my heart had gotten a jump-start. I tried to look for anger or resentment, but there was nothing, just that same hopeful smile that Easton always seemed to be able to give me, even when I was sure I didn't deserve it. "These boxes are for Ari's move."

Of course they were.

"Ah."

When we got to the living room, we made our way to the couch and Easton kept looking at me in that way that meant that serious conversation was not going to happen for much longer, so I said the rest of what needed to be said. "Will that interview affect your job?" I asked as I grabbed his hand, unable to stop touching him now that I'd started.

He smiled again and he leaned back on the couch. "No, Cindy was upset that I pulled out of the race, but she also knows that she should've never pushed me into it like that. And that we all have a lot to answer this community for." He sighed, and even though his eyes looked tired, they had a fire in them that I hadn't seen there before. "As for the interview, I had to say that, because you were right that us keeping quiet is not going to make things any better. I have to step up, we all do. Day called me tonight and said he wants to have a meeting and talk about doing anti-racism training with recruits that we'd talked about."

I nodded, surprised at the news. "Holy shit, that's huge."

"It's a start." There was that strong voice that I'd heard only in the courtroom, the one that said, *I will get this done.*

"He wants to work with some community organizations that do this work, ask for their expertise. I was hoping you could help with that, or if you can't, at least put us in touch with some of the ones you work with."

"Yeah, of course. I'd be happy to help."

Instead of answering, he leaned over, grabbed my sweater and pulled me in for a slow and chaste kiss, as if he needed to work himself up to being like we'd been before.

"You could be it for me, Patrice. You know that right?" Easton was always brave enough to show me his heart, even when I'd handled it so poorly.

But this time I would not waste another minute, second-guessing this enormous gift I'd been given. "I *know* you're it for me. I've known it since that day at the Brew and Wine festival last summer."

He smiled and shook his head as he got close enough to press our foreheads together. "Now, I know *that* is bullshit, but I appreciate you saying it."

I smiled again, in that helpless way that only happened with Easton. "It's true. I knew it then and I know it now. I'm here aren't I? Like Nesto's been telling me since I took the Cornell job, I could front like I was here for a million different reasons, but I knew very well that one big one was you."

This time the smile was big and the kiss was long and deep, when we pulled apart, the glint in his eyes looked a lot like my future. "That's a good place to start."

Epilogue

"How am I expected to be studious when you're bare chested and wearing your hot teacher glasses?" I complained to Patrice as I walked out of his bathroom.

He just shook his head and smiled at me while eying my own bare chest over those glasses that made him look even more delicious than normal. "You're a mess."

"Yeah, but I'm your mess." That got me another sweet smile.

"Yes, you are." Those happened a lot lately. Patrice Denis had sweet smiles and now I got to see them all the time. My heart literally skipped as I hurried to finish up so I could get in bed with him.

We'd come back from the gym and were now in the "before bed routine." We had that now. The last six months had been a remaking of us, together and individually. We'd worked hard on finding ways to be there for each other as we decided who we would be together.

I loved where we'd arrived, even if this new chapter of Patrice and I involved couples therapy, with homework.

"I'll get into bed in a sec, babe, I'm ready to work."

I made a show of taking my towel off and sliding on a pair of boxers as he gave me an amused look.

"Are you going to be serious? We have to focus." Patrice grumbled, as I fidgeted on the bed, arranging myself as close to him as possible while still giving him enough room to write in the notebook he had on his lap.

"I am, I swear, I am just advocating that we figure out a 'strip poker' version." I wasn't whining so much as being bratty enough to get him riled into messing around with me. When he turned to look at me, he scoffed just as he tugged me so that I was sitting between his legs, my back pressed to his chest.

"Here," he said, placing the notebook, pen and sheet from our therapist in my hands. He pressed his lips to my temple as he pointed at the paper. The heat of him made it hard for me to think. Because after almost a year since we started again, and countless nights of getting as much of him as I wanted, being close to him, still made me breathless.

He cleared his throat, commanding my attention, and ran a finger over the paper I was holding. "Today we're supposed to think about shared qualities." The way he said it, like the fact that we could even do this, was a blessing, made my chest tighten. I looked up and found him looking down at me with what I assume was the same lovesick expression on my own face.

I spoke with my lips pressed to his. "I'm so grateful we get to do this." I didn't have to tell him what I meant—that we'd been able to make this work, to makes *us* work.

"Same. I love you, bébé." There was no hesitation in his words, or in the way his eyes locked with mine when he said it.

Since I'd dropped out of the DA race so much had changed for me. I'd stayed in my job, determined to use the power I had to actually make changes in how we dealt with racial justice in the county. My first step, with the new DA's blessing, was heading an initiative to work more closely with advocacy groups in the region.

We were listening to the struggle that minorities faced in our communities and how law enforcement was falling short. We'd been building bridges into parts of the county that we'd neglected for too long. I'd learned more about myself and the kind of prosecutor I wanted to be in the last six months than I had in the previous five years. I wouldn't say being with Patrice had made me do it, but his presence in my life had certainly been the catalyst for me to take bolder steps. To examine how I wanted to show up in my job. To live up to the responsibility I'd been given. I had to be humble enough to admit that being an ally in words but not action was not enough, and in the end, I hadn't learned how to be one for every person I was tasked with serving. But I was determined to do better.

A rumbling sound got my focus back on the man in question, as he gently pressed on my chest. "Did I lose you?"

I shook my head as he ran a hand over my bare skin. The contact bringing me fully back to the moment and him. "Never, you're stuck with me, professor." I felt a ghost of a smile on the side of my face.

"That I know, especially now that you've gone and done this. I have to keep you," he said as he touched the red Scotch Bonnet pepper I'd had tattooed on my right hipbone on our last weekend trip to New York. The little pepper was a hard to find ingredient in all the

Haitian dishes Patrice and I tried to make together. So I got it as a joke, or at least I'd said it was. But we both knew it was more than that. Patrice had claimed possession of that particular part of my body and tended to it like I'd transplanted a part of himself and tattooed it on my skin.

I could not say that I was very upset about it.

"If you keep touching me like this, I'm not going to be able to do this homework," I said as my hand tightened around the notebook and I lifted the other one to his neck. "It's very hard to focus when your lips are only an inch from my mouth." I sounded breathless, but who could blame me?

"Okay, sorry," Patrice said on an exhale and moved a hand to the paper that was now totally crinkled on one side from my tight grip.

"Let's work on this." More hot breath on my neck, making me shiver and my skin tighten. "Then I can do unspeakable things to that tattoo."

I groaned, and tugged on the poor sheet, which was now really at risk of getting torn to smithereens. "Are you sure we can't do this naked, it'll be more fun that way." I could feel his shoulders shaking behind me as he planted a kiss on the top of my head.

"It's a blessing that I didn't take up with you until I was almost done with my PhD or I would've never finished."

"Do I bring you to distraction, Professor Denis?" My heart fluttered in my chest like it had wings as I asked, knowing that now I would get the answer I wanted.

"You know you do." There was nothing in his words other than affection, and maybe just a hint of indulgence. I lifted my face again, needing to respond to his words with a kiss. As I pulled back and settled into his arms I thought of where we'd arrived. Nothing much had changed, and yet it felt like everything was different. Patrice had successfully finished out the academic year. He'd eventually gotten the hang of his classes and with the help of the chair of his department, he'd even started a new research project.

"How was your meeting with Martin?" I asked into the comfortable silence, my body pressed so tightly with his our chests rose and fell in unison.

"It always throws me off that you call him by his first name." My parents had known Patrice's boss for years, and it had been a great surprise to hear he'd offered Patrice his personal support after the police stop. Now they were launching a project to research the hindering effects of systemic racism on social mobility for immigrants.

"It's going well, we got confirmation that we will get the funding for this first phase. So I'll go south in July to meet with the guys from University of Miami who we're partnering with. Maybe you can meet me after I'm done. We'll take a few days after to hang out. Go to Tap Tap."

"Oh I'm in," I said at the mention of the Haitian restaurant he'd taken me to when we'd gone a few months back. "Just tell me the dates and I'll take the time, I can get away for a couple of days next month. Besides, I didn't get nearly enough food and beach time when we were there in February."

Patrice was on fire for the project at work and was also doing more with some of the community organizations he'd gotten involved with over the last year. He was already a big part of the activism in the area, and I was so fucking proud of him.

"Day got back from his trip."

Patrice grunted at the mention of the sheriff. "Oh." Day was not exactly on his favorite people list, but the sheriff had been making some bold moves over the past six months to address the issues in his department. Including a trip to a national gathering of law enforcement leaders trying to address systemic racism at a local level.

"He came back with all kinds of ideas, and is rolling out the anti-racism mandatory training in the department. He's gotten some resistance, but he seems committed."

"He's trying," Patrice conceded. "I hope he sticks with it, because the pushback is not going to relent."

I nodded at his matter-of-fact tone. He ran a hand over my arm again and rested it by mine on the page.

"First question, counselor. As a couple, we're good at—"

I tried very hard not to burst out laughing, and when I looked up saw a matching knowing grin on my boyfriend's face.

"Well that's an easy one, sex. We are excellent at fucking." He nodded soberly at my words as I giggled.

"We're on the gifted and talented track for that for sure. But we're also good at cooking together, and last-minute weekend getaways," he said, and I heard the awe that sometimes tinged his words when he talked about us, the life that we were slowly building together.

I took the dark brown hand, which was a study of hardness and softness, and brought it up so I could kiss the roughened palm. "I love cooking together and I love our little romantic getaways. I also love how well our families get along."

"I like that too," he said firmly. My father was still

an asshole for the most part, but Patrice got along great with my mother, sister and grandpa. And Patrice's mom and stepdad were so fun to hang out with. We were now fully in each other's lives.

I looked down at the second question and raised an eyebrow. "Uh oh, next one is tough." When I glanced at him, his face said, bring it on.

"What are our weaknesses? As a couple."

To my surprise the prospect of hearing what Patrice was going to say didn't make me cringe in trepidation of what he'd say. I knew whatever it was it didn't mean things were shaky or that if I didn't change it was over. Just something to work on, together. So my heart beat steadily in my chest, as I waited for Patrice to think over his answer.

"Hmmm we're getting better at it, but we sometimes wait too long to air grievances." Even as he spoke he kissed my neck and face, soothing the blow.

I nodded in agreement and kissed his palm again. "This is true. We are getting better, *and* we are still not that great at being open about what bothers us in the moment. I wonder if we could use a new tactic—"

"Okay, but why do I have the feeling this is going to go down the fucking path," he said, voice full of humor.

"Uh because you know me and my thirst." I clapped my hands, ready to laugh my ass off at his reaction to what I was going to say. "Hear me out before you veto my idea, are you ready?"

He grinned at my teasing and waved a hand in a "get on with it" motion. "Grievance oral! Whenever we need to say something that we think may be hard for the other person to hear, we soften the blow with a blow job. Pun intended," I added smugly, barely able to get the words out, and Patrice was laughing so hard I had to move out of the way to give him space. I turned around to face him and he had his fist over his mouth like he did when he was practically convulsing from laughing so hard. Which he did a lot these days, because I *could be* a clown.

"Bébé, we need to report back to the therapist. I am not getting into grievance oral with her!" He did sound a little terrified, but he was grinning so hard the corners of his eyes were crinkled.

"I'll report back on this one, I can keep it PG though. But at least admit you like my idea."

I was on my knees facing him and he tugged on my hand to bring me closer. He was still sitting with his legs spread on the bed, that massive chest still moving up and down fast after the laughing fit. "You're lucky I'm so into you."

It was like everything he said was a reason for me to say something corny. But before I did, he got us back on track. "What are the qualities we value in each other?" Patrice asked, making me squirm. That one would go to a place that was hard for me. I did not do well with compliments.

I pointed at my chest. "I'll go first."

Patrice

If anyone would've told me a year ago that I'd be elated to be sitting in bed on a Tuesday night talking about my feelings with my almost live-in boyfriend, I would've told them to fuck right off in no uncertain terms. But here I was, one month out of finishing my first year at Cornell, anxiously waiting to hear what Easton had to say. I knew he'd asked to go first because he hated hearing people say nice things about him. Too bad, because I was going in on all the fucking ways he made me ridiculously happy.

We stared at each other for a bit and as per usual Easton draped himself on me. When we were in bed it was practically mandatory to be touching at all times, and we were in bed together every night these days. We took turns between my place and his, but I couldn't remember the last time I'd slept alone. It was hard to recall much of how it felt to be without Easton, to be honest.

As he moved limbs around, getting us wrapped around each other exactly how he wanted, he started talking. "I love how fiercely loyal you are to your friends. How open you are about your love for them," he said, talking with his face against my neck, warm breath tickling my skin. "I don't get jealous of them anymore, but at first." He paused, nipping on my neck, and then running his tongue over the spot.

"That's not fair play." I groaned, helplessly turned on.

He smiled against my neck and lifted those moss-colored eyes at me. "Sorry." He didn't sound sorry, but there was a vulnerability there. He didn't want to say this next part. "That first time you came back to Ithaca when Nesto opened the restaurant and you totally ignored me." My stomach dipped at how sad he sounded. God I could be such an asshole.

"It was hard seeing you with them, but I still loved how you got along. It's so amazing how you open up with the people you love, how you look so serious all the time, but for them, for *me*, you're soft and sweet."

I almost grimaced at that description. Soft and sweet were not words I associated with myself, but I leaned into how it felt to hear them from Easton. It felt good to be that to him.

"I think I was so distant from you because you scared the shit out of me." I laughed humorlessly as he pressed soft kisses to my neck. "The things you made me want, I was terrified of letting myself have them. I didn't know what would happen if I got you and then you realized I wasn't enough. From that first night, I knew you could be everything I ever needed and the thought of getting so much and losing it…" I shuddered out a gusty breath. "It terrified me."

I shut my eyes hard after saying that, and without speaking Easton pushed up and pressed his mouth to mine. Soft, perfect lips, tongue hot as it stole into my mouth.

Like breathing.

Kissing him was as natural as breathing and it still scared the shit out of me to think about not having that anymore.

"I was gone from the moment Nesto introduced us," Easton continued, making me flush with all the praise. "Gone. But you know what it is that will keep me here forever? The man that you are. Your love for your community, wherever you are. Your courage. You, just you."

Fuck, this man was going to wreck me before I got to talk. "Okay, my turn." I had shit to say too, dammit. "I love that you're my soft landing. I can say things to you I'm scared to even tell myself."

He groaned. "Patrice."

A flush crept up his neck, but I kept going, he was going to hear all of it. "Your willingness to learn. That you're not perfect, and you know it means more work, but you're ready to do it. How you want to know about my history and my people, not like it's a novelty, but because you care and you want to learn how to love what I love. And because you stayed unafraid to love me, even when I let you down." That last part, I had to choke out, as my throat convulsed from emotion. That was another development of life with Easton, I cried now.

"I guess we're really into each other and super sappy." I could only laugh at Easton's bullshit.

"I think Ms. B's evil plan to get us all into our feelings has been a success," I conceded, not annoyed in the slightest.

"She's good," Easton said with genuine admiration. "I really thought I could get you naked while doing this, instead I made us both cry. And we're not even done," he grumbled, as he looked around for the forgotten notepad and paper. He lifted the discarded sheet with one hand while he hooked the other one around my neck.

"Okay, last one," he said with a big-ass grin. "Three goals for the future."

My heart skidded up against my chest at that. It felt so fucking huge, but when I really let myself tune into what I was feeling, it wasn't dread or fear. It was anticipation, excitement…certainty. I couldn't wait to figure out what was next for us.

"Immediate future like in five minutes," I said with a grin to match the one on Easton's lips. "Me fucking you within an inch of your life, because my dick has had about enough of you rubbing your ass on it. I'm not made of stone, Easton Archer," I whined.

The little bastard turned his head and put the tip of his index finger on his cheek, as he wiggled said ass on my achingly hard cock. "Are you sure you're not a least part stone, because from where I'm sitting…"

That was it.

I lunged for him as he laughed his ass off, and within seconds we were both horizontal, with me looming over him. Pressed close, so he could feel me. "Is that what you were talking about?"

"Yup." I gasped as he ran a hand over my cock.

"Easton, we got two more goals for the future to talk about, we're finishing this homework dammit." I groaned as he stroked me over my briefs and nipped my ear.

"I got another one." He sounded as turned on as I was, and how we'd gone from heartfelt declarations to being on the verge of fucking would be surprising if this wasn't just another weeknight with Easton Archer. "I want to take a long trip together. Take that trip to South Africa we've talked about, explore a new place for both of us, together. Cape Town and the beach, safari."

I sucked in a breath, my lungs full of air and the intoxicating thing that was to be in love and be loved back and fearlessly planning for the future. When I spoke there was no hesitation. "I'd love that. Let's do it."

Without missing a beat on that maddening, tight stroke on my dick, he turned his head to kiss me. We tangled our tongues as we rocked against each other and my head was fuzzy with want. I couldn't put thoughts together when Easton got like this. I pushed my briefs off, frantic as he did unspeakable things to my ear. When I went for his boxers though, he stilled my hand.

"No wait, we have to say one more. A long-term goal."

I pressed my forehead to his, because I knew I was the one who had to say this one. I knew what he wanted. He'd told me. He wanted forever, and I'd always been too scared to say it. Before it seemed foolish to ask for so much. To ask for the kind of life I couldn't have even dreamed for myself. But right now, right here I literally had my future in my hands and I needed to claim it. He deserved to hear it, and fuck, I did too.

"*Us.* Living together, because goddammit, Easton Archer, you make me greedy, and I want all of it. Even a fucking dog. How is it you got me acting a fool at all times now?"

"I want it all too." Easton's voice was small, but steady.

A long breath escaped his lungs and we lay there, turned on, in love and ready to plunge into our future. I took stock of everything happening in my body and my head. I fucking throbbed from happiness. All of this was mine, and I would fight forever to keep it.

"So are you going to be able to recap all of this to Ms. B?" I asked with a flustered laugh.

Easton brought his arms up, mouth in a wide grin I could feel against my lips. "I'll do the recap, baby. Now how about we do the naked thing because I've never had 'my boyfriend wants to move in together and we're getting a dog sex' and I'm excited."

"You're so fucking extra."

"And all yours, forever. You said."

That hand went back to stroking and that mouth back to licking and nipping and I was done with homework. I had my hands full for the foreseeable future, and I would not change a thing.

"I did. You are."

* * * * *

Acknowledgments

It's hard to believe we've made it this far! I am so grateful for the readers who have responded so positively and shown so much love to these Dreamers.

I am endlessly grateful for every review, tweet and shoutout, more than I could every say.

When I set to write the stories of Nesto, Camilo, Patrice and Juan Pablo my hope was that I could give readers like me HEAs that they could see themselves in. It's beyond what could I hope for that these books have touched so many, and, what's more, left Romancelandia hungry for more Afro-Latinx romance, literally and figuratively.

As always, there is no way I could do this without the support and love of so many wonderful people:

Kerri Buckley, my editor. I am so grateful for the journey we've been on together. I know that your care and support have made me a better, more thoughtful writer.

The Carina PR and Marketing team, for all your support getting my stories out there and rolling with all my ideas.

Linda Camacho, my agent, for all the positivity and support.

My writing community. My RWA-NYC friends, you continue to inspire and amaze me.

My partner and my girl, for being my two biggest fans. I am so incredibly lucky.

To LaQuette and Robin B for your amazing feedback and enthusiasm for this story. Patrice and Easton's story is better and stronger because of you.

Finally, I have to give a shoutout to the man that inspired Patrice's character, my Uncle O. A gentle, kind and brilliant Haitian man who was not only a role model to me, but to a whole generation of Dominican kids in my family who were blessed to have him in our midst. From him I learned too many things to name, but mostly what it looked like to walk with grace and to know your own worth. Merci merci, pour tout.

Author's Note

All the events in this story are fictional, however, the challenges that so many young black and brown men in America face are far from it. My hope is that like Patrice and Easton we can all continue to show up for hard conversations and be able to walk together as we find ways for every single one of us to feel safe in our communities.

About the Author

Adriana Herrera was born and raised in the Caribbean, but for the last fifteen years has let her job (and her spouse) take her all over the world. She loves writing stories about people who look and sound like her people, getting unapologetic happy endings.

When she's not dreaming up love stories, planning logistically complex vacations with her family or hunting for discount Broadway tickets, she's a social worker in New York City, working with survivors of domestic and sexual violence.

You can find her here:
Twitter: www.Twitter.com/ladrianaherrera
Instagram: www.Instagram.com/ladriana_herrera
Facebook: www.Facebook.com/laura.adriana.94801
Website: AdrianaHerreraRomance.com
Newsletter: adrianaherreraromance.com/newsletter/

*And coming soon from Carina Press and
Adriana Herrera*

*Juan Pablo Campos lives without regrets. He has his
dream job, the best friends and family in the world,
and no time to dwell on what could've been—except
when it comes to Priscilla. The childhood friend who
he's loved for what seems like forever...*

Read on for a sneak preview of
American Sweethearts,
the next book in
Adriana Herrera's Dreamers series.

Chapter One

Juan Pablo

The flex is really fucking real.

I grinned as I tapped the caption onto the photo of me cheesing with my glass of XO on the rocks, in the private motherfucking jet I was taking to the Dominican Republic. I ran my fingers over my mouth as I posted it on Instagram with more hashtags and shit than necessary, but who could blame my ass for doing the most.

"Juan Pablo, get off that phone, sweetheart, and take it easy on that liquor. We haven't even taken off yet."

I rolled my eyes, pocketing my phone as I looked behind me where my parents were sitting. "Okay Ma, it's only my first drink," I protested as I pointed at the glasses of champagne she and my dad were sipping on. "And that's not water."

My father smiled at my whining. "It is an open bar, Irene. Let him live."

My mother shook her head, making her dark curls bop on her shoulders as she pushed up to kiss my dad gently on the mouth, both looking like lovesick teens even after almost forty years. "I can't take you anywhere," she said, without even a hint of annoyance, or specifying which one of us she was talking about. She then turned to the other side of the aisle where the rest of our group was looking on with amusement. "Odette, you have to help me keep these boys in line."

Okay, so both my parents were on the jet with me, as were my best friend Patrice, his partner, Easton, and Patrice's mom and stepdad. We were on our way to our other best friend Camilo's wedding. So I wasn't exactly ballin' on this trip. Camilo was, however, marrying a zillionaire who seemed to live for showering him with every luxury he could get away with. Which meant we were travelling like fucking moguls. That was, we would be if we ever got in the air. We'd been held back because at the last minute a few other passengers were added to the flight.

I turned around to ask P if he knew who would be joining us when I heard the flight attendant's radio come alive with a crackly voice, giving her instructions.

She smiled in our direction and gestured toward the still-open door of the plane. "Looks like our final passengers are here. We should be heading out very soon." With that she quickly went to meet whoever had finally arrived. This shit of travelling in a private jet was pretty fucking swank. I mean, no security line and you basically just rolled up to the plane, which was waiting in a hangar at the Westchester County airport. I could fucking get used to this. Also I needed the vacation, after coming off of what seemed like an interminable off-season, I'd been taking my time decompressing. This trip to the DR was exactly what I needed...

I heard her before I saw her, talking to her mother

and father, whose voices I'd also recognize anywhere, and felt that sickening dip of excitement mixed with barely contained want that always took over whenever Priscilla Gutierrez was near.

Shit. No wonder Camilo didn't respond to my texts asking who he'd put on our flight. That little fucker probably thought this was funny. I wasn't expecting to be in a confined space with Priscilla for four hours today. My heart started pounding in my chest and my vision blurred a little as I heard her chattering with her mother.

I had no clue how to act and for some reason panicked at the thought that she would be caught off guard by me being here. But before I had time to turn around and get some information from Patrice or Easton, she was walking onto the plane.

It was November so even though we were headed to the Caribbean, everyone was wearing fall attire. Pri was in what I always called her Bronx Girl Chic. Fancy leggings and sweater combo with pristine, matching Nikes. The whole thing was a mess of fall colors, olive green and terracotta leggings and a mustard-yellow sweater. She'd taken her braids out and had her hair pulled back into a messy top bun. Glossy baby hair framing her face.

"Oh, wow." She had that sickly sweet tone she used when she was too tired to even look aggravated, and as I stared straight ahead it did not escape me that she was avoiding looking at me. Which in a tight space like that required a hell of a lot of effort.

At thirty-five and after years of working a job that had toughened her on the inside, she still looked so much like the sixteen-year-old girl who made my heart race every time I saw her. When she finally looked up from talking with her parents, her face fell for just a second. Like she didn't know if she was up for having to deal with managing my presence. Like thinking about it made her tired.

Fuck, had it really been almost a year since I'd seen her? There had been a time when we couldn't go more than a few hours without touching or talking. Now months could go by without so much as a word. She of course recovered quickly, not about to give me stank face when our parents were here. Instead she started greeting everyone and giving me an impressively wide berth. Suddenly the luxurious and intimate interior of the plane felt oppressive.

"What's the good word, detective?" That was my dad. He always asked Pri about her job with more than a little bit of pride in his voice. He'd been her mentor since the day she joined the academy. Just another reminder of how our lives were thoroughly tangled together in big and small ways. I'd tried to tell myself for so long that was the reason why we were better off as friends: too many people with their noses in our business. But I'd weaned myself of my habit of not confronting my bullshit. Nosy relatives and friends was not the reason why Priscilla and I didn't work out. No, that was all on us—on me for being a careless fuckboy and on her for being stubborn and prideful.

"Rafa."

Pri's affectionate tone as she went in to hug my dad wrenched me out of my seemingly ever-present regrets playlist.

The kisses, hugs and backslaps went on for what felt

like hours until she finally got to me, and I knew that I wasn't imagining everyone looking at us. Like she always did, Pri kept it surface and polite in front of the parents. We could go at it behind closed doors as much as we wanted, but our parents would never ever see any of it. Not if she had anything to say about it.

"Hey J." She bent down to give me a quick peck on the cheek. But she popped back up so fast I could barely get a whiff of the expensive lemon verbena shower gel I'd gotten her addicted to and now couldn't use myself because it reminded me too much of her.

"Hey yourself, you looking fresh like always," I said, proud of myself for not sounding like a thirsty scrub. "You ready for this?" I asked, looking around the plane full of our raucous family and friends. We were rowdy by nature, but holy shit when we were on the way to our islands we could reach rapture levels of celebration.

Pris smiled, looking at her parents, who were already strapped down on their seats and in conversation with the other couples.

"Let's hope Thomas got us a DR/PR proof plane." My own parents were on their second glasses of wine and we hadn't even taken off. I was about to make an awkward comment about her Nikes when the flight attendant came by asking us to finish up our drinks, since we would be taking off soon.

That broke the tension and by the time she was done giving us instructions, Priscilla was seated next to me. To be fair, it was the only seat left and she had Easton, her best friend, on the long couch-looking thing on the other side. I had no time to fret on things getting awkward or weirdness between us, because within seconds we were all in an easy conversation about the wedding, the obligations and tasks Camilo had given each of us. It was familiar and natural to be with Priscilla—then again that had never been our issue. Coming together had always been too easy. It was staying that way that never seemed to work out for us.

Priscilla

Things *could not* be weirder. I was in a very confined space with my parents, my best friend, my ex *and* his parents. Except it wasn't like that, because Juan Pablo was a lot more than my ex, he was family. Even if things felt awkward now, strained. I felt like my skin was too tight on my face and I didn't know where to look. It was never easy to keep things casual with Juan Pablo, there was too much history between us to act like mere acquaintances. And yet, that was what we were now. We hadn't talked in months and sure, it was partly because we were both busy people, but we'd always been busy.

After that last time we broke up, I told Juan Pablo he needed to grow up and leave me alone... I'd been angry and frustrated, but before he walked out of my apartment he'd looked me straight me in the eyes and said, *I will.* After that, nothing. No booty call texts in the middle of the night, nothing. He'd stayed away like he said he would, *like I'd asked him to.*

As I mulled on that I felt something cold touch the tray that served as an armrest and looked up to see a stemless glass of wine, half full of rosé. The flight attendant smiled as she gestured to Juanpa who was heading toward the tiny, fancy plane lavatory.

"Mr. Campos said you wanted a glass of rosé." I dipped my head and took a sip. That was so much like him, and why I stayed away. Because he fucking lived to take care of little shit like that. Anticipating every little whim of mine and always getting it right. I looked up with a smile at the young woman and gave her a real smile. Like he'd guessed, a glass of rosé was exactly what I'd needed. "Thank you."

"You're welcome," she said with a nod before moving on to my parents and their drink order.

When she got there I saw Irene, J's mom, gesturing for my mom to taste the wine she was drinking and my dad, pointing at Rafa's glass, indicating he wanted one of the same.

"It's like we got a reunion of the old block."

I smiled at Patrice's amused tone. He was right, the old folks were getting on like they'd never stopped living up the street from each other.

I turned so I was facing Easton, who was using Patrice's gigantic chest as his airplane pillow. "Just wait until this plane lands, it'll be utter chaos. Are you sure you're ready for this, Mr. Archer?" I asked teasingly.

He winked at me and then turned so he could bring Patrice's head down for a kiss. It was short and tender, but the devotion flowed off those two in waves.

I'd never thought I'd see Patrice like this, his feelings like an open book for the world to see. It was strange seeing all our friends paired off, settled, how love had changed them. It was bittersweet to think that for Juanpa and me, lack of love had never been the issue. It had always been there, no question. It just couldn't fix all the other things that didn't work.

Easton turned again toward me, his expression content. "I know you'll take good care of me." I knew that by *you* he meant his man. But I nodded anyway as I saw Juan Pablo stepping out of the bathroom.

"Juan, mijo. How you been? You got any gossip for next season?" My dad never missed a chance to ask J about his beloved Yankees. A big smile on her face, my mother beamed at him too.

They fucking loved him.

Like his parents loved me. After all these years of ups and downs with Juan Pablo it was hard to know how to feel with him around. Especially when he wasn't being his usual extra self and trying to act cute or make conversation.

No, he was giving me space, like *all* the space.

I knew that this was going to be weird and deep down I've been on edge, knowing how hard it was going to be to stay off that fucker's dick when we were going to spend an entire week on the beach drinking. But him icing me out was much worse.

I felt like I needed air, from all of it. From my own thoughts, from the friendly ease that everyone seemed to have when I still felt like I didn't even know my place. I realized that on the other side of the wood paneling separating our cabin from the front of the plane there were two empty large leather seats, and I needed a breather.

I got up, and before I could take a step I had five pair of eyes on me. "A donde vas m'ija?"

"Just to sit up front for a second, Mami. I need to send out a couple of emails for work and need some quiet. Since this thing has Wi-Fi I'm going to do them on my iPad." I gestured to the overhead where I'd stuffed my bag. "I'll be back in a sec." I tried my best to keep my tone peppy because there was nothing that put my mother on red alert faster than people needing "to be alone." As kids she'd threatened to "take the doors off the damn hinges" on more than one occasion.

I could feel my mother's eyes tracking my moves, but fuck I was suffocating. Not because being around Juanpa was making feel uncomfortable. No, it was because with him my heart and my head never seemed to want to retain the bad. Things would go up in flames and I'd tell myself to stay away…and after enough time passed I was right back in.

Wanting him.

The seats were back facing, so I had a full view of the cabin. I wondered if they were meant to be for a security detail—they were far enough where you weren't too close, but you had a pretty good view of the cabin. Juanpa was sitting between his mom and his dad. Legs spread and that slick grin that always, *always* did things to me.

My phone buzzed with a message.

You need some company? I'll ditch the hot teacher and come sit with you.

I laughed quietly and glanced up to find Easton looking at me with a knowing expression.

I'm good, just contemplating from afar all the things I can't indulge in this week.

I heard the scoff before I looked up and saw my best friend taking a break from his text exchange with me to whisper something to Patrice. It was hard to remember that only a year ago things for them seemed virtually impossible, their lives at odds in so many ways. And yet here they were, engaged as of a couple of months ago, and so solid it felt like they'd always been together. He tapped me another message as Patrice engulfed him in a tight embrace.

I got your back.

I pocketed my phone after that and took another sip of my rosé as I quietly watched Juanpa. His shoulders were wider than they'd been a year ago, the last time we crashed and burned. Same tight fade, but now he wore a thick beard, which made his broad lips stand out. A shiver ran down my spine as I remembered how they felt grazing the back of my neck. How I could feel the imprint of them for days after.

Fuck, I needed to calm down. My parents were on this plane.

I made myself focus on another part of him that wasn't his mouth and noticed he was wearing his usual "travel ensemble." Fitted sweats, Yankees hoodie and Air Jordan travel combo, nothing different there. Except he didn't *seem* like the old Juan Pablo. There was an ease to him that hadn't been there before. Like he didn't have anything to prove. He had his face turned to talk to my dad and I looked him up and down as he laughed at something.

I could tell you every mole, every scar on Juan Pablo's body better than I could my own. I knew exactly where to touch him to make him moan with pleasure, and he could do the same to me. Except beyond that, nothing ever seemed to work for us. Not since that awful night when we said too many ugly things to forgive. We broke things then, but instead of giving up we kept coming back to take more bites out of each other. Until there was nothing left.

* * * * *

Don't miss
American Sweethearts
by Adriana Herrera,
available January 2020 wherever
Carina Press books are sold.

www.CarinaPress.com